CW01672155

BLACK OAK BURNING

MONIQUE EDENWOOD

Copyright © 2020 by Monique Edenwood

All rights reserved.

This book is a work of fiction. Names, characters, businesses, places, events, and incidents are either the products of the author's imagination or used in a fictitious manner. Any resemblance to actual persons, living or dead, or actual events is purely coincidental.

No part of this book may be reproduced, distributed, or transmitted in any form or by any means, including photocopying, recording, or other methods, without the prior written permission of the author, except in the case of brief quotations in a book review.

Front cover photo credit:

Cloaked woman in forest: © istock/NejroN

Couple (second edition): © Lightfield Studios/Adobe Stock

Cover design by Monique Edenwood

ISBN (electronic format): 978-1-7772249-2-9

ISBN (paperback): 978-1-7772249-3-6

For more information, please visit MoniqueEdenwood.com or Facebook.com/MoniqueEdenwood

ACKNOWLEDGMENTS

I could not have written this book without the help and support of some amazing people that I have met thanks to publishing my first book in July of 2020.

I would like to first say a huge thank you to the readers of *Enter The Black Oak* who took a chance on the book. It was a very personal story to me and I really put my heart and soul into every word. Having people read it has meant so much to me and given me the confidence to keep writing.

I would also like to thank the lovely people that took the time to write reviews. To independent authors, every single review is so important. They allow us to keep writing and also help others to consider reading our work. In addition, retailers are much more likely to recommend our books when we have more reviews and ratings, even if they are just one line long. For small indie authors who are swimming in a pond with some very big fish, this helps us in so many different ways. Reviews and ratings make such a huge difference in our lives and I am eternally grateful to every single person who took the time to leave one.

The first person who ever reviewed my book is Melody Steele. My book had only just come out and like everyone who has left reviews, I did not know Melody before publishing the book. She was one of the very first people to read the book and she left the loveliest review to tell me that she liked it. We then became friends on Facebook and she has given me so much confidence and energy due to her love, support, enthusiasm and her huge heart. She was the first person to give me faith that the book could find an audience who resonated with it and I owe her a million thanks.

Jean Sweeney is the second person to review my book and she took the time to leave reviews on Amazon and Goodreads. I was and still am so grateful to her as hers was my first review in the UK. It helped so much as it took a very long time to get reviews in the UK and when potential readers clicked, they could see her lovely review which made such a difference.

Gina Whited and Giselle Mendieta were early reviewers and like Melody and Jean, soon became Facebook friends and have supported me ever since. I can't express how grateful I am to all of you for your warmth and support and what a special place you have in my heart.

Some other lovely people have left reviews and also supported me by becoming Facebook friends after reading book one. They have given me endless support and encouragement on my posts. I would like to thank with all my heart: Nanzyz Jayz Lotez, Geneva Davies, Kathy Gentry, Jennifer Wright, Karen Warner, Yumnah Isaacs Hajwanie, Devon Bernie, Nichole and Trisha B.

Like the incredibly kind people above, Kelly Marie Gregory and Patricia Johnston contacted me several times to let me know how much they loved the book. Getting emails or messages from people who let me know that they enjoyed the book really has given me wings while writing book two, which, as all authors know, can be challenging at times. Kelly and Patricia also posted about the book in Facebook groups, which makes such a difference and which I am so thankful for. There are some other amazing people who have reached out whom I will be thanking next time.

Sue Graham Edmondson has never read my novel, but she has given me so much love over the last six months and I am so grateful for her amazingly loving energy.

I would like to say such a huge thank you to the following people who have reached out to me about the book and who have also talked about it in Facebook groups: Jennifer Chris, Gisell Butler, Cyndi Arrequin, Jaclyn Combe, Cheryl Woodward, Penny Betcher, Keeana Estrada and Cilla H. It not only fills my heart to have people enjoy the story enough to want to post about it, but it does also help us small authors so incredibly much.

I am so grateful for having met such wonderful people over the last few months and for all of your support and enthusiasm. But most of all, I am just ecstatic and so honored that you liked the book in the first place!

I am part of a small writer's group that has given me so much support over the last six months. I would like to thank my author friends, N. Dune, Nicole Wells, Margot Swan, Shreya Basu, Anouk Roche, Anna White, Ashley Morrison, Maisie Myers, Cadence Keys, Sophy Bannister, Katie Jolliffe and E. Broom for their support, advice and never-ending giggles over vegetable emojis, Stephen Merchant and discussions about fluorescent aardvarks and movie skins. Having a group of people who support your writing and understand all the struggles, big and small, is invaluable.

N. Dune, you are like a life jacket in the storm at times for many of us. Thank you for your steady advice and warmth. Nicole Wells, you have helped and advised me when I have struggled at times. Your wonderful, soulful advice has really helped to lift me up this year. Shreya Basu, in addition to giving me support in our group, you have posted about the book many times and I am so grateful for that.

I would like to thank another new writer friend, Amber Torney, whom I met after she became my first reviewer in Australia and we subsequently connected on Facebook. I am extremely grateful for your knowledge, advice and support.

At a moment when I was struggling a little, as all authors do at times, I received the most incredible review on Amazon Australia. It was so detailed and so lovely and I would like to thank Tracy Wilkin for leaving it. You boosted my spirits that month more than you can imagine.

I would like to thank my two Beta readers, Sophy Bannister and

Cadence Keys. Your advice and input at the end helped me immeasurably and I am eternally thankful. Bringing out a second book in a series can be quite nerve-wracking and you made the last week much more bearable by letting me know that the book was ready to be published. Sophy, you were like a literal angel to me at the end. Your enthusiasm and excitement really lifted my spirits and soothed my frayed nerves.

I did not know any of the people above before publishing book one, but meeting you has been one of the most wonderful things to come out of what can be quite a challenging process at times.

There are other people whom I would like to thank, but am not able to this time. I would like you to know that if you have reached out to me, commented on one of my posts, left me feedback or a rating or review, I have seen it, and I am so grateful to you and just beyond thrilled that you have enjoyed the book.

And to anyone who is reading book two, I am so honored to have you read it. I do put my heart and soul into every line I write.

Sometimes as writers we make decisions not because we approve of certain characters and their actions, but because our desire is to create narrative tension and because we want to explore challenging relationship dynamics.

To find a small tribe of readers who get that and are willing to read the next chapter of the story fills me with energy and so much gratitude that I couldn't begin to express.

Thank you with all my heart.

Monique

BLACK OAK BURNING

Black Oak Burning is the sequel to *Enter The Black Oak*, book one in the *Black Oak* Series.

The child who is not embraced by the village will burn it down to feel its warmth.

- African Proverb

PROLOGUE

TRIBECA

"What should we do about the girl? Jack is still very attached to her. There would be a war if something happened to her."

"We can't touch her for now."

"What about O'Neill? He's determined to have her, no matter the cost."

"And I'm sure he'll succeed. Show me a woman who has ever been able to say no to that man... especially a woman who's in such agony over her husband's *many* thoughtless indiscretions."

"What do you suggest we do about it?"

"*Nothing*. I will greatly enjoy watching the seduction play out."

"Jack will lose his mind."

"Well, it's our job to keep him so distracted that he doesn't realize what's happening. Keep him in the dark for as long as possible. Let Cameron attempt his little domestic experiment with her. Let him hide his true nature, pretend he isn't a dangerous, uncivilized beast just waiting to be let off its leash."

"Tsk, tsk. You are wicked, Sebastian."

"I believe that's why you worship me."

"Very true. But you know that when Jack finds out, there *will* be a war."

"Yes. A most delectable one. I believe this may finally be the way in which the impenetrable Mr. O'Neill is taken out."

"Mmm. How we've longed for that."

"Indeed. I gave him the choice... Return to us or face the consequences. He chose the latter. I think it's only fair we respect his wishes."

"Would it be too late for him to redeem himself? Let's say he were to see the many errors of his ways, would he be allowed to return?"

"I would consider it. Hopefully, it won't happen soon. My hunger for their war is becoming more fervent by the day."

"And what if it's Jack that ends up getting taken out?"

"Hmm. That would be a pity. But Jack has been most problematic of late. Questioning my methods so openly would normally result in severe consequences. If it weren't for my affections for him, I fear he may already have succumbed to some unfortunate accident."

"It *would* be most unfortunate for us to lose such talent."

"Yes. But if that were to happen, then so be it. In the meantime, Cameron's demons will slowly come out. Hopefully, the poor girl doesn't get *too* hurt in the process."

"Oh, I don't know. I'd very much enjoy seeing how much more pain the little one can tolerate. Her distress is so exquisite."

"Yes, it is. I think of it often."

"Well, you have helped engineer it, Sebastian. It's only fitting that you should enjoy your own work."

"Oh, I am. Once Cameron's darkness begins to emerge, we may just see the girl running back into Jack's arms anyway. In either case, there are only two possible outcomes... The destruction of one of them, or mutual annihilation. It is providence. The universe's design."

"Mmm. I will enjoy watching it very much."

"As will many of us."

"The girl's been discrete so far."

"Yes. Luckily for her. But I believe it would be wise to make it clear to her the consequences of speaking up."

"She seems to get it already."

"I know. But I'm bored. I'd like to shake things up a little, see where the pieces of the wreck lie once the collision is over. Having her live in fear for a while would be quite... *sublime*."

"Oh, absolutely."

"I'm also highly curious to know which one of them will be coming to her rescue, if any."

"You are a genius, Sebastian."

"And if our girl doesn't comply with our demands, then she will be brought in to have them explained more... *thoroughly*."

"Mmm. I would savor that moment greatly."

"I'm sure you would, Alex."

"I would like to reward you for your incomparable design. May I?"

"You may."

"Thank you."

"Thank you, what?"

"Thank you, my lord."

"You know what to do..."

1

"HOW DOES STELLA KNOW?" I ask, cold fear cascading through me as I clutch the beige sheet to my chest.

Cameron's tall, muscular frame stiffens at the sight of the anxiety rushing through me. "She didn't have time to explain fully," he responds, his rich voice as stern as his expression, "but she found a tracker on her car. We don't know if they put it there before or after she got back from Redwood, but they may be nearby... or already here by now."

"We have to call the police."

"We can't do that," Cameron replies urgently, grim shadow darkening his face. "You have to get dressed right now. We have to get out of here. I'll be back in three minutes. Clear?"

I nod as his gaze lingers on my face for a long moment before he leaves the room.

Getting up, I let go of the sheet, finding myself naked but for my white panties. Flinging open my little suitcase, I grab a pair of navy-blue sweatpants with shaky hands. I pull them on, the cotton scraping my skin as I yank them up my legs roughly. I forgo the bra and don a white T-shirt and checked blue and gray shirt before tying my long hair into a messy bun at the top of my head.

Cameron reappears in the doorway as I close my suitcase, wearing black pants and a black sweater over a gray T-shirt. "Ready?" he asks.

"Yes."

"Do you have some shoes up here?"

"My sneakers."

"Put them on."

I open my suitcase again and grab my black and white sneakers which I tug on and tie sloppily.

"You can take your purse, phone and laptop, that's it," he says.

I grab my phone, shove it into my purse and join him at the door, flinging my bag over my arm. His strong hand finds mine instantly, his fingers interlocking with mine protectively.

"I'm scared," I whimper, peering up anxiously into his grave but determined face.

He leans down, his lips skimming mine. "You don't have to be. Nothing can happen to you for as long as I'm around. Understood?"

"What about you?"

"I'm not afraid of that man." I see by the scorching fire in his eyes that he means it.

"I'm sorry, Cam. It's all my fault."

"Sorry?" He cups the side of my face, the smooth velvet of his hot palm raising it so that I'm locked into him. "I brought you here, remember?"

A shudder out a heavy breath. "Do you think he's already here?"

"I've checked out front and out back. I don't see anyone. There are floodlights that come on when anyone comes close to the house. They will be triggered if he's nearby."

"Okay." I gulp down the blizzard of fear. "Are security coming?"

"They're ten-fifteen minutes away, on the other side of the bay." He watches me for a suspended moment as his fingers curl around mine, gripping me tightly. "Follow me," he orders, leading me to the top of the stairs. We softly tread downstairs in silence. Cameron nips past the front door of solid wood and over to the living room window to the left of the door.

Before he has a chance to pull open the curtain, there's a click and white light floods in through small gaps at the top of the drapes. A gasp rushes from me as Cameron peels open the curtains and peers through the gap, his brow furrowing in concern.

The sound of a guttural cry sends a shockwave ricocheting through the house. "O'Neill!"

The booming power of Jack's deep rasp cuts through the eerie night, silent but for the shriek of a torrid wind which howls as if in a fit of rage.

"Cameron!" I whisper, clutching my hands to my chest. "We have to call the police!"

My palms press into the engraved front door as I look through the spyhole to see the silhouette of Jack walking determinedly towards us, his right hand seeming to fist beside the dense muscles of his thigh, lit up by the brightest of floodlights. Two men stand either side of him—tall, sturdy, both with fair skin and short light-brown hair, and despite the distortion of the lens, I can see from their faces that they want trouble.

I head over to the living room and pull gently on Cameron's thick bicep as he peeks through a gap in the curtains of the unlit living room. "He's with two of his men," he says, his face a dark storm.

"How did they even get in here?" I whisper.

"They must have jumped the fence." He closes the curtains.

"We should call the police," I urge again.

"No."

"Why not?"

"We can't, Jessynia."

"Why?" I search his troubled amber eyes, trying to understand.

"You need to go upstairs and lock the door. I'm going to speak to him."

"What?! No! Are you insane?! We have to get out of here. Please, Cam. I'm scared."

He peers into me, unspeaking, before pulling on my hand and leading me to the kitchen where he opens a cupboard next to the kitchen door from which he grabs a life jacket, handing it to me. "Put this on," he orders, sliding his feet into walking shoes that he grabs from a cubby beside the door.

"Isn't there another way?" I ask, sliding the orange foam onto my torso.

"We won't make it into the woods," he says. "They'll see us."

He grabs a jacket for himself and gently turns the first lock in the kitchen door. I hold my breath, the click so loud that I am sure it could be heard across the bay.

"I know you're in there, O'Neill!" Jack's voice is a thundering growl set ablaze by violent wrath. "I'll give you *two* minutes to come out and face me!"

Cameron doesn't even flinch at the veiled threat, instead tending to the second lock, a sturdy steel bolt latch. His steady fingers pull down the thick metal rod and slide the bolt free. He turns the door handle and pulls it open, grabbing my hand and tugging on it as we step onto the stone slab outside the back door.

Just as he is about to close the door behind us, his eyes flit to the forest to the left of us beyond a patch of grass at the top of the sandy slope leading to the ocean. He peers into it intently as if looking for ghosts. "Do you see anyone?" he asks, voice low. "In the forest?"

I look, scanning the dark shadows. "No. Nothing."

Jack's raging voice reverberates around the building again. "Are you going to face me, O'Neill? Or are you going to hide like a *coward*?" he snarls.

Cameron stops, looking down, his chest rising and falling in slow, deep breaths.

"Cam?" I whisper to the fizz of ocean waves caressing the small beach, a smooth sound so incongruous with the heavy menace in the air.

"We can't run from this," he responds, pinning me with his earnest gaze. "We run now, we'll be running forever. We have to face this. *I* have to face this. Like I should have done a long time ago."

"What?! No!"

Pushing the door fully open again, he uses his strength to lift me back inside, locking the door behind us.

"Cam, we can't. It's too dangerous!" I say, trying to convey my conviction in a whisper as he removes the life jacket from me and places it back into the cupboard. "Let's call the police," I urge.

"We can't, Jess. The Society has police officers on its payroll. Calling the police on other members is seen as betrayal. There would be fall-out. For both of us. Fallout you could not begin to imagine. I can't risk that."

A thunderbolt rips through my flesh like an explosion at the blast of three loud bangs on the front door. "*One* minute, O'Neill!"

"I'm going to speak to him," says Cameron tensely.

"No! He'll kill you. We have to call the police!"

He doesn't answer, instead silently pulling me back through the kitchen, up the stairs and into his bedroom to the left.

"Cam, are you listening to me?!"

"We can't call the police. And If I don't go out there now, this isn't going to stop, Jessynia. He'll keep hunting us down. You know that."

I walk over to the window and peek through the thick curtains in the unlit bedroom. He joins me, the strong, hard slabs of his chest pressing against my back, his arm snaking around my upper chest possessively as we observe Jack and two of his "men" hovering below us to the soundtrack of leaves blustering in the storm.

Cameron releases his grip and turns.

"No!" I yank his arm in response. "You can't go out there."

He pivots to face me. "I need you to lock yourself in this room right now."

"Cameron, please..."

"This has been a *long* time coming, Jessynia. This goes back to before I even knew you. This thing has been designed by the universe. It had to happen."

"There's three of them out there!"

"Is your phone charged?" he asks.

"Yes." I reach into my purse, grappling for the phone.

"Switch it on now. Put it on silent. I'm going to keep the front door open. If you hear anything *serious* go down followed by nothing but silence, call the police."

"No, please, don't!" I plead, tugging on his brawny arm as he leaves the room.

Reaching the doorway, he turns to face me, his warm fingertips grazing my cheek. "You have to trust me. Do you?"

"It's not *you* that I don't trust..."

"He won't hurt me."

"You give him way too much credit," I whisper, trepidation arrowing through my belly.

"Lock the door behind me," he responds.

"I'm scared."

"He'll never hurt you again. I promise you. Now switch your phone on and lock the door."

As he turns to leave, a thought hits me and I tug on the dense bicep under the black veil of his sweater. "Cameron, you don't tell him about what happened between us, okay? It will make him insane."

He nods.

2

THE CLICK OF THE LOCK THUNDERS through my quivering fingers as I dump my purse on the floor and fumble for my phone's power button. In my jumpy state, I screw up the passcode twice before finally getting it right and putting it on silent. Heading over to the window, I peek through the tiny gap in the black curtains, watching as Jack heads down the steps in front of the house before facing the front door, looking up and around the building's façade. I duck behind the curtain as his eyes pan up to this side of the house. With the room completely unlit he shouldn't be able to see me, but the thought that he could has cold terror wrapping around me.

My heart hammers in my chest at the metallic ticks of the front door lock. Upon the vague creak of the door opening, I see Jack below, watching in horror as he shakes his head, his body tense, hands fisted, his face a tempest of volatile fury as Cameron steps out, stopping on the top step to look down at the man he spent his childhood with.

"Where is my *wife, O'Neill*?" The power in Jack's voice has the sound floating effortlessly through the small bedroom window, open just enough to keep the hot August air from becoming stifling.

"This is over, Jack."

"Over? *You* don't tell *me* when my fucking marriage is over, O'Neill. I'm going to ask you again... Where the fuck is my wife?"

"She's in a safe place, away from you. She needs time to heal from the shit you've put her through."

"Heal?" he sneers, his body bristling in jealous ire. "There will be *no healing* for as long as *you* are *anywhere* near her. Do you understand that? Do you think I'm letting you get your filthy, deviant hands on her?! Do you?!" Jack roars, taking a step toward Cameron. "Do you think this is going to be your happily ever after? With *my* fucking wife?! Is this your idea of payback?"

"I'm not trying to take your wife off you, Jack." Cameron's deep, resonant timbre echoes around the house. "You did that *yourself*. Now I'm trying to protect her, like I should have done from the start."

"*Protect* her?! *You*? I suppose you haven't yet informed her about what a freak you are, have you, O'Neill? Or how *fucked* you are in the head? Have you told her what lengths you have to resort to in order to get pleasure? You'll end up damaging her worse than me. You'd destroy that girl if you got your hands on her, and you know it."

"I'm not the same man I was when that sadistic *cunt* you like so much had her claws in me."

"You're sure about that?"

"Yes. I'm also sure that this is over, Jack."

"Oh yeah?"

My breath hitches at the sight of Jack's bestial form taking two urgent steps forward and lunging up the stairs, ramming his dense frame into Cameron's abdomen, pushing him backwards and inside the house, out of sight. The sounds of scuffling and slamming and a groan emanating from one of them has me rushing to the bedroom door which I unlock before running downstairs.

"Stop!" I shout as Jack and Cameron tear into each other on the floor of the open living room just to the right of the front door.

"Jessynia, no!" shouts Cameron as I make it downstairs and grab Jack whose lip is split and bleeding.

I grasp at the dense mass of his arm under his thin black jacket to pull him off. "Jack, stop! Please! Nothing happened!" I don't like to lie but someone could end up in hospital if I don't. Or worse.

They both get to their feet as I pull Jack away, a gasp escaping me as I pivot to see Cameron's pink, swollen right eye, evidence of one of Jack's punches connecting.

"Please just stop!" I cry, tears streaming down my face as I pull Jack further away and stand between them, one palm on his rock-hard chest, the other stretched out, palm up, as I try to create a pitiful barrier between these men whose history goes so deep that I'm afraid to even ask what happened between them.

As Jack's goons enter the open door, Jack shouts, "Stay out there! I can handle this," which has them retreating.

I take two steps back, unlocking my palm from his chest as he turns to face me, eyes wide, shaking his head in stormy incredulity. "You're coming with me, Jessynia," he roars, the menace in his voice a shock-wave crashing through my shaken body.

"Over my dead body, Wilder," retorts Cameron bitterly.

"Well, if you insist..." And with that, Jack lunges around me, his fist a lightning bolt that connects with Cameron's face so hard that I feel the blow in my body. Cameron staggers back before bracing himself, dodging another of Jack's punches and returning the assault with his own right hook to Jack's mouth.

"Stop!" I cry, pushing myself between them, hoping that my presence will make it impossible for them to keep fighting. "Please! Cameron! Stop!"

They pull apart breathlessly, not from my physical strength but from the danger their continued assault would put me in.

"Jack, please. You need to leave."

"Get your bag and wait outside, Jessynia," he counters roughly.

"You're insane," snarls Cameron, blood trickling down his right cheek from the second collision of Jack's fist with his eye.

"Now!" shouts Jack, his glare shifting between Cameron and me.

"Jack, I can't," I respond. "I'm sorry."

"If you think I am going to stand back and watch my *fucking wife* end up with the man who—"

"Nothing's going on between us," I lie. "My car broke down on the highway. Cameron saved me."

"Saved you?" Jack snarls in jealous fury.

"I mean he helped me."

"Fine," he responds, his body stiff, a tinder box of volatile energy just ready to blow. "You're safe. Now get your stuff and get the fuck out of his house!"

"That's not going to be happening, Jack," responds Cameron, wrath winding its dark fingers around his glowering features. "You've put her through enough shit to last her a lifetime. She's leaving you and there's fuck all you can do about it. It's called *consequences*, Wilder."

"Cam, stop!" I plead as I see Jack bristle, a wounded animal lurking in shadow, ready to fight to the death.

Jack takes a step forward and I hold my hands out, finding the ice-blue of his eyes which glimmer like white-hot embers in the dimly lit room. "Jack!" I wince as I see his mouth filled with blood from Cameron's latest punch. "Oh my God..."

"Jessynia," he says, stunning me with the bleak desperation in his glare. "If you end up with this man, I'll be in so much pain that only the death of one of us will ease it."

Fast tears plummet onto the floor below me as the anguish in his eyes hits me like a bullet, along with the realization that starting a relationship with Cameron is not something I can *ever* do.

How the hell did I think that could happen?

Cameron's safety is the only thing that matters now.

"Jack, I won't," I say. "I promise."

"Don't listen to him, Jessynia!" growls Cameron. "He's trying to intimidate you like he always does." I turn to witness Cameron's pallid face, his breathing quickening as he glares at the man whom he once loved as much as me. He finds my eyes, the silent plea in his face weakening me.

I lower my eyes before meeting Jack's again. "Jack, I can't be with you. I can't put myself through this anymore. This is never going to stop and you *know* it."

"Jessynia, please," he responds. "Let me explain. You don't understand. I had to do it."

Cameron shakes his head, exhaling his contempt. "Don't listen to his *shit*."

"You're going to pay, O'Neill!" Jack roars, lowering his chin as he squares his dense body, legs slightly apart, his fists tight—a provocation of the kind that only men can fully understand.

"No, Jack, stop. This has nothing to do with Cameron. It's just been too much. I'm sorry, but I'm not coming with you. I need some time away from you."

"I can't have you staying here," he responds roughly. "I can't allow it. You know that."

"I'm going to get my parents to pick me up."

"No, Jess," says Cameron.

"I'm sorry, Cam. I can't stay here," I respond as a light blasts through the front door and the crunch of gravel and squeal of fast tires signal the arrival of a white car that careens down the driveway. Through the open doorway, I see two car doors fly open and what look like security guards jump out, both with short dark hair—one with fair and another with deep olive skin, the latter drawing a firearm which he leaves pointing at the ground.

"Get away from the door!" he shouts to Jack's men.

"Jack?" shouts the bulkier of his goons in the black bomber jacket and faded blue jeans.

"Do it," responds Jack and his men walk down the stone steps leading to Redwood's sturdy front door and stand to the side.

The second of the security guards enters. "Are you okay?" he asks Cameron, his cavernous voice booming around the room.

Cameron barely looks at them, his irate glare pinned to the man who was once like a brother to him before Alexandra Frost got her claws into them, weaponizing Jack into blackmailing Cameron's father and using and dumping his sister in some sociopathic revenge ploy.

"Get him the fuck out of here," Cameron growls, dueling silently with Jack who looks about ready to fight again.

"Do you want us to call the police?" asks the guard.

Jack wipes the crimson pool from his lips as I spot a split-second grimace of pain from Cameron at the sight of it.

"No," responds Cameron. "Make sure they leave the street... and don't come back."

The stocky security guard takes a step towards Jack who pivots to face him, legs apart, his huge shoulders squaring to face him him. "Put *one* hand on me and you'll be seeing the inside of your brain," Jack snarls.

The guard retreats a step.

"I will have people watching this house on all sides within thirty minutes," Jack says as he turns to me. "You spend the night with this man, and *one* of us is going to end up in the *ground*. Do you understand that?"

"I'm not spending the night," I say. "My dad is gonna pick me up. I'll call him right now. But you leave me alone after that. And Cameron. Understood?"

Jack's volatile glower darts from me to Cameron and back to me where it softens just the tiniest amount. "The second you leave, I will call my men off," he responds, slick scarlet cells tainting his front teeth, spilling onto his lips. I want to tend to his face, to wash the blood off and make sure he's okay, as I want to do to Cameron. But I can't. Finding his opponent, Jack snarls, his timbre dark and heavy, "I find out that you've touched this girl, and I will make you wish you had taken your life like I once stopped you from doing. You and your entire fucking family will taste my wrath. It will be *war* that *never* ends. Is that understood, *friend*?"

"I'm not intimidated by your threats like everyone else, *friend*."

Jack takes a step forward.

"Jack, stop, please," I plead. "Nothing happened. Cameron helped me. That's all. I'm going to leave."

"You'd better, Jessynia. You're my wife. My property. You touch another man and you'll be responsible for the consequences."

Icy shards of panic shatter my weakened body as his eyes burn into me, watching me as he slowly walks backwards towards the front door before finally turning around and heading down the steps, glaring at the guard outside as he does so, his violent aura intimidating him into backing off.

As he leaves, the security guard inside turns to face Cameron. "Do you want us to stick around?"

"Yes," he replies. "Once they've gone, stay on the grounds. I'll check in every hour. If you don't hear from me, you call me, okay?"

"Yes, sir."

"And there'll be a man coming to the house in about an hour driving a blue sedan," I say to the guard. "His name is Phillip. You can let him in."

"Okay," he replies.

I lower my eyes as Cameron glances at me, pain twisting the usually elegant angles of his breathtaking face. I watch through the front door as the guards leave and order Jack and his men off the property, forcing them down the driveway and out of sight. Heading to the door, Cameron closes it behind them, locking it before turning to face me, the hollow concern in his plaintive gaze clashing with the swollen pink around his eye.

3

"JESUS, CAM." The sight of his bloody, bruised skin tears into my flesh. "Your eye. Come with me."

Taking a few steps towards him, I tug on his hand, pulling him into the kitchen as spikes of cortisol ravage my system. I open the freezer, scouring its contents before grabbing an ice pack and turning to find him right behind me.

"Sit down," I manage shakily.

I grab a paper towel and a bottle of vodka from the drinks cabinet and lead him over to the kitchen table where we sit. I pour the vodka onto the soft towel and use it to stroke away the blood from his eye. Cameron barely flinches at the sting of the alcohol. As the blood wipes away, I observe in utter relief that the cut itself is tiny, though the swollen pink around it only inflames my distress. I raise a quivering hand up to his face, touching the pink skin on his right temple and cheek with the lightest brush of my fingertips before bringing the ice pack up to his eye.

"God, Cameron, I'm so sorry," I manage, tears spilling down my face as my eyes collide with his. "Are you okay?"

He nods, watching me in heavy silence for what feels like an age.

"Does it hurt?" I ask.

"It's not my eye that hurts," he responds, taking the ice pack from me and placing it on the table, his strong hand enveloping mine as he does so, his fingers interlacing mine, pinning them to the table. "Jessynia, what you said—"

"I'm sorry. I can't stay here. Not now. I don't know what I was thinking."

He expels a rough breath. "There's *nothing* that man can do to us. *Nothing*. And he knows it. He's just intimidating you like he always does."

"It doesn't matter. This is wrong and dangerous. You and me. We can't do this. You two were like family for fuck's sake."

"Family? We stopped being *family* when he blackmailed my father, and seduced and dumped my sister on Frost's command. I don't give a fuck about that man anymore and he is certainly no longer family to me after that."

"I know, Cam, but what do you think is going to happen here? That we're just going to be able to walk off into the sunset together and start a new life? He'll *never* let that happen and you know it. We'd be looking over our shoulders constantly. You saw him. He could end up doing something stupid. If something were to happen to you because of me, I would never, ever be able to recover from it. I would spend the rest of my life in pain and grief. Not to mention your mom, Lottie, your sisters. We're dreaming here. This isn't real life."

He reaches an urgent hand up to hold the side of my face, his fingertips curling into the hair at the back of my head, holding me in place. "He's not going to stay like this forever," he says. "In a few weeks' time, he'll calm down. Once he realizes the divorce is going through no matter what tactics he uses to manipulate his way out of this, he'll start accepting that it's over."

"Oh, and you think he'll just sit back and take it as I start dating the man he hates more than anyone?"

"He doesn't hate me," he replies softly. "He tried to make peace with me a few years ago. It was me who couldn't handle his peace offering. I'll go and talk to him, make him understand that if he really loves you, then he has to let you go before he takes you down with him."

"Oh sure, I bet that conversation will go down well. We'll just have to make sure you have a SWAT team on standby..."

"In the meantime, I'll put a security team on both of us." The desolate plea in his eyes leaves a gnawing ache in my chest.

"Cam, we're living in a dream. He will never accept this, security team or not, or at least not anytime soon."

I spot him glancing down at the knuckles of his right hand and I immediately pull it towards me, studying the swollen skin of his beautiful large hand, my fingertips set ablaze by the contact.

"God, Cam..." I shudder as I take the ice pack off the table and put it onto his knuckles. "Does it hurt?" My teary eyes find him again.

"No." He lifts his other hand to my jaw, jolting the side of my face so that I'm forced to look up at him. "Jessynia, I love you. I can't lose you again. I can protect you from him. Please just trust me."

His solemn appeal has me shaking my head as I desperately try to dislodge the temptation to believe him, to fall into his powerful arms and ignore all the alarm bells ringing in my head. I know full well that no amount of security guards will stay the storm of Jack's furor if I were to get together with Cameron now. And it is he who would feel the full force of Jack's ferocity.

"Cam, I'm sorry. This can't happen. I don't know what I was thinking." I pull the phone out of the pocket of my sweatpants.

His hard eyes glance at the phone before cutting to me, anger simmering in his glare. "Jessynia, don't do this. Please stay with me."

A torrent of tears trickles down my cheeks and onto my T-shirt. I glance down to see my bare nipples hard and tight under the thin white cotton, sheer in spots from the wetness of my tears. "Cam, I'm sorry."

"Please," he says.

I call my parents' number and wait.

"Jessie?"

"Dad, it's me. Can you come and pick me up? I'm at Redwood."

"Why— What—?"

"I can't explain it all now. Just please come pick me up."

"What's going on?"

"Dad, please. Just... I need you to come get me. I wouldn't ask if it wasn't important."

"Are you okay? Are you safe?"

"Yeah, I'm safe, Dad. Everything's okay. I just need to come home."

"Okay, just... just let me get dressed. It'll take me an hour to get there. Is that alright?"

"That's fine. Don't rush. Please drive carefully. Not too fast. Promise?"

"Promise. Don't worry."

"Thank you."

"I'm on my way."

I end the call and watch two tears drops onto the screen below me as I try to ignore the dozens of messages I've been sent by Jack over the last few days and text him:

My father is on his way. I don't want any of your men near him, me or anyone else. Call them off now.

His name flashes silently on the screen as he calls me instantly. I reject his call and get a message:

I need to talk to you.

I respond:

I have to pack my stuff. We can talk tomorrow. I don't want anyone near this house or near my father's house. Is that clear?

Jack:

I'll call them off. As long as you swear to me that you haven't and won't let that man touch you.

I swallow hard, having to reach deep into myself to lie to Jack. I've always been a terrible liar. I feel the murderous heat of Cameron's glare on me as I continue to text the man who just assaulted him.

I promise. Please call them off.

Thirty seconds later:

Once you leave this house, they will leave. Not one second before.

I respond:

I'm going to pack and then lie down for an hour.

Jack:

I need to talk to you.

I respond:

No. I can't do this now. I need to be with my parents alone for a few days. We can talk next week.

Jack:

I love you angel. Please let me explain. You don't understand the full story.

Me:

No Jack. I can't. It's too much.

Jack:

When?

I don't answer.

I'm calling you tomorrow. You'd better pick up Jessynia. I'll go insane if you don't.

Me:

Please just leave Cameron alone. He didn't do anything.

Jack:

Once you leave, he will be left alone. Not one second before.

In my final message, I respond:

My dad will be here in an hour. I have to go.

I look up to observe silent torment in Cameron's otherworldly eyes as he watches the screen below, the sharp angles of his face as grim as I have ever seen them.

"Cameron, I'm sorry. I don't want to hurt anyone. This is just way too dangerous."

He exhales roughly. "Jessynia, I've just got you back. I can't lose you again. I won't."

"I'm sorry, but it's not me he'd hurt. It's you." I put my hand onto his, removing it in an instant as a lightning bolt of staticky electricity shocks me, forcing me to take a second to breathe. "I can't put you in this danger."

"I can live with the danger if it means being with you. Life without you is a thousand times more terrifying to me."

"It's not just about us," I respond. "We have to think about your family. If something were to happen to you—"

"He won't hurt me. Not really. Not beyond a punch or two. He couldn't do it. Plus, I can put security on both of us. He wouldn't be able to get near us."

"And what, we live in fear of him trying?"

"The *only* fear I feel is the fear of losing you." He lifts my chin, rubbing a hot thumb over the plump curve of my bottom lip. "The fear that I'll never be able to see you again, to touch you again."

"You'll never lose me, Cam. Never. We'll always be friends. Anything more than that right now is impossible. It's just... *wrong*."

"*Wrong*?" he counters roughly, his gaze darkening like a field falling under a tempestuous thunder cloud.

"I don't mean—"

Before I have a chance to speak, he thrusts his lips onto mine and charges his thick, strong, savage tongue into my mouth. I whimper as he does so and lift my hands up to push against the hard wall of his chest while aware that my sex, already engorged from the half-hour of foreplay we engaged in before Jack arrived is still wet and that I am weak from the desperate need to have him enter me and relieve the gnawing ache within my core and the suffocating stress of both the last half-hour and the months dealing with the bleak darkness of betrayal.

"Cam, we can't," I protest weakly as he lifts me up out of the chair and lays me down onto the kitchen table of polished tigerwood, parting my thighs and standing between them as I look up at him, trying not to give in to the utter defeat of my will, afraid that I have no more resistance to give.

He takes off and throws his sweater to the ground and pulls his black T-shirt over his head as he watches me, his wrathful eyes scorching me with the acuteness of his craving. I inhale sharply at the sight of his sculpted torso and thick, lean arms, densely carved into ridges and valleys of deep caramel. My eyes pan down to the pronounced grooves of his eight-pack as he finds the waistband of my sweatpants with his strong fingers and pulls them down my legs and off my feet leaving just a thin veil of white cotton covering my sex which despite myself is wet, engorged and begging for him.

He leans over me, caging me in, glaring down at me as I glance at the windows quickly to make sure the blinds are drawn before turning to him, trying to muster up some challenge to his advances, to resist the awesome magnetic pull of his body and his overwhelming hunger for mine.

He flexes his arms at the elbow, leaning his face down towards mine. I instinctively lift my hands up to the solid slabs of his pectorals to hold him back as he does so. Using the strength of his arms to hover over me, his face two inches from mine, he glares at me as he asks, "Does it feel *wrong* to be underneath me, Jessynia?"

No. It doesn't. In fact, nothing has ever felt more right.

Jesus, give me strength...

At my refusal to answer, the strong velvet muscle of his tongue slips out of his mouth to lick the surface of my plump lips.

He watches me as I pant my arousal, his eyes narrowing as my lips part. "You like that, don't you?" he murmurs.

I remain silent again, not knowing how on God's green Earth I'm supposed to be able to defy the deep draw of this demi-god's dense body. In response to my refusal to admit the truth of my desire, he parts my lips, licking deep into my mouth which accommodates him without impediment as I melt into the wood beneath me, intoxicated by the sensation of his potent male force claiming my mouth as his own. He pushes, sucks and licks into me, dancing against my tongue, demonstrating his dominance, his exquisite breath heavy on my face.

Pulling out again, he studies me from above, his thick brown hair flopping over his forehead as I try not to drown in the deep bourbon-hued wells of his eyes.

"I don't know how I'm supposed to be able to resist this," I utter softly.

"You're not," he responds gruffly, his moody glare so damn sinful, so delicious. "You were designed to be fucked by me, beautiful. There's nothing you can do to resist it. And you know it, don't you?"

God help me.

At my silence, his hand finds the waistband of my panties, pulling them down before lifting his other hand off the table, uncaging me, standing up straight as he slides the white cotton down my slender legs and off my feet, causing me to blush furiously as he leaves my smooth, naked sex fully exposed in front of him.

His greedy glare meanders down my quivering body as he pulls the hem of my white T-shirt up over my head and throws it to the floor. A rumbling exhale slips from his throat as his fingertips glide over the soft flesh of my ample breasts, skimming both nipples, tugging them to hard points before panning down, his eyes stopping at my sex. A deep, low groan, the noise of a predatory animal, leaves his throat as he kneels down, using his tongue to open the silken folds in a move that has a high-pitched breath escaping me. The tip of his strong muscle finds the tight nub of nerves above my sex which he flicks before pulling away.

"Your sex, Jessynia," he breathes. "Pink. Smooth. Wet. Perfect. It belongs to me now."

A warm swell of anticipation ripples through my body, my clit throbbing as his words come out. He lashes the little bud with his warm tongue before sucking it with a groan, licking up and down and side to side, blowing for a moment before applying his thumb, pressing with a tenderness that seems impossible for this warrior-like man.

God, he feels so good. It feels like I'm supposed to be under him, supposed to have his hands on my body, to have his tongue where it is.

"I'm going to introduce you to realms of pleasure you didn't know existed," he whispers before licking the sensitive knot of nerves again and again and again, his tongue delivering the wettest of caresses before spearing deep inside me as I grip the sides of the table with my hands.

"Cameron!" I exclaim breathlessly as he finds my clit again, lashing it gently, licking rhythmically, working it for several heady minutes as my sex opens up for him, ready to take whatever he has to give. I pant as he runs the full length up and down, feasting on me as though ravenous as I arch my back and breathe, "Don't stop, Cam."

He feasts on me as if he hasn't had a meal in years. Stars blur my vision and I bite my lip to stop myself from screaming his name and begging him to relieve the torture and take me. Take me gently. Roughly. Any damn way he wants.

"That's it. You're going to be coming for me, baby. I need to see that."

On his low utterance and a final flick of his tongue, the intoxicating rush of nirvana undulates through my body in overpowering waves that leave me gasping breathlessly, my limbs stilling, dissolving into the hard wood beneath me. I feel my chest flush hot, my vision going spotty as Cameron stands back up and leans over me, planting his hands on either side of my shoulders, watching me like a tiger would his prey.

"Jesus, you're so fucking beautiful when you come," he says, the rich timbre of his deep voice caressing my skin.

My eyes meet his as my receptive body rides the torrid wave of euphoria that he's pulled me onto. I feel my sex pulse, open and wet in front of him as he straightens back up so that he's standing upright.

My vision clears at the sight of him tugging his pants off his glutes and down his legs to reveal his fully erect cock—thick, long, cut, the head engorged with his blood. As he grips the dense column, I inhale sharply, my pussy pulsating again as it prepares for his entry.

"Are you on birth control, Jessynia?" he asks sternly and I realize he means to fuck me without protection.

"Yes."

"I'm clean," he replies. "Do you trust me?"

I nod again. I trust him. I always have. Since the first minute I met him. I wouldn't give my body to just anyone. I want him so badly that I can barely breathe let alone think.

Clear juices preparing my sex to be penetrated by this godlike man standing before me. He inches his cock forwards, the swollen head lying heavy on the soft pink flesh at the entrance to my body as I part my legs further and bend them up, offering my sex to him completely, aching for him with every cell in my body.

He rubs the engorged dome against the silken opening before grabbing my ankle and lifting it up so that my foot rests on his shoulder. With blazing eyes fixed on me, he softly kisses the creamy flesh of my inner ankle as he holds my calf, before releasing his tongue, the warm muscle tasting me, tracing tingling tracks on the soft skin.

"Cameron," I manage breathlessly as his lashes slip up my leg. I pant and tremble, my heart roaring in my ears as his lips and tongue express how he feels about my body—tenderly at first, and then more fervently, his teeth scraping my flesh, leaving pleasure zinging through my core.

His eyes narrow as his name floats from my throat and he lifts up my other leg, placing both my ankles on his shoulders and leaning forwards, forcing my legs to stretch back as he descends upon me. Fortunately, years of yoga practice make this an easy feat, but the sensation of this man leaning onto me, his erection still lying at the glossy entryway to my swollen, exposed sex leaves me panting in furious anticipation, all reason and sanity escaping me.

He places one hand on either side of my shoulders. "Look at me," he orders and I lock eyes with him, watching timidly, whimpering, my mouth opening wide as he gently feeds his full length into me as the walls of my eager sex contract around him, showing him how welcome he is inside me, something that, deep down, I've wanted to show him for months. I moan as the wet slip of his shaft eases apart my walls—an indecent soundtrack to him slowly sliding into and out of me, his unabashed virility claiming my body. The incandescent embers in his eyes scorch me as his sinfully sculpted lips descend within inches of mine, his exquisite breath hot and urgent.

As my legs stretch further back, he pulls out and rams himself into me in one merciless thrust, extending his thick neck forwards and licking deep into my mouth which opens for him, accommodating his deviant need to fuck me at both ends of my body. As his drives into me become more fervent, my legs drop down on either side of his arms, the soles of my feet hitting the smooth table beneath me as I let out high-pitched breaths of reverence and awe at the sight and sensation of him locking me in possessively, his unwavering eyes penetrating mine with every thrust.

"Jesus, Cam, I'm so wet," I whimper as I realize my sex hasn't felt wet like this for months, since discovering Jack's affairs, and that I could climax a second time if he keeps going.

His deviant grunt of pleasure has my hands gripping the sides of the table. "You like being fucked by me, angel?" he whispers roughly into my lips, cupping the nape of my neck with one of his hands, his fingers threading into my hair as his chest collapses onto mine, the weight of his bulky frame so exquisite, the crush of his muscles so welcome.

"Yes," I respond, licking his pink lips, my whole helpless body aflame, drugged by his lust, his power, his volatile jealousy, his unashamed male competence. It feels like a lightbulb has turned on inside me, illuminating my cells, pulling me out of the darkness I've languished in for so long. "I like it," I add, paralyzed by the devious drive of his greedy cock into the tight tunnel, stretching me open as he uses my body to reach nirvana. I want him to use it. I ache for him to.

"Good," he replies as I part my lips for him. "You'll have to get used to it. Before I impregnate you, I'm going to be spending a couple of years defiling your tight little body." The moody, mercurial bite in his voice and that murderous glare of his is so damn good...

Holy hell, I have no idea how to resist this man.

My sex pulses and I lean my head back as his fingers slide down to my clit and gently use my juices to massage it over and over again, pressing and pinching until I once again feel the tsunami of ecstasy ricochet through me as I pant his name, unable to stay the swell of euphoria released in my body after months of needing it during the dark fallout of Jack's affairs.

"Hmm, you like that," he hisses as he rams his thick length into me with the utmost skill, my face scrutinized by him as I accommodate his diabolical need for my body. "Don't take your eyes off mine," he orders, lifting his glistening torso and standing up so that he can hold my legs together. He pushes my bent knees way up to my chest, groaning as he slowly inserts himself into and out of the glossy hole between my legs. He watches my face as I study him fervently, in awe at the sexual mastery of this warrior of a man. "Jessynia," he breathes, gripping my calves, positioning them exactly the way he wants them.

"Cameron..."

Beads of sweat trickle down his golden neck as he pleasures himself for several minutes with the inside of my submissive body before releasing my legs, my feet finding the table. He places his hands on either side of my shoulders and forms a cage above me, his eyes boring into me as I try not to pass out at the sight, feel and sound of being fucked by what is as close as you can get to a god in human form. We pant, our breaths syncing, the grinding of flesh transporting us into some other dimension.

"Look at me. Look into my eyes," he orders, his swollen eye paining me, making his brutal beauty all the more savage and terrifying.

As he drives into my wet warmth, the hard wood against my back sends a spike of pain into my shoulder blade.

"Cam, my back..."

Without saying a word, he leans over, sliding his hands behind my back and lifting my torso up so that my chest is flush against his. My legs wrap around his hard, sculpted glutes possessively as he cups my buttocks and carries me silently and effortlessly out of the kitchen and up the stairs, the head of his cock pressing into my cervix with each step that he takes.

He takes a left at the top of the stairs and carries me into his dark bedroom, moonlit only through the bathroom at the back, and onto the four-poster bed adorned with gray sheets. He sets me down gently onto his mattress, as if handling some delicate work of art before climbing on top of me and proceeding to fuck me again, interlacing his fingers with mine and pinning them to the pillow beneath my head as his tongue samples my neck, caressing it with unrelenting need.

His head lifts to allow his tongue to find mine, pushing it back, gifting me the ultimate show of dominance as he licks deep into my mouth which welcomes him unreservedly, my body open for whatever invasion he desires.

His unwavering eyes meet mine. "I need you, Jessynia," he breathes into me, thickening the air with his lustful hunger as he works my receptive body like an athlete, his hips thrusting rhythmically as the sweat dripping from both of us leaves us a tangle of hot, slippery bodies. "I need you like I need air. I can't breathe without you."

I want to tell him how much I need him to, but I'm so afraid to do so...

"Dammit," he shudders gruffly, his dense torso weighing divinely on my soft body. "There are things I want to do to you. Indecent things. Things that will leave you shaking for days. But I can't do them with these time constraints. Your father arriving soon..."

"I know. I'm sorry," I whisper as I run my fingertips down the carved contours of his back, set aflame by the contact with his skin.

He lets out a breath of frustration and stops his thrusting, his dick still rock-hard inside me. Afraid he'll stop, I search his eyes imploringly. "Cam, I need to see you come." My sex tingles, aching, desperate for the euphoric release that I know will come with watching him climax as I've dreamed of doing so many times.

He breathes out roughly. "No, Jessynia. You don't get to see that until I am sure that you belong to me."

"Cam, please," I coax, spreading my legs further and reaching around to the hard muscles of his taut ass, tugging him towards me so that his cock slides deep into me, causing a pinch in my cervix. "Please come for me. I need to see you. Please."

He thrusts a few times with a groan and then closes his eyes as his lips find the soft crook of my neck. After a few suspended moments, he pulls his hard shaft out of me and I realize that I won't get to see him climaxing.

I reach down for his cock and he grabs my hand and pins it to the pillow next to me. "No. Not today."

I close my eyes for a second, my body frustrated at not giving this man the release he deserves. "Cam, I can't take not seeing you come. What do I need to do?"

"I like control. And I need to know that you belong to me before you get to see that."

"Let me use my mouth," I murmur, feeling it water in anticipation of tasting his divine flesh. "I've been dreaming about it for days."

He closes his eyes for a second as if contemplating the idea of it before the word "no" finally comes out of his mouth in a rush, as if against his will.

I breathe out in frustration and wriggle out from under him, tilting onto my side to face him as he settles down on the mattress. I lift trembling fingers to touch his unearthly face, brushing sticky hair out of his eyes and running down his pronounced cheekbones. His hot skin glistens, beads of dew running down his neck and onto this square shoulders. We lie there for a minute, our bodies mellowing, recovering from the workout delivered so competently by this deity.

"Jessynia, I can't live without you anymore. You are in my blood. You are part of me. Part of my cells. And I'm done waiting."

I look down for a moment, closing my eyes as I succumb to the weight of the loss I will feel at being away from him, of the fear of Jack finding out, of knowing that I don't feel in full control of myself anymore.

"When will I see you next?" he asks.

"I don't know. I'm scared. If he were to do something to you, I would never survive it."

"He won't hurt me."

"How do you know?"

"Because we were inseparable, for years. And as much as he may despise me right now, he would have to have lost his soul completely to really hurt me. As long as you stay away from him, with time, he'll start to accept that the relationship is over. This won't last forever."

As his hand touches the side of my face, I close my eyes, clueless as to how the hell I got here. How do I begin to navigate this thing when I'm incapable of resisting this man? When all reason leaves me when he pins my hands above my head, his hot body craving me as much as I crave him?

Opening my eyes, I tenderly press my lips to his, defying the urge to beg him to fuck me again. "I'm going to try to do everything I can to have the breakup go smoothly," I say, "but for now, he must never, ever know about tonight. Promise? It's dangerous. For both of us."

He nods and I turn to look at the alarm clock next to the bed.

Thirty-five minutes have passed since I hung up the call with my dad. "My dad will be here in half an hour. I have to take a shower."

"Let me help you," he responds, standing up from the bed and picking me up.

He carries me with ease to the huge en-suite bathroom and places me down in the walk-in shower behind a glass partition. The floor of the shower is rough granite whose various shades of gray match the hundreds of rectangular slate tiles lining the walls. Soft spotlights above leave our shadows bouncing all around. The accents in the bathroom are a mixture of flaxen bamboo and angular stainless-steel hardware. I'd never thought it were possible to be intimidated by a bathroom but this one certainly manages it. It looks like something you'd see in some elite dungeon.

He turns on the shower and I breathe out an exclamation of pleasure as the cool water from the rainfall showerhead above us trickles onto our hot bodies. I run my hands down the solid caramel curves of his arms and find his eyes as the head of his erection prods my abdomen. I can't stop myself from smiling at the sensation of being caressed by tepid water while up against the hard body of this athletic man.

Unspeaking, he takes some shampoo from a thick ledge that juts out from the side of the shower and massages it through my hair while I look into his devouring eyes as he rubs the suds into my scalp. The desperation to drop to my knees and spend half an hour sucking on his thick cock is arrested only by the knowledge that I have to get ready for when my father arrives. Instead, I reach down, sliding my fingers over his taut abs and neatly trimmed pubis, skimming his engorged length until I find his sack, hanging heavy and full. A loud breath escapes me at the feel of it.

"Mmm, I see you're a very bad girl, Miss Avery," he murmurs, eyes gleaming with appreciation as I squeeze the large sack gently, hoping to unleash his need to release his seed inside me so that I get to see him come.

Damn he's big. His cock is easily as long as Jack's eight and some inches if very slightly less thick—which, after months of pain with Jack, is quite frankly a very welcome relief—but his sack is most definitely a little bigger. It feels so sinfully full. I want him emptying himself inside me and only me. His eyes harden as I knead him.

"I think you already knew that, sir," I answer teasingly.

"Well, I certainly hoped so," he replies, a devilish flicker of lust dancing in his eyes.

He untangles his fingers from my hair and I smile in awe at the sight of him rubbing shampoo into his gloriously thick chocolate-brown hair, down his almost-hairless chest and then onto his groin as he runs his strong grip up and down his rock-hard shaft several times as my hand gently squeezes his balls, reminding him of what I know he really wants.

"Jesus, Cameron," I pant as I watch him caress his thick column to the point of utmost attention, watching me, a delectable scowl on his face as he tends to his manhood with strong, talented hands that I don't ever want him to have to resort to using again. I want my body to be his. I want him to use it when he needs to. I just want him, dammit.

Jess, what are you doing?

I tip my head back so that the waterfall rinses the shampoo out of my hair.

"Turn around," he commands as I finish.

"Cam, I don't know if we have time—"

And with that, he spins me around, leaving my hands pushed against the slate wall of the shower. My feet don't slip on the coarse granite floor and he lifts one leg up so that my right foot lands on the ledge, leaving my pink sex open and accessible in front of him.

He grabs hold of a second wall-mounted showerhead and turns it on, placing it between my legs as the cool water pulsates against my clit.

He holds me against him possessively, his massive body curled around me as he grinds against me, the tempo stormy and urgent as he simulates sex, kissing and sucking at my wet skin like a famished beast.

"Fuck," he whispers hoarsely. "I need you again..." The head of his shaft finds my juicy slit and I melt into the menace of his mouth next to my ear as he growls, "I'm going to have to give you something very serious to think about while we're apart."

"Please do, Mr. O'Neill," I invite, moaning at the audacious invasion of his thick girth into my tight pussy, still tender from the hammering it just took. As he begins to thrust, he grasps my throat with his free hand, nipping the side of my neck with his teeth, deviant growls emanating from him as he fucks me mercilessly as the pulse of the showerhead has my clit throbbing.

"Jesus, you cannot imagine the depraved things I want to do to you," he whispers darkly, his desperate yearning leaving me exhaling in pleasure.

"Mmm, Cam," I whisper, dissolving into the hard walls of his lean body. "You have no idea how badly I want you to do them to me."

Jessynia...

Fuck, I know this is wrong. I know it's not allowed. Forbidden. This is the one man that Jack will never be able to accept. But he's also the one man that every ounce of my flesh and soul needs more than anything.

And I have no idea how to stop the penetrating pull drawing me in.

"We'll take it slow, beautiful," he says, lips slipping against my wet ear with a tenderness utterly at odds with the beastly way he's ravishing my slit. "You'll need time to get used to the ways I'm going to love you. To protect you." His thrust into me is so deep. "To possess you. To educate you."

I moan at the promise as he releases the showerhead and grabs hold of my hair with his right hand, pulling my left arm behind my back with his other, twisting and holding it firmly behind me as he locates my neck with his mouth and bites again gently, his breathing raspy as he ravages my delicate body until I feel it turn to mush. As he starts to up the pace and I realize he is going to orgasm, I try to turn my head to look at him.

In response, he tightens his grip on my hair and cranks my arm even further up my back until it twinges slightly.

"Cam, I want to see your face when you come."

"No."

"Please..."

"I told you, you won't see that until I can be sure you belong to me fully."

"Cam, please. I'd do anything to watch."

"I can't, angel. I'm sorry."

Animalistic noises rumble from his throat as he tightens his grasp on my hair, his tongue tasting the side of my neck. He pushes me forward so that my breasts are pressed against the wall of the shower and lets go of my arm, finding my clit with his free hand which he strokes up and down as I whimper in anticipation of this sensational man's orgasm. He presses my clit one more time and my sex starts to clench and pulse around his as waves of a softer, deeper third orgasm hit me, the sensation of his trembling muscles tipping me into ecstasy.

At the sound of my cry, he lets out a deep, guttural roar, his athletic body collapsing onto mine, his arm wrapping around my chest and his mouth nuzzling the curve of my shoulder as he envelops my back just as he did in that hallway at Quercus Velutina. The nirvana of climax ripples through both of us with the soundtrack of our heartbeats almost drowning out the gentle tap of water onto the granite below us as his muscles hold my slippery body tightly in place.

"Do you like the feel of me inside you, Jessynia?"

I nod. "Jesus, Cameron. You're a god."

"This is just the start, angel. I have plans for your pleasure. Nothing will stop them."

Finally pulling out of me, he grabs a bar of black soap from the ledge and traces it down my body, sliding it over the taut curves of my belly, over my smooth pubis and onto the silky folds of my delicate sex before tending to his own and rinsing us both, lifting me up out of the shower and carrying me back through his bedroom and into the guestroom I have been staying in where he places me down on the bed, naked.

God, I could get used to this.

I look up to observe his smile—one of pure male satisfaction. I reciprocate, biting my lip as he stands over me.

"Your father should be here soon. You need to get dressed," he says, his gleaming eyes wandering greedily down to my chest.

"God, Cam, your eye looks red. Here use this..." I jump up and rummage around the purse I had dumped on the floor earlier for a little tube of arnica cream, a smidgen of which I squeeze out onto my fingers as I stand up and massage the skin around his eye as gently as I can. "Arnica is an herb. It helps with swelling and pain. I use it all the time for my ankle," I say as I rub it into the swollen skin around his upper cheekbone. "It really helps."

"Mmm, I like having you as my own personal nurse." He towers over me, glancing down at the nipples peeking through gaps in my long brown hair, his fingers finding the soft teats as he watches me tenderly while I tend to his face with the utmost care.

I ignore his arousal, feeling weakened by the sight of his mesmerizing beauty made all the more terrible by traces of his gruesome war wounds. Luckily the eye itself doesn't look hurt in any way but my stomach sinks at the sight of the mauve skin around it.

"That's going to swell up during the night," I shudder, handing him the tube. "Put the arnica on all day and an ice pack on it for five minutes every hour tomorrow. Promise?"

"I promise. You need to get dressed," he says, picking me up once again and carrying me to the guest room.

"Thank you," I breathe into his ear as he sets me down next to my suitcase.

"You're welcome," he replies. "I'll meet you downstairs." He glances back at me, the flicker of a smile dancing in his eyes as he leaves and closes the door behind him. I sit myself down on the rug next to my case.

Holy shit, did that really just happen?

My head sinks into my hands as I try to make sense of what just took place, and how powerless I feel to resist this man, as well as of my conflicting emotions—the ecstasy of being fucked by this deity mixed with the guilt at having slept with a man I swore to Jack I wouldn't touch.

Maybe Jack does deserve it after the months of him sleeping with so many other women, but I don't want to hurt him. It's just that I don't feel in control around Cameron, and after having lost part of my feisty self under the weight of Jack's power, it's not a dynamic I really should be getting into again.

But Lord knows how I'm possibly supposed to resist the sheer vigor of his lure...

As I take a few minutes and try to calm my respiration and breathe through the waves of pleasure still rippling through my insides, light beams into the bedroom and I jump up and run to the window.

"Oh God," I mutter as my dad's car screeches down the driveway. The poor man must have floored it all the way. He pulls up to the back of the security guard's car which is still in the driveway, and gets out, rushes up the steps and starts ringing the doorbell like an enraged woodpecker. I spy one of the security guards walking up the driveway towards the house and hear the thud of Cameron's steps on the landing and then down the stairs.

As he opens the front door, I throw open my mini-suitcase and grab a T-shirt, jeans and a loose black sweater which I wrangle onto my damp body. Quick as a flash, my hair ends up in a ponytail before I swiftly throw any remaining items lying around the place into my suitcase and zip it closed.

"Is she here?" I hear my dad bellow.

"She's here, Philip." Cameron's smooth, measured tone is infinitely soothing. "Everything is fine."

"I'm here, Dad," I yell at the top of my lungs, opening the bedroom door.

"What the hell happened to your eye?" I hear my dad bark. "Are you alright?"

Oh, Lord.

I yank my bags to the top of the stairs, then head to Cam's bedroom to grab my purse.

"Everything's okay, Dad," I shout. "Don't worry."

"Don't worry?! Do you mind telling me what the hell happened here? Why does this young man have a black eye?"

Cam bounds upstairs, grabs my bag and carries it down.

"Thanks, Cam."

"Well?!" my dad yells.

"God, Dad, you're stressing me out."

"*I'm* stressing *you* out?!"

"It's not black. It's just a bit pink," I respond in an effort to calm the piquant paternal storm.

"Pink?! It'll be black tomorrow, Jessynia."

"God, don't say that. You're giving me anxiety."

He breathes out in exasperation and lowers his tone, feigning a calm demeanor. "Are we going to spend the rest of the night debating the color wheel, young lady, or am I going to get some answers?"

"Jack came to the house," responds Cameron. "There was an altercation."

"An altercation?! How the hell did he know where you were?"

"Stella called the house tonight," says Cameron. "She found out that he had had her car tracked. I didn't have time to ask her for all the details. Not long after, he showed up."

"Well, I hope you got in a punch or two of your own, young man."

"Dad, stop," I moan, my stomach lurching again at the thought of Cameron and Jack exchanging blows and the flecks of crimson running down their faces.

"Well, he may have trouble eating tomorrow in my opinion," responds Cameron.

"Cam, stop," I admonish, energy seeping from my limbs at the image of Jack's mouth filled with blood.

"Good!" exclaims my father. "He's finally met his match, that arrogant son of a bitch."

"Dad, stop encouraging him! I don't want them ever doing that again."

"Listen, young lady. What women don't understand is that the occasional scuffle is what makes a man feel alive. I fought over your mother once."

"What?!"

"Yes, I did. And I still want to do a jig when I remember my right hook connecting with that nauseating snob's bottom lip."

"Well, I'm guessing that the *nauseating snob* is no match for Jack and

I don't want Cameron thinking this is some game. People die or get maimed in these so-called *scuffles*, you know?"

"Yes, well, I have to agree with my daughter, Cameron. I think avoiding this kind of thing in the future is best."

"I'll try, Philip."

"As for that eye, get an ice pack on it ASAP."

"I've already told him all that, Dad. Look, we have to get a move on. I don't want Jack turning up again."

Ten minutes later, Cameron lifts my suitcase into the trunk of my dad's car and slams the door shut as I load my other bag into the back seat. A security guard walks around the side of the house, bracing himself against the bluster of an unseasonably fierce wind.

"Cameron," my father says, extending his hand out to shake my friend's. "I know I was joking back there about the joys of the old right hook, but my daughter is right. You could end up badly hurt, especially if he doesn't play fair which I don't think he does. Please look after yourself."

"I will."

"If he comes near you again, call the police. Or call me. I'd like to kick that prick's ass myself."

"Jesus, Dad," I moan, rolling my eyes.

"Hopefully, it won't come to that," Cameron responds with a smile.

"Well, as far as I'm concerned, you are just as much my responsibility as Jessynia. I want to know about it if he causes you any problems at all. I'll be texting you every day to check." Cam's face softens at the expression of my dad's protective fatherly instincts. I wish Cam's father was still around to help protect his son. "And thank you, young man, for everything you've done for my daughter. Her mother and I are very grateful to you. More than we can express."

"Well, I told you how much she has done for me in the past, Phillip. I wasn't exaggerating. I'm just returning a tiny bit of the favor."

"Okay. You two say goodbye," says my father as he gets into the car.

I turn to face Cameron and find his eyes tender on my face. "Sorry about my dad. I'm fairly sure he thinks he's Chuck Norris."

"Jess, I need you to text me when you get home."

"I will."

"I want to see you again. *Soon*. I *need* to see you."

"I know. Just give me a few days to figure out what I'm doing."

"I'll give you a couple of days," he manages, his expression as somber as the stormy night air.

"Cam, please can you ask the security guys to spend the night here? I'll be worried sick if you don't."

"I will. And I have my own guys driving over from Manhattan right now. They'll be here within an hour. I'll have them spend a couple of weeks with me, just in case."

I touch my hand to my chest, shuddering out a breath of relief. "Thank God for that."

"And I'll have a team stationed on you as well."

"What?! Cam, no. You don't have to do that."

"You won't see them, don't worry. They'll be watching to make sure he doesn't get near you."

I let out a long breath, knowing from his determined stare that I won't convince him to drop the security detail. As we stand watching each other, I don't even know what to say to this man who has protected me so fervently and ravaged me so unapologetically. "Thank you, Cam. For everything."

He bows his head, his gaze colliding with mine once again.

"I'd better go," I finally say, not wanting to at all.

As I turn to leave, his strong fingers wind around my arm, leaving a searing flare in their wake. "Jessynia, you don't mention the Society to anyone, understand? Not your parents, not Stella, not Maddie, not Kevin. *No one*. This is about their safety. Your safety. Mine. Everyone's. What happened the other night was just a *mild* taste of what they will do to people who threaten to expose them. Is that clear?"

"I won't tell anyone. I promise."

"Good." He leans into me, lowering his stern voice to a guttural whisper. "And don't make me wait too long. My body needs you. I already crave you again. I have plans for you, Jessynia. Nothing will get in the way of them. Your body belongs to me now. Understood?"

My sex pulsates at the thought of his and I swallow hard, trying not to drown in the unflinching copper pools of his eyes.

"I have to go," I utter, wishing I didn't.

He walks me round to the passenger door and opens it, letting me in before closing it behind me.

As my dad does a U-turn and drives us away, I watch Cameron in the side mirror as a security guard approaches him. They get smaller and smaller until they finally go out of sight.

Another guard is in a car outside the gate. As we approach, he buzzes it open, allowing us to depart and take a right at the end of Cameron's long driveway, driving through thickets of dense dark trees up to the end of the lane where I spot a black SUV parked on the right side of the road. I turn to look inside and see it empty, but something about it sends a dart of anxiety arrowing through my belly.

I take my phone out of my bag and text Jack:

I've left with my dad. I don't want any of your men near Redwood.

He responds instantly:

Did he touch you?

I pause for five heart-stopping seconds. I hate to lie to him, to anyone, but he can't ever know what happened.

No. Nothing happened. I slept for half an hour and then we talked a little while waiting for dad. Nothing else. Are your men near him?

He responds:

I'll call them off if you promise me he didn't touch you.

My heart jitters in my chest as I type back:

I promise you.

He responds:

I need to talk to you Jessynia.

I can't talk now. You need to give me a few days.

You have to let me explain what happened.

No. I can't do this anymore Jack. I'm sorry.

Please just let me explain. You don't understand. I had no choice.

I shake my head in a burst of frustration and type swiftly:

I need to heal Jack. Give me a few days with my parents. We can talk after that. Please.

I'm warning you not to shut me out again, Jessynia. I lose my fucking mind every time.

Are you hurt?

I know I shouldn't be asking him that, but the thought of his bloody mouth makes me feel weak. Part of me still wants to tend to his wounds despite myself.

No.

OK. Cameron didn't do anything. He saved me when I broke down and gave me a safe place to stay. Nothing more. I want him left out of this.

His messages stop for a full half-minute.

As long as he has not touched you, there won't be any more blood.

I told you he hasn't.

I hope not Jessynia. For all our sakes.

I have to go Jack. I'm too tired to type.

I'll call you tomorrow.

No. I really need a few days to myself.

You're still my wife Jessynia. Nothing changes that. Nothing will ever change that. I'm going to make you understand that.

I'm with my dad. I have to go.

You have to let me talk to you.

Next week. Please respect my need for space Jack.

My hands no longer work and I slide my phone back into my bag.

"Well, you certainly know how to pick 'em, young lady," chides my dad.

"Yeah," I sigh, watching the shadowy tree sentries around us as we drive away.

4

AFTER SEVERAL DAYS spent at my parents' Connecticut home with conversation aplenty and clarity little, I inhale a refreshing lungful of air as my dad drives my mom and me down East Boston Post Road in the direction of Manhattan. He has always refused to take the "soulless"—as he puts it—New England Thruway and as we drive through Mamaroneck and Larchmont and other familiar little towns I've often stopped at throughout my childhood, the familiarity takes the edge off the excitement I feel as I head back into Manhattan.

I'm trying to convince myself that it really is excitement and ignore the whirling trepidation fluttering in my chest and pang of dread settling deep in my belly. Manhattan has always been *my* city, a place whose heartbeat pulsed with mine. The events of the last few months *won't* take that from me. I won't let them, dammit.

As my parents take turns giving opposing styles of pep talk interspersed with irate reproaches that they contradict with jarring moments of gentle advice, I play with the brand-new phone that Cameron had sent to my parents' place a few days ago to solve the problem of the possible tracker on my phone. He also sent me links to firewalls to download so that Jack can't track it ever again.

I haven't spoken to Jack since I left Redwood despite him trying to call many times. I've mainly been attempting lukewarm responses to his incessant texts. At least he had the decency not to turn up at my parents' house, but I'm filled with malaise at the thought of the conversation I have to have with him in a couple of days' time.

Cameron and I have talked a few times though I've tried not to get overcome by his indecent promises of pleasure which I keep asking him to stop engaging in. I try with all my might not to get sucked in by the deep husk of his voice as it gets low and he starts telling me what I mean to him and murmuring all the unspeakable things he will do to me when he sees me next, but I'm struggling to know how any predominantly heterosexual woman could possibly muster up the fortitude to tell that man to stop when they hear him groan his indecent sexual threats down the phone.

He keeps asking me to reciprocate but I don't. It's bad enough that I'm taking his calls and not hanging up when he shares his dark desires with me, but reciprocating would be going too far, though I can't deny that my fingers have found their way down to my clit a few times as I listen to him pleasure himself while whispering delicious words of domination that leave me panting internally, desperate for release.

Every time I get off the phone from him, guilt consumes me as I remember my promise to Jack—guilt that I try to snap myself out of when I realize that for all I know he may be screwing Alexandra Frost or some other woman at that very moment. At that point, I try to cut myself the tiniest slack.

My weakness in the face of Cameron's lust has me struggling to stay in friend zone with him, even though I know that being with him now is just not an option. Jack would never allow it no matter what Cam thinks, and if one of them were to get hurt, I'd never forgive myself. Not to mention that I have to start healing from the split with Jack and delving into another all-consuming romance with a powerful, dominant man like Cameron O'Neill, a coveted icon of Manhattan's high society, would be an exercise in stupid.

But God dammit, why does the thought of it have to feel so good? Why does my sex pulsate and do my hands get clammy at the image of his muscular frame standing over me, the thought of his pulsing, cut erection threatening to invade my fragile body? Images of him glaring at me as he fucks me penetrate my mind constantly. The thought that I haven't yet felt his heavy cock in my mouth or tasted his cum frustrates me. My sex is wet all day long at the thought of experiencing his perverse carnality.

Jess, stop...

Jesus, I thought that no one could ever match Jack for sexual prowess or desirability, but clearly, I was very wrong. But why the hell does he have to be Jack's former friend? Other than for Jack I've never felt lust that compares to this. My body hums day and night in anticipation of being ravaged by what used to be one of my closest friends.

I don't just desire Cameron physically. I care for him desperately and love every moment in his presence. He is razor sharp, cultivated, poised, witty, wise... I constantly want to make sure he is okay and happy and that his eye is healing. I can't bring myself to think the L-word, but I'm starting to feel that heady insanity that hit me when Jack launched his seduction assault in London three or so years ago that had me floating in space for months.

Jessynia, hold it together...

"Are you with us, madam?" my mother squawks at me from the front seat, jolting me upright with the power of her gravelly voice.

"Um, yeah. Sorry, I was just thinking..."

"I really think you should be paying Kevin some rent for letting you stay with him."

"I've tried, Mom. He won't take it. He said I could get the groceries for both of us and do some of the cooking instead."

"You're lucky to have the friends you do. I hope you appreciate them."

"Of course I do! Jesus, Mom. Did you take extra crabby pills today?"

She groans in irritation. She hates car rides and gets moody as hell after five minutes of being cooped up, especially when the traffic is heavy and the early-afternoon sun is blazing like today.

"Kev's been a bit down over his breakup lately. He told me it'd do him good to live with someone for a couple of months," I add. "It was his idea!"

"Well, don't upset him too much talking about yours, Jessynia."

"Jesus, Mom. There's nothing Kevin likes better in this world than picking apart other people's personal lives. He perks up like a cheerleader on acid whenever he can get his tentacles into a juicy divorce or whatnot. He's always asking for more gossip. Plus, he told me that helping me is healing. Helps him move on from his own breakup."

"Well, good."

After a further knuckle-biting forty-five minutes in the car with my parents and a text to Kevin, we finally pull up half a block down from his SoHo apartment. I grin widely as I watch him bound out and run down the street towards us as we get out of the car. He hops up to me and envelops me in a bear hug, lifting my feet off the ground and kissing my neck.

"Hey, you!" he sings, his bright yellow T-shirt standing out like a punk rocker at a cocktail party. "I'm so excited! I've got scalloped potatoes waiting to go in the oven and that fizzy strawberry wine you're obsessed with."

"Oh, Kev, you shouldn't have!"

He turns to my parents. "Hi, Diana. Hi, Phil. How was the drive?"

"Well, my daughter was on another planet the whole time," my mother crows, "but luckily I had her father to keep me company."

I roll my eyes at Kev who grins in response. "How are you doing, Philip?" a smiling Kevin asks my dad.

"Oh, I'm good. Always happy when I've managed to get to the end of a car ride without my darling wife threatening to murder me."

"The engine's still warm, dear," my mother sings. "There's still time."

Kevin bursts into gentle laughter and I grab the keys and pull my bags out of the trunk. "Are you sure you two don't want to come in for a while?" he asks my parents.

"We'd love to, sweetie," replies my mom, "but we have to check into our hotel and we're having dinner with some old friends later and Philip needs a nap before we do that."

"I do?"

"Yes, you do, darling."

"Well, glad you're keeping me informed," responds dad.

Kevin and I stifle a chuckle at my parents' never-ending banter. "I wish I had a third bedroom," says Kevin.

"Oh, don't worry about it, darling," replies my mother. "It'll be nice to spend a couple of nights in a hotel for a change. Spice things up a bit."

Kevin raises his eyebrows at my dad and smiles as my father sighs, "Ah, this is going to be a long couple of days. I can feel it."

My mom delivers a scolding pinch to his arm and turns to Kevin. "We'll be over tomorrow. Lunchtime alright?"

"Perfect. We'll see you both then."

After saying our goodbyes to my parents, Kevin and I carry my bags up to the third floor where he lets us into his open loft-style apartment. The smell of lemon and herbs hits me first and then the sight of the ochre brick walls, the stark white columns leading to the ceiling and the huge red sectional to the right surrounding a low marble-topped coffee table opposite a now-defunct fireplace.

We head towards the back of the apartment, passing a long table of light wood and matching benches lying before the open-plan kitchen to the right.

As we head into the guest bedroom to the left, Kevin plonks down my suitcase. "Hope this is okay," he says.

"Okay?!" I reply, mouth agape at the glorious décor with its periwinkle-blue bedsheets and lemon-yellow walls contrasting against white bedside tables upon one of which lies a tray of snacks, bottles of water and toiletries.

"Kev, you shouldn't have gone to this trouble!"

"Well, what the hell's the point of being an interior designer if you can't show off to your friends a bit."

I throw my arms around him and kiss him on the cheek. "Thank you so much for letting me stay. I was terrified of having to rent an apartment on my own."

"Well, you're doing me the favor, kiddo. I've not been feeling good since I found out that Gary's dating that lawyer asshole."

Gary is Kevin's ex and the "lawyer asshole" is a smoking-hot thirty-three-year-old with the face of an Adonis and the body to match.

"Well, I hear he's a total prick," I respond, rubbing a smudge of something off Kev's lovely face and tucking a loose strand of his ruddy-brown hair behind his ear.

"Yeah, well, when you look like that, you can afford to be," he groans.

"Yeah, I know *that* story," I sigh.

"Mmm hmm..."

"I bet they have nothing in common apart from—" I sigh at my verbal clumsiness. "Sorry."

"You know what? Screw him. If that's what he's going for these days, we had no business being together anyway."

"Couldn't agree more, sweetie," I say.

After enjoying a hour-long nap to sleep off the post-parental irritation, I wash up and join Kevin in the kitchen, taking a seat at his kitchen island with its metallic top which matches his stainless-steel appliances. Stella will be joining us soon and I'm feeling giddy to be surrounded by people I love right now who are distracting me from thinking about Jack—or Cameron—too much.

Jack phoned before my nap but I didn't take the call. Instead, I texted him to let him know that I needed a couple more days to think. Not that two more days will make any difference. I feel as torn to pieces as ever. Staying with him after seeing Alexandra Frost on her knees with her mouth open in front of him is not an option. I will lose all trust in myself if I do, not to mention self-respect. I can't do it. I just wish I didn't love him anymore. I'm still tormented by the idea of him being in pain, a torment made all the more acute by the guilt I feel over sleeping with Cameron which has me responding to Jack's texts instead of ghosting him like I should do.

I shudder at the thought of his last text:

I can't feel light without you, angel. Please help me.

I want to help him, but I can't. I know that the next time I find him cheating I will lose part of my soul. I'll start turning into one of those wives I see at Wall Street galas with glassy eyes, reaching for whatever distraction, substance or person they can get their hands on to numb them to the mire behind the glittery mirage they present to the world on their cheating husbands' arm.

As much as I still love this sensational man with his blazing storm of fire and strength, however wrong that may be, I know that I can't be with him ever again.

I also know that Jack isn't the type of man that takes losing what belongs to him lying down, especially if he senses another man in the vicinity. As for Cameron, I know that's wrong and irresponsible, but I've tasted the drug of his flesh and I can't seem to think of much else right now...

Neither Kevin nor Stella know that we slept together. I've been working up the courage to tell them. I'm sure they'll approve of the idea of another man helping me finally break free of Jack. Stella has told me to cheat on him often enough. Maybe their reassurance is just what I need...

A while later, Kevin and I laugh as Stella recounts asking the shocked lawyer colleague she slept with last night to leave her apartment at 2 a.m. so she could sleep as we tipsily finish off Kev's delectable scalloped potatoes, green beans and braised cabbage, all washed down with bubbly strawberry wine.

I'm grateful for the Dutch courage and for my gorgeous, zany friends who make me laugh despite the nervousness I feel as I build up to telling them about sleeping with Cameron. If anyone will understand, it will be these two...

"Guys, I have to tell you something," I blurt out after my third glass.

"What, sweetie?" asks Stella, glugging down the last of her glass of wine.

"I slept with Cameron."

Silence. Even the music stops. In the quiet between tracks, Kevin and Stella glance at me and then each other solemnly.

Still not a word...

"Good God, guys, say something, please." I grab the bottle of wine off the table and fill up my glass, taking a sip to steady my nerves.

"When did it happen?" asks Stella sitting next to Kevin opposite me.

I explain the events of that night at Redwood, hoping that my vivid descriptions of Cameron's godlike body and enthusiastic virility will strike a chord of understanding in my friends.

"Oh, Lord," mutters Kevin.

"What?" I respond. "You judge me, right?"

"Judge you?" he exclaims. "Hell, girl, I don't know a straight woman on the planet who could turn *that* down. We ain't the judging type, honey," he adds to a nod from Stella. "But that night is over. You have to engage your brain now."

"I'm trying," I breathe out roughly, "believe me."

"Look," responds Kevin. "I get that he may be the hottest male specimen to ever walk the Earth, Jess, but if that asshole ex of yours finds out, he'll set his Bronx goons on both of you."

"I'm not planning on doing anything," I stammer. "I— I— I don't know what I was thinking. You just can't imagine how hard it is to say no to a man like that. Every cell in my body was just like a freaking slave to him. After the nightmare I've been through these last few months, I just... I couldn't say no."

"We get it, baby," says Stella, her hazel eyes soft. "I've been there, many a time. But this is the one man on this Earth that Jack will never allow you to be with. I've seen too much shit from crazy ex-husbands in my job. I can't watch you put yourself in danger like this."

I down the rest of my glass of wine and hang my head. "Shit, I've really messed up. I never meant this to happen. After seeing Jack with Alex, I just... I needed to get the energy of that night out of me... Plus,

Cameron declaring his love for me wasn't exactly something that I knew how to handle."

"He did?" asks Stella, glancing at Kevin who grabs the bottle of wine and takes a slug directly from it.

I nod, my eyes wandering to the gorgeous spattering of freckles on her strong nose. "God, I feel so guilty."

"Guilty? Your husband spent over six months screwing at least two other women repeatedly," retorts Stella. "What you did wasn't calculated for months like what Jack did. It was a moment of passion. We've *all* been there. You have *nothing* to feel guilty about."

"Yeah, well at least he didn't choose one of my friends to do it with." A tremor of anxiety surges through my chest as Kev leans a hand over the table and squeezes mine. "And Cameron... I thought maybe getting what he wanted would be enough for him, but he's sent me about a dozen messages today. He told me he loved me in one of them." I look up at Stella who eyes me, concern coloring her earnest face. "I don't even know how to begin to handle this."

"Look, what's done is done. There's no going back from it," she says, running her stiletto fingertips through her inch-long light-brown hair. "But it has to stop here, sweetie."

"I agree, Jess," adds Kevin. "We love you and we will support whatever you choose, but this is not safe. At all. For either of you."

"What do I do?" I ask. "Jack doesn't seem to fully grasp that I mean it when I tell him I can't be with him anymore."

"Maybe it's because he senses you still love him," suggests Stella softly.

I breathe out a shuddering sigh. "Oh God, I barely speak to the guy. I'm certainly not trying to give off that impression."

"No. But I'm sure he can feel it," she replies.

"And is Cameron saying he really wants to be with you?" asks Kevin.

I nod. "He tells me every day he's been waiting for me for years. You should hear the yearning in his voice. I seriously have no idea how to resist him."

"Look," says Stella, sighing loudly. "In a year's time, when Jack has moved on—*I'm hoping*—maybe things will be different. Frankly, after the way your so-called husband has been putting it about, I couldn't care less about his feelings. But right now, this isn't safe. Jack is damaged. He sees the world as dark and you are what keeps him believing in light. He won't want to let go of that. It's obsession like I've never seen. And I know what lengths these alpha doms will go to to keep what they think is theirs. If I hadn't found that GPS tracker on my car, I wouldn't even have been able to warn you that he was on his way."

"How did you even find the thing?" I ask.

"Sixth sense. The gift of all women."

"God, Stella, I'm so sorry."

"When I saw it, I ripped that thing off and smashed it into a hundred pieces."

"Um, you could have just taken the battery out, Stell," chimes in Kevin, his tone a hair away from mocking.

"Yeah, thanks, smartass." She whacks him with her napkin. "I know that now. Anyway, I'd been trying to call you for an hour at least."

"Cam took me on a boat trip," I say, shivering inside as I think of the trip to that single oak tree in the field and the memory of Quercus Velutina that I would willingly erase from my mind.

"Anyway," continues Stella. "Don't think Jack won't employ similar tactics now."

"I know. I'm so worried about him hurting Cameron that I can't even begin to process my own grief over my marriage ending."

"Baby, trying to escape the pain of divorce by jumping into the arms of another man is just a quick fix, a distraction," says Stella. "You have to feel this thing, all of it, even if you don't want to. You're not in a healthy place right now to start another relationship, especially not with another high-profile man like Cameron. This thing with him is a reaction to what you've been through with Jack. Your hormones are all over the place. You're dealing with betrayal, grief, heartache. It's clouding your judgment. Cameron knows you're weak and vulnerable like this. He shouldn't be pressuring you right now."

"I guess he thinks he's already waited a long time, Stell."

"I know, but the timing is all wrong," she continues. "I don't want to see you in a bigger mess in a year's time. You need to heal. Alone. We love you, baby. We want you healthy and safe. Not in the middle of an electrical storm, which is what will happen if Jack suspects Cameron is on the scene. I know it's hard and I know you don't want to, but you have to break it off with both of them and make sure they both understand."

I sigh—a lonely, unwilling sigh of sorrow and resignation. "Dammit, I hate when you two make sense."

Kevin smiles. "Well, doesn't happen often, but when it does, it's best to listen."

I reach for the hands of my friends. "I love you guys."

"We love you too, baby," says Kev. "You've got this. Whatever happens, we'll be here, no matter what."

5

LYING IN BED LATER THAT NIGHT, I find myself tossing and turning in torment at the thought of Alexandra Frost being fucked by Jack in front of my eyes, and at the idea of telling him that I'm going to file for divorce no matter what he says. As if that wasn't enough, I'm also finding it hard to breathe as I think of telling Cameron that I can't be with him, especially when every cell in my body wants to take refuge in his strong arms.

The bright letters on the sleek cube next to the bed tell me it's 1.05 a.m.

I sit up and turn on my phone, remembering that I meant to text Maddie to see if she's okay. She came down with a stomach bug a couple of days ago and has been off work since.

New messages:

Baby I need to talk to you.

Please pick up.

When can I speak to you?

I need you.

I need you to pick up Jessynia. I'm losing my mind.

My heart drops into my stomach at the sight of the text messages Jack has sent this evening.

"Jack, I'm sorry," I whisper aloud. I wish I could call him, but I know that all that matters right now is making sure I don't get sucked into his maelstrom again even if the idea of him in pain rips my insides to shreds. I worry more about his pain than my own at times. My mother calls it my "empathy-overdrive", a condition I share with my brother but not with her. I wish I could switch the fucking thing off at times, but then I like how deeply I love. My ability to love has gifted me with the most intense of experiences life can offer. I guess this is the downside of it...

I text him back, assuming he'll be asleep:

I can't talk now Jack. I'll wake up Kevin. I will call you tomorrow.

Jack:

Tomorrow.

I love you angel. Please let me explain why I had to go there.

Me:

It doesn't matter. I can't go through this again.

Jack:

I had to do it. To protect us both. There are things you don't understand.

At the exact moment that that message appears on my phone, I inhale sharply at the sight of a message from someone else.

"Cameron." His name rushes from me.

ARE YOU AWAKE BEAUTIFUL? he asks.

My respiration takes off like steeds leaving the stable. I don't answer.

Jack:

Do you believe me beautiful?

Cameron:

I'VE THOUGHT ABOUT YOU EVERY MINUTE OF TODAY. THOUGHT ABOUT YOUR SOFT BODY.

Jack:

Talk to me angel. I need you with me.

Cam:

Thought about what I intend to do to it.

Jack:

I want to tell you everything so that you understand the position I was in.

I lift my fingers to my chest as I try to alleviate the sensation of the room spinning and the ceiling falling in.

Cam:

I crave you like no other. It consumes my flesh.

Jack:

I can't explain everything like this. I need to see you face to face.

Cam:

I crave your mouth. I crave the warmth of your little body. I crave the way you look up at me.

Jack:

You're my wife. I'm not letting go of you without a fight. There are things I haven't told you because it isn't safe.

Cam:

The thought of you haunts me.

Jack:

I'm going to get away from these people.

Cam:

Do you remember what I did to you in the shower?

Jack:

Are you there?

Cam:

Do you remember how it felt when I was inside you?

Jack:

You belong to me, Jessynia. You are my wife and nothing will ever change that.

Cam:

My body yearns for you like no other.

Jack:

I can't lose you.

Cam:

I have plans for you baby.

Jack:

Your heart. It fuels me.

Cam:

I'VE NEVER CRAVED A WOMAN LIKE THIS BEFORE. I PLEASURE MYSELF TO THE THOUGHT OF YOU SLIDING DOWN ONTO ME. I'VE NEVER FELT ANYTHING CLOSE TO THIS BEFORE.

Jack:

I can't live without you.

Cam:

YOU OWN ME, ANGEL.

Jack:

I love you Jessynia. So much.

And with that, my trembling hands manage to muster enough strength to switch my phone off. I clutch it to my chest as I lie back down, trying to calm my frayed nerves.

I don't know how in all holy hell my life descended into this. Eight months ago, Jack and I were in Costa Rica, eating maracuja on the heavenly beach, making love day and night, making plans for the future. He was the *only* man I would ever look at. The only man I wanted.

And now this...

As emotional and physical exhaustion blend with the effects of the four glasses of wine I drank tonight, I let go of the phone and let my eyes close and the welcome weight of sleep take me.

The faintest of noises sets the hair on my arms on end, startling me from my sleep. As I blink into the inky veil of night, I spot a shadowy figure on the bed. The figure lunges towards me, his strong hand muffling my gasp. He leans his face into mine so closely that I can feel his breath. "It's me, beautiful," he whispers roughly, releasing his hand from my lips. Though I can barely see his face, I recognize the rich, deep velvet of his ever-seductive voice.

"Cameron?" I manage breathily. "Jesus Christ, you scared the living shit out of me! How the— How did you get in here?"

"I picked the lock."

"Picked the lock? What are you, a Navy SEAL?" I melt into the weight of his solid chest upon my body as tingling warmth enters my core at the sensation of hard muscle.

"I'm sorry," he whispers against my lips. "I've tried to be patient. My body needs you. I couldn't take another day of not seeing your face."

"You scared the life out of me." As my eyes grow accustomed to the low light, I see him more clearly now, making out disks of burning amber, framed by thick dark locks that brush against his forehead. His strong cheekbones cut into his elegant heart-shaped face.

"I'm not in control when it comes to you," he replies.

"Cam, it's not that I'm not happy to see you. It's just... I told you I needed some time to think. You shouldn't have come here."

"I know that." He slides his full body onto me, his dense bulge pressing into my crotch, rubbing up and down, stimulating me despite myself. "How about I make it up to you?" Without waiting for an answer, he lifts his body and pulls the sheet covering me off my skin which is slightly damp from the cloying mid-August weather. On pulling his T-shirt off his torso, he hitches my thin white cotton nightdress up and spreads my thighs, undoing his belt buckle and tugging his black jeans down his legs and off his feet. Without a word, he slides his body up the bed and onto me, imprisoning me possessively. I feel him, hard and thick, on my pubis as he rubs his lips against mine.

"I want you," he growls.

"Cam, I'm really not sure we should be doing this..."

"It doesn't matter whether you're sure or not. I'm going to be fucking your tight little cunt so hard that you'll barely be able to walk tomorrow."

I squirm at the vulgar roughness of his words and the violence of his tone. "Cam, I— I feel like we really should talk."

"No, Jessynia. No more talking."

He pulls my nightdress up over my head before bending my knee up to my chest with the other and finding my sex with the head of his.

He paralyzes me with his glare, his eyes darkening, burning burgundy in the eerie light, as he rams himself inside me hard without warning, stabbing my cervix as he does so.

One hand muffles the gasp that wants to escape me while his other hand pins mine to the pillow. "You don't get to decide when I fuck you," he whispers into my ear. "You are my property. That means that your body serves one purpose... To be used by me."

I don't know what's got into him, but this dark energy is not something I've seen in him before... and I'm not sure that I like it. I wince at his vice-like grip, searching his fiery eyes, trying to communicate that his roughness is too much.

He narrows his in response. "I started fantasizing about impregnating you the first time I met you," he continues. "And when you are pregnant, you will be my slave. You'll take me five times a day, whenever I choose to be inside you."

I squirm again at the violence of his words and he releases his hand from my mouth. "Cameron, I don't like what you're saying. It reminds me of..."

"Me, maybe?" A second male voice, all grit and gravel, booms into my ear, his hand sinking into my hair, tugging it back. As the avalanche of panic rushes through me, Cameron's merciless hand silences my mouth again as I feel the other man's tongue lashing the side of my neck, the texture rough.

Even in the darkness, I know the rasp in that voice.

Jack.

He pulls on my hair, yanking my face in his direction so that I make contact with glacial eyes glistening like black ice in the glimmers of moonlight seeping through a crevice in the curtains. He watches me in fascination as Cameron continues to fuck me rhythmically, a devious smile on his face as he does so.

Jack leans his devastating face towards me. "Did you think you could play us both forever, angel?"

I struggle to writhe free but between Cameron's dense limbs imprisoning my body, his grip on my mouth and Jack's fist in my hair, I can barely move an inch other than on the merciless impalements by

Cameron which thrust me in the direction of his choosing. Cameron's lips find the other side of my neck, clamping down on it, grunting as he sucks until it hurts as Jack glowers at me while removing his clothes.

I gasp internally at the sight of his monster physique, the defined ridges of his bulky limbs and torso, and the eager erection, thick with engorged veins, that points towards me. In an instant, he finds the other side of my neck with his lips and then tongue. They both lick and suck, animalistic grunts escaping them as Cameron takes my overwhelmed body with fervor that has me trembling.

Tears escape me as Jack's eyes meet mine again.

"Don't cry, beautiful," he says. "You wanted us both. Now you will have us both."

With that, Cameron pulls out of me, forcing me onto my side so that I'm facing Jack as he slides behind me, his strong hand never leaving my mouth for a second. Cameron enters me from behind, arms wrapped around my chest, gently sliding into and out of my sex as Jack leans into my body, his eyes eating into mine in enthrallment, in arousal, his fingers tugging at my bare nipples, hoarse whispers of pleasure escaping his throat as he surveys my domination at the hands of this man he spent his childhood with.

"You'll learn to like this, baby," Jack says softly, licking the side of my face, his hand reaching around my neck which he squeezes so tightly I almost can't breathe. "I promise you."

Cameron's arousal overpowers him as he begins to hammer the inside of my body for long seconds before pulling out of me and pushing me onto my back, climbing on top of me so that he can watch my eyes, his smile darkening at the sight of the tears streaming onto his muffling hand as he enters me again.

"She's good, huh?" Jack murmurs, the thunderous bite in his cavernous voice signaling his arousal as he pins one of my hands to the bed to help his friend better control my body.

"Yeah," replies Cameron, his breath escaping him. "She's something else, alright. She needs training though."

"Well, there are people who'll take care of that."

"I'll certainly volunteer my services."

"As will I," Jack affirms darkly.

I struggle beneath Cameron, using my free hand to try to pry his hand off my mouth. His body is dense and immovable, as if made of stone. I dig my fingernails into his skin but he barely registers the pain, smiling into me at my pathetic attempts to hurt him.

"They've been wanting her for quite some time. I think they've been patient enough," Jack says before tasting my neck with a groan, the head of his heavy erection prodding my thigh without restraint. "Talking of patience..."

"One minute, my friend," replies Cameron as he thrusts more fervently, driving into me, his grunts indecent as he pulls out of my body and pumps his fluid onto my taut belly, a sight which has tears falling from me.

He finally uncages me, a low, bestial roar emerging from deep in his lungs which he discharges in heaving breaths before grabbing a garment and wiping me down. "Your turn," he breathes to Jack. "I'll hold her down." As Cameron lifts his dense frame to the side, Jack takes his place, climbing on top of me, his hand now taking the place of Cameron's over my mouth. I wrap both my hands around his dense forearm as he lowers his heavy body down onto me, the firm enclosure of his chest pushing me into the bed below.

I dig my fingernails into the cool skin of his arm.

"Tsk, tsk, tsk. No, Jessynia," whispers Jack softly, as he spreads my thighs while Cameron pulls my hands over my head. "She's feisty tonight," Jack adds. "I've never seen her struggle like this."

"Mind if I watch?" asks Cameron, pinning my hands above my head.

"Be my guest. She'll have to get used to it sometime."

"He will be *very* pleased," replies Cameron as Jack lifts my knee up and prods my sex with the swollen head of his cock.

"Well, there's quite a queue for this little girl and her tight pink cunt. I've sent them some videos but there's nothing quite like the real thing."

My eyes widen as they plead with Jack's.

"Oh, yeah," replies Cameron, his voice a violent brawl. "There'll be a queue like they've never seen."

The weight of Jack's chest has me struggling to breathe as he slowly starts to slide into me. I try to wrestle my hands free of Cameron's vice-like grip to a groan of his pleasure at the sensation of my resistance.

"Tie her hands to the bed," orders Jack. "I want her wriggling tonight."

Cameron stands up, finding a leather tie which he wraps around my wrists, pulling my arms taught and tying them to the bedpost behind me.

"Hmm," he replies as he finds his way back to the bed, sitting next to Jack, flecks of red flame dancing within his blazing eyes which lock with mine. "I will have to experience that myself once you're done. If you don't mind?"

"Of course not," replies Jack. "She's made it very clear she's our property."

"Good. Enjoy, my friend."

"Cover her mouth," says Jack.

Cameron's hand replaces Jack's so that he can straighten his arms as he cages me in, his face above mine, looking down at me as I search his eyes desperately, silently imploring him to stop.

"Don't worry, beautiful," Jack murmurs. "You'll learn to like this. I promise you."

Cameron's tongue finds my neck as he starts to breathe heavily. "I don't think I can resist anymore," he snarls.

"Tsk, tsk. Bad boy," replies Jack.

"Would you judge me?"

"Of course not," replies Jack. "As long as you share..."

Cameron looks down at me, his eyes half-closed as if enslaved to his desire. With a hiss, he opens his mouth to reveal long, sharp canines gleaming in the gray gloom. I try once again to free myself but can't move as he lowers his mouth into my neck and bites down, spearing pain into my neck, the air filling with the metallic scent of blood. I hear the wild beast growl as he licks and sucks at the gash of my soft flesh, my chest wet from the trickle of slick red cells.

Cameron comes up for air, his eyes two serpent-like slits, his chin and jaw dripping with scarlet blood that looks almost black in the dim light. His breathing is ragged as he lifts his head back and exclaims loudly as if savoring the ecstasy of feasting on my life force.

"Mmm, smells so good," groans Jack.

"You want?" asks Cameron meeting Jack's intense gaze.

"Of course."

"Very well, my friend."

Cameron inches his face towards Jack who licks the full surface of his mouth, inhaling the blood. Cameron's rumbling exhale is deviant as Jack wipes the last of the blood from his face with lashes of his tongue, using it to part Cameron's crimson-stained lips and enter his mouth, their frenzied tongues pushing against each other as they suck and lick on the blood to the diabolical sound of perverse hisses and roars.

Jack pulls away and grunts in delight, exposing his canines as he leans down, eyes silver and serpent-like as he locates the open gash in my neck and begins to suck, all the while fucking my weakening body. He comes up for air, this time allowing Cameron to lick the blood from his lips, lapping up my warm red life force. His hand reaches for Jack's hair, fisting it, tugging it roughly. As Cameron pulls on the back of Jack's head with one hand, finding the flesh of his neck with this tongue, his grip over my mouth loosens for a split-second.

In that second of freedom, I open my mouth wide and bite down as hard as I can onto his little finger, biting with every ounce of strength in my jaw until I feel bone.

"Fuck," he mutters, retreating.

And before Cameron can get his back over my mouth, I shout, "Help me..."

In what feels like seconds, light floods the room and Kevin bursts in.

I sit up, panting, trying to catch my breath as I glance around and realize that Jack and Cameron are gone.

Or rather... they were never there.

I clutch my hand to my neck and try to breathe as Kevin rushes over to comfort me, pulling the hair off my face.

"I'm here, baby. It's okay. Just breathe. You're okay."

"Kev," I whimper as I hold onto him, sweat sliding all over my body. "Oh, God. It felt so..."

"It was just a nightmare, baby."

"Jack... And Cameron... I can still feel them." My body heaves in the dark, discharging the malicious energy of the black vision.

"It wasn't real. I'm here. I'll always be here, sweetie. Always."

"Kev?" I break free of his hold and look up at him as my respiration begins to steady.

"What, sweetie?"

"I have to break up with them. Both of them."

He pauses for a moment. "Yes. You do. There's no other way." He holds me tightly until I'm ready for him to let go.

As the minutes pass by and I start to finally breathe, my fear turns into the hollowest of aches as I begin to visualize what I must do.

I just hope I have the strength...

6

"OH, MAD, YOU STILL LOOK ROUGH," I lament as she holds onto her stomach after taking another bite.

"I think I'd better stop here," she says. It's the following lunchtime at her Chinatown apartment and Maddie and I are tucking into rice and boiled carrots that I made her—the only meal gentle enough on her still-wobbly stomach.

I pick up her plate and take it to the kitchen so that she doesn't have to see it anymore.

"First solid food I've had for three days," she moans.

"Well, at least you've managed to keep this down."

"So far. I'm never eating shrimp again."

"Drink your kefir, my lady." I smile. I gesture to the glass of water kefir that I brought over for her to help her stomach get back to normal.

"My eyes are always too big for my stomach," she complains as she drinks down the fizzy ginger-laced liquid.

"Are you sure it was the shrimp?"

"Yeah. I knew it the first second I bit into the sucker."

"And you kept eating?"

"Yep, my dumb ass did keep eating. Thanks for asking."

I chuckle at her grim self-deprecation. "Were you drunk?"

"I *had* to get drunk to make it through the so-called *comedy*! I mean I know it's a lot to ask to have some actual comedy at a comedy club. Well, technically it was a bar with an open mic. Learned my lesson on that one..."

"Oh, I've been there. Was *any* of it funny?" I ask.

"No! One of the women got up there and did about fifty one-liners. Only about one in ten of them hit... just. The rest of the time we were just looking at her and each other in that *Oh-dear-God* way. Then this moron got up there and started making *jokes*"—she puts air quotes around the word—"about how it's a waste of time to date women in Manhattan and then talked about how he's going to move to Kentucky to date a woman who knows how to treat a man."

"Oh, God. Poor guy thought it was a public therapy session."

"At least I got a few boos in there," she sneers, her blond ponytail gesticulating along with her.

"I'm surprised you didn't run up there and grab the mic and start sharing some of *your* dating stories."

"Oh, I wanted to!"

"I bet," I reply, watching as she grimaces, presumably from nausea again.

"You okay, sweetie?"

"Yeah, I'll survive." She takes a sip of water. "I'm sorry I haven't been much use this week.

"Oh, don't worry about it. You've mainly missed the emotional pretzels I've been twisting myself into."

"Stella told me about Cameron, Jess." I finish my sip of kefir, letting out a despondent sigh. "She was worried about you," Mad continues.

"Yeah, I know. I didn't want to tell you, with you being sick and all."

"You can't keep seeing him, Jess," she says. "I mean nothing would make me happier than you being with him, but it's just way too dangerous right now."

"I know, Mad. I'm planning on telling him tomorrow. God knows how..."

"Look, I know the desire to plunge into a relationship to escape a past one. Remember Pierre?"

I grin at the memory of her torrid five-week love affair with a handsome Ph.D. student from the south of France that she launched into a week after her longest relationship ever ended. The rebound fizzled out before her ex had even taken his name off the lease.

"But Cameron O'Neill is not just some random guy," she continues, her face so earnest that I can't look away. "You know that. And you can't escape this pain. You're walking through this dark, scary tunnel and suddenly someone comes along and says, hey, come back the way you came and get out of that tunnel. But if you had just kept walking, you would have made it all the way through, into the light."

"I know. I just need the strength to do it. Telling Jack is bad enough, but Cam too. I just feel like to crawl into the tunnel and hide for a year."

"You can do it, sweetie. You're one of the toughest women I know."

"Or used to be..."

"No, you're still the same little opinionated asshole you've always been." I break into a grin. "And I love you for it. And we'll be here, Jess. You know that, right? No matter what." She squeezes my hand as I smile into my friend's gorgeous face.

As I leave Maddie's apartment ninety minutes later, the boundless bustle of Chinatown streets barely registers as I keep my head down and slowly make it to the Canal Street Station to get the yellow subway line that will take me to SoHo. I would normally walk the fifteen or so minutes, but I'm feeling tired and decide to do it the easy way today.

Divine odors of garlic and sesame waft in the air, but my appetite is none and I decide against getting something to eat for dinner, turning swiftly to head down the dusty steps of the subway station before getting out my subway card and swiping it through the metallic reader. It's about 2.30 p.m., way before rush hour and I breathe a sigh of relief to find the station fairly quiet.

As I make it down the steps to the platform, I hear the familiar huff of a train about to close its doors and realize it's in the station. I jolt into action, running down the stairs at full speed and making it inside just as the doors close behind me. As I turn around in breathless relief at having made it through, I spot a man rush down the steps and stop right in front of me, the glass of the train doors separating us. Tall and bald with tanned skin, he glares at me and I frown at him as the train begins to rumble out of the station.

I turn and take a seat on a smooth orange chair near the center of the car opposite a couple of women and an elderly gentleman. I close my eyes for a moment and try to breathe through the unbidden stress hormones gallivanting through my body of late.

A minute or so later, laughter from the two women has me opening my eyes and smiling.

And out of the corner of my eye, I spot a figure standing to my right and turn to glance to find him watching me. Upon eye contact, he looks away. Something makes me study him. He's stocky with buzzed hair and ruddy skin and is wearing a black jacket and light-blue jeans.

As I look back down, out of my peripheral vision, I spot a man standing at the end of the car to my left. He glances at the other man to my right before looking up at the subway map above the door.

Shaking it off, I get to my feet as the train rattles to a screeching stop at my station, Prince Street. Getting out, I notice both men alighting and a sudden swell of inexplicable anxiety has me increasing my pace as I head towards the escalator that will take me to the exit closest to Kevin's apartment.

Calm down, Jess. You're just being paranoid. Just breathe...

Damn, this ridiculous feeling like I'm being followed of late is clearly showing no signs of abating.

I mutter reassuring words to myself, but there's that sixth sense again, one that has become so much more acute since discovering the shadowy underworld that was hiding behind the glossy façade of my perfect marriage.

One man is now walking in front of me and throwing a backwards glance I spy the other behind me. I reach into my cross-body purse for my phone, my hand scrambling around for it, cursing under my breath as the damn thing eludes me. I pull my hand out of my bag as we approach the escalator, standing still, afraid to try to walk past the guy before me.

As we make it to the top, I start to breathe again and shake off the fact that both men are walking with me. I keep my head down and take a left in the direction of my exit, my steps brisk as I try to escape the cloying claustrophobia I feel underground and reach the safety of the world above. As I approach the final staircase to the outside world, the man in front of me suddenly turns straight around to face me and I stop dead in my tracks as he pins me with a violent glare.

My heart takes off like thundering steeds as the man slowly prowls towards me. I take a step to my left and he steps in the same direction.

"What do you want?" I shout, panic lurking in the waver of my voice.

He doesn't answer and I turn round, hoping I can run back inside past the man behind me.

Before I have a chance to turn around fully, a sharp breath evades me as I find myself looking into the eyes of two men...

The one from before.

And another.

Jack.

He walks towards me slowly as the other two men box me in, making it impossible for me to get around them.

"What do you want, Jack?" I feel my voice quiver as I say the words.

He takes another step towards me, making it within two feet. "I need to talk to you."

My limbs are paralyzed as I stare into his icy eyes. His face is harsh, unshaven, wilder than I remember it, a shadow roughening his breathtaking features. A woman walks by us, but I don't dare drag her into this.

"You can't do these things!" I shout once she's turned a corner, swallowing hard in the face of his implacable stare.

"You leave me no choice, Jessynia," he replies, a simmering undercurrent of ire in his voice.

"Fine, let's go to a coffee shop."

"I don't think so," he responds, his fingers reaching forward to coil around my arm as he pulls me towards the exit. I pull back on his grip, trying to release myself and he pivots to face me, eyes blazing like white embers sparking off burning wood.

"I'm not your property, Jack!"

"Yes, you are," he growls.

"No, I'm not. You can't do things like this!"

"I'm not going anywhere," he snarls. "We can try this again tomorrow if you like. And the next day... and the day after that... though I presume you don't want to spend the next month looking over your shoulder..."

Upon my silence, he pulls me towards the exit and up the stairs, his two goons on either side of us. As we reach street level, we dodge passersby and I breathe a sigh of relief to see we are vaguely heading in the direction of Kevin's apartment. As we arrive at Thompson Street, Jack leads me to the left.

"Where are we going?" I ask, pulling against him.

He doesn't answer, looking around as we stop in front of one of the first buildings. One of his men pulls out a set of keys and unlocks the door.

"Hey!" I shout, as Jack pulls me inside.

"Wait outside," he orders the men.

They comply as I push against Jack's chest. He responds by lifting me into his arms and carrying me down the hallway, up a single flight of stairs and down a corridor where he sets me down in front of a black door. Caging me in from behind, his breath fiery on the exposed nape under my high braided ponytail, he unlocks the door and ushers me in, locking it behind him.

7

I WALK BACKWARDS TOWARDS THE SPARSE LIVING AREA as Jack paces towards me like a lion trailing its prey in long grass—deliberate, powerful, merciless.

"What is wrong with you?!" I shout.

He stuns me with the ferocity of his silent advance, his stalking unabashed and merciless. "What do you expect, Jessynia? I've asked you to meet me. You keep saying no. I've lost my patience."

"Well, did you ever consider respecting my boundaries for once?!"

"I'm in pain."

I shake my head. "So am I, Jack. You're not the victim here."

I frown at the solemnity in his devastating features, at the vulnerability in his once all-powerful exterior, a look alien to him before June of this year.

"I know I'm not," he replies.

I glance around the room at the beige walls, the room bare but for a black sofa and coffee table, absent of all decoration. "What is this place?" I ask. "Is this where you bring your other women?"

"No woman has ever been here," he responds, a scowl hardening his features.

"So, what, did you set this place up to spy on me, or is this a—" I stop, not wanting to ask Jack about his family's exploits, not wanting him to know that Cameron believes they are involved in organized crime.

"You need to let me explain." His words are weighted with torment... and anger.

"It won't make any difference. This can't be explained away like last time. I can't allow you to put me through this anymore."

"You saw us, didn't you?"

"Yes," I respond defiantly, the image of him on that balcony with Alex causing my eyes to mist over. I still can't bring myself to relive it fully. The scene is so wretched, so visceral that it leaves me clutching my belly for comfort when I think of it for too long.

He lowers his head, breathing deeply as I watch the lightning flash of a single glistening tear spill onto the hardwood floor below him. "I never meant for you to see that."

"Well, if it helps," I utter stiffly, "I wish I had never seen it either."

He lifts his gaze, bleak distress blackening his fierce features. "I'm sorry, Jessynia."

"*Sorry*? Are you sorry in the way you were back in June?" I hear my voice crack as I try not to break down. "Remember how sorry you were then? And remember telling me how you would never, ever do anything like that to hurt me again? That you loved me more than life itself? That you belonged to me and only me? Remember all those lies you fed me?"

"They weren't lies," he replies, anguish hiding in the low grit of his voice as another tear drops onto his sculpted cheekbone, a tear that makes my heart ache. I want to wipe it from his face. I want to hold him, kiss him, tell him it will be okay, but I can't give him a single inch ever again. "She was threatening me, Jessynia. Threatening to damage me. Threatening my job. Threatening to spread lies about me. Threatening my marriage. She's blackmailed me before. I just... lost control."

"Blackmailing you over what?"

He doesn't speak.

"Even if that were true," I continue, "you know a lot about her and her husband. You could hurt them too."

"Yes."

"And you could have told me, Jack. That would have been preferable to what happened."

"I know that. I panicked. I wanted to hurt her. I never tire of wanting to hurt her. I underestimated the hold she has on me. It just... went wrong." I glare at him. The thought of Alex controlling him makes me feel nauseous. "There are things I can't tell you... because it's not safe for you to know."

"You can't tell me? And I'm just supposed to take everything you say at face value?"

He takes another step towards me and I inch back. "Yes. You're supposed to believe me. I'm your husband. No piece of paper will ever change that."

"It's not just her, Jack. What about Lydia? Was she blackmailing you too? And there have been other women, haven't there?" I feel tempted to tell him that I know about Quercus Velutina, but I can't have him finding out that Cameron took me there, for the sake of Cam's safety if nothing else. I know that if Jack knew I had been there, I would have heard about it. I guess for some reason, the forces in charge of that place don't want him to know either... "I don't know how you could expect me to believe you anymore."

He takes a step towards me which has me inching towards the back wall next to the window. "I love you, angel. I can't lose you. It will be the end of me."

"No, Jack. I can't carry that kind of weight. It's not fair to me."

The usual vitality in his strong face is gone, extinguished like a flame snuffed out by a stern wind. "I can't sleep," he says. "I can't eat properly. I don't know how to make it through this life without you."

As he edges me further backwards still, I put my hands up to stop his advance. "Stop!" I shout, a plea that he ignores, pursuing me until my back hits the hard concrete wall.

He glares down at me, taking slow, deep breaths. "I can't live without you, Jessynia. You're in my blood."

"I don't care!" I shout. "The next time I find you cheating, I will lose part of my soul!"

He lowers his head, tears spilling from his eyes—a sight so rare for this powerful man. My heart stalls as I watch this damaged human that I have loved so desperately and shared my life with crumble to pieces.

I want to soothe his pain.

But I can't.

Every other woman gives him what he wants when he wants it. Every other woman is his slave. I can't be like them. I can't lose any more of my self-respect on top of everything else.

His haunted gaze catches mine. "Jessynia, the emptiness I feel without you consumes me." He places one hand onto the wall behind me.

I push against his chest but it doesn't retreat. "Yeah. How about the emptiness I feel when I find out that my husband is sleeping with other women? Do you enjoy causing me pain like that?"

"Enjoy it? It kills me. It eats me alive. Seeing you in pain rips out my insides."

"And yet it's not enough to stop?"

"I don't know why I'm pulled into the darkness like this, attracted to evil people. I've tried to stop it. It's like it's part of my blood, my insides. The same way that you are. There are two forces inside me that pull on me every day. And they're polar opposites. Incompatible."

"And they both make you feel good?"

"Yes. Even though I know that one of them will be the end of me."

"You know that and you can't stop?" I ask, scouring his eyes, trying to understand.

"There's rage inside me, Jess. Rage that you haven't really seen. Rage at myself. Rage at the world. Being near that woman and her... *friends* soothes that rage. Channels it. Turns it into energy that I use in this world. I don't know why."

"Or maybe they are the reason for your rage and you don't even realize it? Maybe they feed into it and then act like they can help you to diffuse it..."

He nods. "You're too smart for your own good, angel. You are the smartest woman I've ever known."

Clearly not smart enough if I'm still afraid of succumbing to his words...

"The path of people like Alexandra Frost is just... pain and misery," I say.

"And death."

I swallow hard. "Don't say that word, Jack."

"I feel its pull. Something inside me wants to self-destruct. Maybe it's something that all men fight. I don't know if I can stop it anymore."

"Well, you will. For me. Whether we're together or not, I know you won't do anything that will leave me tormented for the rest of my life. You won't do that to me, Jack."

"You know that you still belong to me, don't you?"

"No. That's not how this works."

He edges his face closer, his restless, beautifully carved lips hovering inches from mine, his ravenous gaze roaming over my face, studying the lines, melting into me. As he does so, tingling warmth enters my core as I succumb to the primal sensation of his height, his broad shoulders and transcendent virility and thoughts of him ravaging me in every room of our apartment explode in my mind.

Dammit, so he still does that to me, I moan internally, wondering if I will forever be enslaved to the dominance of his shameless expression of masculinity.

"We could make this work," he says softly, seductively almost.

"How? By me turning a blind eye to everything you do?"

"You're the *only* woman I love. The only woman I will ever love. There is nothing I've ever felt for another human that comes close to what I feel for you. What I do outside our marriage isn't about love. It's... a need that I can't control. It's a drug. It's a release of rage which has nothing to do with my love for you. You could... overlook it, like other wives do."

"Overlook it?! Are you insane?! I'm supposed to just pretend it isn't happening in exchange for your love? Is that what you want for me?!"

"Could you?"

I peer into him, scrutinizing the unique lines of his face—his strong jaw, wide forehead and cheekbones that could cut glass, the golden hair, the ferocious azure eyes that hold your gaze until you're mesmerized and giddy, unable to look away.

I shake my head. "No. And if I could, our love wouldn't be the same anyway."

My eyes pan down to the light-blue collar of his T-shirt protruding out from under his thin black jacket. He doesn't speak for the longest time. "You're right. I love you because of your purity, your innocence, your compassion, your sense of honor..."

His other hand lifts to my face, his fingers setting my skin ablaze before cupping the back of my neck. I reach my hands up and wrap my fingers around his strong wrist to pull it off, a gesture which transports me back to the vampiric nightmare I had last night. His hand doesn't move. The man is about ten times stronger than me.

"I want you, baby," he says.

"No, Jack. That's not happening."

"You know what I can do to you."

My face flushes, anger seeping into me. Anger at his shameless words. Anger at his arrogant presumptions. Anger at his belief that I will capitulate to his whim like every other woman does. And anger at myself for knowing he's right. I do want him. And I do want what he can do to me. I want him to relieve this never-ending tension I feel in my body when he's near me. I want him to relieve the stress of the last few days.

The cold, hard truth is that something inside me yearns for the savage beast within this man. I yearn for his brutal carnality and deviant domination. Part of me even yearns for the darkness of the hell he takes me to the edge of.

Oh, God.

Jess, you have to fight this...

Please fight...

His fingers sink into the hair above my nape. "I know you, angel. I know by the way your eyes dilate and your face flushes pink that you want me inside you."

I frown, irate that this arrogant, cheating prick is right and that my nipples are hard and my sex is wet, pulsating, at the thought of being penetrated by him.

Be strong, Jess.

Please be strong.

"I want you, Jessynia. Let me remind you what I'm capable of," he murmurs, clenching my ponytail in his fist in a move that has a whimper escaping me. "I always know when you're hot, wet. I'm very hard. But you know that, don't you? I'm always hard for you. Without fail. My cock craves your soft, wet body every second of the day. I know you want me inside you. I can see it in your eyes. I know you want me to lift your skirt and enter you, fuck you against this wall. Hard. I know you want me to show you what your husband is made of. You can't conceal what I do to you, Jessynia. I see into you."

I feel my sex throb and hot air escape my lungs as he leans his lips towards me, my eyelids falling heavy under the weight of arousal.

"Let me show you, baby," he murmurs. "Let me show you what I'm made of..."

And then, like the tail of a comet exploding in the night's sky, the image of Alexandra Frost on her knees performing fellatio on my husband blazes into my mind, leaving shards of shrapnel in their wake.

I push against his chest, hard. "No!" He stands up straight, his breathing labored, his stiff body a slave to his arrested arousal. "What, do you think you can just fuck your way out of this?"

"Maybe I can," he counters roughly. "Do you know another man who can do to you what I can?"

Only one... but I think I'd best keep that thought to myself for today.

"You can't manipulate me anymore, Jack. Do you know what I saw you doing?! Do you know what that did to me?!" The rage I thought was gone floods my system leaving my body filled with gunpowder just ready to detonate. The emotion releases in the form of a tear that tracks down my face.

He looks down at me, grimacing in torment. "Don't cry, baby. Please. I can't see that."

"I'm not like every other woman you know, Jack. I'm not letting you just have my body whenever you want anymore. I did that for *three* years. Multiple times a day when you demanded it. I never said no to you and look where it got me."

"What are you going to do?" he asks coldly.

I wipe the tears falling fast down my cheek. "I have to file for divorce. I have no choice."

He shakes his head, his chest expanding as he tries to discharge excess energy from his unsatisfied body. "I can't allow that, Jessynia."

"Jack, there's—"

"Give me a year."

"What? What difference will that make?"

"I'm going to break free of these people. Take them down if I have to. I will be free of the poison. I promise you."

"I can't stay in limbo, Jack. I'm in too much pain like this."

"One year, baby. I will be free of them. For good. I'll get help. I'm still seeing Dr. Vorigun. I saw him last night. I will see whoever it takes to be free of this need for... darkness."

"And did you run today's little kidnapping plot by Vorigun for approval? Is this one of the conflict resolution strategies he suggested?"

There is the glimmer of a smile which instantly fades into obscurity. "No," he replies. "I doubt he would approve."

I take a deep breath. "Cameron told me about you and Alex." Jack's eyes widen in response. "He told me how young you two were when—"

"Well, he had no fucking right to do that," he growls, leaning into me.

"He was defending you. He was trying to explain why she has her claws so deep in you."

"How considerate of him," he sneers. "And does he realize he's putting my fucking wife in *danger* by letting you into that woman's world? Or is that part of the fun for the sanctimonious Mr. O'Neill?"

"He doesn't want to hurt me, Jack."

"He doesn't? You're sure about that? Because he wants to hurt me... and maybe *you* are the perfect vehicle to do it. You have *no* idea what that man is capable of."

"He's not trying to hurt either of us. You should have told me about

Alex yourself, Jack. You were fifteen, for God's sake! She was in her late twenties. It's wrong! Why don't you go to the police?"

"The police?" he scoffs, eyes narrowing into keen slits. "They... Her and her friends, shall we say, they *own* the police. You live in some fantasy land filled with fairies and unicorns, Jessynia. You have no fucking clue who you're dealing with. You haven't seen the things I've seen. You don't understand the forces at work here. Not to mention, that if she ever wanted revenge on me, there is only one way to get it. There is only one thing I give a fuck about in this world. Nothing would give her more pleasure than to have an excuse to hurt you."

I swallow hard as the deep pools of his watery eyes weaken my resistance to him, a resistance holding on by the threads of pain and principle.

He looks down before facing me again. "Give me one year. Please. I can fix this."

"I can't wait that long. I need to move on. I can't take this torment anymore, Jack. It eats out my insides."

"I'm begging you, Jessynia. We can separate. However fucking nightmarish that may be, I will cope with it... as long as you promise me you'll give me a year before filing."

I shake my head. "Jack..."

"I can't breathe without you, Jessynia. I feel sick to my stomach every day, insane with jealousy at the idea that you could meet another man. Sick with worry that I can't protect you in this godforsaken city. I miss you. I ache from it." His piercing eyes blaze cerulean as radiant mid-afternoon light streams through the window. I can't look away, wondering for a moment if this is the last time I will see the deep ocean of his irises so closely. He strokes the side of my face with his thumb. "I love you. It's in my DNA. My bones. My flesh. I can't do anything about it." This time it's his tears which fall onto the blue T-shirt between the sides of his jacket which does nothing to conceal the hard cuts of muscle beneath.

"Jack, stop," I utter softly, the pain of losing him making me tremble inside.

"You still love me too, don't you?"

I don't respond, but I know he can see the truth in my teary eyes.

"I will agree to the separation while I deal with certain... people around me, but don't file for a year. If you file before then, I will fight it *every* step of the way. I will put ten lawyers on the case, stalling it over every little thing, and it will take years to get through the system. If you wait a year and you still want it, I will sign and set you free."

I pause for a while, locked into his solemn gaze. "I will give you six months," I finally say. "Until the end of March. After that I file."

He nods on a deep breath. "March."

"And I don't want people following me. I don't want you turning up at my place. And I may end up going on date at some point, Jack. I don't want any trouble if I do."

He shakes his head, letting out a raspy breath of irritation. "I'm gonna end up in prison, I can feel it," he mutters under his breath.

"No. You're going to accept it, Jack. It won't be happening any time soon, but if it does one day, you have to accept it, just as I've had to accept my marriage falling apart when I didn't want it to. And I can't be looking over my shoulder all the time worried that you or one of your *men* are there. It's not fair."

"They won't follow you anymore."

"Good."

He leans into me, his fingers reaching behind my head as I look up to find eyes suddenly stormy, brimming with rancor. "But if I find out that you have gone *anywhere near* Cameron O'Neill," he growls, bringing thunder into the room, his forehead skimming mine, "there will be a *war*. It will annihilate me, and in exchange, I will annihilate *him*. I will rip out his insides and feed them to the fucking dogs. The strength I've lost will come back one thousand-fold and I will make him wish he'd ended his life like he once planned to do. Do you understand that?"

"Jack, stop. You're scaring me."

"I'm. Not. Fucking. Kidding. Here," he roars into me, the ferocity of his furor forcing my hands into his firm chest to keep him back. "You touch that man, and I will rip his fucking throat out with my bare hands. I will drink his blood. And I'll get away with it as well." He says the sentence slowly, his breathing accelerating as his face hardens, wrathful and merciless. "Is that clear?" he asks.

I nod, feeling hollowed out.

"I'm not going to have you followed. I'm not going to spy on you. But if you touch that man, believe me, I will hear about it. I have people all over Manhattan who answer to *me*. Is that understood?"

Despite my dry mouth, I manage to swallow. "Yes."

"Good. What happens here is in your hands, Jessynia. I need you to understand that."

"I need to get my stuff out of the apartment," I say, still shaking internally at the vivid threats of violence against his childhood friend. "I need some time alone there. Without you, I mean."

"I'll be in Brooklyn Saturday morning. You can come then."

"I'm going to bring Kevin or Stella."

"Very well."

"I have to go home."

Fifteen minutes later, we pull up outside Kevin's SoHo loft in a car that was waiting for Jack as we left the building. As I get out, I wince at the sight of Kevin walking down the block towards us, engrossed in his cellphone.

"Jesus. Jack, you have to go," I blurt out as he joins me on the sidewalk. "Get back in the car."

I look up to see Kevin's eyes wide in shock as he spots us both.

"Fuck," I mutter as he approaches us.

"What the hell are you doing here, Wilder?" Kevin's voice is as shrill as a fire alarm.

"Hello, Kevin," Jack replies, his tone measured despite the black malice in his voice. His hands delve into pockets as if to restrain them, his usual warm demeanor towards Kevin visibly chilled. "Nice to see you," he adds, cold as ice.

"Well, it's not mutual," retorts Kevin. "And you're not welcome in my fucking apartment."

"Well, we didn't go inside your apartment, Kevin. Not *this* time."

"Jack, stop," I say, gently pulling Kevin towards the front doorsteps.

"I hope you're pleased with yourself," Kevin shouts at Jack. "I hope that Frost whore was worth it."

"Kevin, stop! Seriously, don't do this." I pull on his arm, which seems to do nothing but irritate him further. "We had to talk, sort things out. We're done now. Let's go inside."

"My marriage is no one's business but mine and my wife's," sneers Jack, "and certainly not some undiscerning *cunt* like you who'll fuck anything with a pulse."

"Jack, stop," I shout, positioning myself in front of Kevin.

"Not my business?" Kevin yells as passersby give us a wide berth. "It is my business when I'm helping pick her up off the floor, you prick."

"You're lucky you're Jessynia's friend, little boy," Jack smirks.

"Oh yeah. You want a piece?" responds Kevin taking a step towards Jack as he puffs out his chest. He's at least half a foot shorter and about a third as strong, and Jack doesn't even flinch at Kevin's display of aggression.

"Stop it!" I shout. "Please, Kev, you're giving me anxiety. Just go inside. I can handle this."

He takes a breath, glowering at Jack before muttering, "He's not worth it," and turning to head up the stone steps. As he gets to the front door, he turns around. "You coming, Jessie?"

"Yeah, just give me three minutes."

"Three minutes. Then I'm coming back out."

He heads inside. "I'm sorry," I say to a scowling Jack. "He's got protective instincts on par with a grizzly bear that's just given birth."

"Well, he ever hurts you and he's fair game," Jack replies frigidly.

"I have to go." A lump forms in my throat as I say it.

I shudder as I observe a quiver in Jack's usually impenetrable façade. His countenance is solemn, his body language defeated, so at odds with the dominant, virile god of a man I'm used to. "I have something for you," he says finally, a crack resounding in that resonant rasp of his. He reaches into the deep pockets of his pants and pulls out a small velvet box of deep violet which he holds out for me. I stare at it for a moment.

"Jack, I can't accept this."

"Please. I want you to wear it. I haven't taken my wedding ring off since we split up." I glance down to see it on his ring finger. "I need you to wear this, for me."

"What is it?"

"Open it."

I reach shaky fingers forward and open the box to reveal a delicate gold chain at the center of which lie two small intertwined circles twice the size of the other chain links—one rose gold, one white gold. He watches me as I run my fingers over the delicate chain.

"Take it out," he says.

I look up at him for a moment before pulling the necklace out, laying it on my palm as I study the elegant intertwined circles. My eyes run down the length of the chain to the clasp. There is a long, solid oval piece with a hole in it, into which slides the arm of a lobster claw clasp. Studying it further, I spot something engraved into both sides of the lock. I lift it up and see two letter J's, one on either side.

"Jack, it's beautiful, but I can't wear this," I say, tears spilling onto the chain in my hand. "It will hurt me every time I put it on. Please just take it." I hold it out to him, pleading with him silently.

Dew mists his eyes. "I need you to wear it, Jessynia. I need to feel close to you. Feeling close to you is the only thing that keeps me from spinning out of control. Becoming...one of *them*."

"Jesus, I can't be responsible for that. It's too much to put on me."

"I'll try to break free for as long as you wear that... or keep it on you."

I study the devastating plea in his aquamarine eyes, the tremor of weakness in this powerful man.

"Please."

"I will keep it with me... as long as you try, Jack. Not for me. But for you. You have to get free of her. Promise me you'll try?"

He nods.

I take the box from him and put the necklace inside.

"I have to go," I utter, feeling like I'm going to break into a million pieces. "Bye, Jack."

"Bye, Jess," he says, a tear falling from each eye down the panes of his savage face. I turn and walk up the stairs, my feet feeling like lead weights, unable to stop the tears at the thought that this may be the last time I see this man whom I have loved so desperately and whom I still feel in my blood.

Our eyes meet once again as I climb the steps, stopping at the top. As I reach for the door handle, I look across the street towards the end of the block to spot a man, tall and bald, watching me from behind a black car. He gets inside it and sits there as I look down at Jack a final time and enter the building, closing the door behind me. After taking a few minutes to quell the flow of tears and dry my eyes, I head upstairs and into the apartment, quickly slinking into my bedroom while Kevin is tending to something on the stove with a podcast to distract him.

I plunk my purse down on a chair and look at the violet box in my hand. Opening it, I take out Jack's necklace which I ponder for a moment before unclasping it, putting it around my neck and locking it in place. I don't fully understand why, but I need to wear it... for now. I glance at the delicate string of gold around my neck in the mirror opposite the bed before heading back to the kitchen and joining Kevin where I listen to him rant for fifteen minutes about the "cheating prick" of a husband of mine. What he's saying is true, but his black and white way of seeing Jack has something inside me bristling.

I can't tell Kevin everything I know about Jack, about how old he was when Alex ensnared him, about how damaged he is, how prone to self-destruction, about the death of his mother and him feeling like an outcast infiltrating Manhattan's high society as a boy. I don't want Kevin, Stella or Maddie to know how deep the rabbit hole goes with Alex, her husband Steven, Vallen Markov and that psychopath they all seem to answer to, Sebastian Gravier.

The only person I can really talk to about these people is Cameron, and I can't talk to him anymore, not just because of the promise I made to Jack, but because it suddenly feels wrong.

I need to heal. Alone. And not drag anyone else into this mess with me.

As Kevin starts to calm down and serves both of us a glass of sparkling wine to temper our frazzled nerves, I ask him if he can sit with me tonight as I tell Cameron that it's over between us.

Later that night, Kevin holds me as I sit on the floor, half an hour after telling Cameron that I can't see him anymore and then listening to him plead and try to reason with me and talk me out of the decision.

Guilt and trauma overwhelm me as the words he uttered and the desolation in his voice continue to send shockwaves into me.

"Please don't do this."

"I've waited for you for five years."

"It's him, isn't it? He threatened you, didn't he?"

"I'll wait."

"What did he say to you?"

"Please let me come see you."

"Don't do this, Jess."

"I love you."

The exhaustion of holding my ground finally got too much and I ended up hanging up in a move that has left me feeling more hollow than I have ever felt, not least because I know that this man that I care for so desperately needs me to be there for him now and I can't unless I undo everything I've just said to him.

Kevin holds me until the tears finally cease and I manage to breathe normally again. "You did the right thing, baby," he whispers, kissing me on the forehead and wiping my slippery face.

"You think?" I manage as I find his gaze through my tears.

"I know it."

"Then why does it feel like this, Kev? Why does it feel so wrong?"

"There was no other way. You have to protect him. The pain won't last forever, baby. I promise you that."

. . .

Kevin forces me to sleep in his king-size bed with him that night so that I'm not alone. His presence comforts me, though does nothing to help me sleep. I toss and turn, my body a live wire of unstable electricity.

Visions of Jack and Cameron haunt me—their words, their pleas, their pain. I feel it all, inside me.

I only pray that this pain really won't last forever.

8

DECEMBER 17TH.

Over four months have passed since I split up with Jack. Despite his incessant requests to, I haven't seen him since. In fact, his text messages became so overwhelming a couple of weeks back that I had to threaten to block him to get him to stop. After making good on my threat for a day before unblocking him, he has responded by sending me handwritten letters several times a week, most of which I can't bring myself to read.

He's not the only one sending me letters. After realizing how much pain Cameron's calls and texts brought me, and how unfair they were to him and to me—stopping both of us from fully moving on—I also asked him to stop calling and texting. I now receive his letters in the mail too, sometimes on the same day as Jack's.

I somehow seem to have managed to get involved with the only two men left in Manhattan who actually still write letters on paper.

Though it doesn't surprise me; there are so many coincidences when it comes to those two that I sometimes wonder if they weren't the same person in another life.

After reading the first two of Cam's letters, I had to stop reading the rest. I don't know how to fully move on yet, but I know that having as little contact with either of them is the only way for me to do it.

I haven't been out too much of late. The winter has been a particularly cold and somber one, gray clouds and blighting wind the soundtrack to the increasingly obscure, shadowy days and interminable nights in this metropolis of brick, concrete and steel.

I don't think I've ever felt the bleakness of New York winters quite so acutely. When I lived back on Central Park West with Jack, it was located opposite Central Park. Looking out onto those trees every day and walking through the park with Jack seemed to take the edge off winter. I guess just being with him, this vibrant, radiant source of fire and energy also helped. Even when I lived with Kev at the end of the summer, we lived just down the block from a park and his street was lined with trees and cozy brick buildings which always made me feel at home.

I'm grateful to have found my apartment in Hudson Square though it's made of gray concrete and other than the tiniest of parks opposite my apartment, there is a distinct absence of flora on the block where I live which doesn't help the mid-winter blues.

The place is a little more than I can really afford seeing as I'm still only doing some freelance journalism at the moment, but I have some savings that I'm using to subsidize my expenses. I still have access to our joint account, though I haven't used it since we split, despite Jack's very vocal and frequent insistence that I do, if only to compensate for the fact that he now lives alone in our apartment. It is in our name, though Jack paid for all the deposit and is still paying for the mortgage. I just don't feel right taking his money, and I don't want to give him power over me or an excuse to think I owe him something. Luckily my year working at the investment bank on Wall Street let me put away some good savings. I certainly need them now.

To distract from the disaster zone that is my private life, I've thrown myself into writing. I now work for about eight online news platforms and magazines, all freelance, which means I'm basically at the whim of the hiring editor and whatever mood they're in that week. I've started my own non-partisan blog focusing on social, health and environmental issues that I believe need more attention without the polarizing and alienating filter of politics getting in the way. I paid a web designer to create a site that looks something like a popular online magazine. I'm trying to turn the thing into a one-woman news site. I'm aware that may sound ludicrously ambitious at this stage, but as my favorite college professor once pointed out, who the hell are we helping by playing small?

I spend about ten dollars a day on online ads to try to get visitors. So far it's working and I'm up to about nine thousand unique views a day. I've even managed to harass a couple of socially and environmentally conscious advertising agencies into putting a few ads on there for a cut-price rate which more than pay for the costs of running the site.

Writing has helped take my mind off things, though the subject matter can get heavy at times and I sometimes find myself simmering with anger as I think about our poor planet and its citizens.

As for socializing, other than going out a handful of times with my friends, either to bars in the area and once to my friend River's concert, I've mainly cocooned myself but for my daily treks to the yoga studio which keep my mind calm and my body strong and supple, and occasional cups of chai with some yoga buddies and cups of coffee with journalist friends.

My brother came to stay with me for a few days. He's an engineer working in San Francisco so I don't see him nearly as much as I would like. Spending days ambling around with him was wonderful, but I fear telling him too much about my life. He's a little hot-headed and has a very pronounced overprotective streak which causes me no end of anxiety when he threatens to rip Jack's face off.

I've done my best to move on. Between the obligatory few pints of ice cream, the Gloria Gaynor records and endless love from my gorgeous friends, I've moved through some of the pain. I wish I could say that I'm starting to fully heal, but there is a pit of longing and sorrow that has taken up residence within me and I can't seem to shake it no matter what I do.

Tonight, Kevin has convinced me to go to an art gallery in Chelsea to see the opening night of our artist friend Gerry's newest exhibition.

There's a bitter sting in the damp air and I rearrange my scarf around my neck and nuzzle my face into it as I walk through the West Village in the direction of Chelsea. I haven't worked out for a couple of days so I've decided to walk the twenty-five minutes from my apartment to the gallery.

As I make it onto 10th Avenue, I just about hear my phone ring above the shrill wind and calamitous cacophony of Saturday evening traffic.

"Hey, Kev," I sing as I pick up, excited to see him soon. I haven't seen him at all since I finally moved out of his apartment at the end of November.

"Hey, I've been trying to call you."

I glance down at my phone and see two missed calls from him and realize the traffic and bluster must have drowned them out. "Oh, sorry, I must have missed them."

"You haven't left yet, have you?"

I stop dead in my tracks. "Um, I'm like ten minutes away. Why? Where are you?"

"Oh, shit. I'm so sorry."

"Oh, please don't tell me you're bailing on me! You're the one that convinced me to come out tonight!"

"Fuck. I'll make it up to you."

"Why can't you come?!" I yell.

"I— Oh, God. I feel like such a shit."

"You *are* a shit! What's going on?"

His voice lowers. "Jessie, you would not believe the specimen I've just met at the gym. He looks like a young Idris Elba. He's only in Manhattan till tomorrow and... well, you get the gist."

I breathe out audibly in irritation. "And I guess your libido is more important to you than your best friend, huh?"

"Will you hate me forever?" he asks.

"Well, not forever," I moan grumpily.

"Look, you go. Have a few canapés, a glass of wine and enjoy silently judging those stuck-up art snobs."

I stop at the corner of 10th and West 19th for a second, not sure what to do. "I think I'll just go back," I say. "I'm not much in the mood for socializing right now."

"Listen, Jess. You better get your backside in that place. You need to get out a bit. It's no good moping at home every night. You need to get your sparkle back. Go on. Have a glass of wine, maybe chat up some hot millionaire art collector. Plus, Gerry's expecting us. We can't *both* not turn up. Go on, please. You'll have a great time."

I let out another sigh. Every fiber in my body wants to just turn back and curl up with a hot chocolate and a magazine, but Kev is right—I need to start going out more, and not just when harangued into it by my friends.

"Fine!" I say. "You better make the very most of tonight, mister. I don't want to be stood up unless I know you're going to be having some ridiculously hot sex."

Kev chuckles. "It'll be swelteringly hot, just for you."

"And be *careful*, huh?"

"I'll try."

We say our goodbyes to the flutter of butterflies in my belly as I walk the last six blocks to the gallery. I'm really not used to talking to strangers much these days. This last year has really taken its toll on me emotionally and whereas you once had to strap me down to stop me going out, my idea of a good night is now some green curry, cashew ice cream and a good book. Not to mention that I don't fancy bumping into people who ask me how Jack is or who grill me about the rumors they've heard about our separation.

As I make it to the gallery, I look through the floor-to-ceiling windows, observing strangers aplenty mingling in the lofty rooms. I take a deep breath and enter against the will of my body. The sting of the merciless wind dissipates in an instant as the heat from inside blasts my cheeks.

"Hello, miss," says a strapping security guard as I enter.

"Hello."

On my immediate left as I enter is a coat rack and I stuff my hat and gloves into my pockets before exchanging my full-length black coat and turquoise scarf for a token that I place in my petite purse whose skinny strap I drape cross-body to ensure it doesn't get left on a table somewhere by accident after I've had a couple of glasses of wine.

I must say I had not expected this gallery to be as opulent as it is. I've been to a couple of art exhibitions in Chelsea in the past but this is a level of chic that I haven't seen before.

Unlike the typical white walls you see at most galleries, these are a rich, deep blood red that is uneven and mottled in places so that parts of the wall are light maroon and some the deepest of crimsons, the color of congealed blood. The ceiling is a stark ivory and so high a trapeze act could happily contort overhead. The floor is polished concrete, a glossy mix of grays and browns and gold.

Gerry's artwork is offset from the wall, each piece standing against a chalk-white background which frames it, separating it perfectly from the dark façade behind. Strong spotlights accentuate the art but the overhead lighting in the room is soft, elegant.

I take a stiff breath in and venture further into the main room to the sight of glistening jewelry adorning well-dressed folk with expensive haircuts who mingle gracefully, watched over by the silent works of art on offer tonight.

Gerry's paintings are large, mostly about eight feet wide by six feet tall and consisting of the splashes, dashes, spots and streaks of color that abstract art experts fawn over, but that I would have a hard time differentiating from the result of giving a two-year-old a brush, canvas and some paints. That is not a commentary on my gorgeous, amazingly talented friend's skills, but on my lamentable lack of knowledge about abstract art which leaves me utterly inept at discerning the genius behind what look like random splotches on canvas, or at least to my weary eyes right now.

I spy a few people glancing in my direction which for reasons unknown makes me feel paper-thin and exposed. If I'm being totally honest with myself, it's at times like this that I think back to being on Jack's arm. No matter what social situation we found ourselves in, we would always amuse ourselves, trying to discretely make each other smile as we would weed out the absurd in the little things that people say or do, exchanging knowing glances most of the night. Jack radiates power. It's by default, part of his aura, his history, his supreme self-confidence and the ruthless way he interacts with the world, unafraid to be himself.

Sometimes his eyes would burn into mine, signaling his ferocious arousal. Other times his hand would ease round my back, squeezing the side of my hip when no one was looking. At times when heads were turned in the opposite direction, his lips would find my ear, his voice low as he would whisper the deviant things he wanted to do to me when we got home... or before then if he had been given half the chance.

I'm going to gag you while I fuck you tonight.

You're going to be pregnant by tomorrow.

You'll be swallowing my cum tonight.

Your tits look indecent in that dress.

We'll have to get a hotel room when we leave. I won't last the forty-five minutes back home without needing to fuck you.

I'm hard. I need you on your knees tonight.

I'm going to end up in prison if another man looks at you.

I know you're wet. I can feel it.

I'm going to make you scream when we get back.

Quite frankly, the list is endless. One time at our friend's birthday party, he dragged me out of the main bar without saying a word and downstairs into the cellar, pulled me behind some boxes of booze, lifted my skirt and fucked me silently against the wall, glaring into my eyes as he did so, before leading me back inside by the hand. He watched my face all night after that. The energy was so mercilessly dominant that it felt like he was fucking me again just with his smoldering stare.

I used to blush with embarrassment every time he growled his indecent threats into my ear, but I now realize how vivid they made every outing and how alive they made me feel. I realize how protected I always was by him.

That's enough, Jess.

I take a lungful of perfumed air and bat off that hollow feeling that seems determined to take up residence within me these days like the most unwelcome of house guests.

As I head towards the left-hand wall on the lookout for my friend, I gasp as I spot faceless strangers standing against the wall—three waiters, all male and wearing dark-gray full-face masks with black trim. One of them steps towards me carrying a tray which he holds out.

"Champagne, miss?"

I don't speak for a second, peering into inscrutable eyes hidden in the shadows of the mask.

Christ, which genius came up with this bright idea?

Apparently, there are no lengths to which Manhattanites won't go to add a little extra thrill and pizazz to a night out, even if it is impractical and eerie as all hell.

"Um, sure." I take a flute of champagne off the silver tray. "Thank you."

"You're welcome."

He eyes me, unmoving until I smile and walk away.

I take a sip of my champagne, only to hear my name called from behind me over the elegant music. I turn to see Ruth Sternburg, a forty-something Fifth Avenue staple, making a beeline for me with her more docile sixty-something property developer husband in tow.

"Oh, hi, Ruth," I say, suppressing a sigh of regret that I couldn't have made it through the night without bumping into this notorious gossip. I greet her husband. Obligatory air kisses all round. "How have you been?" I ask.

"I've been fine, dear." Jesus, even that suspicious tone of voice of hers is annoying. I'd forgotten how grating this meddlesome broad can be.

"More importantly, how have *you* been?" she asks, eyeing me keenly.

"Oh, I've been... you know, good."

"Really? Because I heard this frightful rumor that you and Jack were separated."

Wow, this lady really does go straight for the jugular. I spy the wavy brown hair tumbling from her tight ponytail and wonder for a moment whether it is long enough for me to wrap around her face and gag her with it...

At my silence, she starts to speak again. "Because that's what I've been told, but my friend said she saw him out in a restaurant with his wedding ring on not two weeks ago, and now I see that you don't have yours on, so I don't really know what to think anymore."

As she speaks, my eyes wander to her face-erasing plum-sized mauve earrings in an effort to dull the piercing shrill of her voice, my heart aching at the idea of Jack still wearing his wedding ring in public.

"Well?" she asks. This is the side of Manhattan that I struggle with —the invasive sense of entitlement of the likes of powerful people like Ruth who think they can question you about the most personal parts of your life as if you are a defendant on trial.

"Well, um... Jack and I are not divorced."

"Yes, but are you separated, Jessynia?" Madam clearly has no self-awareness of how inappropriate the stern reproach in her voice is given the circumstances.

Making up my mind not to explain my private life to the entitled elite of New York, I respond, "I'm sorry, Ruth, but I need to find my friend. Please excuse me." I bow to her husband and walk around them, heading through the well-heeled throngs and into the second room behind a large wall.

I take a deep breath, trying to ignore the growing sense of claustrophobia I feel and the sense that the walls are closing in. The chicest of people turn to look towards me as I amble through the room looking for Gerry, trying to make him out while simultaneously trying to avoid eye contact with others at all costs.

As I turn, a masked waiter approaches. "Finished with the glass, miss?"

I spy a half-inch at the bottom of my flute but put it back on his tray anyway, freeing up my clammy hands. As I head towards the left wall, out of my peripheral vision, I spot a man watching me—tall, dark hair.

It can't be...

Cameron?

My heartbeat takes off like a freight train as I slowly turn to look at the man only to find a perfect stranger looking back at me.

He smiles at me, his eyes narrowing, his gaze flitting to my lips for a second. I know that look—unabashed, naked desire. I don't say that about every man that looks at me, but there is a special breed of Manhattanite that navigates social functions in this way. They use their eyes and body language to communicate their readiness to jump into a cab with you at a moment's notice. Subtlety isn't on the menu. This guy is that type. I know them well. Not that there is anything wrong with it, but one-night stands are most definitely not my cup of tea.

He takes a step towards me and I turn around, slowly wandering back through the merry guests towards the exit as I realize that I'm not really up for socializing alone in such an opulent setting after all.

As I make it within a few feet of the coat rack, trying to resist the urge to leave, a voice booms out.

"Jessie!"

I turn and breathe out the longest sigh of relief at the sight of a grinning Gerry making his way towards me. He envelops me in a big hug. "Oh, so glad you've made it!"

"Me too! Gerry, this exhibition is insane. I'm so proud of you!" I hug him back.

"Aw, thanks, gorgeous," he replies, a glint of his Irish accent still there after almost fifteen years living in New York. "Let me get you some booze." He leans in to whisper. "You can't be surrounded by stuck-up art snobs without something to make them more bearable."

I grin and watch as he nips to a table a few feet away and brings back a flute of champagne for both of us. I sip my second glass willingly, happy to have something more to take the edge off.

"Did Kev text you to tell you he can't make it?" I ask.

"He did. Bastard!" Gerry replies jovially, his shaggy light-brown hair waving as he does.

Kevin and I met Gerry on a snowboarding trip to Quebec about five years ago on our first night in a local bar in the village we were staying in. Gerry finding out that they serve Guinness led to one of the most memorable nights of my life as he set the bar on fire by jumping on a table and crooning out *The Whole of the Moon* with the rest of the bar turning into his back-up singers, gleefully spending the night crooning along as this charismatic man filled the entire village with his larger-than-life personality. Wow, that was an innocent time...

"So, how's it going tonight?" I ask, wiping a slight smudge of glossy lipstick off his cheek, a gift from one of the admiring fans around here no doubt. It always makes me laugh to see this potty-mouthed Irishman being fawned over by the art elite of Manhattan.

"Well, I've sold three paintings already and it's only been an hour, so I'm ecstatic. Though I suspect the four glasses of Moët heavily influenced one buyer's decision," he whispers with a wry grin. "And the gallery owner forced me to insinuate I was in the closet to get the second sale" —I suppress a laugh—"so all in all, this has been disastrous for my self-esteem."

He flashes a smile and downs his champagne. I consider warning him not to drink too much but don't want to put a dampener on his special night, even if I always worry about his inability to stop drinking once he's started.

"So, how've you been, gorgeous?" he asks. "You and Jack haven't managed to work things out?"

"No," I reply softly.

"I am sorry, Jess. I liked Jack a lot."

"I know. He liked you too."

"You mean once he got past that phase where he wanted to rip my limbs off my body for being a straight male friend of yours?"

"Yeah, after that phase," I laugh.

"He's quite the caveman that one."

I look down for a moment as Jack's face blasts into my mind.

Gerry's expression turns more serious as I take a deep breath in and take a sip of champagne. "How've you been coping, Jessie? Really, I mean."

"Oh, good and bad days, you know. I'm in a better state than I was a few months ago."

"That's good."

"Yeah."

"But?"

"But... I don't know. I've just kind of... lost my sparkle a little bit. It'll be back."

"Okay, right, that's it," he pipes up resolutely.

"What?"

"Sparkle retrieval is one of my specialist subjects."

"Oh God..."

"We're going out this Saturday night. You, me, a couple of friends. I'll invite this new girl I've been dating. We'll hit a few Irish pubs. Drink a few pints. Get you dancing on the tables like you used to do."

"Oh, I'm not sure anyone needs to see that spectacle again."

"Well, *I* do. I'm not taking no for an answer. You with me?"

"Sure," I smile and kiss him on the cheek. "If anyone can help me snap out of my self-pity, it's you, Gerry."

"Challenge accepted."

"Okay."

"Oh, and speaking of challenges... I've got a very hot single friend coming by in about half an hour. Ewan. I'll introduce you to him. Multi-millionaire. He'll *definitely* like you... You need to get back in the land of the living, girl."

I shrug and down my champagne, putting it on a tray a few steps away. "Hell, why not?"

As Gerry grins at me, a tall middle-aged lady with glasses holding back her wild red hair pops up next to him, planting a manicured hand on his shoulder.

She gives me a curt *hello* before turning to my friend. "Gerry, I have some buyers I need you to be extremely charming to in about thirty seconds. Think you can manage that?"

"Oh, I think so," he responds with a grin. "What do you think, Jess?"

"I have every faith in you, lovely."

"I'll catch you later," he replies, squeezing my arm as he does. "Hey, Sandy," he calls over my shoulder.

A smiling platinum-blonde wearing a loose black shirt and black pants strides up to us confidently.

"Sandy, I want you to meet a good friend of mine, Jess. She's a journalist as well."

"Hello, Jess," she says.

"Hi, nice to meet you," I reply.

"Could you show her around a bit?" asks Gerry. "I'm still trying to get her to finally appreciate my art."

Gerry squeezes my arm as he bids us goodbye as Sandy offers me a warm, open smile which I reciprocate gladly. "Wow, I love that blue dress!" she enthuses, looking over my tight long-sleeved ankle-length robe.

"Oh, thank you. My mom got me this. It's one of the only things she's ever bought me that doesn't make me look like a Christmas present."

Her eyes twinkle in response. "So, you're a journalist?" she asks.

"Just freelance so far."

"Oh really, what type of thing?"

"I mainly write about health issues and the environment, animal rights. How about you?" I ask.

"Well, I'm on hiatus, but I used to work for a couple of national newspapers in Washington. Arts section."

"Wow, you must have some stories to tell!"

"Oh, you can say that again. Have you seen Gerry's paintings?"

"Just quickly. If I'm being perfectly honest," I add in a whisper, "when it comes to abstract art, I can't much tell the difference between a Kandinsky and a plate of spaghetti."

"Well, let me show you around and see if I can fake my way through an explanation."

I chuckle as she loops her arm into mine with the über-familiarity that is typical of Manhattanites at social functions involving alcohol.

Sandy spends ten minutes showing me around the gallery, pointing out the symbolism in Gerry's paintings as I nod along and take her word for it, grateful to be feeling a little more like my usual sociable self now that I've shaken off the nerves I had earlier and can enjoy this lovely woman's company. I spot a couple of men making eye contact with me and manage to smile back at them, just about. It still feels so alien to do so, as though Jack is around every corner, ready to pounce.

Not to mention Cameron whom I feel in my blood every second of the day, pulsing through my veins, the thought of him haunting me constantly, the phantom feeling of his fiery flesh upon mine stopping me from sleeping at night.

A while later, Sandy leads me into a very small empty fourth room tucked in at the back that I hadn't even noticed. On the walls hang some smaller paintings by Gerry, all landscapes if I'm interpreting them correctly, which, let's face it, I may not be.

"Wow, a tree!" I exclaim. "Finally something I can identify!"

She touches my arm with a giggle. "Listen, let me tell you a secret. Art critics and artists are so full of shit. They're all seeing these amazing things because they don't want to admit they have no idea what's going on!"

"Yeah, I can believe that."

"Jess, I'm gonna leave you. I need to use the ladies' room. There's a queue so it may take a few minutes. Feel free to wander around, okay?"

"Sure. Thanks so much, Sandy."

"You're welcome. Hope I see you later."

I smile as I turn to look at Gerry's gorgeous paint renditions of trees and lakes and what look like mountains. I can just picture him scraping the brightly colored acrylic on the canvas and rewarding himself with a cold glass of beer once he's done. Or maybe the beer came before the scraping...

As I turn to observe a small green and gray number with a price tag about three times as much as my monthly rent, there is a shuffle from behind me—someone else walking into the little room.

I look up to say hello.

But the words don't come out.

For as I glance upwards, I feel myself tremble, my breath leaving me at the sight of Steven Frost, Alexandra's husband, slowly making his way towards me with Vallen Markov in tow, blocking the way out.

I manage to suppress a gasp at the steady way Frost is prowling towards me and at Vallen's gleeful, unflinching stare before starting to walk past Frost in the direction of the exit which I intend to get through if I have to punch Vallen in the throat do it. As I brush past Steven, he grabs my arm forcefully, holding it and stopping me from moving.

"I wouldn't do that, Jessynia," he growls. "I'll only have to find you at some other place where there may not be as many people around, and I'm sure you wouldn't like that very much. Let's not make a scene."

I yank my arm away from his, indignant with rage that he would put his hands on me. "You touch me one more time, Frost, and they won't be able to tell the difference between these paintings and your face!"

He breaks into a smile and puts his hands in his pockets. He's taller than I remember, scraping six foot, with raven-black hair that's mottled with gray at the sides. In contrast, his skin is pale and his eyes so dark that they almost look black under the dull spotlight above. He must be in his early forties, but his skin shows little evidence of wear, and his features are still crisp and defined, as are the thick muscles under his suit.

"Well, I'm glad to see that recent events haven't dampened that spirit of yours," he says smoothly, his disquieting voice contrasting sharply with the faint laughter drifting in from nearby rooms. "That would have been a shame. There's nothing more tedious than a beautiful woman that has nothing to say for herself."

"What do you want, Steven? Did you know I was going to be here?! Did you have me followed?!"

"Don't worry. It's only been for a couple of days."

"A couple of— How dare you?! You have no right to do that!"

I flick a glance behind him to observe Vallen's trademark toothy smirk that has me wanting to grab one of the sculptures on display around here and use it to rearrange his face into something more civilized.

"Well, it won't happen again," Steven responds. "I just felt the need to... have a little chat with you."

"A chat? What about?"

"We're tied together, you and I."

"You know about them, don't you?" I ask.

His eyes narrow and his lips curve into a wicked smile. "Of course I do."

"And you don't care?"

"Hmm," he chuckles. "Why on Earth should I care? I encouraged it. I even watched a couple of times."

A sharp breath escapes me without my meaning it to. I search his gratified face, trying to breathe, hating that I allowed him to observe my feelings. I hear Vallen snigger, filling the doorway to this enclave with his malignant presence as Steven takes a step towards me, the narrow slits of his eyes glistening in utter jubilation at my distress. "Your husband is an extremely talented man," he adds. "You're a very lucky woman."

"You watched them?" I can't hide the tremor in my voice.

"Of course."

"And... and you're just happy as Larry to watch another man make love to your own wife?"

He sniggers. "I'm not sure what narrative you have going on in your head, Jessynia, but your husband doesn't *make love* to my wife. *Hate* is closer to the mark. He gets pleasure from dominating her, hurting her. She is a very smart woman but doesn't seem to pick up on the fact that he is in fact hate-fucking her. Every time. Denial is a very powerful thing when you have feelings for someone, you see."

I shake my head if only to try to dislodge the vision of them together.

"As it turns out," he continues, "I enjoy him hurting her very much. I enjoy the hatred in his eyes. I enjoy him violating her. I take great, great pleasure in it. She does too, despite slowly but surely losing the power she once wielded over him so effectively."

I shake my head in incredulity. "Do you... know how insane that is?"

"My wife is a uniquely fascinating creature. I want her to have an enjoyable life, Jessynia. And if that means enjoying *talented* men like your husband, then so be it."

My breathing quickens. "And I suppose you think that's normal, do you?"

"We've been together for thirteen years. She no longer has"—he slowly runs his gaze up and down my body, pausing at my breasts with relish before finding my eyes again—"what it takes to satisfy me sufficiently. And I'm sure she could say the same about me." He gestures with his hand as he speaks and I notice his gold wedding band sparkle, witness to the façade of this man and his "wife".

"So, what, she can't go for single men, or men whose wives don't care if they screw about? I'm just acceptable collateral damage, is that it?"

"You're young, Jessynia. Naïve. Inexperienced." I turn to observe malicious mirth on Vallen's face, my gaze returning to Steven whose eyes I find moving down the curves of my body again. I wish my hair were loose and not tied into a tight bun at the back of my head, to at least provide some protection from his indecent, ravenous lust over my form. "You still believe there are couples out there that are faithful to each other, don't you? Well, let me tell you, there aren't. One or both of them are fucking around... or are planning how to fuck around... or are trying to find a way to fuck around without getting caught. My dear wife and I just have the guts to face the truth about our urges."

"Sounds like a match made in heaven," I scoff.

"Well, I highly recommend finding a partner with whom you can be honest about your basest of urges. If you don't, it leads to all sorts of trouble... as you've discovered to your cost."

"Well, I don't pick up my partners at Sociopaths Anonymous, so I guess they're not as open about their *base urges*."

He smiles, his glare deviant on my lips. "You're quite a fascinating creature yourself, Jessynia." I stare at him, unmoving as a sudden spike of pain stabs the ankle that was operated on seven months ago. "You know, I have learned a great deal about giving and receiving pleasure in my life," he says. "I hope to be able to share what I've learned with you one day."

I shake my head in incredulity. "Yeah, keep dreaming, Frost," I retort, utterly aghast, my cheeks suddenly hot.

Clouds darken the troughs of his face and his voice roughens in haste. "I've been a patient man, Mrs. Wilder. I've allowed your husband to fuck my wife for *years*. I think it's only fair he reciprocates."

"Well, I'm not Jack's property."

"You still are by law. And I believe you would greatly benefit from being instructed by an older, stronger, more experienced man than your husband. Men in their twenties, even men as talented as him, really have no idea what they're doing compared to trained and educated men like me." I swallow hard to the sound of Vallen's quiet laughter, trying to hold my ground in the face of Frost's perverse glare and unmistakable arousal. "Wouldn't you say so, Vallen?"

"Most definitely."

"What is it you want from me?" I ask, rage causing my chest to flush pink.

He watches me for a few moments, scrutinizing every movement of my face before speaking. "There has been some concern from my wife, and from a few other... *friends* about how many people you are telling about my wife's little... *exploits* with your husband. In particular, we are concerned about the divorce petition you will file next year. We most certainly hope that she does not feature in it."

"What, do you think people don't know what she is?" I ask, glancing down at the white shirt hiding under his expensive gray dress suit.

"I don't care what they know," he retorts. "Most people are smart enough not to discuss my wife in public. I would hate to have to have another run-in with you if you did not exercise sensible discretion."

"*Discretion*?" I scoff. "Such a civilized word for what's going on here."

"You know what I'm saying here, Jessynia," he snarls, a murky shadow obfuscating his eyes.

"Yes, you're saying that you don't want me broadcasting to the entire island that your wife is a soulless succubus from hell who sucks on other people's life force because she's so empty inside." His lips widen into a broad smile as he watches my face in something akin to amusement, glancing at my lips with indiscrete relish. There's not an ounce of protectiveness in his demeanor over his maligned wife. "Well, sorry, but you're about five years too late on this one, Steven," I continue. "The cat is well and truly out of the bag. Maybe consider moving to a different state where her reputation doesn't precede her everywhere she goes."

He watches me for a while, seemingly diverted, before turning to Vallen and asking softly, "Can you give us a moment, Mr. Markov?"

"Certainly," says Vallen, bowing his head.

"What are you, his bodyguard?" I throw at Vallen as he runs a hand through almond-brown hair that matches his pale brown eyes.

"Just a good friend, Jessynia. It's always a pleasure for me to spend time in your company. I've enjoyed watching the show. Watching you has certainly given me some... interesting material for later this evening." There's that pernicious smile on his face that I want to sandpaper off again. "Enjoy the rest of your chat."

He leaves the room and disappears out of sight and I shoot a glance through the doorway in the hopes of catching someone's eye... to no avail.

Steven studies my face before running his greedy gaze down my body, his lascivity leaving me feeling violated. "You're quite the specimen, Jessynia. I've always enjoyed your rebellious spirit. I can certainly understand why men lose their minds over you. Your turquoise eyes, your plump lips, your soft skin, your slim body, your big, round tits, that long hair of yours, very useful for pulling you around with." My breathing turns shallow as I try not to gasp aloud at the licentious assault of his words. "I can only imagine the pleasure of fucking your soft, wet cunt, your hands tied behind your back, unable to get away..."

"You don't have the right to talk to me like that," I manage, my voice small.

"And what's more... I know you would like it. Very much. There is no greater honor nor pleasure for a beautiful young woman like yourself than to be educated by an older, more experienced man, a man who can appreciate her unique gifts, a man unburdened by the impulsivity of youth." He leans his face in closer. "And I've certainly given your pleasure enough thought."

I take a step back as I spot someone enter the tiny room out of the corner of my eye.

"You know," he continues, his black hair creating a shadow over his eyes, "sex is merely an exchange of energies. And when I fuck my wife after I've watched her being violated and sodomized by your husband, I *almost* feel like I'm fucking you. Sodomizing you." He takes a step towards me as a subtle groan escapes his throat, his eyes dilating, his mouth opening slightly. There is no doubt what he is imagining doing to me.

As vertigo seizes me and I feel my limbs weaken, a male voice cuts through the silent duel.

"Excuse me, miss?"

I look up to see a man, handsome and in his mid-twenties, shift his glance between me and Steven Frost. He must see my fearful, likely ashen face for he takes a step towards us, his brow furrowing in concern. "Is everything okay here?" the man asks.

"I'm leaving now," I respond as firmly as I can muster, half to Frost and half to signal to this new arrival that I want to get out of the room.

I spot Steven glaring at him as I start to walk away. As I glance down to steady my gait, Frost's strong hand curls around my forearm, the power in his well-used muscles chilling me.

"You tell *anyone else* about my wife and your husband," he growls, leaning into me, his eyes a cauldron of fury, "and we will have to have another of these little chats."

The stranger takes a step towards us. "Hey, let go of her," he urges.

I yank my arm away from Frost's grasp. "I won't tell the lawyer her name... or anyone else," I yell, a yell luckily drowned out by the bustle in the other rooms and the civilized elevator music wafting through ours, "but you have anyone follow me *ever* again and I will tell Jack and you can answer to him. Is that understood?"

He bows his head with a smile. "Then we understand each other. Good evening, Mrs. Wilder."

I burst out of the room and turn to the stranger. "Sir, please come with me," I urge, tugging on his arm when he hesitates. "Please, just trust me. We have to leave," I add pulling him in the direction of the exit where I let go of him and fumble for the coat-check token which I hastily exchange for my coat and scarf before watching him do the same.

I glance at him as he slides a long dark-gray coat onto his muscular body and then pull on his arm as we make it outside where we are blasted by the winter frost. In what may well be the single most inappropriate gesture I've subjected a complete stranger to, I hold onto his arm and march him in the direction of my apartment just to get him away from that place.

"Um, miss?" he says as I grip his coat tightly, pulling him as we cross the street.

I don't answer, finally letting go of him when we have cleared three blocks where I stop and let out a long, audible breath. "I'm so sorry about that," I say, angst and embarrassment making me tremble. "I don't normally manhandle perfect strangers. I... I just... That man is... He could be dangerous. I don't think you should go back there... back to the gallery, I mean."

The handsome stranger frowns at me as if waiting for an explanation.

"Look, that man is kind of... powerful and... unhinged. It's a very bad combination."

"Yeah, it certainly sounds like it," he responds. "More importantly, are you okay?"

"Yeah, I'm... fine. Look, thanks so much for helping me out there."

"You're welcome. You, um, you know that guy?"

"Unfortunately, yes. Hopefully, I'll never have to see him again."

"I hope not."

"Look, sir—"

"Mika." The tiniest of smiles brightens the man's cool light-brown eyes.

"Jess," I say. "Look, thank you. I really do appreciate what you did. Not everyone has the guts to step in when something weird's going down."

"You're welcome," he replies. "I'm sorry you had to go through that."

"Well, I'm sorry you never got to enjoy the exhibition."

"Oh, I'll survive," he replies. "One thing that Manhattan is not short of is art exhibitions."

"Yeah. Just, um, promise me that you won't go back..."

"I promise."

"Good." I finally let myself breathe, taking in a ragged breath and slowly letting it out. "Okay, well, I'm gonna head home. Thank you again, Mika."

"You're welcome again, Jess."

"Bye," I say and turn, continuing my brisk walk down 10th Avenue.

A half-minute or so passes and I sense a man behind me, turning around to see Mika fifteen feet behind. He lifts his eyebrows cutely. "I'm sorry. I just... I live in this direction too. In the West Village."

"Oh..."

"I can take a different route if you prefer?"

"No. That's okay. I don't mind."

He joins me and we walk side by side for a block. I would make conversation but my mind is whirling, troubled by the things Steven Frost said to me. I little know how I got involved with the living dead of Manhattan like him and his so-called wife, but part of me wants to fly off to another country for a year just to escape the energy that I can't seem to extricate myself from.

"You, um, like the West Village?" I finally ask to break the silence. "I've always wanted to live there. Those russet bricks are so beautiful."

I glance up at him and he smiles. "I love it. Do you live nearby?"

I don't answer, my voice lost and my insides shaky as we walk a couple of blocks. "Mika, I'm sorry, I'm usually more talkative than this. I'm still a bit shaken up from before."

"Yeah, well, I kind of sensed that. Think maybe it's best I don't barrage you with questions."

I smile at him as he stops in front of a coffee shop. "Jess, I... I think I'm going to get something to warm me up." He tips his head in the direction of the shop.

"Oh, sure."

"Do you want to, um, join me?"

"Um, no. I really have to get home."

"Okay. Are you sure you're okay to walk by yourself? You don't want a cab?"

"No, no," I reply. "The walk will do me good."

"Okay, well, it was very nice to meet you, Jess. Sorry it had to be like *that.*"

"It was nice to meet you too, Mika. You won't go back there, right?"

"No. I won't."

"Okay, good. Bye, then."

"Bye."

He watches me as I turn, wrapping my scarf tightly around my neck and nestling my mouth into it.

After twenty minutes of walking, barely registering the passersby on the street or the biting sting of the harsh December air, I turn the key to my apartment, a shiver running through me as I scramble for the light in the pitch black. I half expect the spectre of Steven Frost to greet me in the living room.

After locking the door and engaging the safety latch, I take off my coat, scarf and boots and head into the little area between the kitchen and living room which I've transformed into my office where I stand still, my mind short-circuiting, my body inert, unable to move as pieces of the deviant things that Frost uttered whirl before me like debris in a tornado.

My hand moves towards the bottom drawer of my white armoire-style desk where I keep all the unopened letters that both Jack and Cameron have sent me over the last few months.

My heart aches as I see Jack's scrawl on an unopened letter and remember how safe the world felt a year ago compared to now where I see insidious ghouls lurking in shadows that I didn't know existed all around me. Or rather I finally see the shadows that his protective shield kept me oblivious to throughout our relationship.

I can't stop myself from grabbing the silver letter opener and sitting on the hardwood floor next to the drawer. My hand moves to the last letter I got from Cameron three days ago which I slice open, afraid to look at it, but unable to stop myself. I pull out and unfold a single piece of thick, cream paper embossed at the top with the initials **C.O.**

Jessynia,

I feel you with me.

Your light.

Your warmth.

Your face.

Your scent haunts me.

I feel the touch of my lips on your skin.
I see the turquoise in your eyes as they look up at mine.
Sensing that you are near me is the only thing keeping me moving forward each day.
Knowing that one day I will be with you is the only thing keeping me alive.
Please come back to me.
Yours, Cameron

Cameron...

Where are you?

I'm suddenly numb, unable to process anymore. Holding his letter, I get up and head into the living area and onto the warm gray rug that reminds me of the one in Cameron's Fifth Avenue penthouse. I grab a throw from the armchair and drape it over me, not having the energy to take my clothes and makeup off. The palms of one hand rest on Cam's letter while I touch my neck with the other, intertwining a finger in the gold chain Jack gifted me a few months ago. Touching it is ridiculously comforting. Jack always made me feel so safe from the world. This chain is the little I have left of that feeling. And I hate that I still need it...

As I lie in the stillness, I close my eyes and hope that with morning, that bold sense of joy and fearlessness I used to awaken with every morning comes back to me.

9

"SO HOW WAS THE EXHIBITION?" asks Stella the following Monday as I use a large mug to water my poor flailing plants. I hear her walking in the street, the familiar beeps and shouts that make up the daily symphony of Manhattan sounding off even from afar.

"Oh, it was..." I pause. I can't tell her about Steven Frost and drag her into this quagmire I've found myself in. "It was... great. You should have seen Gerry. He had Manhattan's glitterati fawning all over him. It was absolutely hilarious."

"I bet he enjoyed that," she laughs. "How was the art?"

"Well, I'm told it was sublime."

"Tsk. You mean you could not decipher the intricacies of abstract art!"

I chuckle. "No, it's not my forte."

"Mine neither, darling. How've you been feeling? You sound a bit tired."

"I've been..." I feel a lump form in my throat which I swallow down, trying to make sure my voice doesn't crack as I feel a fast, unexpected tear drop onto my cheek. It happens a lot these days when people ask me how I am.

I know I'm supposed to be okay. I'm supposed to be great. I'm twenty-four, living in Manhattan, in fairly good health but for a temperamental ankle. I have a career that means a lot to me, that makes a difference in the world. I have wonderful friends, a close family. Even my feisty battle-axe of a mother has a loving, protective side that I'm grateful for which is more than what some kids get. On paper, I should be doing great.

Is it even okay for me to say I still have days when I struggle to feel good?

I don't remember ever having moments when I felt low and hollow like this before. Sometimes I catch myself wondering if it's even allowed. Am I weak for feeling down? Am I depressed or just grieving? Is this just totally normal after a breakup? That I can't taste food like before, that music no longer makes me want to dance, that colors look dull? Am I deluded for mourning my marriage given how it ended?

It's not just about the precious marriage that meant so much to me falling to pieces. I miss my old life with Jack before the curtain dropped. I miss the singular bond I had with him so much that my insides hurt from it. The grief is trapped inside me, feasting on my life force, hollowing me out from the inside like a vulture feasting on flesh.

I know I'm not supposed to miss him. He cheated on me so I'm supposed to just hate his guts and move on without giving him a second thought. He's now less than human and I'm a fool if I think of him ever again. It's supposed to be black and white. Not a single shade of grey, never mind fifty of them.

That's what I've been told anyway. And if I don't relegate him to the category of pond scum and don't forever cast aside the person who hurt me without a second thought, does that make me weak? Is my love weakness? My lingering compassion for a man who nursed me back to health and traveled the world with me, protecting me every step of the way for years... Is it naïve? Stupid? Is it even allowed?

I know there are women out there who get cheated on and then guillotine all emotion towards the man who wronged them. I don't blame them. I fight that urge myself depending on the day.

But when I think of Jack, I don't just think of the cheating. I wish I did, but I also think of the six months he took out of his life to nurse me back to health after my skiing accident. I think of him renting the house off the coast of Georgia because it was better for my recovery. I remember him sitting with me, watching me, his strong hands holding mine, reassuring me when I could not even turn my head without wanting to throw up. I remember him carrying me from room to room, carrying me into and out of cars, taking me to physiotherapists, neurologists, canceling work plans, not seeing his family for weeks at a time in order to stay with me, watching terrible movies that would give me the occasional light relief, not having sex for weeks at a time. I remember him holding me, kissing me, telling me he loved me when there was no guarantee I would ever overcome those health issues. I remember him telling me that he would never let me go, that he would stay with me no matter what happened.

How do I erase those memories? Are they allowed to exist anymore? Am I allowed to mourn the loss of that man? I've found the strength to leave him and will *never* go back, but do all the things he once did for me now disappear into the earth? Should the sting now be dulled forever? Should my love have already vanished into the ether?

I find myself afraid that people will judge me for telling them I'm mourning the breakdown of my marriage after the way he cheated on me so I keep it inside a lot where the sorrow builds and builds until it becomes so deep, so heavy that getting up some mornings is a challenge.

It never used to be. I used to leap out of bed with so much enthusiasm that it would make Jack grin before he'd even fully woken up. How the hell did I lose that?

And while I will never go back to him after all that has happened, I can't help but ache at no longer sharing my life with someone so vibrant, so strong, so passionate, so smart who got me and all my quirky little ways. Not only got them, loved and encouraged them.

I miss his presence. I miss his strength. I miss the boundless momentum that came with being part of his team. I miss his eyes boring into me day and night. Jack got me, eccentricities and all. And that type of connection doesn't happen every day. I miss the heat I felt when I was with him. I miss us laughing, melting into each other. I miss life feeling like it made sense before the veil was pulled off this tenebrous underworld.

And then... there's Cameron.

Cameron whose presence I feel with me every minute, even more acutely than Jack's at times. I miss him in a different way. It's not the grief of loss and layers of memories stacked one on top of each other.

It's the grief of having something so powerful cut down before it had a chance to blossom like it wanted to, to explode, to radiate light and heat.

It's the grief of reconnecting with this sensational, mind-blowing man, this person who knew me so well, who could sense my thoughts before I even spoke them... and then having that energy handcuffed and locked away in some somber cell, not because I wanted that, nor him, but because there is no other choice. It's the grief of having a light extinguished which lit up my flesh, my insides, my soul, which poured flame into me, into us, which lifted me, which lifted him...

My body yearns for him desperately. The very thought of him ignites my flesh some days... until the cold dawn of realization sets in. Flashbacks of making love to him at Redwood leave me looking around the room to see if he is there. I see unbidden spectres of him when walking down the street. I feel him near me in stores and turn to look into the eyes of strangers.

My hands constantly pick up the phone and hover over his name to call him... if only to check that this man I care about so desperately is okay. But I never do. I asked him not to call nor text, so I have to respect that myself. I can barely face looking at his letters. I can't face more heartache.

I should go on dates with other men. I've had at least ten friends ask if they can set me up with someone. The idea of it just leaves me hollow.

How did all this happen?

I've always been told what a little powerhouse I was, ever since I was a kid. As early as I can remember, people used to call me the *tornado*, or the *stick of dynamite*, or the *ray of sunshine*. They would say, "*Oh, watch out, the little dynamo's coming.*" Boy, did I have some unyielding opinions to proffer to the unsuspecting world when I was younger, even up to a year or so ago.

I remember being fearless.

And I loved that girl. She was a total badass.

Where did she go?

I still feel her with me. I feel her stuck in a room deep in a labyrinth inside me and she wants to come out... but I can't find the room, nor the key. I try but there are too many paths to take. And it's too dark. And her voice echoes in different directions. And I'm trying to rescue her but I can't.

I've always thought of myself as a tough, feisty, take-no-prisoners kind of gal. Are women like us allowed to have moments of weakness? Do we have to be ball-busting badasses right out of the gate until the day we die? Are we allowed to have moments when we feel low? When others throw us off balance? Are we allowed to second-guess our choices? To feel despair and have to learn to pick ourselves up and walk again?

Some days I wonder...

"Sweetie?" Stella's voice snaps me back to the real world in front of me.

I wipe away a tear with feeble fingers once so strong. "I... I'm doing good, Stell. How are you?" I ask, trying to sound upbeat in the hopes that my melancholy doesn't register.

"Oh, I'm okay. This bastard from that competing firm is trying to blackmail me."

"What?! That's illegal, isn't it?"

"Don't worry. I have a plan. He won't know what's hit him."

"Oh, I believe you, my friend. Is there anything I can do to help? Expose the fucker? I'll do it, you know..."

"I'll let you know," she laughs. "What are you doing today?"

"Just some more research and then I need to start writing."

"Is this still the fracking one?"

"No, they want one on bitumen sands," I groan.

"Sounds, um, fascinating."

"Yeah, it's a hoot," I jest.

"Fancy some company later?" Stella asks. "You, me, some wine, Indian food. How about I bring it all round? 7 p.m.?"

"Oh, Stell, are you sure you want to go to all that trouble?"

"You just make sure you let me in."

I smile. "Will do. And there'll be wine and dessert waiting for you."

"Can't wait."

A couple of hours later I find myself sitting in one of my favorite coffee shops in Greenwich Village sipping a spicy chai coconut-milk latte. After procrastinating by pottering around my apartment restlessly all morning, tidying things that didn't need to be tidied, scrubbing at surfaces until I feared they could wear thin, I decided to just grab my laptop and get the hell out as my brain is way too frazzled to be of any use at home.

Studying the horrors of factory farming for my last article and an offshoot entry for my blog took a lot out of me and I'm currently relieved that I'm instead reading various scientists' contradicting views on the health and environmental impact of bitumen sands for an article commissioned for the environmental section of a prominent online magazine.

As I curse under my breath while studying pictures of a polluted lake, thick with a layer of some black substance, I take another sip of chai and look up, my eyes almost popping out of my head as I spot the guy from the other night at the gallery—Mika, I think.

I forget to breathe as he heads to the counter and orders something, pays, then waits for a moment before collecting a Danish and a cup of something hot. He turns and looks around for a free table, heading in my direction while spying an empty table near the window. As he heads towards it, he glances absently in my direction before doing a double-take, his mouth opening a little.

He walks towards me tentatively. "Um, hi," he says cutely, a little blush of coral pink appearing on his alabaster skin.

"Um, hey," I reply. "Mika, right?"

"Yeah. Jess?"

"Yes."

His lips slowly widen into a nervous smile. "I, um... I'm not stalking you, I promise," he says, probably noticing the ridiculous flicker of anxiety in my frown. "I live like four blocks down. I come here all the time." He raises his brows cutely as if waiting to see if I believe him.

I smile, partly in relief and partly at my own ridiculous jumpiness. "I know that."

He smiles back, the skin around his eyes crinkling cutely. "I guess you're working on something. I think it's best I don't join you," he says, a question mark hanging in the air. I can tell by the way his window-bent momentum has stopped cold and by how his fingers are leaning on the chair opposite me that he wants to sit with me.

My instinct is to politely refuse and just get on with my work, but Mad and Stella have been bugging me for weeks now to start interacting with more people—men, specifically—and I know I have to do it at some point before my hymen grows back. Plus, the guy is hot as all hell and I feel my body vibrate slightly at the sight of his modelesque face and tall, well-built frame.

"You know what, I could use a break," I reply with a smile. "Unless you have something you have to do?"

"Nothing urgent."

I pull my laptop towards me and close the screen so that he has enough place to put his cup and plate. He pulls out the wooden chair opposite me and sits down.

I check out his cute dimples as his eyes dart around my face, stopping in short bursts on my lips, cheeks and then my eyes.

"So—" We break into a grin as we both attempt the same word at the same time.

"You go," I urge.

"I was just wondering how you're doing after the other night."

"Oh, I'm... I'm fine. I've dealt with my fair share of insufferable Manhattanites in my time. He's just another one to add to the list." The truth is that I do still feel contaminated by my little chat with Steven Frost.

"Yeah, if there's one thing Manhattan has no shortage of, it's insufferable pricks," he replies. "The art world is full of them."

"You're an artist?"

"Trying to be. I'm, um, in negotiations to have my first joint exhibition in March."

"Wow, that's amazing! Congratulations. I know from Gerry how hard it is to make that happen."

"Yeah, it's been a trip, alright."

"Are you two friends?" I ask. "You and Gerry?"

"Friends? No. I just... I heard about the exhibition from the gallery owner. She's a friend of mine. I thought I'd check out a fellow abstract artist."

"Do you like his work?" I ask.

"Yeah. Feel like it puts mine to shame."

"Well, don't repeat this, but I saw him painting at his studio a few years ago and he kept saying he had no idea what he was doing. I have been told that self-doubt is an obligatory rite of passage for most artists."

He tucks a strand of his ashy-brown hair behind his ear before grasping his cup of coffee with both hands as if to warm them up. As he does so, slate-blue cuffs peeking out from under his black coat settle on his sturdy hands.

I look up to find his eyes soft on mine, a small smile tugging at his lips. "And what do you do?" he asks taking a sip of his coffee before placing it down and removing his coat.

"Well, I guess I'm a journalist."

He raises his brows as his gaze hits my lips. "You guess?"

I grin. "Well, I've only been doing it since the start of the year. Just freelance. I've had a few dozen articles published this year, but I still haven't quite assumed the title fully."

"I get what you mean. I still struggle to officially call myself an artist."

"Oh, I feel you," I respond. "Plus, I made the mistake of telling my mom I have my own website, so now she keeps introducing me to her friends as a *blogger* rather than a *journalist*." I shake my head to stifle a smile. “Not that there’s *anything* wrong with that, at all but... you know. I think she likes it when I’m knocked down a peg or three.”

“Let me guess... It’s character-building, right?”

“That’s what she says!” I chuckle.

“I feel you, Jess.”

“She honestly drives me nuts, that lady...”

“Who needs critics when you’ve got moms, huh?” He takes a big bite of his glossy Danish.

“I’ve already banned her from reading my last three articles. She had way too much to say about a few I wrote earlier this year.”

“She sounds like she’d get along with mine. Mine tends to roll her eyes when I tell her I’m still trying to make the art thing work.”

“Oh, that’s terrible. Don’t listen!” I urge.

“Moms, huh?”

“Yeah.”

He watches me as I take a sip of chai. “What are you working on now?”

I gulp down the spicy brew. “Well, I’m exploring the *thrilling* world of tar sands.”

His eyes brighten and he rubs a hand across his strong jaw. “Sure, that sounds... um, quite thrilling. What can you tell me about it?”

“Um, well, did you know that because bitumen has the consistency of peanut butter, it has to be diluted with a satanic cocktail of petroleum compounds to allow it to flow through pipelines?”

“Satanic?”

“Yes. That is the technical term the top scientists are using.”

“I see,” he grins. “I take it you’re not on board?”

“Well, as a journalist we’re supposed to give an unbiased analysis, but after reading some of the case reports, let’s just say that I feel sorry for our poor little planet when I study these things.”

“And it pays the rent?” He finishes off his Danish, licking delicate crumbs from his lush lips. “Just about. Hopefully, in another year, I’ll have made a name for myself and won’t have to guilt-trip people into hiring me anymore like I do now. I’ve actually got an interview for a part-time staff writer position for a New York newspaper the second week of January. It'll be my second interview with them."

"Wow, that's awesome. Do you want the job?" he asks, leaning into me a little. A shiver rolls through me as I realize that his face suddenly seems familiar to me, as if I've bumped into him briefly at some function a long time ago. On second thoughts, probably not. I'm sure I would remember meeting a man as smoking hot as this one.

"I don't know," I respond, shaking off the ghost of mistaken déjà-vu. "I kind of like working from home and setting my own deadlines if I'm being honest. But... I've always dreamed of working for a newspaper, ever since I was a little girl."

"It sounds like you have a lot that you want to share with the world," he responds.

"Yeah. I can thank my parents for that one. They've always been very... *vocal about their opinions*, shall we say."

He smiles broadly. "Good for them."

"How about you?" I ask. "Do you like your career?"

He pauses while he gulps down some coffee, his pale brown eyes watching mine from over the cup. He licks his lips as he places the cup back down on the table. "Yeah, I do. I like being creative. I like working with different artistic media, using my hands."

"You work with acrylics like Gerry?" I ask.

"Mmm hmm. My heart is with oils if I'm being honest, but acrylics are just so much more practical."

A beep suddenly sounds and I watch as he reaches into the pocket of his coat and brings out his phone. "Sorry," he says.

"Not a problem."

"I said I would help a friend with something today. Just need to check it's not him."

"Oh, sure. No problem at all."

His face darkens as he looks at the screen. "Damn," he mutters quietly under his breath.

"Problem?"

"Yeah, my asshole friend needs help *right now*," he sighs in exasperation.

"Oh, well. I guess you'd better go help him."

"Yeah."

"It was nice to see you again, Mika."

"Yeah, it was nice to see you too, Jess." He watches my face silently, looking like he's about to say something... but he doesn't. Instead, he reaches around and slides his coat off the back of the chair, standing up to put it on his muscular frame. "Well, bye, then. Maybe I'll see you around here sometime."

"Sure," I respond.

"Do you, um, come to this coffee shop often?" he asks and we both smile at the line.

"Um, every time I can't getting into my writing groove, so... fairly frequently."

"Well, I hope to see you soon."

I nod. "Bye."

As he turns to walk away and I open up the screen of my laptop, out of the corner of my eye, I see him stop dead in his tracks before looking down as if muttering to himself. My breathing quickens as he pivots on his heels and marches back to the table.

"Jess," he says on a deep breath in, "I don't wanna... I... " He shakes his head at his clumsy attempt at formulating a sentence—a feeling I know all too well which I convey with a warm smile of reassurance. "I know this is a bit... forward of me, and I'm probably freaking you out right now, but... I just—" He looks down, taking another deep breath in. "I wanted to ask if you're dating anyone because I... I was hoping that I could ask you out on a date. I mean, a proper one. No Danish, coffee shops or asshole friends involved."

I feel the flare of a blush come over my cheeks and I swallow hard. "Mika, I— It's really sweet of you, but I—" I'm about to stammer that I can't when I stop myself. "Actually, I'm not dating anyone, but I am married. Well, *separated* from my husband."

"Oh, I'm sorry to hear that. Is it recent?"

"No. Well, about four months."

"Are you dating now?"

"I haven't since... the breakup."

"Okay. Well, in that case, I would like to know if you would like to go to dinner this weekend, or whatever you want, a movie or... just go for a drink..."

My respiration quickens and I feel my palms start to get clammy. I swallow hard as his intense stare burns into me, hot as the sun. My instinct is to say no, but I hear Maddie's words ricochet around my head.

You need to get out there, Jess.

It just takes one man to break down the barrier.

No woman as hot as you should be single for this long.

Once you've slept with someone else, you'll feel so much better.

I take a deep breath. "Yeah. Thank you, Mika. I'd like that," I utter, watching the sides of his lips tilt upwards into the most adorable of smiles as he runs his fingers through his almond-brown hair.

"Awesome," he replies, his body relaxing as if in relief. "Can I get your number?"

"Sure."

As we exchange numbers, a thought hits me—a thought that would help take the pressure off this date, the first I've had since meeting Jack. "Hey, you know Gerry has invited me out on a pub crawl on Saturday night. Fancy doing that instead? We'll be eating along the way and you can pick his brain, maybe."

"Hmm," he responds, seeming to contemplate my suggestion with the intensity of a president contemplating whether to go to war. "I guess that would work too."

"How about I text you on Saturday to let you know when and where we're meeting?"

"That sounds good," he says. "I'm really looking forward to it."

"Great."

"I'd better go. It was great seeing you, Jess."

"You too. Bye."

As he reaches the door, he turns around and breaks into the most stunning of smiles at the sight of me looking at him.

Wow, that is one hell of a gorgeous man. I smile back and watch as he heads left and out of sight.

10

"ANOTHER ONE!" Gerry shouts to the barman as the rest of us mock him mercilessly.

Twenty minutes earlier he'd sworn that he'd had his fill for the night.

"Gerry, stop for fuck's sake! Leave some for the other patrons!" moans Sarah, his new girlfriend who busts his balls with the familiarity of a woman who has known him for years.

"You'll have a half pint and it'll be your last one!" admonishes Roan, the witty barman, in his thick Irish lilt as he hands a moaning Gerald his short glass of ale.

"I had thought the whole *Irish people like to drink* thing was a myth, Gerry," says Mika with a smile as his arm slides against mine in this cramped booth in Gerry's favorite Irish pub in Manhattan.

"Oh, you've seen nothing yet," I respond. "I once saw him down five pints and then debate some guy about quantum physics... and he wiped the floor with the guy!"

"Oh, I remember that!" responds Eric, one of Gerry's oldest friends who has brought his gorgeously bubbly girlfriend, Kerry, along for this pub crawl. Well, I say pub crawl, but this is our first pub and by the looks of it, it'll also be the last of the night. "What an arrogant prick that guy was." Eric's face contorts haughtily as he mocks Gerry's erstwhile opponent. "I don't *think* that that is *pertinent* to the *current* conversation."

Gerry bursts into booming laughter at Eric's impression and lifts his glass in the air before downing it in one go as Sarah whacks him on the arm.

"Your liver's not going to be happy with you tomorrow morning, sir," I reproach playfully.

"It never is!" replies Sarah.

Gerry turns to Mika. "Are you still on your first, son?"

"Yeah, I... I have to confess I'm a bit of a lightweight. One of these is about my lot."

"Ah, so you're a pussy," smiles Gerry.

"Gerry!" I shake my head, throwing him a piquant look of outrage. "Not wanting to fry your liver does not make you a pussy!"

"Oh, in Ireland it does."

"You're such a dick!" I laugh.

"And that's why you love me, Jess."

Sarah and I roll our eyes at each other as Gerry chuckles at his own joke. "So, Jess tells me you're a friend of Donna's," he says to Mika, referring to the owner of the art gallery where Gerry had his exhibition.

"Yeah, that's right."

"Where did you two meet?"

"Oh, it was just at a couple of other exhibitions," replies Mika. "We just got chatting and then she gave me her number. I don't actually know her *that* well."

"Oh, that sounds like Donna. I bet she was *drooling* over you! Her hormones have been going nuts since she hit forty-five."

"And how would you know?" asks Sarah. "She hasn't tried it on with you, has she?"

"She tries it on with every man under the age of forty! When she was in her twenties, she only dated men twice her age, and now that she's in her forties, she's done a swap and she only dates men *half* her age!"

Mika looks down at me as we smile into each other, his eyes glistening in amusement as his arm rubs against mine. I feel my body tingle from the sight of his handsome face and penetrating stare. I really do feel like I've met this man before... or maybe I just really want to know him, want to have something pull me out of the blues I've been languishing in of late.

"Well, she'd better not pull the old cougar seduction act on you in front of me!" gripes Sarah.

Gerry sighs and plants a kiss of appeasement on Sarah's lips. "Listen, sweetheart, I'm almost thirty-five. I'm getting too old for the woman. Plus, you're about five women in one. You're more than enough to keep me occupied."

As Gerry uses his wily charms to diffuse Sarah's irritation, Mika and I share another amused glance which quickly transforms into a lingering stare on the part of Mika whose eyes flick to my mouth before meeting my gaze again. He moves his hand onto his thigh, his little finger resting against my leg. I swallow hard as he taciturnly communicates his desire, suddenly more serious, more focused, absent of the cute, playful smiles he usually shoots at me.

"So, how did you two meet?" asks Kerry from the other side of the table.

"Us?" I reply. "At Gerry's exhibition."

"You did?!" responds Gerry. "You never told me that. I don't remember seeing you there, Mika."

"Well, I didn't end up staying as long as I'd planned. I saw you though. I was gonna introduce myself but you seemed pretty busy."

"Yeah, pimping myself out all night," replies Gerry. "It was fucking exhausting."

"I can imagine," Mika says. "Maybe I'll get to experience it one day."

"You're an artist too, Jess tells me."

"Yeah, that's right," replies Mika. "I haven't had any exhibitions yet. I'm working on it."

"Do you have a website I could take a gander at?" asks Gerry.

"Oh, it's down right now. We're doing a revamp."

Gerry rubs his jaw. "Did you go to art school?"

"Um, no, I'm self-taught."

"Really? Don't see many of those these days."

"Gerry, not all artists go to art school, you know," I butt in.

"The ones I know do. You didn't fancy it, Mika?"

"No, I just... I studied finance actually and then, I just knew that it wasn't for me and started painting."

"Hmm, haven't heard that one for a long time," retorts Gerry, arching an eyebrow. "He's mysterious this new friend of yours, Jess."

"Well, maybe that's because you keep giving him the Spanish Inquisition, Geraldo."

"Don't mind me," Gerry smiles. "I like to bust people's balls, especially little upstarts that swan in wanting their own exhibition when they haven't paid their dues yet," he chuckles.

"Gerry!" scolds Sarah.

"I'd forgotten how delightful you can be when you're drunk, my friend," I counter with a slow shake of the head.

I turn to glance at Mika who smiles. "Well, we can take it outside and I can pay my dues that way, old man..."

Gerry's head tilts backwards as he bursts into throaty laughter, reaching over the table and tapping Mika on the arm heartily. "That's more like it! That's what I'm looking for. The boy does have some spunk in him!"

I lean into Mika, his eager lips inches from mine, heat radiating from his gaze. "Don't mind him," I say purposefully loudly. "As well as being a world-famous artist, he's also a professional dick!"

We spend another hour enjoying each other's company before fatigue and the strong ale finally get the best of us and we call it a night.

Mika and I decide that we'll share a cab to Hudson Square after which he'll go on to Greenwich Village. As we pull up to my apartment, I open my purse but Mika hands the driver twenty dollars before I have a chance to pay.

"Thanks," I say, kind of wishing we had split the bill like I wanted.

"You know, I think I'm gonna get out here," he says, exiting the vehicle and slamming the door behind him as we thank the driver. "I feel like walking the rest of the way."

"Gerry didn't get to you back there, did he? That's just his default way of bonding with men."

He raises an eyebrow. "What, busting their balls?"

I try not to laugh. "Yeah. I think he thinks if they can roll with the punches, he can trust them."

"It was fine," he grins as we move out of the way of some passersby and stop at the bottom of the steps leading to my apartment building. "I've got some pretty sadistic cousins and uncles so I can handle him."

"Good... about Gerry, I mean... not the sadistic cousins."

He shoots me another stunning smile. "Yeah, I got that."

As he locks into me, I suddenly feel a bit stifled and pull off the turquoise scarf that my mom gave me for Christmas last year as I prepare to say goodbye.

"It was fun tonight," he says, lifting his shoulders as if to brace against the sting of the frigid December wind.

"Yeah. It was."

As he takes a step towards me and I prepare to say goodbye to him, Mika threads his gloved fingers through his thick locks. "Jess, I'd love to see you again sometime."

"Yeah," I nod. "I'd like that."

I shift a little. Man, I'd forgotten how awkward first dates can be.

"Look, I know I'm breaking every single rule of first dates here," he continues, "but... I really like you, Jess. A lot. I know that you're going through a separation, but I really hope that I can take you out on a proper date again, like for dinner or something."

"That sounds good. I'd like that."

He takes a step towards me and I quiver internally as I see in his eyes that he wants to kiss me. I haven't had to dodge a doorstep kiss since I was still in my teens and didn't want my parents catching me outside with a boy.

He encroaches on my personal space once again, his eyes focused on their target—my lips. "Can I kiss you?" The question is gentle yet his eyes are not.

I swallow hard, unsure of what to say.

It's not that I don't want to kiss him. It's just that it feels so alien to be kissing anyone other than the two men who have so consumed my mind, heart and body this year. Mika is gorgeous and smart and lovely, but he just seems so sweet. I'm not used to it. I'm used to dominance and unabashed assertiveness.

Jack would never have asked me such a question. By the time we had our third date in London, he was like a machine in motion. He knew exactly what was going to happen and I was so overwhelmed by his determined virility that I was powerless to stop it, not that I wanted to. If Jack had been here now, he would have stared me into submission and then seized the back of my neck, locking my head into a receiving position and penetrated my mouth with his tongue as his erection threatened me from under his pants. He would have carried me up the stairs without asking and grabbed my key from my purse himself, opening the door and leading me into my own bedroom before ripping my skirt, tights and panties off and devouring my clit with his tongue as he prepared to ravage me for hours until all force had wilted from my limbs. And I would have let him. But then every cell in my body hummed in desperation for his touch, his scent, his power.

Mika is beautiful and interesting, but I just don't really feel that "I want to rip your clothes off" thing I had with... both of them.

Maybe this need for brain-melting passion is where you're going wrong, Jess.

Good point...

I feel Mika studying my profile as I glance up at the dark window of my empty apartment and realize that the way I've been shutting myself off the last couple of months is just not healthy at all.

Remembering my resolve to make changes to my life, I reply, "Yes. You can."

Without a moment's hesitation, Mika steps forward and cups my face in his hand, gently pressing his soft lips to mine before sliding his tongue against my lips and using it to pry open my mouth. His other hand finds my neck as his tongue delves deeper into me, a gentle groan slipping from his throat. I'm relieved to find myself turned on by the penetration and begin to reciprocate as the kisses deepen, his tongue writhing as his hips meet mine, his hand sliding from my face into my loose brown hair.

The icy air whips us as we lose ourselves in the drunken kiss, the erotic tango becoming more fervent with every second spent locked into each other. A minute or so passes in this oral exploration until a couple of passersby whistle at the spectacle.

We pull apart and grin at each other in amused embarrassment. His eyes stun me with the fervor of his arousal and the dominance of his stance which has morphed suddenly, emboldened perhaps by my clear receptiveness to his advances.

His glare is laser-sharp. "Can I come in, Jess?" he asks as we try to catch our breath.

Oh, Lord...

My gut is telling me to say no. I'm not ready. I don't like to sleep with men on the first date. I made Jack wait a few dates and we'd known each other for over a year before that. I trusted him. I don't even know this guy.

Just as I muster up the strength to say no, Maddie's words hit me:

It'll just take one man for you to feel like yourself again.

"Please," he adds, his gaze soft, open.

I take a deep breath, contemplating the fear of waking up tomorrow with that same hollow ache I've done the entire last month.

"Yes," I utter gently.

He smiles, the yearning in his eyes unmistakable.

I hesitate for a moment before leading him inside, past Sammy, the cheery sixty-something concierge who is only around during the day and during evenings at the weekend. My feet seem to have turned into lead weights as I lead Mika up the stairs to the second floor and along the narrow hallway to my apartment where I manage to slot the key into the lock with jittery fingers, open the door and welcome him in.

As I fumble for the ridiculously positioned light switch and close the door behind us, the shrill chime of my phone suddenly rings out.

"Shit, sorry... Let me turn that off," I say, reaching into my tan purse and sliding my phone out.

My eyes widen and I suppress a gasp as I see Cameron's name flash upon the screen.

What the hell?

I stare in disbelief.

Christ.

Talk about timing.

I haven't spoken to Cameron on the phone for over two months and although his letters haven't slowed down, he has respected my wishes for him not to call or text me anymore.

I reject the call only to have him call straight back. This time I reject it again and put my phone on silent, placing it back into my purse.

"So sorry about that," I mutter nervously, trying to shake off the errant crackle of electricity whipping through me like a live wire at the sight of Cameron's name.

"Not a problem," Mika replies. "A friend?"

"Yeah." I take a moment to shake off the stun-gun-like effect that seeing his name on my phone has on me. "An old friend."

"Cool."

I head over to the window in the living room which I left open earlier this evening for some fresh air, a decision which has left my apartment feeling like a commercial fridge. As I close the window, I glance out onto the street below where we were standing a few minutes ago. Part of me wants to open the window and rappel out to escape my date, no matter how lovely he is.

Jesus. Pull yourself together, woman, I yell at myself internally, groaning inwardly at my sudden attack of nerves. Anyone would think I was a virgin bringing home a man for the very first time in my life.

I turn on the radiator full blast as well as two small lamps and walk back towards him as he watches me from the kitchen, my feet still feeling like they've been swapped with those of a particularly large elephant.

"Fancy some water?" I ask, trying to ignore the fact that my body is sending me clear signs that this isn't quite right.

"No. Thank you," he replies as I pour myself a glass to quench my thirst and relieve my dry mouth.

"Mind if I take off my coat?" he asks.

"Sorry. Of course not. There's a coat rack on the door."

With my jelly-like arms, I remove my coat and hang both of them on hooks hanging over the door as he does the same.

Get a grip, Jessynia, I moan as I try to temper my nerves.

I've never felt this awkward around a man before. Mind you, I've never invited a man I didn't know well back to my apartment either. I'm half-tempted to make my excuses, go out into the hallway and call the experienced Stella for a pep talk before resuming, especially when I realize Cameron's call just now blazed through my flesh like a thousand flaring embers, annihilating in an instant the sweet attraction I feel to Mika.

"Nice place you've got here," says Mika, walking through the apartment towards the living room.

I pause for a minute before joining him, sitting down on the taupe sofa next to him as his stare wanders over my face as if in utmost fascination. He smiles, most probably amused at my awkward-as-all-ass attempts at navigating the moment.

"You're nervous," he says, his studious eyes eating into me.

I flush a little, tempted to remove my cardigan. Despite the cold room, I feel like I'm being sautéed alive. "Sorry, it's just... I haven't really been on a date since..."

"You and your husband split up."

"Yeah. I'm not usually this... *weird.*"

"Well, don't worry," he laughs. "I have picked up that you're normally a pretty feisty girl."

"Yeah, well, she's in there... *somewhere.*"

"It's understandable that you'd be nervous," he responds smoothly, running his hand over his jaw.

Is it me, or does he suddenly seem much more confident than he did when we were outside?

"What happened with your husband?" he asks.

"Oh, we just... It's kinda complicated."

"Try me."

I bristle a little. I'm not sure that discussing my husband's infidelity is really something that is going to get me in the mood, if you know what I mean.

"Oh, we just... grew apart," I lie. In reality, before I found that secret phone of Jack's, I'd never felt more connected to another human being in my life.

"Hmm," he responds. "Well, I certainly hope I can help you forget him."

I bristle again, wondering where the sweet, shy guy from outside was. I study his face as he scrutinizes me. His light-brown hair glistens in the soft light of my living room and his pallid eyes look almost vampiric as they pan down to my neck for a few suspended moments.

In my gut, I suddenly know with certainty I'm not ready. I like Mika. He's lovely, but something doesn't feel right and getting Cameron's lighting strike of a call before only cemented in my mind how much I'm forcing myself to get into this date.

"Do you mind if I get that water after all?" he asks.

"No, not at all," I respond, jumping to my feet. I'm honestly relieved to get up and out of there. I'm half-tempted to make the most of the moment to run downstairs and ask the concierge up for moral support as I ask Mika to leave, but my fear of looking like the world's most ridiculous female is stopping that from happening.

Plus, Mika has done absolutely nothing wrong.

I'm just not ready. And I'm sure he'll be fine when I tell him that...

I fill up a glass with filtered water and walk towards him only to find him standing in the passageway between the kitchen and living room that I've turned into a makeshift office.

I frown at him as I hand him the glass which he starts to drink while peering at me from behind it.

"Are you leaving?" I ask, momentarily flooded with relief. He must realize that I don't really seem ready for whatever is going on here...

He doesn't answer, instead finishing the last of the water and placing it behind him onto my desk. I watch for a moment as a sparkling droplet of condensation trickles down the outside of the glass, pooling between its thick base and my white desk.

Mika's stare is unflinching as shakes his head, and with a firm voice replies, "No."

I frown at the sudden assertiveness in his demeanor, searching his eyes to understand who the hell this man standing in front of me is. Just at the moment I decide to politely make my excuses and ask him to leave, without warning he thrusts me up against the bare wall opposite the desk, his hands finding the wall on either side of my head as he rams his tongue deep inside my mouth with an animalistic groan.

I haven't been kissed like this for so long and waver for a moment as he presses his body into mine, his strong chest pushing into me as his hand slides into the loose hair at the back of my head. After a moment, I push against his chest, forcing him to stop kissing me.

He looks down at me, breathless. "What's wrong?"

"Mika, I'm really sorry. I'm not sure that I'm ready for this..."

"You're just nervous," he responds after a moment. "It's been a long time."

"I know. I just... I need to go a bit more slowly. Maybe we can try this again another day..."

He holds his position, not shifting backwards as my stomach sinks at the idea that I may have to be more direct in a minute if he doesn't get the hint faster.

"Look, I get it, okay?" His eyes flick to my mouth as he leans his body into me again. "It's a big deal... You don't have to be afraid. I want you, Jess, badly, and I know I can make you feel real good. Make you forget your husband..."

He charges his cool lips onto mine and his tongue into my mouth again, groaning as I press against his chest, gently at first, then more forcefully, arresting the kiss once again.

"I'm sorry, Mika," I pant. "I can't. It's nothing to do with you. Really. I just need to get to know you before we do this. How about we try again next week?"

Or never, if you keep insisting like this...

"Look, I'll be gentle," he murmurs. "Really gentle. You won't regret it. I promise."

I shake my head. "I'm sorry. I can't."

He breathes out heavily in exasperation, his eyes suddenly colder, the smile disappearing from his face like smoke fading into the night air.

I scan the memory banks of my numerous self-defense classes, picking out targets—his eye, his Adam's apple, his groin.

Just relax, Jess...

"I need you to consent, Jessynia. This can't happen without your consent."

My stomach lurches and the hairs on my arms prickle, a cold tremor zapping down my spine as he says my full first name, for I don't recall giving it to him. I usually call myself *Jess* with people I've only just met these days. My name is pretty unusual and I just feel safer not giving it out to people I don't know that well as it's easy to find me online with it. Gerry *always* calls me Jessie or Jess. Did I give it to Mika in my tipsy state without realizing it? Maybe he heard someone saying it when I was in the washroom of the pub...

"*What* can't happen?" I ask. "This isn't a business deal."

His breath is of heavy frustration. "Look, you're overthinking things." His muddy eyes are suddenly harsh, betraying the soft smile he is attempting as he leans into my lips. I glance at his Adam's apple again, deciding it will be the target of my fist in the unlikely event that I have to force him off me. "You're just nervous because it's the first time since you split up with your husband. I intend to fuck you *very* nicely. Very gently. I know what I'm doing. You won't regret it. And you don't have to be afraid." I shake my head. "I need your consent, Jess," he says. "Please just say yes..."

"I'm sorry, but I want you to leave!" I push against his chest hard to the sound of a vehicle screeching down the street below.

As the thunderous roar of an engine outside stops, Mika's lightning bolt of a fist flies into the drywall as he sandwiches me against the wall.

"Fuck," he growls, silencing my mouth with his hand and pinning my arm against the wall, pushing his whole body into me, his bulge dense against my crotch as he turns his head towards the window and grins, before finding the barrier of his hand with his lips, his eyes an inch from mine. "Well, it looks like someone is here to save the princess," he sighs, his keen glare indecent as I push against him. "I wonder which one of them it will be..."

I attempt to strike his neck with my free hand but he grabs it, pinning it against the wall, freeing my mouth in the process.

"Get the fuck off me!" I shout.

He smiles, a grumble of arousal leaving him at the sight of my panicked eyes. He greedily devours my desperation to the sound of a sudden commotion in the hallway which doesn't make him flinch despite the violent banging on my front door. "It's a pity, Jessynia. I've wanted to experience you for a long time... ever since I heard what a state you'd left the formidable Jackson Wilder in."

I whimper, my eyes widening in fear as I muster all my strength to try to extricate my arms from him... unsuccessfully.

"Jessynia!" a man's voice yells to the sound of the concierge ordering him out. "She's in danger. Open this fucking door!" shouts the man.

I know that voice...

Sammy's weathered cry rings out. "I'm going to call the police!"

After a few more bangs on the door, Mika hits me with the most venomous of smiles before finally letting go of my arms, raising his hands in defeat as I push against his chest and run to the door, my heart somersaulting as I open it to find Cameron standing there, his tall, dense frame bristling, his savage eyes wild with fury. Without a word, he rushes at Mika whom he knocks down with one punch to the cheek that breaks through the barrier Mika tries to erect with his hands. He stumbles backwards as I dash to Cameron, pulling him away.

"Cameron, stop! He'll call the police!"

Mika breaks into a demonic-sounding cackle as he looks up, checking his jaw with his hand as he studies Cameron's wrath in delight.

"No he won't," Cameron snarls, fury twisting his breathtaking features as Mika stands back up, a thick grin on his treacherous face.

"Do you know this man, miss?" shouts the concierge, pointing at Cameron.

"Yes, he's my friend. But I want this piece of shit out of here!" I shout, signaling at the sneering, wide-eyed thing in the room.

"Right!" responds the concierge purposefully, turning to face Mika. "Are you leaving or am I gonna have to call the police?"

"I'm leaving," he replies. "Don't worry." Turning to Cameron, he snickers, "I was wondering which one of you would be turning up... Does Jackson know you're still obsessed with his *wife*?"

"Get the fuck out, you *filth*," responds Cameron slowly as I pull back on his arm. "And if I see you anywhere near this girl *ever* again, I'll be instructing the three lawyers who are holding onto my dossier about your uncle and his friends to send it off to the D.A.'s office. Is that clear?!" he roars.

His uncle? Who the fuck is this man?!

Mika laughs, a wicked noxious laugh. "You wouldn't *dare*, O'Neill."

"Get out!" I shout.

"Tsk, tsk. It could have been good, Jessynia," Mika sniggers, swiveling to face me as he takes a step towards the door. "You have no idea what you missed out on. Maybe some other time, huh?"

And with that, I take a step forward, allowing my right foot to take sharp and fast aim at his groin, colliding with it perfectly. A groan rushes from him as he is bent over by the blow allowing me to punch him as hard as I can in the side of his face. Cameron grabs me by the waist, pulling me back as soon as the punch makes contact.

The winded Mika starts to laugh inanely as he gets his breath back. "See, there she is," he sniggers. "I'd been warned you were quite the feisty little bitch. We could have really had some serious fun."

"Get out!" I bellow as the concierge grabs him by the arm and pulls him out.

As Mika grabs his coat, he turns around to face me. "My uncle will be disappointed I don't have the full report to give to him, but he will enjoy me telling him about the panic in your eyes as you realized how powerless you were before me. That look of fear in your eyes was quite exquisite. I shall remember it."

Cameron takes a step towards him and I pull him back.

"That's it!" shouts the concierge, shoving him out of the apartment.

"Let me help you," says Cameron as he follows them out the door. I head to the doorway, watching as they lead Mika down the hallway and down the stairs.

Aware of a sudden stab of pain in my ankle, I open the freezer and grab a bag of frozen blueberries and wrap it in a tea towel. I head to the window where I see Cameron and Sammy on the sidewalk below talking to another man I've never seen before as Mika heads off down the street.

Upon another twinge of pain, I sit down on the sofa and remove my black tights from under my ankle-length burgundy skirt, placing the ice pack onto my ankle, closing my eyes as the cold soothes the spike of pain from my cathartic kick to the nuts before lifting it onto the knuckles of my right hand which collided with Mika's cheekbone.

A few minutes later, Cameron enters without knocking, hurriedly finding me in the living room.

"Jessynia," he says, kneeling down in front of me and breathlessly glancing at my hand. "Are you hurt?"

I don't answer, for looking up and locking eyes with him stuns me, leaving me jolted into some other realm. Cameron studies me, unspeaking, hair longer than it was when I saw him last, framing the insanely beautiful angles of his strong face so boldly.

Flames of copper swirl in his piercing eyes, his expression bordering on desperation as his gaze darts over my face, meeting my eyes every few seconds. I see his chest rise and fall deeply as he leans his muscular frame and broad shoulders in just a tad, swallowing hard, searching my expression before lifting the ice pack off my hand and running his fingers over my knuckles, studying them as if they are some fragile piece of exquisite porcelain.

"Does it hurt?" he asks again.

Finally recovering from the heady dizziness I feel at seeing this man again, I shake my head. "It was worth it," I respond.

He places the bag of blueberries back on my hand and lifts his dense body up and onto the sofa where he sits facing me, his expression vivid, attentive. He removes his gray coat to reveal a white T-shirt under a navy sweater which hugs every ridge of his massive muscular frame.

I swallow hard at the intensity of his unflinching stare and move the pack of blueberries onto the knuckles of his right hand, the contact with his flesh leaving flaring imprints crackling on my skin as I do so. "Cam, you need this. Did you hurt yourself?"

He pushes it back onto my hand, another lightning bolt shocking my cells. "I don't need it," he insists. "He's not the first scumbag I've punched in my life either... if you recall?"

I smile half-heartedly. "Yeah. I guess we'll both have to get out of the habit one day." I look down, not knowing how to cope with the collision of the cavernous depths of fear I just felt with the elation at seeing my old friend again.

"Jess," he says, his chest taking in and releasing deep, challenging breaths as if building up the courage to ask a question. "Did he... *hurt* you? I need you to tell me the truth."

"No. He just scared me. I thought he wasn't going to leave... I started to panic."

"Did he touch you?"

"We kissed, but he didn't go further once I got cold feet. Cam, who the hell is he?"

He reaches his hand up to my face, studying my lips as he does so, before stroking a lock of my wavy brown hair off my face, his fingertips skimming the two silver hoops in my lobe before lingering on the soft shell of my ear in a gesture that has flares of effervescent energy sparking off my skin.

"They'll never get to you again, Jessynia. I promise you. *Never*. I thought they had moved on. I should have never stopped having you..." He stops talking, his forehead dropping, hitting his hands as his breathing becomes audible, erratic, his face suddenly hardening, his expression a frenzy of fury.

"Cam?"

He looks up at me, somber. "His real name is Ilya Mikhail Markov."

"What?!" I whisper. "Not... related to..."

He nods, bitter wrath glowing behind his fiery eyes. "To Vallen Markov. Vallen is his uncle."

"Wha—" I clutch my hand to my chest, feeling like I want to cry. "What do they want from me? I haven't told anyone about the Society. I did what they asked! I kept my mouth shut! Isn't that what they wanted?!"

"I don't know what happened here. This isn't their usual M.O.," he replies. "Things must be brewing behind the scenes. I will find out what happened, Jess, if I have to kill someone to do it."

"Did Vallen organize this?"

"Possibly. But nothing involving the Society happens without the go-ahead of Sebastian Gravier. Vallen answers to him. He must have approved this."

"Why?"

"I don't know. Maybe they wanted to plant a listening device in here, bug the apartment. Plus, it's no secret that Vallen..."

"What?"

"Considers you to be his most sought-after prize." My blood runs cold at the thought of that monster. "Maybe this was his way of vicariously satisfying that need."

"Well, he kept asking for consent. Mika. I mean, Ilya. He asked over and over."

"Yes, that would make sense," he responds. "Non-consensual acts are strictly banned by the Society... unless consented to in writing beforehand, if you can make sense of that."

"What, these lunatics suddenly have some honor?"

"It's enshrined in their codes, written by their founding fathers. Those types of act are too risky, could cause too much fallout if people tell outsiders, lawyers, police, etcetera. Anything non-consensual"—he watches as I shift back in distress at the thought of it—"would mean banishment for life, at the *very* least. There are rumors of people losing their lives for doing such a thing."

"But if I did what they asked for, why would they do this?"

"Maybe Vallen couldn't control his curiosity anymore."

"Cam, don't tell me that. It makes me feel ill."

"I'm sorry." He runs a strong hand through thick, glossy locks of chestnut brown. "It's possible they wanted to see who would come to the rescue." I swallow hard, trying not to drown in the deep earthy pools of his eyes. "But most likely, this is some game concocted by Sebastian Gravier to get back at Jack for questioning his methods. If what happened tonight were to get back to Jack, Jack would start a war. And I think Gravier is just waiting for an excuse to press the detonation button."

I gulp down a stone in my throat. "Jack is still *involved* with these people?" I ask as the bottom drops out from under me.

Cameron's nod is solemn, his answer unwavering. "Yes. Very much so."

"I... I can't believe he would still go back to that place and those people."

"The hold they have over him is very strong, Jess. Until he gets to the point that the poison is so toxic that he can't function, they will always have power over him. Always. He won't even understand how much."

"And so what, he's fallen out with Gravier? He's going to get himself killed." Cameron nods, unspeaking. "What, because he doesn't agree with their scorched Earth tactics?" I ask.

"Something like that. And he's becoming more vocal about it. Gravier has been abusing his power. Having people *disappeared*. Threatening people. Having them followed, blackmailed. From what my source tells me, Jack is part of a small group of high-level patrons that have had the guts to be vocal about the Society needing to tone it down before they get into trouble. Gravier seems to be losing patience with those that criticize him. Luckily for Jack, he's always been fond of him, but it seems that that fondness has its limits. If Ilya had"—his head drops, his breathing ragged for a few seconds before he looks back up—"managed to seduce you, Jack would have lost his mind, and Gravier would have a reason to start his war, make an example of Jack."

"God... He needs to get away from those people."

"Well, I wouldn't hold your breath."

"I just want to be left alone..."

"You will be, Jess. I promise you." His voice—smooth, elegant, confident—soothes the deepest fear within me somehow. "I'm not leaving you alone *ever again*."

"How did you know what was happening tonight?" I ask, searching his moody eyes in the low light.

He looks down for a moment before finding my face again.

"Tell me," I urge, aware that my cells are suddenly alight, drawn in by the merciless magnetic pull of his virile body.

"For the first two months after... we last saw each other, I had you watched," he replies.

"What?! Two months?!"

"Yes. After that, I switched the surveillance to mornings, evenings and at night times. That is when they strike. They have a very specific M.O. They don't deviate from it."

"What, like a great white shark or something..."

He smiles for just a moment. It's ever so slight but it's there. It's the first time I've seen that smile of his in months. Boy, it could light up Times Square.

"Who followed me?" I ask.

"My men. Security. They've been with the family for years. They know what they're doing. I wanted to check that Jack or the Society wasn't having you followed."

"And they weren't?"

"Jack had some men stationed on you for a month or so, then he withdrew them. I'm assuming he was satisfied that you weren't seeing me. His goons aren't as smart as the men I can afford to hire. They had no idea they were being watched."

"They're not the only ones. How did I not see them?!" Though as I say it, I do recall seeing a couple of guys lurking in the shadows back in August and September...

"You're not supposed to. The average person would have no clue at all if they were being followed, especially in a city like Manhattan. I made the mistake of withdrawing my men a few weeks ago. I thought you would be safe."

"Well, who could have predicted something as deranged as this?"

"*I* could have," he replies roughly. "I know these people. I know how they operate. I should have been smarter."

"How did you know about tonight?" I ask.

He pauses for what feels like an age. "I always feel you with me, Jessynia. It's this constant pull that I can't escape... I feel your presence. It's in my blood. I woke up this morning and had the same panicked feeling I had that day I went driving down the highway and found you. I tried to shake it off but by the evening, I knew something was wrong. A few hours ago, I called one of my security guys, stationed him outside your apartment. I guess he must have got here after you'd already left. When you came back, he managed to get some shots of you and Markov outside the apartment and sent them to me. They were dark and grainy but I made out Ilya in one of them. He tried to get in, but the concierge wouldn't let him past. I've been staying a few blocks away at my SoHo place for the last few weeks so I was able to get here fast. And no human could have stopped me from getting in..."

I part my lips without meaning to as the edges of the room fade to black and we peer into each in silence for a long minute, watching one another in the soft glow of the salt lamps perched on side tables.

"I met him in a weird way," I finally say. "It was at my friend's art gallery the other night—Gerry. You remember him? I introduced you once. He came to see me at Brown."

"I remember." I'd forgotten how deep Cameron's stunning voice is. "But you didn't meet Ilya by chance. They must have set it up for you to meet him."

"Jesus," I manage, my chest hollow as I contemplate telling him about my run-in with Steven Frost and Vallen Markov, ruling against it in case Cameron decides to seek revenge of some sort and put himself in danger.

"Who knew you were going to that exhibition?" he asks.

"Well, Gerry, Kevin and Stella, I think. That's all."

"And they all knew you were going alone?"

"I was supposed to be going with Kev but he bailed on me at the last minute."

"Bailed?" His brow creases, his eyes narrowing. "Why?"

"He met some guy at the gym and... I guess his *other* brain took over."

"Hmm. I don't think that guy was just some random meeting."

"Are you serious?" I feel strength seeping from my limbs like blood from an open wound. "I asked him about the guy. He said he had an amazing night. Nothing weird happened. Only that the guy now seems to have blocked him, Kev says."

"Well, the Society have people on their payroll who can offer services like that."

"Oh my God..." I shudder at the thought of my friends being used as pawns by these people.

"How did you arrange to go to the gallery in the first place?" he asks. "I mean, did you call, text..."

"It was all by text."

"And you're still using the phone I got you? With the software I asked you to install."

"Yes."

"Hmm," responds Cameron, hints of anger deepening the shadows of his face. "They've probably hacked his phone."

"They would do that?"

"Yes. They're very good at it."

"Or maybe they just followed me that night?"

"That's also possible. In any case, I'll send Kevin a new phone tomorrow. Early Christmas present."

"God, Cam. I don't want him mixed up in all this."

"He doesn't have to know the details. I'll chalk it up to me being protective over you because of Jack. Or maybe I can get Mason to give it to him, pretend it's from him."

I run my hands through my hair in a sudden burst of frustration. "I can't cope with my friends being dragged into this. I just want to be left alone! I haven't done anything to expose them. I haven't told anyone, not Mad, Stella, Kev, my parents, no one! It's not fair! I'm respecting their rules and they're still targeting me." My face crumples and fat tears spill onto my cheek as I realize that I may never be free of these people.

He raises a strong hand to my face, lifting it to look at him, his thumb wiping away tears, leaving behind a fizz of white-hot effervescence at his touch. His scowling eyes peer into me in distress as he watches me cry silently. "Jessynia, they will *never* do this to you again. I promise you. Do you believe me?"

I nod, putting the ersatz ice pack down on the coffee table. He releases his hand from my skin, placing it on top of my mine, pain etched into the usually graceful lines of his face. After a long minute of silence, he speaks. "I've missed you, God dammit. You can't even begin to imagine how much."

I want to say the same to him. I want to tell him how much I've missed him, how many times a day I've imagined he were with me, I've wanted to talk to him, to see him, I've dreamt of him, wished things were different. But things aren't different and until such time as Jack is no longer in the picture, they can never be different.

"Did you read my letters?" he asks.

"I tried to. I couldn't face reading them all," I reply. "It was just too much for my heart. But the ones I read were...beautiful."

I study his face earnestly and am once again caught off-guard by the strength and potential of his powerful body, by the breathtaking masculine beauty of his face; by the silent fire in his golden-brown eyes; by the sharpness of his cheekbones and the shadows carved under them. His lips are a dusky pink above a strong chin. The slight stubble on his face and extra inch in his wavy chocolate-brown hair makes him look wild somehow, savage almost.

"How have you been, Cam?" I ask him.

His eyes wander over my face without flinching. "I've been... in pain. I crave you day and night. Your face, your body, your beauty. I miss you. I miss your wit, your spark, your strength, your tenderness. Every time I experience something, you're the only person I want to share it with. And I can't. I'm in constant pain."

"I'm sorry, Cam. I didn't really have any choice."

"I know that. But you do now. Jack is moving on, albeit slowly."

I don't bother telling him that Jack has had two letters delivered to the apartment in the last two days. I opened one of them which didn't exactly suggest he was moving on. The sentences he scribed in his distinctive handwriting flicker through my mind like fireflies:

Baby, none of the distractions I use take the edge off being without you.

I'm going to get well. I promise you.

When I'm free of this poison, I'm taking you back.

I'm starting to see through these people.

I intend to take you far away from this place.

Without you, there's nothing pure in the world.

I get through the nights by imagining your body sleeping next to mine.

My desire for you is as fervent as ever. I pleasure myself to the thought of your tight little body.

Writing to you is the only thing that keeps me sane.

I will make this right, Jessynia.

Don't give up on me.

I wonder for a second whether I should tell Cameron about Jack's letters, but decide against it.

"How have you been?" Cameron asks, scanning my eyes in that way he does that makes me feel like he is seeing inside my soul.

A feel my eyes mist over and I look down instantly, leaving the question unanswered, lingering like the smell of smoke in a room once the candle has burnt out.

"Jess, answer me."

When I don't, he lifts my chin up, forcing me to look at him, the caress of his flesh burning a hot trail on my skin. Cameron and I have always had this connection that was raw and honest and I don't know how I could begin to lie to him.

"It's been... hard," I finally reply. "This year has just..."—I feel the tear I had tried to conceal trickle onto my cheek—"taken a lot out of me."

Cameron tracks the solitary drop of salt water as it slowly trickles down my face, the furrow in his brow deepening with every second spent watching me. "Have you been sleeping okay?" he asks.

I don't answer. I don't want to tell him the truth that I have not slept through the night since the breakup. "Getting better," I answer, though as I utter the last words, I realize I don't believe them... and my friend has always been able to read me like a book.

He takes a deep breath. "That's it." He removes his hand from my face. "I'm taking you away from here."

"What do you mean?"

Unlocking his gaze from mine, he stands up and strides to my bedroom in a thunder of that wild energy that emerges in volatile bursts from that poised outer stance of his.

"Cameron?"

"We're leaving in ten minutes." He disappears into my bedroom which has me getting to my feet.

"What are you talking about? I'm not going anywhere..."

"You don't have a choice, Avery," he snaps, mercurial and moody as all hell.

Incredulous, I follow him into the bedroom and watch, mouth agape, as he opens my closet from which he grabs my large green weekend bag and throws it onto the teal blanket messily draped over my bed.

"Um, what are you doing?" I ask.

He ignores me and returns to the closet where I watch him grab some T-shirts, a few cardigans and sweaters and a couple of pairs of pants.

"Cameron! Are you listening to me? I'm not going anywhere with you."

"Yes, you are," he replies firmly.

"No, I'm not! I'm supposed to be going to my parent's place on the twenty-fourth."

"I'll take you there after you spend a few days with me," he responds sternly as he slides open a few rickety drawers in my cramped closet before finding my underwear drawer, grabbing some bras, panties and socks and putting them into a small mesh bag languishing on top of the drawers and into the bag on my bed.

"Cameron, I'm not kidding. I can't go with you! What if Jack finds out?!"

"He won't," he says. "I've just put a team back on you to make sure no one ever follows you again without my knowing about it."

"Well, thanks for telling me! I suppose I don't have any say in the matter..."

"No, you do not."

"Well, I'm not coming with you. I've already been down that road. It's just asking for trouble."

"I'm not having you spending one more night in this apartment alone. You're coming with me, Jessynia, whether you like it or not." The rich, deep timbre of his voice rolls through my body like the roughest caress. "Besides, there are some people who want to see you."

"What people?"

"My mother, for one. Evie, for another."

"Evie? She wants to see me?"

My heart skips a beat at the thought of seeing Cameron's sister, a woman who was once like a sister to me and who stopped talking to me shortly after I got together with Jack, who, unbeknownst to me, had seduced and then callously dumped her a year or so before on the orders of Alexandra Frost.

"Evie isn't planning on coming till later, but I want your relationship healed. I'm not waiting any longer. I'll ask her to drive up early."

"Cameron—"

"There are a few other people who want to see you."

"Others? Who?"

"You don't know them, but they know you. They're enemies of Gravier's clan and they protect people targeted by them. They want to meet you."

"Well... I'm sorry, but I can't just go swanning off to—"

He ignores me and leaves the room, striding with imperious nerve into the bathroom where he rummages around my cupboard for my toiletry bag and starts shoving my toothbrush, toothpaste, brush, some random pots of cream and items of makeup into it.

I follow him swiftly, watching in indignation as he disrespects all my boundaries. "Cameron, what the hell?! That's my stuff!"

"I apologize, but we need to get out of here fast, Miss Avery, and I'm not sitting here for an hour as you fuck around attempting to convince me not to drag you out of here."

"You know, you can be such an overbearing *prick* at times!"

He turns to look at me, amusement brightening his smiling eyes. "And you still happen to be the single most infuriating woman I've ever dealt with in my life, so I guess that makes us even."

He zips up my toiletry bag, his tall frame brushing past me, leaving smoldering imprints on my flesh as he skims my arm, goes back into the bedroom and throws it into my weekend bag, carrying it out and dumping it onto my desk. He scans my study, grabbing my laptop and charger which he also dumps in my bag before zipping it up.

"Listen, I know men have a need to problem-solve, but this is ridiculous! I can't go with you!"

He pays me no heed, scouring my desk with sharp eyes once again before reaching down to grab my phone charger which he yanks out of the socket.

Finally done with his selective deafness, I grab his arm and shout, "Cameron!" in an attempt to get him to listen to me and abort this trip.

In response, he drops the charger onto the desk and whips around, hitching me up against the wall, sandwiching me between his wildly muscular frame and the light-green drywall behind me. My feet hit the floor as he closes the gap between us, planting his hands on either side of the wall behind me, towering over me, caging me in, leaning into me as he studies my flushing face with an irate scowl. It's a cranky look that is hot as hades and I have to trap my bottom lip between my teeth to stop myself from gasping at the sight of his angry heat.

"Yes, Jessynia?" he responds to my previous insolent cry. "What can I help you with?"

I don't speak, mesmerized as I am by his power and dominance and the unflinching way his ferocious eyes duel with mine, occasionally drifting downwards towards my plump lips before meeting my defeated gaze again.

I had forgotten quite how stunning his heart-shaped face was, forgotten how his thick, wavy brown hair caresses the warm honey skin of his forehead, forgotten how the strong planes of his cheeks glide down to meet a mouth so wickedly enticing that it's all I can do to stop myself releasing my tongue and licking the length of it.

The violent devastation of his beauty is only matched by the supreme self-confidence of his poise, of his obvious awareness of his strength and power and indecent sex appeal. Ferocious eyes penetrate me, his breathing deepening as his gaze roams avidly over my face, lingering on my lips, challenging my timid stare.

I swallow hard and pant at the unabashed display of savage virility, conscious that my sex is instantly wet and swollen at the sight and sensation of this divine specimen of masculinity.

In my defense, I haven't been touched by a man in four months, so I'll be giving myself a pass for being instantly aroused by the incomparable beauty of this most mysterious of men.

"Well?" he asks, drinking me in in all his hot-headed glory.

"Um..." I respond.

"Having trouble thinking, perhaps, Miss Avery?"

"Hmm. Unfortunately, it seems my IQ has dropped about fifty points in the last ten seconds... and my verbal skills have taken a beating as well."

"Good," he replies, the corner of his lip twisting upwards in a display of wry satisfaction. "I'm glad to see I still have that effect on you."

I whimper a little as he repositions his hands on either side of me, aware that my sex is pulsating at the proximity of this godlike man. Before locking eyes with me again, I notice him look down at my panting chest, exposed between the two sides of my cardigan, hard nipples protruding through my tight indigo T-shirt.

"I'm not coming with you," I reiterate, my voice meeker this time, echoing my weakening resolve.

"Oh yes you are," he responds stiffly, dauntless determination written on his torrid features.

"Why?"

He removes one hand from the wall, stroking his fingers down the side of my neck, placing his hand loosely around my throat, tilting his head and studying my jawline as he does so. He closes his eyes for a second before opening them, astounding me with the unique kaleidoscope of warm whiskey tones in his large irises.

"Because I've spent the last four months dreaming about you to the point of insanity, staying away because you asked me to and because I had hoped you were happy, like you told me you were when I asked. It seems you were not being entirely truthful."

I look down for a moment as he slides his hand up to my jaw, lifting my chin with strong fingers, dipping his head towards mine, breathing heavily as he restrains himself from doing what I know his body wants him to do.

"Why didn't you tell me how much pain you were in?" he asks stiffly.

I don't respond.

"I'm not staying away when I know you're in pain like this," he continues. "I can't bear the thought of it. It tears my insides out. No one else's suffering has ever had this effect on me. Not to mention that you are now most definitely on their radar. That changes things, and until I find out why, I won't be able to function if I'm not around to protect you from their insanity. I will not be leaving you alone again. The decision is final. You don't have a say in the matter."

"Cam," I manage, mustering every ounce of resistance within me. "What if he—"

"He won't find out. I'll make sure of that. Plus, there are forces he's involved with who want him away from you and your influence. The allure of your purity is highly inconvenient to them, and they're doing everything they can to keep him away from you forever, including feeding him all sorts of distractions."

My heart sinks at the thought of Jack being in the clutches of Frost and Gravier and the maniacs they frequent.

"Cam, I can't."

"Like I said, Avery, you don't have a choice in the matter. I would rather not have to unleash the, um, inner neanderthal if I can help it. He can be quite... *uncivilized,* to put it mildly."

"You mean, that wasn't him?!" I tease in mock-exasperation, tipping my head towards the bedroom, scene of his determined bag-packing exploits.

He breaks into the gentlest of laughs, his delicious masculine scent entering me as he does so. "No." He shakes his head slowly. "Not even close."

"The real one must be quite the brute."

"He is not very gentleman-like. You *are* coming with me, Avery, whether you like it or not. You either comply or I may have to use less sophisticated techniques to negotiate compliance out of you... though I do suspect you may enjoy the process..."

I sigh inwardly, trying to be outraged, but secretly wishing he would throw me onto the bed and show me exactly what he means.

Hold it together, Jess.

You can't do this.

I shake off my hormonal brain fog and finally manage to grab hold of myself, wishing I could say no but knowing that every cell in my body wants to be near this person who has been so dear to me for so long, and not just because the thought of spending another night in my apartment alone in the middle of the deep gloom of this Manhattan winter has a dark rock forming in the pit of my stomach.

"Do I need to use more extreme measures to procure your compliance, Jessynia?" His eyes gleam as I shoot him a carefully crafted unimpressed look.

"I'll come with you, but as a friend, okay? Jack still hasn't fully moved on, and it's more than I could bear if something happened to you because of me. Agreed?"

"We'll see."

"No, not *We'll see*... I need you to tell me that you agree to the parameters of me coming."

"I don't agree to them, but I will do my best to respect them."

"Good."

"Though it's challenging when I see your soft little body succumbing to my strength." I shake my head in indignation, my face suddenly hot. "I know what's happening in your body, Jessynia. I can always see it in your eyes, no matter how much you try to conceal it from me."

"Cam, stop," I manage weakly as glossy juice pools at the outside of my pulsating sex. I restrain myself from telling him I know he's hard. I can see it in his face.

"I see it in the way the apples of your cheeks flush pink," he continues. "Like they're doing now..." I shift a little in embarrassment. "I see the craving in your innocent eyes, the yearning to have your little body ravaged by me. I watch you lick your plump lips without even realizing you are doing it. You'll have to take pity on me as all of these things make self-restraint *challenging* when I'm around you."

He watches me from above, contemplating my blushes and the meek way I look at him.

"See, this is the opposite of the whole *Let's be friends* spiel I was trying to convey just now," I mutter, trying to sound scolding.

"Hmm," he responds, the slight crinkle in the skin around his eyes signaling his amusement.

"Are you going to respect these boundaries if I come or not?" I ask.

"You are coming, Avery. That's non-negotiable. And I shall do everything within my power to control what my body wants to do to you."

I shake my head in admonishment at his devious smile, watching as I look up at him, swallowing hard as I waver under the magnetic pull of his outrageous virility and the brutal resolve in this face.

"Let's go," he finally says.

11

SEVERAL HOURS LATER, I jolt awake as the car we're in goes over a bump. Opening my eyes, I see Cam in the passenger seat watching his assistant-slash-bodyguard-slash-surrogate father, Charles, maneuver the car down a twisting snow-covered lane. The dashboard clock tells me it is just after 2 a.m. The SUV's floodlights illuminate a tunnel up ahead composed of the path below and a seemingly endless row of mammoth firs which greet each other from either side of the trail, closing us off from the onyx sky. The slow slip of windscreen wipers gently pushes aside the delicate dusting of snowflakes that caress the windscreen.

"Best hug left down this bit, Charles," Cam says softly as we roll up the snowy path.

I lean forward and put my hand on the shoulder of Cam's seat and he turns to look back at me.

"Sorry, I didn't mean to fall asleep," I say with a yawn. "I think falling asleep has always been my body's way of coping with car rides with my parents."

He smiles at me and turns back to face the front.

"Do you guys want a snack?" I ask, rummaging through my purse for a granola bar to offer the men.

"No. We're nearly there," responds Cameron.

"No, thank you," responds Charles whose big brown eyes I study through his rear-view mirror.

I met Charles a few times when Cam and I were studying at college together. He used to be Cameron's father's right-hand man, running everything from logistics to transport to just fixing things for the powerful O'Neill clan. From what I gather, he now works directly for Cameron, which I'm sure they both enjoy as I know he adores Cam, having watched over him since he was a child.

He is one of those old-school types who vows allegiance to those that treat him with respect. Although he is technically an employee, I've always seen the O'Neill's treat him more like a family member than anything else, and as he has never really had a family of his own, I imagine this is where he feels he belongs.

Jack's father stopped working security for Joseph, Cameron's father, when Jack and Cam were in their late teens. I'm not entirely sure what happened but I know Jack's father well enough to know that he may not have done things by the book and that his battle with alcoholism after Jack's mother died probably didn't help matters. And with Cameron's belief that Jack and his family are somehow involved in organized crime, some of the mysterious secrets I had often wondered about are starting to make more sense.

I sit up straight to the sight of an imposing metal gate looming up before us. As we pull up, a security guard appears from a small lodge next to it. The guard peers into the car before giving a thumbs up and pressing a button which opens the sturdy black gate. As we drive through, I turn back to look at the guard who eyes me as we disappear out of sight.

As we take a final turn to the left, my eyes widen as a huge house with wooden exterior rolls into mesmerizing view. Its triangular rooftop lies under six inches of snow. Short icicles hang from caramel-colored gables and various window ledges lying under large windows. The exterior walls are made of wood that is stained black and there are cameras pointing around the property. The place looks like some kind of sci-fi ski-lodge.

To the left as we pull in behind imposing hedges that encircle the property is what looks like a guest house, about the size of a small studio. The soft light around the house turns into a garish floodlight as Charles deftly pulls up in front of it.

On the dark paneling to the right of the front door hangs a sign:

BLACKWOOD

As we unbuckle our seatbelts and get out, our breaths create a tango of mist in the icy night air. The crunch of fresh snow beneath my feet makes me understand why Cameron ordered me to put on the closest thing I had to snowshoes before we left my apartment. The arctic bite in the wintry breeze makes me relieved I also stopped resisting him and agreed to wear my thickest winter coat and bring a scarf and a beanie.

I don't mean to resist him so much but I can't help it. I know that he leans towards dominance, especially this new version of Cameron who has transformed into such a *man* since I knew him at college. But I spent three years with Jack who is like a case study in alpha, and I'll be damned if I lose my power to another dominant man, even if he is just a friend.

Cameron pulls our bags out of the trunk as Charles grabs another. As he does so, a man emerges from the door of the guest house. "Cameron!" he shouts over. Tall, bald with deep olive skin, he looks like he may have just got out of bed.

"Go back to bed, Aaron. It's all good," replies Cameron.

"You sure?"

"Yeah. Oh, and, my friend Jessynia will be staying with me for a few days." The man's gaze shifts to me, his eyes widening as he takes me in, before smiling as if remembering to do so. He nods at me and I shoot him a *Hi*. I feel like I've seen him before somewhere... "We'll catch up tomorrow morning, huh?" shouts Cameron.

"Sure. Goodnight." The man disappears inside.

"This way, miss," says Cameron and I watch my feet plunge into a thick layer of pristine snow as I follow them to a side door which

Cameron opens with a key that he retrieves from the pocket of his graphite-gray winter coat.

We enter a mudroom, all beige with tiles of taupe, where we take off our shoes and put them into a small cubby near the floor before hanging our hats and coats on the ample black hooks lining the room. Cameron hands me some guest shoes and puts a pair on himself.

"You'll have to excuse me, young lady," says Charles. "Nature calls... quite frequently at my age."

"No problem, Charles," I smile. "Thank you so much for driving us."

He disappears into the house and I watch Cameron as he ruffles his hair, shaking off the specks of snow that settled there on the walk from the car. The brush of hair off his face leaves me momentarily mesmerized by the preposterous perfection of his wildly masculine elegance. He catches me checking out the indecently sexy way his fingers slide through his thick brown tresses, his gaze strong, the shadow of a smile tugging at his lips as I take in the otherworldly beauty of his rich brown eyes with their dancing dots of warm ochre in the center.

"This way," Cameron finally says and leads me through a huge unlit kitchen and into the foyer of the house, to the right of which is a carpet-lined staircase with a wrought-iron baluster under a glossy walnut handrail. He carries my bag and his up one flight of stairs and then another. On this smaller level at the top of the house stand only three doors—two white ones on either side of the hallway and a black one at the end.

"Charles is staying downstairs," Cameron says as he places his bag on the beige carpet next to the door to the left before opening the one opposite it and leading me inside. He places my tatty old fair-trade bag onto a chair next to the wall and turns on a small lamp stood on a bedside table which brings into view the stunning, understated elegance of all residences owned by the O'Neill dynasty. The walls are mint-green, the furniture all white with black hardware. There is an olive-green rug lying over the dark hardwood floor and a large oil painting of a willow above the bed.

Well, at least it's not an oak this time...

"There's a bathroom through here," Cameron says, opening a door to the right.

"Thanks," I respond. Though I'm not entirely sure what I'm doing here, the sadness permeating through me for months and months seems to have dissipated for now, and I can only be grateful for that. "Cam, are you sure he can't find out I'm here?"

"I'm sure. Charles made sure there's no tracker on your phone. I trust the men here with my life. Plus, I'm having Jack and his men monitored."

"Oh, God," I moan, anxiety flooding my body at the thought.

"Don't worry. My men have never been spotted yet. If Jack hears anything, we will know about it instantly."

"Okay. Is Evie here?"

"She hasn't confirmed if she'll be coming. My mother is here though."

"She is?"

"Yeah. In the house opposite us. She's bugged me to bring you to see her about five hundred times over the last few years. She'll be ecstatic to see you."

"Good," I sigh. "Cam, you should go to bed. You must be tired."

He watches me in the low light for ten long seconds before speaking. "I'll be across the hall if you need anything. And there's a lock on the door," he says, pointing to a black barrel bolt on the ivory bedroom door. "I want you to use it. The Wi-Fi code is on the table next to the water. There's a radiator against the wall in case it's too cold. The guards put it on before you got here. There's also a key to the room on the table over there. You can lock the room when you go out. If you need anything from the kitchen, just help yourself. My house is yours, Avery. Always."

"Okay, thank you," I respond.

He doesn't reply, but watches my face as I swallow hard at the intensity of his stare. He takes a step towards me, a crease in his brown showing his concern. "Jess... are you okay?" he asks. "After tonight, I mean. Ilya..."

I sigh out deeply. "I'll be okay."

"If you need to talk about it, I want you to... with me. I don't want this stuck inside you. If you need to get it out, I want to help you to do it. I don't want that maniac inside your head. Promise me you'll come to me if you need to talk."

I smile. "I promise."

"They will *never* hurt you again, Jessynia. I promise you that."

I nod, stunned by the anguish in his face. "I believe you, Cam."

"Goodnight," he says, his gaze lingering on mine as he leaves the room and closes the door behind him.

"Goodnight."

12

I AWAKEN TO SUNLIGHT gleaming through gaps in the pewter curtains and the sound of men's voices at the side of the house. I jump up and draw open the curtains to see Cameron and Charles talking to the security guard I saw last night when we arrived and a second man I haven't seen before.

This man is older, in his early fifties by the looks of things, same age as Charles, with dark-gray hair that reaches just past shoulder-length. He's wearing a regal-looking umber coat and a thick burgundy scarf.

The men talk intently, pointing things out around the property. I see the older long-haired gentleman pat Cameron on the arm a few times, the proximity and intimate gestures suggesting they are closer than mere acquaintances. A few minutes of conversing pass and the men enter the house through the mudroom door.

Making my mind up to go downstairs, I quickly jump in the shower and wash my body. On getting out, I envelop myself in a plush bathrobe, put some lip balm on and apply a split-second swish of bronzer to liven up my pale winter complexion. I brush through my long hair and then pull on a black bra and panties, some thick black leggings, a sleeveless high-neck white T-shirt with a wolf print on it that I got at a vintage store, and the beloved mottled-gray cardigan that my godmother Babs knitted for me, before pulling on some socks with a drunken frog motif on them that Kevin bought me for a goof as well as the house shoes Cameron gave me last night.

I take a deep breath in to ease the trepidation fluttering in my chest as I open the door, lock it behind me and head downstairs. Voices lead me down the hallway at the end of which I see the kitchen where the three men are now conversing around a large table of stained wood. Charles pours coffee into three large mugs and then sits back down as the men lean into each other and talk.

"Oh, I need this today," says Charles bringing the cup to his lips.

"Well, you're getting old, Charles," replies the security guy, slight Brooklyn accent, who is totally bald with three-day-old stubble in that hot, rugged Jason Statham kind of way.

Charles chuckles as he places the cup back down onto a thick tile of a coaster. "Well, you're only twelve years behind me, Aaron. Watch out, they'll go by fast!"

Having reached the kitchen without anyone seeing me, I decide to clear my throat so as not to startle anyone. "Ahem," I manage with a nervous smile.

Cameron immediately jumps to his feet and walks towards me. "Did you sleep well?" he asks.

"Yeah, I did. You?"

He nods.

"Good morning, miss," says Charles, peering at me over his glasses as I say hello to the two other men. "Fancy some coffee?"

"Oh, no thanks, Charles. I'll make myself a tea in a few minutes. Did you sleep well?"

"Well enough, young lady," he replies, his umber cheeks plumping up as he smiles to reveal the cutest of dimples below them.

"This is Aaron," says Cam of the guy dressed all in black whose walkie-talkie is lying on the table in front of him.

He stands up to shake my hand firmly and I realize that he is even taller than the almost six-foot-three-inch Mr. O'Neill.

"Jess," I respond.

"I know," he says. "I'm glad to finally get to talk to you."

"Finally?" I respond with a frown. "You're not one of the guys that Cameron got to stalk me, are you?" I ask, shooting a glance of exasperation at Cameron whose eyes bear an amused glint.

"Um, I'm afraid I am, miss," he replies, his tone utterly unapologetic as he sits down to the warm smile of the other man with the long gray hair.

"Oh," I say. "Well, I hope you weren't bored out of your mind." I think back to my uneventful life in September and October when I barely left Kevin's apartment.

"It wasn't too bad."

"I still don't know how I didn't spot you," I say.

"We weren't spying on you. Just trying to work out if anyone was following you."

"Did you ever lose me?"

"A couple of times. The bright pink yoga mat certainly helped."

I burst into a gentle laugh. "Oh, yeah, well, yoga has been pretty much the only thing to get me out of the house these last few months. Glad it was useful at least."

"This is Silas," says Cameron about the other gentleman who gets to his feet to shake my hand, his face bearing a few glorious lines and the beginnings of folds, suggesting he is in his early fifties. There is something regal about the way his loose waves of multiple shades of gray frame his face. His expression is kind and open with a warm self-confidence that comes with being smart and experienced in society. He's the kind of man who makes you feel instantly safe.

"It's wonderful to finally meet you, Jessynia," he says as he sits back down. "Cameron has told me so much about you."

"Oh, dear." I glance over to find Cam watching me, his eyes never leaving my face. "I always get nervous when I hear that."

"All wonderful things, don't worry," adds Silas.

"Oh well, I do try," I reply in jest.

"I hope we'll get to spend some time together over the next few days," he adds.

"I hope so too."

"Jess," interrupts Cameron. "My mom's been pestering me to send you over. She's in a house across the street. She's made breakfast for you."

"Oh, sure. I'll go. Leave the men to it."

"Aaron, can you get Christian to walk her over?"

"I don't need help walking," I reply as Aaron radios for this Christian guy on his walkie-talkie.

"Well, you're gonna get help whether you need it or not," Cameron counters.

I breathe out in exasperation. "This must be what the president's children feel like," I mutter to Charles who smiles back and scratches the scalp under his tight black and gray curls.

"Miss Avery," Cameron retorts. "For as long as you are under my roof—"

"Yes, da—." I shutter my mouth quickly, stopping myself from saying the word *daddy* around these men.

A minute or so later, there's a knock on the back door and another man—equally tall with the palest of skin, short light-brown hair and pallid brown eyes, the skin around them a little dark—steps through the mudroom, hovering at the entrance to the kitchen.

"Ready, miss?" the man asks. "I'm Christian."

I shrug and sigh. "Sure. Thanks. Jess." I bow my head slightly and say goodbye to the group as Cam follows me to the mudroom where I put on my coat and beanie.

As I sit on the small bench and pull on my boots, I shoot a glance up at Cam in the doorway and find him regarding my ridiculous socks in gentle mirth.

"Present from Kev," I explain.

"Who else?" replies Cameron dryly, his gaze soft on my face as Christian steps outside.

"Well, you packed my bag, sir, so I won't hear one word of complaint about my attire while I'm here."

He grins broadly and for a second, breath leaves me as I have one of those recurring moments with Cameron when I am stunned to my very core by the self-assured way he occupies space. Sunlight floating through the glass pane in the mudroom door caresses the smooth panes of his cheek and large light-pink lips. The expression in his almond-shaped eyes is frankly sinful as he watches me silently. I know that my sassy independent streak has me often playing the defiance game with him, but there are times when I feel truly weak in the presence of his ridiculously bold masculinity. Tingling warmth shoots through me at the thought of his rock-hard body and the visceral way he protects me.

As I finally get to my feet and pull my beanie on, I'm observed by shrewd eyes under tousled waves of chestnut brown.

"Enjoy," he says. "I'll be over later."

"Bye," I respond, swallowing hard.

Lord, give me strength, I mutter internally as I step outside as the memory of this mass of savage muscle and beauty standing over me at the kitchen table at Redwood while he plowed my slim body slices through me, leaving goosebumps prickling all over my skin.

"Ready?" asks Christian.

"Yes. Thanks."

The caustic chill in the wintry air is welcome relief as we walk down the driveway, cooling my skin which flushes as I'm suddenly unwillingly besieged by a flashback of Cameron standing behind me, lifting my leg up and fucking me in the shower, his dense limbs holding me in place, his sex hard and thick and merciless.

Jesus, Jess, let's pull it together, I grumble inwardly as I endeavor to distract myself from my indecent thoughts by taking in the bulbous clouds of white snow perching on the bushes and trees all around.

The snow on the central part of the driveway beneath our feet has been topped with a layer of grit and sand to stop us from slipping, but I still manage to slide on a glistening patch of ice, shadowed by a tall shrub next to it.

Christian reaches out and grabs me to stop me from falling on my ass. "You okay?" he asks, eyeing me keenly.

"Yep, just... spatially challenged as usual," I reply. "I'm amazed I've only broken two bones in my life."

"Well, I've slipped around here a few times myself."

As we leave the driveway, I look around at the stunning tree giants watching over us. "This place is so beautiful," I say.

"Yes. I love coming here."

"Have you worked for Cameron long?"

"Two years."

"Wow, that's a long time."

I'm grateful for any meager small talk with Christian to distract me from the trepidation I feel at seeing Cam's mother, Valentina, again. We were once so close when Cam and I were friends at college, to the point that there were times when she would call me more often than her son, something that used to amuse Cameron to no end.

I haven't seen her since I married Jack, although she did send me a few letters on that exquisite embossed cream paper of hers when Jack and I first started dating before Cameron and I fell out so badly.

God knows what she thinks of me staying in this house when I'm still married and there is so much bad blood between Jack and her son. I have no idea what Cam has even told her about us, if anything, but the thought of facing her sends a shudder of anxiety into me.

"I'm nervous," I say to Christian who glances at me inquisitively as we walk up a quiet path lined with magnificent conifers sheathed in white. "I haven't seen Val for so long."

"Well, she's been asking after you since this morning. She seems to be chomping at the bit to see you."

As we turn a corner and emerge from this tunnel of trees, I spot a large wooden house, modern like Blackwood with a front façade made almost entirely of glass. There is a wooden veranda out front and accents of dark metal adorn the property.

As we start making our way up some wooden stairs lined with metal grate, the shriek of a breathy voice makes me jump. "Jessie!"

I look up to see Valentina emerging from the front door. She's dressed in khaki pants and a cream sweater and is wearing sober house shoes. Her brown hair is shorter than I remember, now skimming her shoulders. Man, this gorgeous lady is something else.

"Val!" I respond and bound up the final steps where she envelops me in the tightest of hugs that I reciprocate in relief.

"It's been so long!" she moans.

"It's so good to see you!" I reply breathlessly as we pull apart and she cups my face with her delicate hand.

"Oh, let me look at you! I've missed your stunning face, sweetheart! I've begged my son to bring you to see me so many times."

"Oh, I was so nervous that you wouldn't want to see me..."

"See you? Darling, you're one of my favorite people. I always want to see you." The relief at her kind words leaves me enveloping her in another crushing hug. "Did you sleep well in that house?" she asks.

"Um, amazing, actually," I reply, surprising myself as I realize that this is one of the few times I've slept right through the night in recent months.

"Good." She pulls on my arm as we prepare to head in. "Christian, do you want to come in?"

"No, thank you, Mrs. O'Neill. I'm gonna get some fresh air and then hang out in the lodge," he responds, gesturing to the small building just below Val's house. "I'll be keeping an eye out."

"Okay."

With that, we disappear into the house and Val double-locks the door behind us, instructing me to remove my shoes and coat which she puts into a little closet next to the door.

As I inhale the delicious odor of freshly baked bread, she plops her arm onto my shoulders giddily and leads me through the spacious living room—all white walls with green accent pillows, throws and plants to offset the eye-catching wooden ceiling and prominent beams.

"How have you been, darling?" she asks as we head into the kitchen and she beckons for me to sit down opposite some plates of food.

"I've been...." My programming has me wanting to say that I'm doing great like I usually tell people no matter what I'm feeling, but Val knows me too well, and doesn't hesitate to call me on my bullshit when she sniffs it out. "I guess I've been better," I finally reply.

"Oh darling, it's normal to feel a bit low when you're going through a divorce. You're doing great. A friend of mine was in such a state after hers that she took up smoking, drinking, binge-eating and not showering for a year."

I sputter at the way she says it. "God. Is she doing better now?"

"Well, she's still smoking and drinking, but she's more functional now at least."

"Oh, poor woman."

"Divorce hurts, Jess. It goes very deep inside."

"Yeah."

"I'm so glad Cameron dragged you out of Manhattan. It's one of the toughest cities to spend the winter in, especially when you're on your own. I remember when Joseph was away one winter on some business trip, before the kids were born, I was so miserable that I hopped into the car alone and just drove in the direction of Canada."

A gentle laugh escapes me. "Did you get there?"

"No, not quite. I ended up in Vermont," she laughs, "but that trip was when I first discovered Woodstock and this whole area."

"Is that where we are? I didn't even ask Cameron."

"We're not far from Mohonk Lake, about twenty minutes south of Woodstock."

"Well, I've never been to either before."

"I'll ask my son to drive you around a bit. It's absolutely stunning around here."

"Is this your house?"

"Yes, this one and the one opposite that you're staying at belongs to the family. Several families we are very close to chose this area as a safe place to meet up every few months. I suppose you'll meet those that haven't been able to come this time tomorrow."

"I will?" I frown.

"That's the plan."

"Oh, your son hasn't really filled me in on *the plan* as of yet."

Val chuckles. "I think he enjoys seeing how you will react to the things he springs on you."

"Yeah, I've noticed that!"

"Anyway, more importantly… la comida!"

Valentina's long wooden breakfast table, laden with bread, eggs, salmon, avocado and tomatoes, isn't dissimilar to the one that Cameron had his way with me on at Redwood.

"Earl Grey," she says with a smile, pouring some tea into two delicate floral cups.

"What else?" I respond.

"Now eat!" she commands warmly.

"Val, you shouldn't have gone to this trouble."

"For you, no trouble at all, sweetheart."

Valentina and I spend the next few hours utterly lost in each other, talking through lunch and into the early afternoon where we lounge on sofas drinking tea and eating homemade oatmeal cookies on the enclosed veranda at the back of her house which looks out onto a sublime forest of firs.

I feel as giddy as ever to be in her soft yet intensely focused presence. We laugh easily, bringing out each other's tactile nature with the touch of an arm or the stroke of a lock of hair. She is in her mid-fifties and as mesmerizingly ethereal as ever with naturally bouncy chocolate-brown hair, stunning amber eyes that Cameron gets from her, golden olive skin, a broad face with angular cheekbones and slim, delicate limbs which make you feel like she may float off into the air at any moment.

Conversing with her is as effortless as it is with Cameron. We always have something to say and when we don't, silences are easy and light, no stagnant energy or awkwardness, obviously without the injection of sexual tension that I've experienced with Cameron since rediscovering him this year.

Valentina and I talk about her late husband Joseph's death, her charity work, my journalism, my nutty parents, Cam's ball-busting grandmother Lottie, and Val's younger daughter, Lauren. Her voice is gentle and breathy, but her expressions are bold and fearless and light just radiates from the lady effortlessly. Boy, that light is something else. Being in her glowing company makes me feel like getting my own back after the divorce from Jack really is possible.

Maybe Val notices the tiniest of shifts in my face, for she suddenly stills for a dozen silent seconds, her wide-set eyes drifting over my face the way Cameron's do when there's a lull in conversation.

"You're thinking about Jack, aren't you?" Val isn't into artifice and her precision-strike of a question, however well-meant, leaves a lump in my throat as I look down and let my failed marriage sink in with aching clarity as it still does several times a day.

"I try my best not to, Val. I just get these moments when it comes flooding back. This time last year, we were with my parents for Christmas and then Costa Rica for New Year's. If you had told me that a year later, we would be preparing for divorce..."

"What happened, darling?"

"Did Cameron not tell you?"

"He told me a little."

"What?"

"I know that that monster, Alexandra Frost, was involved." The tiniest remnant of a Spanish accent comes out on the word *monster*. Valentina moved to the US with her parents when she was still a young child. She has lost her accent since but occasionally that gorgeous Latin inflection emerges from deep within.

"Oh God, Val. He shouldn't have told you that," I respond, feeling blood drain from my face as I remember Steven Frost's threats about the consequences of being indiscrete about Alex's affair with my husband. "These people are really dangerous."

She smiles and puts her hand onto mine with a squeeze. "I've known that since you were still a girl, my dear. I once trusted her with my most precious gift—my son. The betrayal I felt when I found out... I wanted to commit murder. A few people had to stop me. The families that reunite at this compound have been dealing with the Society for years."

"Cameron told you about them?" I gasp.

"No, it was Silas and Gabriel who did. You'll meet Gabriel soon. They told me about that place after my son fell into a deep depression that nothing seemed to be able to pull him out of... until he met you, that is." She strokes the side of my face as she says it. "You were like an angel to him, you know? To the whole family."

"Does Cam know that you know about them?"

"Of course. We've talked about it many times. I wanted him to release the shame that had been eating him up inside. This compound is for those who resist them to meet up in safety as we try to figure out how to protect ourselves and our kids, not to mention the greater New York population."

"Are they really *that* dangerous?" I shift position on her soft cream sofa, placing a sage-green cushion under my hands.

"Yes. They've become so. They have people infiltrating the mayor's office, the governor's office, police departments, hospitals, you name it. They've become way more powerful than any of us could have imagined. In the past, we have let them *be,* more or less, on condition that they leave us and our children alone—not that they fully complied with that. But I believe we have reached a point where we can no longer sit back and watch as they take over New York, kidnap people, blackmail people… kill people."

"You think they do that?" I ask breathlessly.

"Yes. And I think that we finally have enough people now that are willing to make a move and do something about them. That's what we are meeting about tomorrow."

"God, Val. These people seem like monsters."

"Some of them are. The Society has existed for many years, never causing much trouble for anyone. Unfortunately, one particular *monster* took over a few years ago and promptly axed anyone who didn't comply with his ruthless way of running things."

"Sebastian Gravier?"

She nods. "Since then, the more reasonable patrons who just wanted a place to… express their desires, shall we say, have started to leave, and the dangerous sadists who see the place as a way to get power and control have been promoted to the top. And things have started to get… messy."

"God, I'm so glad that Cam got away from them. I hate that—" I stop.

"Jack is still mixed up with them?"

I nod.

Val takes a deep breath. "Jessynia, Jackson is a grown man. I know this may be hard for you to accept, but no one is forcing him to be around those people. If he wanted to break free, he could. Cameron has managed it."

"Not as cleanly as he would have liked," I suggest gently.

"Yes, you're right. It is not easy, but he could have tried. It was a choice between them and his marriage, and while this may be hard to face, he chose them."

"I know that," I reply.

"You still love him?" she asks. "I want you to be honest with me."

"I find it hard to stop loving him completely," I reply solemnly. "We went through so much together. He's left this imprint on me that I can't seem to fully shake off."

"And you want to work it out with him?"

"*No*," I say with an emphatic shake of the head. "I can't. It's over, for good."

"You're sure?"

"Certain. My lawyer has already prepared all the paperwork. I told Jack I wouldn't file until March, but everything is ready to go for then."

"And did you mention the adultery in the filings? New York allows for *fault* divorces, you know?"

"Yes. The lawyer insisted I tell him the full story just in case something happens, but I'm not going to include it when I file. We have a prenup that supersedes any fault. Plus, I wouldn't want to do that to Jack."

"And I don't think that Frost bitch would take kindly to being mentioned," says Valentina. "It could put you in danger."

"I didn't give the lawyer the names of the women he slept with anyway. It will be a no-fault divorce, but once March thirty-first comes round, I am filing, no matter what Jack says."

She breathes a sigh of relief. "My son will be very happy to hear that." I study her face as she smiles back at me softly. "Cam loves you, you know." I swallow hard as she peers into me. "Do you love him?"

"I'm really trying very hard not to allow myself to feel that way. I'm so afraid of something happening to him, of Jack finding out. If something were to happen to him because of me, I would never forgive myself."

"Cameron's a big boy. He knows the risk."

I search her gentle eyes. "You want him to be with me, don't you?"

"Nothing would make me happier."

"But... But how could you want that when you know that Jack may hurt him?"

"I don't believe Jack will hurt him. Not really. I watched him play with Cameron their entire childhoods. They were inseparable. Not to mention I held Jack in my arms for months after his mother died. I loved him. He was the feistiest little boy. Adorable. Charming. Irreverent. He would *not* do that to me."

"Val, he's changed a lot. He's not that cute little boy anymore. He's become powerful and ruthless. I've heard him talk to people on the phone and it's sent shivers down my spine. Can you imagine your life if something happened to Cam? I'm amazed you want him anywhere near me."

She smiles. "I want him with you because I remember what he was like in the years before he met you. He was a shadow of the man he is today. This was when that Frost psychopath still had her claws in him, and afterwards when he was dealing with the fallout of that place. I suffered such horrific anxiety during those years that my hair started falling out. Every night I would struggle to sleep, wondering whether my son would still be alive in the morning."

I frown as I remember that hollow look in Cam's face the very first time I met him.

"As soon as he met you and started spending time with you," she continues, "I saw something lift. It was like this cloud had gone away. He told me how you looked after him, dragged him out of his room, fed him, made him laugh, made him engage in things on campus. As I watched him talk about you, I saw a light return to him that I had thought would be gone forever. When you burst back into his life in June, I could see a shift in his whole being, as though he was floating. Every time he talks of you, it's like he's recharging his batteries. No one else has ever done that for him."

"Val, stop. I don't know if I can hear any more."

"It's true, Jessynia. For three years before he knew you, I was terrified every single night that I would get a call telling me my son had ended his own life. Even when he was with Olivia, it was like he was checked out. It was you who stopped that. It's you who he lives for. I don't think he has really told you the full extent of his feelings. He's told me."

I feel a pit form in my belly as I think of how dangerous it would be for me to consider dating Cameron. "I wish it were that simple, Val."

"Nothing in life is simple, sweetheart. And loving two men at once *is* possible. I've been there."

"You have?" I ask, putting a hand to my chest in relief that I'm not the only one who struggles like this.

"Oh yes. When I met Jo, I was actually dating someone else. This dreamboat called David. Star quarterback on the college football team. And boy, did he ever like me. Then Jo met me and pursued me relentlessly and I was torn to pieces. In the end, I went with my gut... and my hormones," she laughs. "I picked Jo."

"Did you ever regret it?"

"Not for one minute. With Jo, I always knew I was home. *But*... it took me well over a year to really get over David. I still think of him from time to time, even to this day."

"I used to feel at home with Jack. Now the thought of living with him makes me feel physically ill."

"And my son?"

"I don't know, Val. If Jack weren't involved, I would have been begging Cameron to be with me by now. But he is. I can't just ignore that."

Val suddenly opens her mouth as if a thought has just dawned on her. "Wait here!" she says, rushing from the room.

A minute later, she comes back in holding something in her hand. "I found this the other day!" she exclaims, handing me a dozen or so photographs which I begin to flick through. "Remember this day?"

I exclaim at seeing pictures of me, Cameron, his sister Evie, his then-girlfriend Olivia, Val and his badass grandma Lottie on a boat trip we took to Fishers Island off the coast of Connecticut a few years ago.

There's a few taken inside a gorgeous golf club overlooking the ocean and several of us on the beach. Olivia is breathtaking, and to her credit, was pretty open-minded about Cameron having a close female friend like me and a few others.

"Wow, that was such a fun day," I sing as Val scoots closer towards me.

"Notice anything?" she asks, her breathy voice soft as air.

I look up at her tenderly then look down at the pictures. My stomach sinks into the floor as I spot it...

Cameron.

In every single picture that both of us are in, he's looking at me.

Even when we're supposed to be making goofy faces for the camera.

Even when he's standing with his arm around Olivia.

Even when we're on opposite ends of the frame.

His eyes are always on my face.

My hands tremble a little as Val takes the pictures from me and puts her hand onto mine.

"He loves you, Jessynia. You're the one. You always have been. And that's worth a little bit of danger."

13

"HOW'S IT GOING?" Cameron asks from the doorway of Blackwood's library later that evening.

"Oh, I've got distracted again," I respond as he walks round to sit next to me on the carpeted floor. I shift away from him slightly, laptop in front of me on the low tigerwood table as I study a photograph of a fluffy young humanoid primate, orphaned and displaced, clutching onto his human rescuer.

"I'm never eating palm oil again," I announce sorrowfully as he looks at the pitiful image.

"I'm sensing an article brewing," he says as I look up at him, trying not to blush at the intensity of his gaze on my face. "I've never before devoured a journalist's every article."

I smile at him. "Yeah. If I have the guts to face the horror of what humans put these poor creatures through."

"The guts? You're the bravest, most fearless woman I've ever met, Avery."

I look down at my laptop. "I'm not feeling too brave these days if I'm honest."

"You're not? Well, I still remember a certain madam that organized a sit-in in front of the Dean's office as a protest for them not banning plastic straws on campus." I smile as he leans into me. "And I remember when that same little loudmouth got a hundred people to turn up to lectures wearing duct tape over their mouths to protest free speech censorship. And then there's the little asshole who dragged me out of my room on threat of violence to go hiking in the rain when she sensed I was down."

I peer into those deep, large coppery-brown eyes and try to smile. "I don't really know where that girl's gone, Cam. I feel like she's locked in some room and I don't know how to get her out."

"She'll be back."

"She will?"

"Yes. You're grieving, Jess. When my dad died, I couldn't face going out in public for a while. My mom thought I was going to turn into Howard Hughes at one point."

"What changed?"

"Time. Waking up day after day and slowly realizing there can be a life after it. The thought of you." I shift a little as his otherworldly eyes scrutinize my expression. "When I think of you," he continues, "I feel my strength coming back. I see light...or as close as a fucked-up man like me can get to it."

I don't ask him if what he's saying is true. One thing I've learned over the years spent with Mr. O'Neill is that his sense of the truth is acute. He doesn't lie or say things to impress. He speaks boldly, his words reflecting how he feels, no matter the consequences.

We sit in silence for what feels like an age, sparks flaring through our outwardly still bodies. "Do you want something to eat?" I finally deflect.

The way he narrows his eyes at me is quite frankly deviant. "Yes, there is something I would very much like to eat, Miss Avery."

I can't stop the sheepish grin appearing on my face at the devilish way he answers my question. "I mean, are you hungry?"

There's the subtlest of flicks of his tongue on his bottom lip. "Ravenous. Is there anything you have to offer me?" Amusement brightens his eyes at the sight of the blush that rushes over my cheeks. I shake my head at him slowly, shifting nervously. "Well?" he asks gently.

"I know what we need to perk us up..."

"I'm not sure it would be safe for me to be more *perked up* than I am now," he responds dryly.

"Stop," I laugh.

"Tell me your idea," he grins.

"Do you have wine and fruit?"

"Wine and fruit? You're teasing me, Avery..."

"Do you?" I ask, trying not to laugh.

He stands up. "Let's go find out."

I close my laptop and take the hand that he reaches out to help me stand. His robust fingers clamp down on mine as he pulls me to my feet and drags me into the kitchen.

"What kind of wine would madam like?" he asks.

"Um, do you have anything sweet, white and sparkling?"

"You still have the wine tastes of a teenager, Avery."

"I know. My dad still threatens to disown me each Christmas when I turn down his prize-winning Bordeaux in favor of a local apple cider."

Cameron opens a wine fridge behind him and pulls out a forest-green bottle of Moët et Chandon Demi-Sec from the door.

"No! I meant some cheap bottle of table wine."

"I don't buy cheap bottles of table wine, Jessynia."

"No, Cam, it's too much."

"Have you ever thought that I enjoy getting you drunk on expensive wine?"

I shoot him a look of disapproval as he unpops it with his strong hands, his thick biceps flexing under his white T-shirt as he places two flutes on the countertop which he fills up.

"Cheers," he says, handing me my glass.

"Cheers," I respond as his strong fingers curl around the stem of the glass which he slowly brings to his lips. I watch as he takes a sip, peering at me as I inelegantly down the whole glass. "Oh, good God, that is *so* good. Can I have another?"

"Just one," he says, pouring me another glass. "I prefer you coherent. *Most of the time.*"

I smile and take a sip of my second glass before putting it on the countertop. “Okay, so, now the fruit,” I announce purposefully.

A few minutes later, Cameron’s fingers find the top of my hand, removing the knife from me that I’m using to hack open a bag of frozen berries after deciding that we need a smoothie bowl. “I’d rather not have to take you to ER, my friend,” he says as he takes the bag and rips the top off in one fell swoop, handing it back to me.

Christ, those strong, dexterous hands do sinful things to my insides.

“Thank you, sir.” I dump the contents into the high-speed blender followed by a tiny wedge of lemon and a smidgen of apple juice. “Do you have agave syrup or coconut nectar?” I ask.

“No,” he responds, shaking his head slowly in sardonic amusement. “We’re not a raw food café, Miss Avery.”

He reaches up to a cupboard, bringing out a bottle of maple syrup which he hands to me. I begin to croon a Duran Duran number as I pour a couple of dollops into the mixer and blend the whole lot up until it’s smooth, all the while watched by Cameron who smiles at the sight of me singing over the roaring blender.

“When you’re *hungry like the wolf*,” I finish crooning as I turn off the machine while he grabs two white bowls from a cupboard and places them on the countertop. “Do you have chia or hemp seeds?”

He shakes his head slowly.

“Nuts?” I ask.

“I think *eccentric* is more the word I would use to describe you,” he deadpans, his eyes gleaming as he observes my grin of appreciation. He opens a cupboard next to me and hands me a small container of mixed nuts.

“Can I open it?”

“You’ll be in trouble if you ask that again,” he responds. “Anything in this house is yours.”

“*Anything*?” I ask cheekily, the champagne wreaking havoc with my attempts at self-control.

“Yes,” he responds, mischief written on his lips. “*Anything*.”

"What kind of *trouble*?" I ask, my tone impish.

"If I didn't know better, I would say you wanted to find out..."

Okay, Jess, let's tone it down a little.

I pour some nuts on top of the sorbet in each bowl. Conscious, despite the champagne, that I'm now playing with fire, I give myself an internal whipping and promise my inner disapproving wise sage that I will behave myself and forgo all sassy comments for the remainder of the evening.

"Do you like it?" I ask Cameron back in the library as we sit on opposite sides of the coffee table.

"It reminds me of college," Cameron replies. "Or specifically your room and that shitty blender of yours."

"You bought me a new blender in the end, remember?"

"I think it was the sight of yours sputtering while giving off fumes that smelt like burning rubber that inspired the purchase."

While distracted by a face and body that shouldn't be allowed, I'd somehow forgotten how witty this sharp man is.

I try not to smile as he takes a mouthful. Unless my friend has changed radically since we were in college, I don't think that this is his typical fare.

"What's funny?" he asks.

"Nothing."

"Don't make me get it out of you."

"It's just funny to see you eat this type of food again. Do you remember when I used to force those açaí bowls down you?" I giggle.

"Vividly," he responds. "The date and mulberry cookies are also emblazoned on my mind."

"Hey, they were good!"

He smiles as I enthusiastically tuck into my delicious frozen berry bowl. I lift my gaze to see him watching me, seemingly enjoying the entertainment.

This time it's my turn to ask. "What?"

"I'd forgotten how much I like watching you eat. There's no one I've ever got pleasure from just by watching them attack their food. I think it's something about how serious you get about it... and about your plump lips when they're covered in liquid."

I shake my head, trying to suppress the blush I feel coming on. "You better not be getting off on this, O'Neill."

"You're a messy eater, Avery. I like watching you lick your lips to clean your mouth."

"Stop," I moan as he narrows his eyes at me.

"I enjoy watching your throat when you swallow as well," he continues.

I roll my eyes as a diversion tactic as he smiles at my timidity. "Okay, that's enough," I reply playfully.

We spend the next few minutes sitting in silence as we finish our bowls, smiling at times, other times not, our eyes tracing each other's mouths or straying up each other's cheekbones. Cameron and I have always been able to look at each other's faces without feeling awkward, but tonight as my mind goes to indecent places, and his gaze becomes an implacable stare, I find my cheeks flushing as he watches me eat the pink berry blend.

I shift a little, suddenly feeling self-conscious as I am devoured by his glare. I down the rest of the second glass of champagne to distract myself.

"Did you like it?" I ask to the sight of his empty bowl.

"I like it because you made it."

"Good." I clear my throat nervously.

After washing up and following Cameron upstairs, laptop in hand, my entire body hums as we arrive at the third floor. As we reach the landing, I pull the key out of my pocket and unlock the door to my room, turning the light on before turning to wish him goodnight.

"Thanks," I say, visibly gulping at the sight of his towering physique and his indecent, unrelenting glare. "For the champagne, I mean." I feel heat rise in my cheeks as he watches me. "And the nuts..."

"You're most welcome. Do you have everything you need for the night?"

"Yes," I stammer. *Lord, those damn nerves again.* "Goodnight."

"Goodnight."

And with that, I close the door behind me, leaning my back against the door, eyes closed, as I cringe at my awkwardness around this man and my inability to stay in friend mode after I've had a few.

After changing into my pajamas and climbing into bed, I lie awake for what feels like an age, my body buzzing as I picture Cameron lying in bed in the room opposite me. I bite my lip as I visualize his heavy limbs settling into his mattress, his thick, glossy hair melting into the pillow, the hard, defined slabs of his chest rising and falling as he breathes.

I wonder if he's hard.

I wonder if his hand is wrapped around his thick shaft.

I wonder if he's pleasuring himself.

If he will come...

That's enough, Jess.

As I close my eyes, I promise myself that tomorrow I will do a better job of not flirting with the devastating Mr. O'Neill.

14

6.03 AM.

After tossing and turning for the last hour, trying to shake off the remnants of the nightmare I had this night involving Ilya Markov and other restless men at Q.N. in Tribeca, I finally resign myself to the fact that I'm unlikely to fall back asleep like I'm trying to convince my body to do, my negotiations with my own self falling on deaf ears.

The radiator has been on all night, yet I feel a nip in the air as I get up and open the curtains. It's still dark outside and silent and I feel like I'm privy to a secret world that no one else but me is experiencing. A couple of small lamps illuminate the snowy trees and bushes around Blackwood. Fluttering moths are the only sign of life.

I sit back down on the bed, wondering whether I should do some writing. Instead, I find my mind wandering to the man in the room opposite mine.

I wonder whether he's dreaming.

Whether it's a good dream...

I wonder whether he's hard, whether his thick cock lies heavy on his abdomen.

I wonder whether he wakes up with a hefty erection every morning like Jack does, desperate for a release so that he can concentrate on his work that day.

Does he like morning sex?

Did he pleasure himself last night?

Did he come?

The thought of his throbbing erection has my sex aching. I still haven't tasted him. I wonder what giving him head must feel like. Does he like you on your knees? Does he like to give instructions? Does he grab you by the hair as you're pleasuring him? What does his cum taste like?

Jesus, Jess. Snap out of it, I groan.

No more.

I jump to my feet to distract myself from inappropriate thoughts of his morning wood entering my starved body. Switching on the bedside lamp, I turn my phone on to text Stella.

Before I have a chance to, a notification tells me I have a voicemail message... from Jack.

He has respected my wishes not to call or text me for so long, but in the last couple of days, he has broken that promise, maybe because it's the first holiday he'll be without me in three years. My hands tremble a little as I prepare to listen to the message and not have the thought of it bother me all day long.

I dial voicemail and lift the phone to my ears.

The sound of his solemn voice makes my heart sink.

It's me. I know I'm not supposed to call you. I had to hear your voice. I guess you're with your parents. I miss you. I think of you every second of the day. I'm struggling to stay afloat without you. There isn't a day that I'm not in torment over it. I dream of your body. I dream of holding you in my arms. Do you dream of that too? Tell me you're still here, Jessynia. I can face the next few days if I know that. Please let me call you. Bye.

I clutch my hand to my throat as his sudden presence wraps around me as if he were in the room with me.

Jack, please, just be strong.

I want to call him back. I want to tell him I'm here and will always be here. That I'll never abandon him. I want to help him break free of these people. But I'm so afraid of giving him an inch... and of being sucked in by the sheer power of his magnetic pull.

After much contemplation, I text back:

I'm with my parents.
I'm here Jack. I will always be here as long as you fight them.
I can't text much. I'm trying to spend time with my family.
Please don't call. We can text a little if you want.
Bye.

I wait a few minutes but there is no answer. I hope he is asleep.

I feel a momentary wave of guilt at being at Cameron's place. I mean, I guess I have the right to be. Cameron is one of my oldest friends, someone I met way before meeting Jack. I have the right to spend time with him. But Cam and I are not really just friends, no matter how much I pretend we are and given their history...

Then I think about the numerous women Jack's probably had since we split up. Not to mention the many he had while we were married.

I put my head in my hands for a moment, wondering what cosmic force always draws me back to these two men...

Knowing that there is no way in hell that I will be able to sleep now between Jack's messages and my lewd—and dangerous—lusting after Cameron's hard body, I drink down the water next to my bed, open the bedroom door and make my way downstairs, taking care to tread as lightly as I can so as not to waken him or Charles sleeping on the floor below us.

There are a couple of dim nightlights on in the hallway which allow me to make my way to the library and turn the door handle gently, flinching as it clicks and the door creaks open.

It is pitch black inside and I fumble for the light switch, having a split-second moment of panic as the darkness of the room cloaks me. The light finally comes on, dazzling my eyes, and I instantly pull down the dimmer switch to soften it.

The room is large with a single wall of floor-to-ceiling shelves lined with books from top to bottom. A few black leather armchairs sit atop a rug of cerulean wool. Accents of cyan are dotted around the place bringing out the hardware of polished chrome. The contemporary look of this house is distinct from the classy Old-World vibe that I've seen in the other O'Neill properties that I've visited around New York. I guess that makes sense seeing as this must be one of their newest acquisitions.

I take a few steps forward and observe the books on display, my gaze strolling around the shelves until I spot the shelf marked *Classics*. After a few minutes spent contemplating the books on offer, I pull out Emily Brontë's only novel, *Wuthering Heights*, one I last read when I was still in high school.

I shift from one foot to another as I open the book and run a thumb over the name before starting to read. As I revel in the glorious melodies that her words create, get to the end of the first page and turn it gently, I pivot slightly and gasp at the sight of a tall, black figure standing near the door. The book falls from my hand as I spin around, clutching my hammering chest as I spot Christian standing just inside the room. His face, grim and focused at first, suddenly opens into a stiff smile as I begin to recover from the shock.

"I'm sorry, Mrs. Wilder," he says dispassionately. "I didn't mean to alarm you. I heard a noise."

"It's okay," I pant, trying to catch my breath. "Please call me Jess," I say as politely as I can, wishing he didn't know my married name.

"Sure. Jess."

"How... how long have you been here?" I ask as my breathing begins to steady.

"Just a couple of seconds," he replies with a smile... though it doesn't seem to reach his eyes.

"Oh."

"You're jumpy," he observes.

"Yeah, sorry, I'm always a bit jumpy when it's still dark out."

"Oh? Afraid of the dark? Or the night, maybe?"

I see that the door behind him is almost completely closed for some reason.

"Um... I guess so." This guy clearly has a penchant for personal questions.

He doesn't move, watching me as I shift awkwardly. "Can I get you anything?" he finally asks, the smile he had now dissipating, leaving behind a keen stare and stiff posture. I notice his right hand form a fist that he swiftly unfurls.

"No, no. I was just gonna read here for a while. I hope that's okay?"

"Of course it is. It's not my house."

"Okay, well, thanks for checking on me."

"You're welcome." He doesn't move. His obscure eyes—all black pupil in the dim light—study me with all the warmth of a vampire bat in a pitch-black cave as I shift nervously at his unmoving stance. I search his pallid face, waiting for him to move or speaking or... *something*. But he doesn't. Ten or so seconds go by to the sound of my heartbeat accelerating in my chest.

Just as I prepare to go back upstairs in the face of him not budging, there is a shuffle outside and I see the door being pushed open. Relief has my body feeling light again as Cameron walks in, barefoot but for blue socks and dressed in black sweatpants and a gray sweater.

"Good morning, sir," Christian says, his face lighting up with a big smile as he steps forward to let Cameron enter properly.

Cameron's eyes shift from Christian to me. "It's *Cameron*, Christian. We're about two years past the *sir* thing. Looking after Jess?"

"I heard a noise," he responds. "Just wanted to check."

"Good. Thank you. I'll be taking care of her from here on in."

"Sure. I'll go check the grounds. Bye, Jess," he says, bowing his head to me politely.

"Bye," I respond, trying to pretend I'm not a little shaken.

We listen to Christian walk through the kitchen, open the door and step outside, the dissipating sound of the crunch of snow under his feet signaling his departure.

"You okay?" Cam asks, walking slowly towards me, his eyes exploring my face.

"Yeah. I can't sleep. I think it was those conversations with your mom. They were kind of... intense. Brought some stuff back up to the surface."

"She has been wanting to talk to you for a long time," he says, glancing down and picking up the book I dropped.

"I know. I'm glad we did," I respond as he hands it to me. "It was just a bit... emotional."

"You need to get this emotion out, Jess. To heal."

"I know."

He takes a step closer to me and I feel my bare nipples harden under my baby-blue pajama top at the sensation of his tall, competent male body encroaching on my personal space. My core aches as he shocks me with the most intense gaze, placing his hands in his pockets as he studies my flushing cheeks.

I glance down without meaning to and spot his indecently large bulge under his gray sweatpants. I guess that answers the morning erection question I had...

"Did you sleep well?" he asks. "You look pale."

I pause for a few moments. "Christian kind of... shook me up a little."

"Oh?"

"He's a bit... intense. Don't you think?"

"Don't worry about him. He's just a little socially awkward. He's always been that way. Once he gets to know you, he'll relax."

"He was just kind of standing there. Not making conversation or anything."

A wry glimmer seeps into his eyes. "He's a security guard, Jessynia. He's not here to debate Kierkegaard."

"Um, don't let him hear you say that!"

He flashes one of those smiles of his that should be illegal, banned by local authorities for being a danger to women's mental health. "I'm just being an asshole. These guards can outwit most people on any given day."

"How long have you known him?" I ask.

"A couple of years." He watches me for what feels like an age. "You don't like him?"

"No, I… I do. He just—"

"Creeped you out?"

I shrug, not wanting to malign a poor man who may just be a bit stiff in public. "You trust him?"

"He protects my mother… and now you. I wouldn't trust him with anything that precious if I didn't."

I sigh. "You're right. I'm sorry. I'm just seeing ghosts around every corner these days."

"Well, once you get used to feeling safe, you won't see ghosts anymore. And Jessynia, I'm going to make sure you are safe. I promise you that."

I nod, smiling at him in gratitude.

"Now get dressed," he orders. "I want to take you somewhere."

"Um, not another boat trip is it?" I ask. "I've decided I'm refusing to put on another life jacket for the next five years."

"No boats involved this time, Avery," he smiles.

15

"I'LL HAVE A COFFEE," says Cameron. "Black. Thank you."

The pretty thirty-something woman serving us at the empty roadside coffee shop christened *Tammy* that we've stopped at on the way to wherever it is Cameron is dragging me to doesn't move, pausing to salivate over his face and body in a manner most reminiscent of a guppy fish if they could go into heat. Phil Collins' *Easy Lover* plays on the radio. Apt.

"And I'll have a matcha soy latte, thanks," I add. "I have my own flask." I glance down at the name Tammy on her blue name tag and back up at the lady who I assume owns this merry establishment. "Um, madam?"

She flicks her suddenly apathetic gaze back down towards me. "Yeah?"

"Um, a matcha soy latte, please." I place my flask onto the sky-blue countertop.

"We don't have soy. We got milk."

Cameron's eyes pan down to me and glimmer in amusement at my unimpressed expression. I've seen it all before when it comes to women making asses of themselves around him but this time my patience seems to be thinner than a slice of flatbread that's been run over by an eight-wheeler.

"Um, do you have almond milk or coconut milk, maybe?"

She does the slow-eyed-blink thing and shakes her head at a speed that would make a sloth look like an ostrich in a sprint.

"Oh, well, then I'll just have a plain green tea. Thanks."

"Sure." She eyes me up and down with borderline contempt before offering Cameron a frankly ridiculous pageant-worthy smile. I mean it's so blatant that she might as well just strip butt naked right there and spread herself over the countertop. It would be just about as subtle.

As madam swivels round and heads off to the machines opposite us to start preparing the drinks, I shift a little in agitation, feeling my cheeks flush hot as I eye the crisp ends of her fried peroxide ponytail and think about how enjoyable it would be to swing her around the parking lot with it.

I tilt my face up towards Cameron's ear and stand on my tiptoes. "Do you think I should tell her what a day in the life of a dairy cow is like?" I whisper.

He pivots slightly so that his gleaming eyes lock with mine, inches away. "I'm not sure you have the most receptive of audiences."

We stand to attention as Tammy returns. She pours his coffee first —of course—and places it on the countertop with an *I'm wet* expression that she catapults at Cameron who watches her, hands in pockets, face unmoved.

My breathing takes off like horses careening out of the gate as I start to wonder how much momentum I would need to generate to get her feet off the ground if I were to swing her around by her ponytail.

He glances down at me again, a smile concealed in his gaze at the green-eyed monster I am failing miserably to conceal.

"That'll be two-fifty, sir," she coos, her carnation-pink lips puckering ludicrously. If I cock my head slightly, she kind of looks like that female Chucky doll when she's in seduction mode.

"I think we're missing a drink," says Cameron coolly.

"Oh, yeah," she replies with a disdainful throwaway glance in my direction.

Cam's eyes meet mine again as I open my mouth in mock-outrage before reaching into my pocket to grab the little coin purse my father's mother gave to me that I stuffed two twenties into before leaving.

He takes it from me. "Avery, you will never be paying for one single thing for as long as you're in my presence."

I stretch my neck upward to impart vital information and he leans down a tad, reading my cue. "How do I leave a negative tip?" I whisper into his ear as I watch her pull a sachet of tea out from a box while thinking that if I ever knowingly flirt with a man who is next to a woman who could be his wife or girlfriend at any time in my life, then I will consider my entire life a colossal fail. "I mean, could she at least *attempt* subtlety?"

He tilts his head, his lips hovering near my ear. "If it makes you feel any better, whenever a man looks at you for more than five seconds, I want to tear his throat out with my teeth."

I blink at him slowly. "Nice visual for 8 a.m."

There's the faintest of smiles on his talented lips as he observes the irritation in my face as madam places a steaming paper cup of green tea on the counter, fastening a white plastic lid to the top.

"I wanted it in the flask," I respond.

"Oh," she says. "Why?"

"Well, you know, the environment." I'm tempted to inform madam proprietor of the sixteen billion disposable coffee cups and lids we use a year, most of which end up in landfills, but decide to refrain from unleashing my inner sanctimonious asshole on her this time.

"So, just pour it in there," she responds. "Knock yourself out."

"Will you be able to reuse the cup or plastic lid on another customer?" I ask.

"No. They're contaminated now. We'll just throw them in the trash."

"So, that kind of defeats the entire purpose of bringing the flask."

"Yeah, I guess it does," she shrugs with a smile that is really just screaming to be pressure-hosed off.

"Can I at least put them in the recycling bin?" I ask.

Oh God, I'm turning into my mother.

"We don't have those," she responds flatly.

"Um, have you thought of maybe setting up just a basic recycling system so you can reduce your environmental footprint a little?" I ask, deciding the sanctimonious asshole can come out just a tad.

"Our environmental *what*?" she yawns, flashing a few amalgam fillings at us in the process.

Most probably sensing that my self-righteous self is now imagining pouring the tea into an entirely different receptacle, Cameron removes the lid and does the pouring into the flask himself before holding out his credit card.

Birdbrain punches a few numbers into a card reader before holding it out for Cameron to pay while demanding he fuck her with her eyes. I am more than used to this type of thing around Cameron, though it's usually at least slightly more subtle than this. This one will go into the *come-hither* hall of fame.

"Thank you. Have a nice day," says Cameron.

"You too, sir," she smiles in a puma-in-estrus kind of way.

"Yes, thanks, Tammy," I say as we turn to leave, drinks in hand. And in an oh-so-classy moment of uncontrolled irrationality, I stop after a few feet, turn around, and with as much sass as I can muster towards someone whose IQ seems to be on par with an aging mollusk, I spout, "Also, just an idea... Some people find it can be quite enjoyable to actually have a soul. Maybe look into that one day. Just a thought..."

With that, I pivot on my heels, loop my arm into Cameron's and sashay out the door.

"Enjoy that?" he grins as we cross the parking lot, handing me back my purse. "You're definitely your parents' kid, my friend."

I groan audibly at the embarrassingly transparent reaction I had in there, burying my face with my free hand. I'm hoping that Cameron thinks I'm more annoyed by her environmental incompetence than her attempts at flirting with him.

"I like it when you're jealous, Avery."

"Excuse me, I'm not—" I stop my protest mid-sentence at the sight of his wry smile. The man knows me way too well for denial. I sigh out in frustration at being caught well and truly red-handed. "Well, let's just say I have newfound respect for Olivia. I'm amazed she wasn't arrested for assault in the time you were together."

"She's not the jealous type."

"Well, she needs to be studied in a lab."

"We didn't have that kind of passion. If it makes you feel any better, I had never experienced jealousy before I met you. Now a man looks at you and I have to restrain myself from ripping his limbs off."

"Well, I suppose that does make me feel slightly better about my desire to go back in, tie her to a chair and pour my green tea down her throat."

"I'm not a teenager, Avery. This stuff used to occasionally do something for me. I'm twenty-eight. To me, this shtick feels cheap and soulless."

I cock an eyebrow at him. "Nice line, O'Neill."

"I barely see women anymore, Jessynia," he says, his voice low, his exquisite lips locating the shell of my ear. "All I see is you."

"Alright, keep talking," I respond as the irritation at the unabashed gal-on-gal sabotage starts to dissipate. I thought the brazenness was bad with Jack, but it seems that with Cameron it is even worse.

In reality, I have no right or business feeling this spike of jealousy piercing me. Cam and I are just friends, or that's what I keep reminding myself anyway.

"Like I said," he continues. "I like it when you're jealous. It *affects* me greatly."

"Oh, well, I'm glad you're getting something out of it at least."

He scans my face, a smile tugging at his lips. I groan inwardly at how visceral my reaction to seeing a woman flirt with Cameron was. I used to take it with a pinch of salt, more often than not finding it quite amusing. Now I want to channel my inner club-bearing cavewoman to mete out justice neanderthal-style....

I guess my body is trying to tell me something that my mind is trying desperately to conceal.

Not to mention that my plan to give off the friend vibe has just failed spectacularly, and in plain view for him to see.

And to top it off, my body is now a live wire of unstable electricity that needs some way to ground itself.

Just wonderful...

Half an hour later, I delight in the ethereal scenery as Cameron drives us through stunning fields of sparkling white topped with a steely-blue layer of icy haze. The sun has finally started to rise, cleansing the air with its silvery rays and turning the clear sky a glorious kaleidoscope of hazy blues and muted golden tones.

I take a sip of my green tea and eye Cameron's cup of coffee languishing in the drinks holder. "You want some coffee?" I ask Cam who drives with a brand of control and concentration that I'll never not be enthralled by. I check out his steady fingers which turn the steering wheel with graceful ease, shifting over the leather sublimely before gripping the firm charcoal-gray tube firmly.

Great.

I'm officially so starved for physical contact after four months without sex that I'm actually getting turned on by a man's hands.

He catches my gaze lingering on his hands. "I'll have some when we get there," he replies, glancing in the rear-view mirror as I have seen him do a dozen times since we left despite the roads being almost completely clear.

"Get where, may I ask?"

He doesn't answer and I take a sip of tea as my eyes wander over to his powerful hands, drooling internally as I witness his competent male body and its various flexing parts.

"Patience, Avery."

You can say that again.

I wonder if he knows that no man has touched me since the day he last ravaged my body in the shower at Redwood.

Fifteen minutes later we park at the bottom of a tree-covered slope and get out. I hand him his cup as we shake off the drive and watch him as he takes a sip, his eyes tracking mine as he does so, his throat contracting, drawing my focus to his neck which my tongue feels so drawn to that it's a miracle it isn't hanging out of my mouth Golden Retriever-style. He places the cup back in the car and zips up his thick winter parka, his neck thankfully now off-limits.

Scanning me over, he says, "You don't need the hat," and pulls my black beanie off my head, throwing it inside the car.

"Excuse me, I can make my own vestimentary choices, sir." I smooth back errant strands of hair that are boycotting my high ponytail as the frigid air around my mouth mists. "It's freezing."

"You'll be hot soon. Don't worry." He eyes me as he says it, always studying, observing the minutest expressions of my face, responding with glimpses of amusement, groans of exasperation or furrows of concern depending on which transparent emotion is registering on my face at the time. Cameron has always been able to read me so well. It drives me nuts sometimes. I wonder whether he can also read how turned on I am to be in his proximity, how clammy my skin gets when my eyes pan down to his light-pink lips, how wet my sex is every time he throws me one of those salacious stares that he does ten times a day.

"I'll let it slide this time," I tease, the jest a ruse designed to cut the tension I feel mounting within me, "but I'll be making my own clothing decisions from now on."

"Hmm, we'll see about that. Follow me."

My boots crunch into packed crystals of pristine snow as I follow his athletic form up a little track leading up a spruce-covered hill.

"This way," Cameron commands a while later as we veer off the path and into the forest.

"Um, shouldn't we stick to the path?"

His firm fingers appear swiftly, curling around my gloved hand, pulling me behind him with a force that I had forgotten he was capable of. The sensation of his strong grip and the powerful kinesis of his body sends a savage shudder through my cells.

"You have trust issues, Avery," he responds, looking back at me.

No kidding.

It's not the steepest of hills, but we nonetheless make our way up tentatively over snow and the occasional patch of ice, stepping over sinewy roots, navigating our way over lumps and bumps in the cold earth. I stumble a couple of times and he catches me instantly, his lips brushing against my cheek in one impromptu rescue maneuver and his hand clasping my waist in another. Both of them leave me jittery inside as I do everything in my power not to make eye contact with him as his robust limbs grasp parts of me to stop me from falling on my ass.

I realize he was right—as usual—about the beanie as the uphill climb has me heating up from the inside like a calzone despite the chill seeping through the air. I unzip my winter coat and take off my gloves, shoving them into my pockets, getting more and more breathless and sweaty as we make it up the hill. Not that I mind a bit of exercise. After the tenebrous energy I've felt assailing my body over the last month, exerting myself by climbing up this forested hill in the early morning light feels invigorating, even if my ankle still twinges when I step onto it too hard.

As we finally make it to the top, Cameron's arm bands around my back and eases me up to the very crest of the summit which overlooks a stunning valley of ivory tones below.

"Wow," I manage breathlessly at the sight of snow-topped trees cascading down the hill joining a gathering of stunning firs cloaked in white in the valley below. The snow is immaculate and glistens like clusters of stars in the rays of the rising sun. "It's so beautiful!" I suddenly realize I haven't been on top of a snowy slope since my skiing accident three years ago. "The light is spectacular," I add, wanting him to know how appreciative I am, and have always been, of the little adventures he has always dragged me on, whether to bear-strewn campsites on breaks from Brown or ice-cold lakes in Pennsylvania.

"Look," he points out as a bald eagle glides over the other side of the valley.

"Oh my God, Cam," I gasp at the magnificent animal soaring with effortless grace over the treetops. The easy way he glides reminds me of the masterful competence Cameron accomplishes any physical task he's faced with.

"And if you look at that tree right there..." he says, crouching down slightly to reduce the nine inches in height difference between us as he points to a tall spruce that juts out above the others to the right of the hill opposite us.

"Oh, I see it!" I exclaim at the sight of a bulbous eagle's nest, a conglomeration of goodness knows how many hundreds of tiny twigs, in which I can just about make out two large birds. "I've never seen an eagle's nest before..." I watch in awe at the sight of these most iconic of birds in their private treetop dwelling.

Out of the corner of my eye, I see him study my profile. "You like it?"

I turn to find his expression so tender that I feel my heart ache at the sight of him. "Yes," I nod, swallowing hard. "It's sensational, Cam. How did you know about this place?"

"I used to climb up here with my father when I was a child," he says.

"Oh, I had no idea."

"After a few years, it became a kind of ritual. Before we had Blackwood, we would drive up here and stay in a hotel in Woodstock for a few nights, but would always climb up here together, just the two of us, every year without fail. I haven't been able to come back here since he passed away..."

"Cam, that's normal," I respond softly taking in his large coppery-brown eyes in the silvery light which bounces off his thick brown hair leaving strands of gold in its wake. The lines of his mesmerizing face are so strong, so genius, as though sculpted by a higher power. They almost distract me from the spectre of grief hanging from him. Seeing his pain makes my heart ache. I wish I could hold him, take away some of the pain of him losing his beloved father. "It's hard to go back to places you visited with someone you have lost," I say.

"Well, I suspected I would be able to come back up here if I was with you," he utters. "I was right."

We don't speak for what feels like an age, partly due to how paralyzed I feel in the spotlight of his steady gaze. Finally, I find my voice. "You never talk about your dad. He was such a great man."

"Yeah, he was something else."

"I wish we hadn't been estranged when he passed away, Cam. I wish I could have helped you through it."

"I know that."

"You can talk about these things, you know? You don't have to keep everything inside."

"I've learned that it's easier that way sometimes," he says.

"I know. But there are hidden costs to doing that."

He raises an eyebrow. "Jessynia, I also feel like you hide things from the world. Painful things."

I drop my gaze only to have my chin lifted by his strong hands. He strokes a cold thumb over the side of my toasty cheek as he holds me.

"I've had a hard time trusting people these last ten years," he continues, his face that particular brand of Cameron-O'Neill-severe that makes your legs almost buckle out from under you. "You are one of the very few exceptions. How about we make a deal? I will trust you enough to open up when I need to... and you do that same?"

I nod. "Sounds like a good deal."

"Good," he says.

I inhale the crisp air deep into my lungs as we lose ourselves in that ethereal space beyond time where I hear no sound but the echoey drumbeat of my heart. Words evade me once again as I am taken hostage by his grace, his poise, his vulnerability and his power.

Sliding his hand to cradle my jaw, he runs his thumb over my lips which part for him, my mouth opening instinctively as he leans his head towards mine.

"Jessynia," he breathes, glaring at my lips for a long moment before leaning in and licking the full length of them with his large, eager tongue.

"Cameron, we..." I try to muster up some feeble verbal resistance but I feel my body pulsate at his yearning and he repeats the gesture with a quiet groan, this time forcing his tongue into my mouth and grasping my ponytail with his hand, pulling it back slightly so that my chin is lifted, easing the invasion of my mouth.

His tongue does the speaking as it dances dominantly against mine, licking, sucking, setting off fireworks in my core that have my limbs feeling like they are barely touching the earth. He tugs my ponytail back so that I have no choice but to welcome his tongue into me, the velvety muscle pressing against mine, encircling, imparting his exquisite breath, owning my mouth with ease, reducing my body to a receptive vehicle.

Stirring seconds pass and he stops, his large hands finding and cupping the round cheeks of my ass to lift me so that I'm straddling him, my legs wrapping around the defined curves of his glutes. He carries me over to the trunk of the evergreen behind us and continues to kiss me, pressing his dense body into me, holding me up so that I'm floating, held in space by him and the tree behind me as his rock-hard bulge rubs against my sex.

Reason miraculously jolting me out of the stupor of desire, I push against his chest very slightly and release myself from the grip of his greedy lust. "Cam, I think we should stop," I finally manage as a frail protest but he doesn't respond, expelling icy mist as he kisses me again with unbridled desperation, my body offering not the slightest bit of resistance, desperate as it is to be ravaged by his.

As I feel him reach down for his belt buckle, I try again to stop the act, knowing that I have to engage my brain at some point whether I want to or not. "Cam, we said we wouldn't do this," I say softly, meeting his hungry gaze. "I'm sorry."

He lets go of his belt, his respiration ragged, scouring my face for a long half-minute as the sun's rays behind brighten, illuminating the day. He lets go of me and gently places me down onto the roots of the tree below me, his panting subsiding.

"I'm sorry for my lack of control, Miss Avery," he finally says, composing himself.

I burst into a warm smile. "That's okay, Mr. O'Neill."

"I can't say that resisting you is something that comes easily to me. In fact, not touching you is bordering on torture at this point."

I know the feeling.

"I shall do my best to restrain myself in the future," he adds.

"Same," I smile.

His gleaming gaze remains for a while before we finally set off back down the hill.

I've managed to hold him off this time, but Lord knows if I will have the strength to do it again...

16

AS WE PULL UP TO BLACKWOOD AN HOUR OR SO LATER, I spot a man in the driveway talking to Aaron, the security guard. He smiles as he watches us approach and walks over to the driver's side as we park and get out.

"Gabriel," says Cameron as they envelop each other in a long hug.

As they pull apart, Gabriel lifts a hand to Cameron's neck. "You're looking better, my friend," he says.

Cameron nods. "This is Jessynia."

Gabriel releases Cameron and turns to face me, eyes warm and bright. "This must be why." He speaks while running his gaze over every inch of my face. In fact, his stare is so intense that I feel myself blushing and shifting from one foot to the other, especially in the light of how breathtaking this man is. "It's so nice to finally meet you, Jessynia. Cameron has told me so much about you."

"Oh, dear. Well, I can probably explain at least fifty percent of it." They both smile. "Though I wish I could say the same thing about you..."

"I haven't been very forthcoming with Jess about all the degenerates that are part of my life," explains Cameron to Gabriel.

"Probably wise," he responds with a sinful grin. "In any case, it's wonderful to finally meet the person my friend has spent the last four years talking about. I was very afraid that this day would never come."

"Oh, well," I stammer, disintegrating under the weight of the handsome Gabriel's penetrating poise. The sight of the two of them next to each other, both peering at me avidly, dizzies me for a moment. They look like brothers or models you'd see on some suggestive billboard poster standing in their underwear on either side of the girl. Gabriel's tan is slightly deeper and he is a couple of inches shorter than Cameron, but still scraping six foot at least, and it's clear from the shape of his arms and shoulders, even under his coat, that he is toned and densely muscular. Quite frankly, my mouth waters at the sight of them, no doubt aided by four months of total sex drought. Man, one day I will learn inscrutable self-possession like other Manhattanites manage, but clearly not today. "I... um... Is anyone up for lunch?" The deflection stumbles from me.

"How about you join us, Gabriel?" suggests Cameron. "My mom has made some food."

"I'd love to."

"So how do you know Cameron?" I ask Gabriel as we tuck into the scrumptious tofu and yam red curry that Valentina has made.

Cameron doesn't take his eyes off my face as we eat, his lips curving between mouthfuls as he watches me attack my food with my usual lion-chomping-on-a-carcass gusto.

Sitting directly opposite me at Val's long kitchen table, Gabriel, dressed in an exquisite dark-blue shirt, finishes a mouthful as his eyes wander over my features, lingering too long at times. He has that same habit as Cameron of watching you with total poise and engrossment as if studying a rare work of fine art. Like Cameron, he's self-possessed and doesn't fidget or try to fill silences, but embraces them as opportunities to study his interlocutor, see what they are made of. I've known men like him before—bold, resolute, deliberate, in total control of themselves. If I hadn't spent all those years interacting with Jack, I may very well have found myself intimidated by him.

It's hard not to lose yourself in his forceful presence and striking beauty. He must be in his late twenties or early thirties at the most, with a mop of wavy dark-brown hair, ever so slightly lighter at the sides, which stops an inch below his jawline. His skin is the color of golden caramel, his eyes dark-brown and almond-shaped, tapering upwards at the outer corner. His face is unshaven with tufts of thick black hair sprouting from his upper lip and jaw.

He leans in ever so slightly as he speaks. "We've known each other all our lives. My father was Cameron's godfather," replies Gabriel to my question. "Luca."

"Oh, I'm so sorry," I respond, understanding from his use of the past tense that his father must now be deceased.

"Thank you. He died the year after Cameron's father died. They were very, very close. And I promised myself that I would try to fill those roles in Cam's life... even if I am only one year older than him."

"One year that he never lets me forget it," adds Cameron with that characteristic blink-and-you've-missed-it wink of his.

"Wow, that's wonderful of you," I respond.

"Well, it's been a joy and a privilege to become Cameron's new *godfather*."

Cameron laughs. "You're not my godfather, asshole."

"Cameron doesn't like the authoritative role I take in our friendship," a smirking Gabriel says to me, "so I like to bust his balls by calling him my godson."

I look at Cameron who smiles and shakes his head. "Don't mind Gabriel," he says. "He's not happy unless he's making me squirm."

"I see," I giggle, taking a sip of sparkling water.

"In truth," says Gabriel softly. "Cameron is my closest friend."

"That's because I'm the only person who can tolerate you for more than an hour at a time, Gabriel."

"Very true," Gabriel responds, eyes gleaming in amusement. "But really"—he fixes me with an implacable stare—"us getting so close over the last couple of years is the only good thing that has come from our fathers dying. He's family to me."

"And you are family to us, Gabriel," responds Val, sitting at the head of the table. "You always have been."

"You've had a tough year, Jessynia," Gabriel says to me, eyes sharp. "Your separation from Jack. Alexandra Frost..."

"Gabriel!" barks Cameron as Val swats him with her napkin.

I bristle at the uninvited observation. "Cameron told you about it?" I ask, my voice wavering like a flickering candle.

"Yes."

"Gabriel, how about we go gentle on this girl," says Cameron roughly. "I wouldn't want you to end up needing medical attention today."

"I'm sorry to be so blunt, Jessynia. We will only have a couple of days together and I want to understand you so that I can better protect both of you. There are many of us who work tirelessly behind the scenes to stop this group. I need to know where you are in the healing process. I need to know how attached you still are to your estranged husband. I need to know where your allegiances lie, for our sake, for Cameron's, and for yours."

Cameron breathes out as if in irritation at Gabriel's stun-gun style of conversing. I don't answer him, trying to control my breathing in the face of this brazen man and his irritating questions about the most intimate and painful parts of my life.

"Maybe you prefer I not speak my mind?" Gabriel questions, raising his brows.

"No. It's not that," I counter. "It's just we've only just met, Gabriel. I mean, I prefer... you, know... just a bit of foreplay before we go deep."

Val breaks into a gentle roll of laughter as Gabriel responds to my playful rebuff with a stroke of his chin below a broad smile, his shrewd gaze wandering to my lips.

"I like your spirit, Jessynia. It will serve you well as you navigate this next phase of your life."

I sense a firestorm brewing inside me at the arrogance of this near-stranger who seems to take such pleasure in picking apart my life and dishing out unsolicited advice. Cameron can read me well. His eyes flit between me and Gabriel, his steady posture staying the mounting tension.

"I'm not sure how much I like being unwillingly psychoanalyzed over lunch, Gabriel," I respond.

"Well, that is my job, unfortunately."

"Jessie, Gabriel is a clinical psychologist, psychoanalyst and in the end stages of becoming a forensic psychologist," explains Val. "He is one of the most renowned psychoanalysts in the country, even at his young age. He has some very avant-garde theories in his field."

Oh, Lord.

"Well, forgive me if I'm being rude," I say, irritation brewing, my voice sharpening and glare hardening, "but you're not, by any chance, one of those really overbearing ones that subject the unfortunates around them to public psychoanalysis without their consent, are you?"

Gabriel bursts into deep, unabashed throaty laughter as Cameron conceals a smile by tucking his chin before looking back up at the scene.

"Give it to him, Jess," whispers Val, her demeanor impish as she finishes off the creamy crimson sauce at the bottom of her bowl.

"Well," Gabriel responds, regaining his composure. "Under normal circumstances, I do restrain myself, believe it or not. But seeing as the time we have together is so short and the stakes are now so high, I have no choice but to be an *overbearing* prick for a few days."

My sigh turns into a smile at his good-natured absorption of my jab, a smile reciprocated by him as we reach a tentative entente cordial, meaning I don't have to subject a person very dear to Cameron to one of my colorful tongue-lashings.

The momentary comic relief gives way to a sense of unease as his words begin to imprint themselves on me. "What *stakes* do you mean, Gabriel?" I ask.

He mulls over the question as I finish my curry. "I mean that the Society is getting powerful, much more powerful than we could have ever predicted. And this coming year will be a decisive one. If we stand down now, we may not ever be able to challenge their power again. But if we stand up, fight, make hard decisions, we should have enough evidence and momentum to take them out once and for all, like we should have done years ago before they became as formidable as they are now."

"What do they want?" I ask as Valentina takes Cameron's empty bowl and hers and places them in the sink before returning to her seat.

"They want *power*. They want influence. They want control. They want to play games. To them moving chess pieces around so that people's lives implode is all in a day's *entertainment*. These people are vampires. There are no morals, no ethics. They have no souls and survive by feeding on other people's. They cause suffering for the sheer thrill of it."

An eerie shiver makes its way down my spine as his words linger in the air around us. "It's Gravier that runs the show, isn't it?" I ask.

"Jessynia," interrupts Cameron sternly. "I think that's enough questions for today."

"She has to know what she's dealing with, Cameron," retorts Gabriel.

"She knows enough! There's a limit to how much a human can be put through in one year."

"If we are serious about finally trying to take this group down, then the people involved have to know everything."

"He's right, sweetheart," adds Valentina, placing a delicate hand onto Cam's dense forearm as he bows his head and takes a deep breath to calm himself down.

"Is he really as evil as people say he is?" I ask. "Gravier, I mean."

"Yes. He is human in outwards appearances only. Do you know much about his life?"

"I don't know anything. I only know that he is friends with... some people I try my best to forget. I've only had a couple of brief and unsettling encounters with him at social functions."

"Jack never spoke to you about him?"

"No, other than to ban me from ever talking to him."

"Sebastian is what a psychiatrist would call a psychopath. Although I'm not entirely sure that that word goes far enough if I'm being honest.

He suffered severe abuse as a child. Emotional and psychological abuse —abuse that is just as dangerous and damaging as any other in my experience.

"His parents were from Eastern Europe, the late communist era. Not the most empathetic of societies at *that* time, one might say. They moved to a suburb of Chicago when he was about three. From what we know from multiple sources, his mother was a case study in sociopathy —domineering, demeaning, totally devoid of empathy. She belittled him, criticized him constantly, gaslit him, obsessed over his appearance to the point that she erased his personality, his needs, his desires, and turned him into some living mannequin, a walking representation of her, something purely to impress others with. His soul, his spirit, his personality, his needs, they were irrelevant to her as long as he looked like the respectable little boy. He spent his life walking on eggshells, afraid of his own shadow, constantly afraid that he would do something to set off his mother's rage—even the littlest of things that all children do like... humming, dancing, singing, just being a dumb kid. Every part of him was picked apart relentlessly. Textbook narcissistic abuse. He spent his childhood afraid, being hurt, abused, insulted, accused of crimes which were in reality him just being a child... until one day he snapped."

"What happened?" I ask, glancing at Cameron whose eyes burn amber, never leaving my face.

"He was thirteen when it happened," replies Gabriel.

"What happened?" I ask as Val gets up to the sound of the whistle of a kettle.

"From what I've gathered from the case file, she had spent a week alternating between screaming at him for his supposed crimes and ghosting him for them, refusing to talk or acknowledge his existence. He was timid back then, submissive. He tried to keep her happy. On the last day, she was screaming at him for doing another thing wrong and he pushed her back. She attacked him as she had done many times before and he punched her. And then again, and again, and again... and at some point, he grabbed hold of a rosewood sculpture from a table nearby..."

My hands clasp my cheeks as the image of that young boy permeates my flesh like damp on a winter's day.

"They found her with her face caved in," he continues, rubbing one tanned hand with the other. "There was blood everywhere. He was found sitting next to her body, covered it in. Rocking backwards and forwards. Crying."

"Jesus," I breathe. "Didn't his father do anything to stop it?"

"His father died when he was ten years old. Not that he would have got his son out of there. He was the archetypal flying monkey, submissive to his wife, desperate for her approval. He also had a sadistic streak himself, possibly from his own childhood abuse. From what we gather, he did nothing to protect his boy when he was alive."

"God," I utter quietly. "So, what happened after that?"

"He was given eight years in a young offender's institute, was tried as a child in a display of mercy from Cook County's then-State's attorney. When he came out, he was... *gone*. His soul was fractured. He had disconnected from whatever humanity was left that she hadn't berated out of him over the years."

"Why don't we know about this?!" I ask. "You would have thought it would have gotten out in a place like Manhattan."

"He changed his name when he got out. His real name is Stefan Koval."

"And he chose Sebastian Gravier? It's a pretty ominous choice of name..."

Gabriel smiles for a split-second before a cloud darkens the strong lines of his face. "Subtlety is not his cup of tea. When his father died, he left him a large trust fund that he couldn't access until he was twenty-one. When he got out, he used that to erase his past, make sure no one knew who he really was."

"How do *you* know?"

"There are people who have gotten away from them. People who frequented Q.N. when it was more just a place for libertines to... *express themselves*, before Gravier took hold of the Council and their tactics become so extreme. We have learned a lot from them. Or rather those brave enough to speak out. You'll meet a couple of them tonight."

"No," responds Cameron firmly. "She will not be attending the meeting."

"I want to come," I retort, daring him with my glare.

"I said *no*. It is not negotiable, Jessynia."

"She's involved, sweetheart," says Val, bringing a pot of tea over to the kitchen table. "That's not something that we can change. And they haven't forgotten her. She needs to know what she's dealing with."

"I said *no*. I'm protecting her now. The less she knows, the safer she will be. She is not coming. The decision is final."

17

MY FEET DRUM THE FLOOR, the perfect percussion to the frenetic tapping of my fingertips on my laptop keyboard, as I write a post for my blog using the content that didn't make it into the article that was commissioned last month.

I'm trying my best to concentrate, but in truth, writing is a futile effort to distract myself from the meeting going on a few houses down.

I look at the view count of my blog—over eleven thousand unique visits yesterday alone. I know that's small—nay, tiny—beans compared to the big news sites, but I can't help feeling proud that my articles are resonating with more and more people. I should be ecstatic about it, but I'm still irked that my thirty minutes of protests with Cameron this afternoon about wanting to attend the meeting fell on deaf ears. I can't bear the feeling of being locked away in some ivory tower for my own protection. It reminds me of the shroud of ignorance that concealed Jack's affairs.

I click on a tab I had opened earlier—a search for Sebastian Gravier. Little shows up beyond the shiny façade of his professional achievements, which no doubt were built on his father's fortune and left a trail of devastation in their wake that has been omitted from the dazzling descriptions of his professional accomplishments. There are a few images of him—his face is rugged and masculine, the angles sharp and strong with large, icy gray eyes framed by cool natural-blond hair, slightly darker at the roots. He is utterly and completely breathtaking, a fact that makes his malice all the more unsettling.

"This is ridiculous," I mutter, finding my playlist and stopping the rousing Tina Turner track that usually fills me with buoyant energy. "He's treating me like a child."

I sigh. I do appreciate Cameron's protective instincts, but I've been in the dark about so much for so long that the darkness now feels like it's contaminating me, as if gray spores of dirt and dust are seeping into my lungs. It feels like the walls of some dank, somber cell closing in on me, inching ever closer until I have no room to move or breathe. The need to knock the walls of that cell down and have light flood into me has never been so acute, even if that means my hands will be left broken and bloody from pulling down the bricks.

Not to mention that the more in the dark I am about these people, the more likely I am to fall victim to some Machiavellian nightmare involving the likes of Ilya Markov.

I look down at the bottom-right corner of my screen.

9.33 p.m.

It's too late to call Maddie. She'll probably be in bed already. It's Saturday night so Stella will almost certainly have company and Kev will be with his family in Trenton, a small primarily working-class New Jersey town which he returns to most fleetingly every Christmas. Not that it isn't lovely. It's just that with his natural flamboyance and effervescent personality, he never felt that he quite fit in.

Deciding against calling my parents, I burst to my feet and head to the window, looking out at the rooftop of the house I believe Cameron is in.

"This is *ridiculous*," I mutter again.

All he's doing is leaving me more ignorant and vulnerable. How can I possibly defend myself if I have no clue who these people are or what they want?

I'm tempted to just go over there and knock on the door. I mean, it's not like I'm not involved at this point. And I've never really been the type to follow orders. Plus, Gabriel and Valentina clearly wanted me there. It's Cameron who is the sole roadblock in all this. I shudder as I picture his severe face earlier this afternoon when he reiterated his ban on me attending in the most uncertain terms.

God, he'll go nuts if I go.

As I turn around, my eyes widen as I spot something that wasn't there earlier this evening.

A note, pushed under the door.

I walk over to it, assuming it's a peace offering from Cameron.

I unfold it to read:

PLEASE JOIN US.

I stare at it in confusion. It isn't Cameron's handwriting. I know his distinct script by heart, just as I do Jack's or my parents'. This doesn't have the slants and curves of Cameron's elegant letters.

I tentatively open the door, looking to see if anyone is there.

No one.

Who would have left it? A security guy maybe... sent by someone else.

It definitely isn't Val's delicate writing.

Gabriel, perhaps.

But would he defy Cameron's wishes so brazenly?

Maybe it's someone I haven't even met yet...

I crumple the note up and put it in my bag so that Cameron doesn't see it at some point. Heading over to the window, I watch as bright flecks of snow dust the rooftops that peak out over tops of tall trees.

I want to go.

If they hadn't pulled their stunt with Ilya, I would have dropped the subject, happy not to be involved. But I can't sit back oblivious as people plot to hurt me like that. Plus, I want to know what Jack is mixed up in. I know I shouldn't care at this point, but I have to at least know if he's in some kind of danger.

Turning around, I pull my pajamas off and change into thick black leggings and a black cold-shoulder crocheted sweater.

Well, I think he's figured out by now that I'm not exactly the submissive type, I decide, connecting to my inner rebel, channeling her zeal as I grab my keys, lock the door behind me and tiptoe downstairs, walking down the hallway, through the dark, empty kitchen and into the mudroom where I grab my winter coat and shove my feet into my walking boots without bothering to tie them up.

The sound of light banter from two security guards outside has my heart hammering as I prepare to open the kitchen door and slip out. I don't want them seeing me. They no doubt have instructions from Cameron to keep me inside my beautiful cage.

I glance out of the window to my right and watch them—ones I've only seen in passing while walking back from Val's with Cameron—at the front of the house. They shouldn't be able to spot me as I slip out of the side door and head to the back of the house.

Okay, Jess, let's do this.

Just as I prepare to turn the door handle, I hear their voices get louder and realize that they are making their way towards the kitchen door.

Fuck!

Heart pounding furiously, I dart out of the mudroom, panicking as I realize that the kitchen is too long for me to make it out of without them seeing me first. I skirt to the right into the pantry, trying to steady my breathing as I push the pantry door closed and hide behind it as the two men enter the room, switching on the kitchen light as they do so.

"I'm gonna take a leak," says one to the dull clomp of footsteps leading out of the room.

I hear the other open the fridge and then pour something into a glass by the sounds of it, burping as he finishes and then rinsing the glass from what I can make out. There's a clink and some shuffling and I raise a jittery hand over my mouth to stop any sounds escaping my chest at the tread of slow, heavy footsteps in the direction of the pantry.

God, please tell me he doesn't want something from in here.

I hold my breath for thirty interminable seconds until I hear the other one return.

"I checked upstairs. All quiet. She must be asleep."

"Think she wants some company?"

"Sure. If you want O'Neill to rip your fucking throat out."

There's a chuckle and the light goes off as footsteps lead to the kitchen door which they open and close behind them.

I tiptoe out of the pantry and watch as the men amble around the front of the house. Deciding it's too risky to try the kitchen door again, I head through the kitchen, down the hall and into the unlit dining room to the right at the back of the house. I make my way to the window which I unlock and push open, climbing onto the window ledge as I prepare to ease myself onto the floor below. The ledge is about three feet off the ground and as I drop down and land on the snow below, a sharp twinge stabs at my ankle.

Fuck, Jess. What are we doing here?

My internal wisdom is clearly more aware than I am about the ample signs the universe is giving me that I should abort this mission.

Oh, well...

I pull the bottom of the window towards me, hopefully just enough that the security guys don't notice it's open if they patrol the full perimeter of the house. Reassured by whispers of conversation floating across from the other side of the property, I step onto the snow, hoping that the snow flecks dancing toward the ground like fairy dust will cover any dents I make.

I walk a few feet and enter the woods behind the house which I will use as camouflage, except without a flashlight or the light of my phone, I can barely see where I'm walking. The ground is lit up just the faintest amount by the floodlights around the house and I walk gently and with the utmost care, afraid to trip and twist my ankle.

I clear Blackwood and then the house next door which lies even further away from the edge of the woods. As I take another step, a lightning crackle of snapping twigs rebounds through the air, stopping me in my tracks as I spin round to see where it came from. The floodlights barely touch this area of the woods and I can just about see two feet in front of my face.

I turn and look down to see where my feet are, pan up and gasp at the silhouette of an immobile, expressionless man ten feet before me.

"Good evening, Jessynia."

"Ch... Christian?" I whisper, my voice trembling as I try to match the face to the voice I heard.

Oh God, not this guy.

"Yes."

"You scared me."

He still does.

"It's late for a walk in the woods, Jessynia." I can just about make out the lines of his face enough to see that his glare is unflinching and this time, there is not a hint of a smile on display.

"I... I couldn't sleep."

"I would much prefer that you called me to take you for a walk. I'm not sure that Mr. O'Neill would be impressed to find you walking around the compound at night. You never know who could be watching..."

Insidious cold creeps down my spine at the severity of his words and his unyielding posture. "Well, I—" I start.

"You want to attend the meeting."

"How... How did you know?"

"Well, the walk through the woods at night is not something I see women do alone very often."

"I guess that's not an option now?"

He doesn't speak as I stare into obsidian discs in the tiniest of light. I know Cameron said Christian was socially awkward, but surely even he must be able to see that just staring at someone like that without speaking is intimidating?

"I don't see why not."

"Will you get into trouble?" I ask.

"It's not my shift. I'm supposed to be sleeping. I just fancied a walk."

"What about the other guys?"

"The ones guarding Blackwood are just reserves. They don't work for the families. The ones guarding this house are the big guns. They've been with the families for a decade. I'm sure they'll be forgiven for this slip-up."

"Okay. Well, thank you. I would be very grateful."

"Good."

We walk in slow and painfully awkward silence towards the third house with Christian leading me towards the very periphery of the woods.

"Here it is," he whispers, turning to face me, his expression austere.

"Oh, isn't it the next one? I thought it was four houses down."

"No, Jessynia. It is this one."

"Okay."

"Here is the key," he says, reaching into his pocket and bringing a single key out. "They're meeting in the basement. You unlock the door then place it under the mat outside. See it?"

"Yes."

"I'll pick it back up once you're inside. Then take off your shoes and coat and make your way through the kitchen, take the first door to the left, go down the stairs and the meeting will be taking place in a large room. You'll hear voices. Just follow those."

"Okay. Thank you, Christian. I really appreciate it."

"And I would appreciate it if no one knew I had helped you, including Cameron. Can you do that for me?"

"Of course. I won't tell him, or anyone."

"Enjoy your meeting."

I swallow hard. "Yeah. I'll try."

As I take a single step out of the shadow of the forest, a thought hits me and I turn around. "Christian, did you leave me a note tonight?" I whisper. "Under my door?"

He doesn't speak for a while, his lifeless eyes watching me, expressionless. Finally, he responds. "No."

"Okay. Thanks," I reply, turning round to carefully make my way over the patch of earth between the woods and the house, up two steps sprinkled with salt and sand, and to the heavy, royal-blue door which I open as gently as I can.

"Just me," I hear Christian say nearby, presumably to the guards come to investigate the noise at the back of the house. "I fancied a walk."

As his voice trails off, I swiftly take off my coat and shoes, hanging the coat on a brushed brass hook.

Trepidation saps strength from my limbs as I make my way through the large kitchen, open the door to its left and head down the stairs to the murmur of voices below. The hallway at the bottom of the stairs is carpeted and dimly lit and at the end, I see the door, four-fifths closed with light emanating from it.

I creep closer, hugging the wall before tucking myself into the corner a few feet away from the doorway. In the throes of my headstrong indignation back at Blackwood, I had planned to march up here with conviction, fling open the door and demand that I be allowed to participate, but now that I am here, the fear I feel is so acute that all I want to do is run back upstairs and get my sorry ass out of here.

"How close is he to agreeing?" asks a voice—male, soft, slightly muffled by the wall and almost-closed door between us and bearing the slightest of rasps that come when one is in middle age. I recognize it instantly as being the voice of Silas, the man I met yesterday morning at Cam's place.

"He won't do it alone," replies a woman, her voice sharp, clear as crystal, the vaguest hint of a Scottish accent hidden within. "He'll do it if we can get the numbers together."

"We would need five men at the very minimum to make any kind of impact." This time I recognize Gabriel's deep rasp.

"Well," replies the same female voice. "We have David, Lee, Andrew, Rohan and Cameron."

"Cameron hasn't given a firm yes yet, Francis," retorts Charles, his cavernous voice distinct despite the distance between us.

"Where are you in the process, Cameron?" asks the woman.

"I'm still coming to terms with it, Francis. You'll have to give me a couple more months."

"Cameron, you know you would have the right to anonymity as a victim of a sex crime... What's holding you back?"

There's silence but for the clunk of a glass on a table before he begins to speak. "Many things, Francis. Shame. Guilt. Some twisted sense of loyalty to that woman. And... fear. It's not just about me anymore. If it were, I wouldn't have to think this hard. I have someone else to think about now. Someone whose life I could endanger by speaking out. Someone who means more to me than anything on this Earth."

"Jessynia is already in danger just by being the woman you love," responds a new voice—male, bold, resonant, with no pipes or whistles in his sound, suggesting he is in his thirties.

"And that Jack still loves, lest we forget." Gabriel's voice. "That puts a target on her back every day. To get that target off her, we need to take these people down."

"And if the D.A. doesn't take it seriously?" replies Cameron. "This is statutory rape against hormonally challenged *pubescent* boys who were not exactly fighting her off at the time. This type of crime is not exactly on the D.A.'s list of top priorities in New York City. What if they decide not to press charges? What if Gravier decides to avenge his friends for their public humiliation?"

"The D.A. is the one office they haven't managed to infiltrate... *yet*," responds a new female voice, low-pitched and as smooth as single-malt scotch poured over ice with an expensive Upper East Side accent. "And these savages are working on it. It's only a matter of time. We have to act now before they do."

"That's easy to say, Beth," responds Charles. "If the D.A. doesn't take this seriously, then Cameron will have a target the size of the Hoover Dam on his back, and I'm not sure even we with our combined forces could protect him... or those he loves."

"Well, we have some women who are ready to come forward about Vallen," adds a third female voice with the strength, depth and flow of someone in her early forties, "with a whole host of unpalatable accusations—underage sex, coercion, theft, fraud. The women are afraid, but they are getting there. Living in fear is starting to get to most of them anyway. If we can unite voices, have the men and women come forward in one fell swoop, then the pressure on the D.A. would multiply exponentially. Both Markov and Frost have enough dirt on Steven Frost to put him away for a long time for securities and wire fraud among a host of other things. He's notoriously paranoid. If he senses the D.A. sniffing at a plea deal for either of them, that will stop all involvement with Q.N. and it should keep him behaving himself for a few years."

"And what about Gravier?" asks Charles somberly. "He is the head of the snake. If we don't cut it off, this plan won't work."

"He's been more careful to cover his tracks," responds Gabriel. "And about respecting the age of consent. But if Alex and Vallen really think they are going down for a long time, they may decide to take Gravier down with them, throw him under the bus if they can get a deal out of the D.A."

"Would they really do that to a friend of theirs?" asks Valentina.

"They aren't friends," replies Gabriel. "They're tied together through their misdeeds. I doubt they even like each other."

"I agree," adds Silas. "The hardcore members are still there, many out of fear of their missteps being exposed... and of Gravier's wrath if they were to leave, but the old-school ones like me who remember how things used to be have left in droves—or are trying to. I suspect many of the law-abiding ones would queue up to tell their stories if it meant taking Gravier down. And in my opinion, the not so law-abiding ones are not far behind."

"And you would take that risk by speaking up, Silas?" asks Charles.

"Yes, though I would prefer not to be alone when doing it."

"Do you think we could get Jack?" This time I recognize Valentina, her voice soft as a spring zephyr, a welcome relief to this heavy conversation. "If we could get him to report Alex for statutory rape along with Cameron, then that would open the floodgates for these other young men who don't have their power."

"From what we know, Jack is as involved with these people as ever," replies Charles. "He's there every week."

The thought makes my stomach sink to the floor.

"But all our sources confirm that he's starting to fall foul of Sebastian," adds the first sharp female voice, belonging to Francis, I believe. "He's been too vocal in questioning his methods and intimidation tactics and need for control. If Sebastian starts a war on Jack, going to the D.A. may be his best line of defense."

"Yes, and Jack was fifteen, possibly fourteen when she seduced him," adds Gabriel. A current of rage cascades through me. "If Jack turns on them and comes forward with Cameron, the two most high-profile men of the lot, then it will be like a house of cards."

"Perhaps Jessynia could work on him," suggests Silas.

"No," responds Cameron firmly. "She is not going to be involved in this."

I take a deep, trembling breath and force my legs to tread the few steps to the doorway. With a silent prayer for strength, I push open the door.

"I'm already involved," I say to announce my arrival.

18

CAMERON VAULTS TO HIS FEET, dangerous and volatile. "Jessynia!" His voice is the low growl of a brooding animal. "How did you—?"

"I'm sorry. I don't mean to interrupt, but I feel very strongly that I should be part of this."

I scan the faces of the people around the room. Gabriel gifts me a smile of approval at my presence. Charles's eyes shift between me and Cameron. Val smiles at me with her usual warmth and scoots over to her right to make space on the loveseat she is occupying.

The others eye me with interest, their faces welcoming, curious, gracious, but for one blond-haired man who observes me coldly.

"How did you get past the guards?" asks a glaring Cameron.

"It wasn't their fault," I respond in a snap. "I went into full-on stealth mode. I was going at one foot a minute to make sure I wasn't spotted."

I detect an amused smile on the faces of Gabriel, Silas and Valentina, in stark contrast to Cameron's simmering frustration.

A woman, early forties I would guess, with auburn hair with golden highlights around the front and the most striking of bright blue eyes gets to her feet, sidestepping a long ottoman adorned with trays bearing drinks and snacks in order to take a few steps towards me. She holds her hand outstretched to shake mine. "It's a great pleasure to meet you, Jessynia. My name is Frances Ingraham." She's wearing a long-sleeved mauve kaftan with gold embroidery snaking around the neck and down the center to the hem.

I stretch out my hand to hers. "Same to you, Francis."

"Cameron," Francis says, turning to face him. "There comes a point where Jessynia being in the dark becomes just as dangerous to her as coming into the light. I think we've reached that point."

"I agree, sweetheart," adds Valentina, looking up at her incensed son.

"Same," adds Gabriel, patting Cameron on the arm. He is sitting on a sofa to Cameron's right next to a beautiful heavily made-up woman with thick blond hair stopping an inch above her shoulders.

A few more words of agreement float around the room as I look into Cameron's irate face, swallowing hard, trying to silently communicate to him that I didn't take this decision lightly, but that being uninformed now feels like the darkest of prisons for my soul.

His face softens slightly as he observes my taciturn contrition. "Very well," he utters stiffly. "But if there is something that I decide you can't listen to, then you will have to leave. I won't have you learning things that will cause you unnecessary pain. Is that agreed?"

"Agreed," I nod.

As Cameron sits down as if against his own will, Silas stands up from an obsidian armchair. He's wearing an ornately woven slate-blue tunic with five buttons running down from the center of the mandarin collar. "It's great to see you here, Jessynia," he says, his hand squeezing mine firmly, his kind face lit up with the warmest of smiles.

"Thank you," I respond.

The blond next to Gabriel gets up and greets me. "Beth," she says, her voice deep, bold and assertive, matching the striking orange bodysuit and tight black pants that put her stunning body on sublime display. Her face is oval with a strong nose and the most striking of jade-green eyes. Her skin is flawlessly smooth, her lips lush, her gaze unflinching.

"Nice to meet you, Beth."

"Jess, come sit down," beckons Val, patting the empty spot adjacent to her on the brown loveseat. I skirt the table and sit down next to her, relieved to be in her comforting presence. "Jess, you know Charles," she says, putting her hand onto mine.

"Of course. Hi, Charles." He nods with a smile.

My eyes pan around the room to meet a slim but muscular lady with very short and tight black curls framing a beautiful round face, her skin a luminous chocolate brown. Her legs are crossed under a shimmery violet A-line skirt below a fitted black top and gold necklace in the shape of a serpent. She must be in her early forties at the most, with a poise and elegance that stun me.

"Remi," she says, her rich voice radiant. "It's an honor to finally meet you."

"Thank you."

"And finally, this is Nathan," says Francis about the man sitting opposite me at the very end of the semi-circle.

"Nice to meet you," I say to the handsome man, early thirties at the most, with hazel eyes, wavy dark-blond hair and stubble darkening his jaw.

"Likewise," he says, his glare icy, his tone flat. "I've heard a lot about you."

I swallow hard at the revelation in the silent moments before Francis speaks. "Are you enjoying your time here, Jessynia?"

"Yes, thank you. This area is just breathtaking."

"Indeed."

I glance around the room. I've never seen a basement like this before. It's elegant but entirely futuristic. The walls are matte tiles of various tones of gray. A beautiful, tasteful oil painting of a nude couple in the throes of passion—their most intimate body parts hidden in shadow—dominates the wall opposite me. The ceiling is a stark white dotted with soft spotlights with paneling of dark wood around its edges. The furniture is dark, modern and expensive with sleek angles and accents of glass and steel. I spot a wine rack behind a small bar on the other side of the immense room.

Panning back to the people peering at me at this late hour, I decide to spare them having to make the obligatory small talk and instead, go straight for the jugular.

"I really didn't mean to eavesdrop," I say as I look around the room. "It's not something I like to do. I meant to just march straight down here and knock on the door. I guess I lost my nerve." I inhale deeply. "I heard what you were saying about Alex and Vallen. About the... statutory rape case. I know I don't know as much about all this as you, but for what it's worth, I want you to know that I support that action one hundred percent and I will support anyone who is brave enough to do that."

I don't dare look at Cameron but instead glance at Gabriel who conveys his approval of my statement with a nod of his head and a smile.

"It's not as simple as that, Jess," replies Charles. "If things go wrong and the D.A. doesn't press charges or the Society intimidate some of the men and women into retracting their statements—and they *will* try to do that—then the remaining victims will be left hung out to dry, exposed and vulnerable. We need a united front. We need a plan in place. We need protection."

"Yes," I nod. "But to get into this house, I had to basically recreate that rappelling scene from *Mission Impossible.* I dodged five guards to walk three houses down. You already need protection. And from the little I've heard, it is only getting worse. I know I don't know as much about this situation as you, but this may be the last chance to do something to stop them."

"Unfortunately, only the victims can make that decision," says the blond Beth in the clementine top. "We can't make it for them. And they have valid reasons to fear for their safety if they do come forward."

I take a deep breath, my mouth so dry it's a miracle I can converse at all. "I don't know if Cameron told you, but I'm... a journalist," I say, trying to finally own that word. "I know a lot of journalists and editors at this point. I also have a website, which I'm trying to turn into a news aggregator. I'm getting more and more visitors every day. I could maybe help bring this story to life. Plus, I'm friends with some journalists who would jump at the chance of covering the story. Maybe bringing the story into the light will provide protection."

"Jesus, Jessynia. You live in some fantasy world," sneers Cameron, fire burning in his voice.

A ghostly shiver floats through my flesh as he repeats the exact words Jack said to me four months ago after he cornered me on the subway. "No," I respond calmly. "I just see things with different eyes. I haven't been around these people for as long as you, so I see light and possibility and hope where you see none."

That goddamn moody glare of his that he casts in my direction makes me want to sink into the chair. "Do you have *any* idea what they would do to you, or your loved ones if they couldn't get to you, if they—"

"That's enough, young man," interrupts Silas. "We're here to put cards on the table. No idea is off-limits."

"I will not allow her to put herself in any more danger," responds Cameron stiffly. "Over my *dead* body will she do that."

Don't say that, Cameron.

The room is silent for a few moments before Silas starts to speak, his gentle but confident aura so reassuring. "We have talked over the idea of going public. It is a good idea and something that we have been considering ourselves for after a complaint is made with the D.A. But we have some contacts in the media and we can get the story out ourselves if we decide to do that. The risk if you were to get involved would be too great, Jessynia."

"Agreed," adds Francis. "Your involvement should be limited to the bare minimum."

I nod, though deep down, I'm not sure that *I* agree. "It seems like it's Gravier who has made the place as dangerous as it is," I say.

"Yes," replies Silas. "He has turned the Society from... an *alternative* social group into something akin to a horror movie. I should know. I used to serve on the Council."

My eyes widen in surprise. "You did?"

"Yes. Remi too, if you don't mind me saying, Remi?"

"Of course not," she responds. "This was ten or so years ago. It was a time when people came just to experience the kind of pleasure they couldn't get elsewhere. The place wasn't like Fort Knox back then. And there were no *non-consensual* areas, nor people being followed, threatened and blackmailed. There were no *paid* patrons. It was just a group of open-minded libertines who wanted to enjoy each other within a structure that they could not really get in the outside world."

"There was a time when it was all about pleasure," adds Silas. "Now it is about terror. The more casual of patrons are fleeing. Sebastian is distilling the types of people that frequent the place into those of a more extreme disposition. We call Quercus Velutina Q.N. because its founding name was Quercus Nigrum. In the nineteenth century, it had become a perverse and dangerous place. They stopped at nothing to procure pleasure for their most powerful patrons. People ended up maimed, imprisoned, murdered." I rub one hand against the other to soothe my fraying nerves. "After a series of unfortunate incidents that led to the police getting involved, a group of more moderate patrons fought to overthrow the heads of council. They called themselves Quercus Alba."

"White oak." The words float from me without thought.

Silas nods.

"And did they overthrow them?" I ask.

"Yes. They did. The name was changed to Quercus Velutina to cleanse the energy of that dark time. Both phrases mean Black Oak. They kept the abbreviation Q.N. to provide some distance and some plausible deniability if those initials were found on the Society's documents, but mainly it was to remind patrons of what can happen when the wrong people get into power. Make no mistake, that *has* now happened. Sebastian would happily turn the place into the dangerous hell it had once become. He has to be stopped."

"How did he get so much power?" I ask.

"When Sebastian became a member, he was taken under the wing of the then-president, David," says Silas. "He was a wonderful man. Open, caring. His vision was in line with the forefathers—to create a place where people could come together without judgment, without being shamed, without fear of repercussions in their normal life. But

Sebastian had a different vision, and little by little, once he made Council, he pushed for changes that transformed the whole feel of the place."

"He was the one that pushed for the security cameras," takes over Remi, her gorgeous doe eyes sharp on my face. "The holding rooms, the security guards, the insane membership fees. David was an empath, able to feel compassion for the cruelest of people. He had not studied the pathology of the likes of Gravier. Had no idea that showing compassion to sociopaths and narcissists is like giving them carte blanche to destroy people's lives."

"By the time David had come to realize that Sebastian was dangerous, he had collected a little handful of flying monkeys, enough to swing the vote in his favor during Council meetings." Silas' voice is somber, with the tiniest hint of anger roughening his words. "About five years ago, Sebastian led a coup to oust the man who had taken him under his wing. He managed to persuade enough people that David was weak and putting the survival of the Society in danger with his naivety. Nothing could have been further from the truth."

"Gravier was voted in as president that same year," says Gabriel. "His first order of business was to make sure that David was banned for life for treason."

"Treason?" I ask, frowning.

"For putting Q.N. in danger by not enforcing the harshest of their codes which hadn't been enforced in over a century anyway," replies Gabriel. "He was banned for life."

"Where is he now?" I ask.

"He died a year later," replies Cameron, turning to face me, his tone tenebrous.

"How?" I ask, afraid to hear the answer.

"Drug overdose," replies Nathan, his harsh glare on my face still unsettling. "Heroin. Another of their methods of choice."

"And it was definitely them?" I ask.

"Yes," replies Silas. "We have some evidence. Not enough to go to the police, but enough for *us* to know."

"I can't believe they can get away with this stuff," I utter.

"They know what they're doing," replies Nathan.

"And if anything, they are becoming even bolder," adds Francis.

"This is why we have to take them all out," says Gabriel. "Him, Steven, Alexandra, Vallen, Jack."

I sit up straight upon hearing Jack's name. "I'm sorry, Gabriel," I respond firmly, "but Jack is *not* one of them." I'm loath to defend Jack in front of Cameron and Valentina in light of what he did to Evie, but I don't think I have a choice.

Gabriel arches an eyebrow. "He isn't?"

"No. He's been caught up in their world, but he isn't a monster like them. I'm sorry, but I know him much better than you."

I see Cameron bristle visibly at my defense of his old friend. It makes my heart sink to defend Jack aloud in front of Cameron. Beth scrutinizes my reaction intently as Gabriel watches me in silent curiosity, his shrewd gaze tracking the lines of my face, wandering over my chin to my lips then panning up to my cheeks before meeting my eyes. "Do you know what Jack has been doing since you split up in August?"

"No," I answer truthfully. "Do you?"

"Well, let's just say that if you had hoped that he would have extricated himself from that group once and for all, I'm afraid that you would be sorely disappointed."

The stares from around the room hit me hard.

Gabriel threads a hand through his thick dark locks. "Hmm. You still care about him. And *still* defend him. After everything. In your defense, you are not the only one who does that around here," Gabriel adds, glancing at Cameron who meets Gabriel's stern regard head-on. "Does it occur to you that he would not hesitate to hurt you both if you crossed him in some way?"

"Look, I'm not saying he's some boy scout," I respond. "He isn't. I know he's... highly problematic, but he doesn't take pleasure in actively hurting people like they do."

"Not unless they have their claws into him, in which case all bets seem to be off," replies Gabriel. "Remember what he did to Evie? Are they the actions of a man who has compassion for his fellow man?"

I feel my face flush as I glance at Val. I don't know how I can begin to defend him in front of her. "I'm not trying to justify his actions. He's done a lot of things that were *completely* inexcusable. I cannot defend him on those *at all.* All I'm saying is that he's... he's not some two-dimensional monster like Frost or Markov or Gravier. I know him. I lived with him for three years. He has another side to him."

"He has?" retorts Gabriel. "Or maybe he *had.* Maybe it was *you* that allowed him to keep his humanity. Maybe without you, he is indeed the monster you would deny him to be."

"That's enough, Gabriel," says Francis softly. "Jess was married to him. She has an attachment to him that we don't."

"And as you know," adds Nathan, glancing at Cameron, "she's not the only one around here who doesn't see Jack as being a big part of the problem."

"Indeed," replies Gabriel. "But I've seen first-hand the naivety that allowed Sebastian to take power... I wouldn't want us to fall victim to it again with Jack."

"Jack isn't our biggest concern," interrupts Silas. "We have no evidence that he has been involved in the types of serious crimes some of the others have. He could in fact end up being a huge asset for us... if he agrees to testify against Alexandra. He *is* a victim too, Gabriel."

"You give him too much credit, Silas," he replies gruffly.

"Don't forget that Jack has fallen out of Gravier's good graces," adds Beth, placing an elegant, perfectly manicured hand on Gabriel's dense forearm and squeezing it once. "That means that he must be pushing back on some of that maniac's more extreme behavior."

"There's no evidence that Jackson's a totally lost cause as of yet," adds Francis. "Until we see such evidence, we have to try to bring him over to our side."

"I'm sorry if I sound harsh, Jessynia," says Gabriel taking a deep breath. "It just that I've had these debates with... certain people around here many a time and I still stand by the fact that if we are going to cut this cancer out, then that means taking Jack down as well."

"But, for what crimes?" asks Remi, her rich voice comforting. "Beyond blackmail, we can't find much that he's done within the structure of Q.N. that is illegal, or certainly nothing as serious as the others. I'm not saying he hasn't, but we don't have concrete evidence of it."

There is a pause for a few tense moments as Gabriel exhales, his tense body finally loosening up. "Well, it seems that I'm outnumbered on this front," he finally concedes.

"No matter how you feel about Jack, we would be stronger if he were with us," says Remi. "Maybe Jess could be the one to talk to him."

Cameron gets to his feet in a simmering burst of frustration. "I think maybe there are ways of handling Jack without involving Jessynia," he responds, his body just about containing his firestorm of fury.

"I agree," responds Francis quickly. "Jessynia's involvement should be kept to a minimum."

"Especially in light of what happened to Luca and Joseph," adds Nathan.

"What do you mean?" I ask, my voice quivering like jelly at the sight of grave glances around the room.

"She doesn't know?" asks Beth turning to Cameron who reaches the taupe wall to my right and leans his athletic frame against it.

"No," he replies soberly.

"I thought he died in a car crash," I utter, trying to control my respiration.

My glance shifts from Cameron to Valentina who watches me, pain registering in the valleys of her beautiful face as she puts her hand on mine. "He did," replies Val. "He was coming back from..." Her voice falters and she stops.

"He had been staying at a resort in the Adirondack mountains for a few days," takes up Charles as Cameron's eyes find the plush cream rug below his feet. "He used to go there alone, every year, just to recoup and... get his head together. It helped him with his health issues. The morning he left the resort, as he was driving down to the bottom of the mountain, he lost control of the car and swerved and ended up going head-first into a tree at a hundred and twenty miles per hour. He died three days later from his injuries. We had originally thought that he had had a funny spell or something while driving, but when the police investigated, they found that his brake pads were worn right down to the backplate."

I feel my breathing shallow as I swallow down a gasp.

"Joseph was a *very* serious, methodical person," adds Silas. "He did a yearly tune-up on all the families' cars. He'd had one done on that car just months before. We knew when we read the report that someone had changed those brake pads during the night."

"He had been the driving force behind wanting to take down the Society," says Nathan grimly.

I squeeze Valentina's hand. "And the police investigated?" I manage shakily.

"Yes," says Val. "They determined it was a car accident caused by the owner's failure to maintain his car in good working order. I know my husband. That is not something that could have ever happened on his watch."

I lower my head as I try to take in what they are saying in the midst of taciturn heaviness all around that never seems to end. I glance at the others who watch me, their faces kind with the exception of Nathan whose dark glare never leaves my face.

Finally, Francis speaks, cutting the tension. "It's been a long night, boys and girls. We're making great headway."

"We are," adds Silas with a nod. "I think we've earned the right to call it a night."

"Myself and Francis will work on encouraging the women to come forward about Vallen," says Beth. "Silas and Gabriel, I believe you will be speaking to the men again?"

They both nod.

"How about we leave the issue of Jack for now?" Francis adds. "Discuss him at the next meeting in a few weeks' time."

"Agreed," says Charles, glancing back at a tense Cameron.

"Cameron, I believe you will be putting a security detail back on Jess when she gets back to Manhattan?" asks Francis.

"Yes."

I restrain myself from protesting it when I see the resoluteness in Cameron's expression. Plus, I suddenly feel like I may need it after all.

"We will meet again late-January," says Francis. "Most of the others will be able to join us for that one as well as the lawyers. In the meantime, I would encourage everyone to exercise the same precautions as before. And please post in the group if anything feels out of place, even the tiniest thing."

"It's been a pleasure to have you with us, Jessynia," says Silas, getting to his feet, followed by others.

"Same here, Silas," I respond, getting to mine.

"And don't worry, these meetings are always a little tense."

I smile, grateful for his reassurance.

After spending a few minutes saying goodbyes, we head upstairs and out through the front door.

"Gentlemen, let's have *all* doors locked next time," Cameron says to Aaron and another security guard outside, tipping his head in my direction ever so slightly.

They turn to me, perplexed. "I was sure I'd locked it," says Aaron, eyeing me curiously.

"Well," I say to them. "In your defense, it was the most nerve-wracking attempt at gaining access to a house I have ever had."

"Okay," says Aaron, suspicion lingering in his tone. "I'll double-check next time."

I manage a smile as Valentina hugs Cameron and me goodnight before turning to do the same to Remi and Beth.

"You two go ahead," says Charles to us. "I'm going to have a nightcap with Silas."

"Okay, goodnight Charles," I respond.

Cam and I walk in cumbersome silence, our feet making new dents in the fresh evening snowfall, glistening under lamps stationed along the path down the hill. The sorrow of hearing of Joseph's death is mitigated by the fear I feel of Cameron's reaction to me defending Jack. I hate defending him in front of Cameron. I'm not doing it to antagonize him. I've always had the overprotective instinct of a mama bear with cubs towards the people I care about, and that includes Jack. I just can't stand by and say nothing as they lump him in with psychopaths like Gravier and Markov.

Heading into the mudroom, we take off our coats and boots to the sound of the two security guards from before talking in the kitchen.

"Gentlemen, I'd appreciate if you did a tour of the grounds now. And please check all doors and windows as you do."

The men get to their feet. "We're on it."

"We won't be needing you in the house for the rest of the night."

"Okay. Goodnight."

After watching them leave and then heading through the kitchen and up the second set of stairs, I decide to break the ice. "Cam—"

Before I have a chance to finish his name, he spins around and cages me against the wall next to my bedroom door, his breathing labored, eyes scorching, blazing into me in jealous wrath.

19

I TAKE A DEEP BREATH and try not to pass out at the sight of this storming mass of muscle, watching him with soft eyes as I try to soothe his ire without speaking.

"I don't like it when you defend that man," he breathes into me, his energy tempestuous, eyes all fire and storm.

"I know. I'm sorry."

"Do you have any idea what it does to me to hear you say those things about him?"

"You defend him too."

"Yes. But when you do it—"

"If it makes you feel any better, if you defended an ex-girlfriend in front of me, I would start fantasizing about pulling her fingernails out with pliers." His face softens the tiniest amount. "I don't want to do it, Cam. If things weren't so serious, I wouldn't say anything."

His glare dissolves, his breathing quietening. "I can't stomach the thought of you still loving that man."

"That's not why I'm defending him. I just can't watch him become totally lost, lumped in with those monsters. I think you can understand that urge, no?"

He doesn't answer.

"Cam, you once told me that my compassion is what you... like about me. This is one of the side effects of that. If I just stopped feeling anything for him because of what he has done this year, then that would make me cold."

The stiffness in his arms begins to ease and he removes his hands from the wall on either side of me, standing up before me, dizzying me with his height and broad shoulders which he squares in front of me. He studies my face without speaking as I look up into his troubled eyes, trying to soothe him with my acknowledgment of his pain, with my contrition about defending Jack, with my submission.

"When you defend that man, it rips out my insides," he says, the vulnerable eyes under tousled hair causing my cells to melt.

I nod, my face solemn, giving him the space to breathe through his anger as a heavy minute passes by and his expression begins to thaw, his body releasing its wrath, his wide shoulders untensing.

"Cam?"

"Yes..."

"Why didn't you tell me about your father?" I ask as gently as I can.

He watches me, unspeaking, for the longest time, looking down before finding my gaze again. "Because I haven't fully faced his death myself," he finally answers.

I observe his eyes mist over and lift one wavering hand to his face, tracing the sharp angle of his cheekbone, enthralled by his unearthly beauty, by the depths of his gaze, by the innate grace of his stance and the physical potential packed tightly into his bristling body. Tingling current sets the skin on my fingertips alight on contact with his warm cheek and I withdraw my hand quickly as we watch each other, time and space disappearing into the ether.

"Can you stay with me tonight?" he finally asks, his tormented eyes feasting on my face. "Just to sleep. I need you with me."

I swallow hard, trying to muster up the strength to say no.

"Please," he says.

I nod. I should engage my brain more effectively than this but there are forces at play—physical, emotional, spiritual—that are stronger than even me. I don't know how to say no.

He glances at my lips for a few suspended seconds before turning, removing a set of keys from his pocket and opening the door to his room.

I turn to face my door so that I can get my pajamas for the night but before I have a chance to get my key out, I am hoisted in the air, finding myself in Cameron's thick, lean arms as he carries me into his room.

"You'll be wearing my clothes tonight, Avery," he whispers into my ear, his delicious breath a hot lash on my skin.

After the briefest of body showers to wash off the murky tension of the evening and brushing my teeth with his toothbrush on his urging, he hands me a pair of his light-gray cotton pajama bottoms and a white T-shirt which I put on alone in the bathroom over my naked skin. The clothes positively swamp my petite frame and after tugging my long brown hair out of its ponytail and running his comb through it, I leave the bathroom and prepare to enter Cameron O'Neill's bed to my left.

He's already in it, watching me from the right-hand side nearest the door. I once heard that men instinctively pick the side of the bed closest to the door in order to better protect the person they are sharing it with. It doesn't surprise me to find the über-protective Cameron on that side.

I glance around quickly. The walls of the room are painted a dark taupe, offset by accents of olive green and touches of burnished metal scattered here and there. A thick sage-green rug lies over the dark hardwood. Two black armchairs stand beside a black table with curved legs of brushed metal. Every accent, angle, material and piece of furniture in his room is rugged and masculine. The place looks like something you'd see in an elite dungeon.

I lift the charcoal-gray duvet cover and climb into bed, turning to face an unspeaking Cameron who surveys me as my head hits the plush pillow, lying a foot and a half away from him in this king-size bed.

"Are you still mad?" I ask as he plunges us into moonlight by flicking a switch on the side of the headboard—solid oak if I'm not mistaken—to turn off the bedside light.

"I find it difficult to stay angry at you for more than five minutes," he responds slowly. "It's something about your face and the way you look at me..."

"Oh, well, lucky for me."

"Indeed." That cranky tone of his should be obnoxious but it secretly sends my senses whirling and shoots pleasure between my legs.

I study the gorgeous lines of his features in the violet light of this moonlit room. His eyes are the hue of warm, dark honey, deep as the cosmos, and fixated on my face in a way that would remind me of Jack if I let them. Even though he's wearing pajama bottoms and a black T-shirt, the sheer size and density of his muscles and the force of his glare fill the bed with the threat and potential of a naked man.

The way his gaze flits between my lips and my eyes unravels indecent thoughts. "You think I'm a jealous asshole," he says, a low growl hiding in his voice.

His words make me smile. "Well, I'm just very relieved I'm not the only jealous asshole around here. Remember Tammy?"

Now it's his turn to smile. It's hard to understand how I can be so enthralled by his volatile masculinity while at the same time able to gaze into his eyes in silence without feeling uncomfortable.

I wonder if he knows that my pussy is wet and throbbing just by being in proximity to his warrior-like body. It feels like my entire blood supply has descended on my sex which pulsates as I think of his hard body.

Jess...

Stop.

Jesus, how in all fresh hell do I control desire like this?

"Well, goodnight," I finally utter with a deep exhalation.

"Goodnight," he responds.

I let out another heaving sigh before closing my eyes, desperately hoping I can fall asleep in these heady conditions.

After a few minutes during which my body is so restlessly aroused that I know falling asleep will take a miracle, I open my eyes to find his open too, his face soft as he watches me.

"Hey," I murmur.

"Can't sleep?"

"I'm not sure the conditions are conducive to sleeping."

"I'm sorry. I enjoy watching your face."

"Why?" I ask.

"There's something about it that soothes me."

"What about when I'm not around? What do you do then?"

"Things feel dark. Heavy."

"That's not healthy, Cam. You don't need me to feel good."

"It's not a choice. It's designed this way by the universe. I can feel you in my blood, Jessynia."

"And what if something were to happen to me? What would you do then?"

"Nothing will *ever* happen to you. And if it does, I will have lost my life trying to stop it."

My fingers grip the gray pillow beneath my head. "Cam, please don't say words like that. It gives me anxiety."

"I want to be with you, Jessynia. Nothing has changed in that regard. In fact, the feeling only amplifies with each day." His expression is so earnest that it has my heart racing. "Do you want to be with me?"

I take a few deep breaths. "I'm going to file in March. I can't make any decisions until then."

"And you think he will have magically moved on by then?"

"I hope so. I feel like if I wait until March, I will have respected his request and I won't have all this anxiety over seeing you. I'm so afraid of him trying to hurt you. It gives me nightmares sometimes."

"And what if he hasn't moved on by then? Are we supposed to wait forever?"

"I'm scared of his reaction, Cam. He can be so unpredictable. What if us being together is what finally makes him lose all the humanity he has left? I never really saw the goons he has lurking in the shadows when we were married. He was careful to keep that side of things hidden. Now that I've seen them and the way they are loyal to him, I'm even more afraid of him trying to hurt you if he went... over the edge."

He sighs out heavily. "I told you that I don't believe he will hurt me. Not to mention that he has nowhere near my wealth or power. I can damage him as easily as he can damage me. In any case, I'm willing to take the risk. I'm already in pain without you, Jessynia. And as for him losing himself to them, that is *his* choice. He has made many, many choices over the years. Only he can stop what he's doing. Make better choices."

"You care about him too, don't you?"

I observe the sudden furrow in Cameron's brow as the silence between us lengthens. "I've tried not to..." His voice is uncharacteristically shaky. "I can't stop it completely. Maybe it's because... part of me understands him. I understand him being pulled to that side—I feel the pull too, still to this day."

I sit up, pivoting towards him, taken aback by his storm and his grace. "What?" I whisper, the wind knocked out of my voice.

"Yes," he replies, sitting up to face me.

"No, Cam. You can't be serious..."

He doesn't speak, watching me in the silent semi-darkness for what feels like an eternity. "I don't feel it often, but... it comes back at times."

"Why?"

"That group is dangerous... and seductive. They appeal to the basest of needs. They push you to the edge, allow you to have experiences that are... outside the norm, shall we say. You don't have to think, don't you have to engage your conscience. Don't have to *feel* much of anything..."

"But... you've been there. You remember the state you were in after a while. I still remember your face when I first met you. It was like you were... gone."

"I was in that state because I still had a soul and a conscience. Maybe it is possible to disconnect from those things, like they do. Sometimes I wonder if life isn't easier that way..."

"No, Cam. It isn't. It's a mirage, fool's gold. Plus, just look at what they did to your father!"

“I asked Alex about that,” he replies grimly. “She denied it vehemently. They all do. My father had other enemies. Maybe someone else did it. Maybe the auto shop messed up and didn’t check his brake pads. We can’t prove it was them.”

“That’s a rationalization and you *know* it. Aligning yourself with someone who you even *suspect* could be capable of that is just… insane. And what about Evie, what Alex did to her… And you said they had a friend of yours beaten up. And that they drugged you and left a syringe full of heroin in your room one night…”

“I don’t like this pull I feel, Jess,” he responds his voice low, his cadence slowing with every word. “They’ve tried to get me back many times over the years. If it weren’t for the thought of you, I may have gone. I almost did a couple of times. Part of me feels like if I came back to them, the fear I feel at times would be gone. And the pain…”

“No. That’s not how it works. That place is… like a drug,” I continue. “The drug is what is hurting you, and when you're in pain, the drug is what takes that pain away… for a moment. But you eventually need more and more of it until it kills you.”

He nods. “I know that.”

I swallow down the hard lump I feel in my throat as I feel his pain, his torment, his need to have something, anything take that away. I want to touch him, to caress his skin, to lean my lips into his, to stroke his mouth with my tongue, offering him my body to relieve his tension…

But I can’t…

“Do you feel that pull often?” I ask.

“Not often. And never when I’m with you.”

“Cam, there is *no* light in that direction.”

He nods as I watch his face in the gloomy shadows, his divine almond-shaped eyes tracing the soft curves of my face as we peer into each other.

I lie down, my head nestling into the pillow. “We should sleep,” I say softly.

He follows suit.

“Are you going to watch me again?” I ask.

"Most definitely."

"It calms you down?"

"Yes." He pauses for a moment, eyes twinkling in the obscurity of the room. "That and… the less civilized reason is because every time I look at your mouth, I get hard."

I part my lips at his brazen utterance.

"Your lips are plump and pink and beautiful. I can't stop myself thinking about pushing my hard cock through them and into your wet mouth."

"Cameron," I manage, barely concealing a whimper.

"I think about your insanely beautiful eyes looking up at me innocently as I fuck you."

I feel a drop of glossy juice trickle from inside my pulsating pussy. I'm so aroused that I'm on the verge of pulling down my pants and pleading with him to fuck me as mercilessly as possible.

I know that's what he wants. I know he's hard. Rock-hard. And big. And powerful.

My chest expands causing my breasts to push out.

"You're wet, Jessynia," he murmurs. "I can see it in the way your eyes glisten."

Suddenly I feel his hand at my waist, his fingers lifting my T-shirt, making their way under my waistband, sliding into my pajama bottoms, and down over my smooth pubis. I move my hands up to his forearm which I clutch in a half-hearted attempt at resistance, but I am attempting to stop him on principle only, so my muscles barely contract, desperate as I am to have him inside me.

As his fingers delve into the juicy syrup which reveals everything I had tried to conceal from him, he lets out a groan, studying my reticent face as he runs his fingertips up and down the pink velvet of my sex without going in.

"You have no idea what it takes every day to stop myself from ripping your clothes off and claiming you as my own," he says.

I swallow hard as he slides his thumb upwards to meet my eager clit which he strokes gently up and down and round in circles as I try to hold onto my composure and not lose myself to long-awaited pleasure.

He pulls his hand out and takes hold of mine, using his other one to yank his pajama bottoms off the tight muscles of his taut glutes. He firmly leads my hand under the covers until I gasp at the contact with his rigid erection—throbbing, silky, engorged.

He places my hand onto it, my fingers instinctively curling around the soft, warm, dense column as he begins to run my hand up and down his thick shaft.

"Tighter," he orders, his voice brimming with delicious dark command.

After a moment's hesitation, I tighten my grip and he closes his eyes in response.

I'm trying to convince myself that anything less than penetration doesn't count, but I want him inside me so badly that if he climbs on top of me, I will submit to his penetration without the tiniest fight. There will not be one ounce of resistance I can conjure up from anywhere if he does decide that he wants my body… unless I find the strength to stop him.

He removes his hand from mine and lifts my T-shirt up so that my round breasts are exposed in the dim light. He groans before gliding his hand down my body, toying with the entrance to my sex, groaning as if restraining himself from penetrating the wet tunnel with his strong finger.

His ravenous gaze meets mine as we melt into the exploration of the body parts that want nothing more than to have his seed released inside me.

As he begins to shift closer to me, I withdraw my hand from his cock and find the strength to tug his hand out of my pants. "I think—"

"*Don't* think. Let me love you, Jessynia."

I wince at the words, feeling torn to pieces. "Cam, I'm sorry. We can't do this."

"Why not?"

"You know why."

He bristles, shuddering out violent frustration. "Jesus Christ, are we *still* here?!"

"Look—"

"Do you realize that you are concerned about the feelings of a man who cheated on you constantly for *months* and *months*?"

I pull away from him and sit up.

"Stop!" I shout as he follows suit, his formidable frame huge in front of me.

"Or are you still in denial about that, maybe?" he sneers.

"I am not in denial!"

"You're not?! Well, let me remind you that apart from Frost and Lydia Bulgova, he spent the last nine months of your marriage fucking multiple other faceless women at Q.N. *Multiple*."

"What is wrong with you?! Are you trying to hurt me?!"

"I just can't believe we're still here! I love you, God dammit. I love you like I've never loved any woman. I desire you so much that my body *aches* from it day and night. And yet I can't make love to you because you're worried about the feelings of some fucked-up prick who—"

"I'm not worried about his feelings! That's not the point! He's dangerous. What if he did something to you?! It's me that would have to live with that!"

"He's not going to do *anything* to me."

"This isn't about my feelings. This is about your safety! He loses his fucking mind when it comes to you. You were like a *brother* to him. Am I expected to just ignore that?"

"A brother?" he snarls. "I stopped being that man's brother the day he made the decision to seduce my sister and dump her on Alex Frost's command. I stopped being his brother when I watched her cry for months, not eating, not sleeping. I stopped being his brother when I found out that he had blackmailed my father into handing over huge sums of money. Or do you just not give a fuck about all the things he did to my family..."

"Of course I do! Jesus, Cameron, what do you take me for?!"

He leans in towards me, his breathtaking features hard as nails. "I take you for the woman who is dripping wet, whose body is begging me to pin her to the bed and fuck her, and who won't let me out of some twisted sense of loyalty to that—"

And with that, I pull the covers off me, the heat of humiliation careening through me as I jump out of bed, grab my key from the side table and head towards his door.

As I reach it, unlock it and pull it open, I feel a towering force behind me and a strong hand braces against the door, hemming me in. I try to pull it open again, but it is immovable against the barrier of his flesh. "Let me out!" I shout, tugging at it roughly over and over again, to no avail. "You can be such a prick sometimes!"

"I'm sorry," he says softly.

I stop pulling.

I feel him behind me, heat radiating from his tall, powerful frame. Out of the corner of my eye, I see strands of his dark locks, his head lowering, leaning into my left ear as silent tears drop swiftly down my face and onto the floor.

"I'm sorry," he repeats, suddenly soft. "I'm a fucking asshole who is insane with jealousy."

"I don't want you throwing his cheating up in my face all the time," I respond, still looking down at the floor. "It hurts me."

"I'm not doing it to hurt you. I'm just trying to get you to understand that you do not owe that man *anything*. And neither do I."

He takes hold of my shoulders and swivels me around gently, grimacing as he sees my tear-strewn face. "Don't cry, angel. Please." He wipes a tear from my face. "Christ, please don't cry. Your tears kill me. I say these things to you because... I love you. And I'm out of my mind with jealousy because I want you to be mine. And to do that, you need to understand that you are free."

"I'm not worried about his feelings, Cameron. I'm worried about your safety. That's what you don't understand."

His fingers slide onto the side of my face, tilting my chin up, his solemn gaze watching my tears as they fall onto my chest. "I do understand that. But if it means being with you, I'm willing to take the risk. You are meant to be with me, Jessynia. I know it in every fiber of my cells. And unlike in every other area of my life, I don't have control over you and it drives me out of my fucking mind."

"I shouldn't have agreed to come here," I utter. "I've just made everything worse."

"You didn't agree. I dragged you here kicking and screaming, remember? Like I've wanted to do for months." He leans his bulky mass into me. "These last couple of days have been the only source of light I've felt in months."

"I hate when you say things like that..."

"There hasn't been a minute since you left me in August when I haven't been restless or in torment without you. Nothing has even taken the edge off. I want us to start a life together. Or maybe the problem is that you just don't love me..."

"Cam, that isn't it. I want to be with you. It's just—"

His fingers curl into my hair as he dips into me. "You want to be with me?" he asks, scouring my eyes.

I nod earnestly. "Yes."

"It's the first time you've said that."

"I know. I'm just trying to be... responsible. I guess I'm making a mess of it all."

"If I know you want to be with me, I can wait. I can do anything I need to do."

"I don't want to keep you in limbo while I wait to file officially."

"You don't have to wait till March, Jess. *Fuck* what he wants. He gave up his rights to you when he—" He pauses at the sight of another tear spilling over my waterline. "You are a free woman, Jessynia. You were a decent, faithful wife... and he took that loyalty and betrayed it. Multiple times. You owe him nothing. Neither do I. Do you see that? Please tell me you see it." His thumb caresses my bottom lips as I peer into him. "Do you see it?" he asks.

I nod.

"Good. That's the main barrier here, Jess. Not him. You need to understand that you are free. At some point, he'll have to accept us. He won't have a choice. I intend to talk to him in the new year anyway."

"No, Cam. It'll just make things worse."

"I'll wait until March in the hopes he signs. If he doesn't, I will be paying him a visit." I tremble internally at the thought as he looks down at the floor, breathing deeply as he finds my gaze again. "I want you with me tonight," he says after a pause, running his thumb across my tear-stained cheek.

"I don't think it's a good idea. We're just playing with fire."

"I won't be able to sleep if we end the night like this."

I buckle under the weight of a gaze that sees so deep into me that I feel him inside me, and of a magnetic pull that is so strong that I have no idea how I have withstood it so far. "How about we stay in my room?" I suggest after a long pause.

"Why?"

"Well, your room is... It's..." He raises his eyebrows in curiosity at what I'm going to say. "It's ludicrously masculine," I blurt out, shaking my head at him.

A breathtaking smile brightens his previously grim face and he begins to laugh, the gorgeous deep booms from his lungs like the most joyous of symphonies. He arches a thick brow. "*Ludicrously* masculine?"

"Yeah, you know... the gray walls and sheets, the black bed, the dungeon-esque furniture. It's just... I feel very strongly that we need some yin energy tonight..."

"Yin energy? What does that involve exactly?" he asks, eyes mischievous.

"Not the type of yin energy *you're* thinking of," I respond to his composed stare. "We just need some softer energy."

"I can live with your *yin* energy tonight, Avery."

Fifteen minutes later, lying in my bed, his face is the last thing I see as my eyelids fall heavy, sleep consuming me, saving me from the unrelenting fervor of Cameron's glare.

"Jessynia..."

The voice is faint, distant.

"Jessynia..."

There it is again. Deeper, this time. Louder.

"Who's there?" I shout, looking around the clearing, scanning the trees all around as I try to figure out which direction the voice is coming from.

"Help me..."

The voice echoes around me.

"Help me..."

The deep rasp is unmistakable.

Jack.

I run through the featureless dark, trying not to slip on the wet grass under my feet.

"Jack?! Where are you?!"

I strain to see through the obscurity, studying each tree on the periphery.

"Jessynia..."

I pivot as I realize the sound is coming from behind me and start to run in that direction, the moon the only source of light, a beacon in the inky sky. "I'm coming. Hold on!"

I dart through the first row of tree guards before me, entering the somber forest, twigs crackling under my feet which slip and trip on twisted roots and stacks of wet leaves.

"Jessynia..."

"I'm coming!" I keep stumbling forward until suddenly, in a sparse patch of forest, I see him, illuminated by the blue moon lying low and heavy in the sky.

"I can't hold on..."

Though far away, his voice echoes through me as I race towards him, making out a rough shape standing with his back against a sinewy tree, a mammoth onyx canopy reaching up above him.

As I run forwards, dodging trees and tripping over branches which leave scratches and welts and specks of blood on my arms and legs, I finally see him clearly, naked from the waist up, his back against the dark tree, sanguine licks of orange and crimson flame emerging from its center, billowing behind him.

"Jack! I'm coming!"

"I can't hold on." His blood-stained mouth doesn't move, but I hear his words inside me.

"Yes, you can..."

As I make it within thirty feet, ebony branches emerge from inside the fiery trunk, reaching out to clasp his waist, bursting to life, twisting, contorting, grabbing onto Jack's weakened body.

"Goodbye, Jessynia." The gleaming ice of his irises cuts through the dark and into me.

"Jack, no. Hold on!"

"I'm sorry."

"No!"

Corrupt branches shroud his face and neck, yanking him into the blazing inferno of hellfire within.

"Jack!"

As I make it within ten feet, there is a final tug and he is swallowed whole, the opening in the wood closing around him, returning the tree to its natural form, all sign of flame extinguished.

Reaching it, I shove my hands into the treacherous wood. "Jack! Where are you?!" I scream, banging and clawing against the jagged, fibrous bark, blood trickling from my hands as I do so. "Let him out! Let him out! Jack!"

A second later, I'm sitting upright, jolted out of my vision to the sight of Cameron's muscular silhouette heaving in the night.

"Cam?" I manage breathlessly, trying to get my bearings. "Are... are you okay?"

He doesn't speak, hyperventilating, his skin drenched in glistening sweat. I pull the cover off me and pivot to face him, running strands of thick hair out of his damp face. "Cam, what's wrong?"

He doesn't acknowledge me as he struggles to catch his breath. I move a hand onto his brawny arm which is slick from the rivulets of perspiration running down it.

"Cam! Can you hear me?" I ask more urgently, pulling on his arm.

He turns to look at me, finally seeming to register that I am here, his respiration tempering ever so slightly. "Jess?"

"It's me. You had a nightmare."

"I..." He looks down at his hands.

"It's okay." I touch the strong line of his jaw with my fingertips. "It was just a dream."

His tormented gaze finds me and he nods before reaching behind his head and grabbing his black T-shirt which is soaked through, pulling it off his body to leave his gleaming torso oscillating slightly as his strained breaths begin to ebb like tempestuous ocean water still holding onto turbulence after the storm has lulled.

To the outside world, the man is a god—impenetrable, elegant, poised, one of Manhattan's most coveted icons, his body a work of art, his mind sharp as a knife. Seeing him like this—so open, so raw, so brutally human—is jarring, like seeing a glimpse of the shadowy underworld hiding beneath the glossy surface of Manhattan's high society.

I want to take his pain away.

On the collision of his brutal eyes with mine, I dissolve into his hounded glare, swallowing hard at the savagery of his aura and the dense curves of his feverish body. I know it's hardly the time, but I can't help noticing that he's even bulkier than he was back in August. His shoulders are fuller, his arms thicker, his muscles even more pronounced, if that's humanly possible. I glance down at his abdominals which are as though sculpted from granite, then up to his pecs, his strong neck and finally I'm swallowed whole by his thirsty regard. He must have spent the last four months working out tirelessly.

"Jessynia..." The desperate plea in his haunted eyes overwhelms me. "I'm done waiting to claim you as my own."

"Cam—"

I don't finish the word, silenced by the charge of his lips onto mine which part without my consent. His raging hunger explodes as he grabs my neck before driving his tongue deep into my mouth in a move that has my limbs melting into nothing. In a burst of panting, our tongues begin to push against each other as he seizes my body, cupping my ass cheeks and pulling me towards him so that I'm sitting, knees bent, on top of his thighs as he fucks my mouth with his tongue, his crude groans vibrating into my chest.

In a tousle of hands, my T-shirt is ripped off me so that I'm naked from the waist up, a sight he greets with a moan as his hands slide up my back and pull me into him so that my taut nipples tickle the solid mass of his glistening chest.

We speak using tongues and hands, the only sound emanating from me being the slight whimper that escapes as I feel the solid heft of his erection beneath the cotton of his pants which rubs against my throbbing clit.

Our famished bodies undulate as if by design, crashing into each other, pawing restlessly, the stormy choreography of lust and desire swaying us backwards and forwards and into each other as we claw and stroke and pant and gasp as our bodies do what nature is ordering them to. My fingertips greedily graze the muscular curves of his back, leaving a trail of smoke fuming beneath them.

He lifts me with ease so that he can pull his pajama bottoms down before reaching behind me, grabbing the thin cotton of mine and ripping it to shreds with his bare hands, leaving a hole through which lies my swollen, dripping sex. The solid, engorged head of his cock locates the glossy entrance to my pussy in an instant.

"I'm clean," he whispers into my lips.

"Okay," I reply, our lips an inch apart, our breaths ragged.

On the word, he pulls me down onto him, ramming his thick shaft into me, leaving my head dipping backwards as I exclaim in ecstasy. His diabolical tongue finds the hot cream of my neck, the wet muscle lashing me with fervor, gliding upwards to my jaw which he nips with his teeth. Tipping my head forwards to find his hot gaze, I contract the muscles in my legs to slowly lift and lower myself onto him, sliding my pussy up and down his large cock, his strong arms helping to lift and lower me as he uses my insides to pleasure himself with.

Nothing but notes of exhaled pleasure break the silence as we drink each other in as he fucks me slowly in the moonlight, the slick slip of him entering me an erotic soundtrack to the feast of our entangled bodies.

"Jessynia," he breathes as I slowly lick the perfect curves of his lips with a moan, nipping the tender flesh ever so slightly as he fists a handful of my hair to hold me against him.

I whimper as he mercilessly impales the most intimate part of me, his arms around my back, his pull on me possessive and needy as if wanting to own every inch of me. The deep grunt thundering from his throat has me exclaiming his name, breathing onto him as our lips slip against each other and I melt into the preposterous masculine beauty of this ravenous beast.

His unwavering glare leaves me cowering with the stark force of its impact. The sheen of moonlight illuminates the deep fiery wells which eat into me as he slowly slides me up and down his greedy erection. The friction of his hard length claiming the inside of my body has me moaning as I revel in the sight of this godlike man taking his pleasure.

"You are mine, Jessynia," he growls into my lips, stealing the gasp from my throat. "I intend to show you what that entails."

A moment later, I'm on my back as he pulls the remnants of cotton from my legs, the head of his cock finding its target once again. To ensure that my invitation is clear, I part my legs further and bend my knees up so that he knows that my body is his and that my submission to him is unequivocal.

"Look at me," he whispers as his full length invades the wet warmth of the most sacred part of my flesh.

I inhale audibly at the sound of his brutal moan, watching him tenderly as he straightens his athletic arms, forms a cage above me and begins to thrust as I bend my knees further. His impalement becomes more savage as he spears himself in and out of my welcoming slit, pivoting his hips ever so slightly, varying the stimulation divinely.

He finally lowers himself down so that his chest is on top of mine and I can't move but for his say-so. He licks my neck, his flesh strong and warm on my skin, before forcing his tongue into my mouth which accommodates him without question, a willing vessel for his deviant desire. I melt into the heat of him, his hefty weight so welcome, so wanted, so needed after the months without his touch. I know what we're doing isn't allowed, but that only makes my craving for him all the more impossible to defy.

"I need you, Jessynia," he moans, his yearning a heavy stroke on my lips. "Tell me you belong to me."

Upon my silence, he rams into me roughly, filling me over-capacity as he thrusts with the utmost competence, savagely demonstrating his stamina. Sharp breaths escape me at the sensation of being fucked with such animalistic manners by this brooding mass of muscle. The deep, murky blue of moonlight dances off the flexing bulk of his shoulders which press me down into the bed, a device for ensuring his total physical dominance over me.

His voice is a thunder into my ear as his fingers find my clit which he tenderly presses over and over again as I feel the climax build. His teeth nip the curve of my shoulder with silence between us but for the sound of his thick sex slipping into and out of my glossy insides. Taking his full length is hard but I'm so wet that the stretch is the most welcome of pain.

"Cam, I want to watch your face as you come," I murmur as his groans become more fervent.

"No," he replies gruffly. "You will see that once I am certain you are my property."

"Cam, please."

"I can't, angel."

With that, he thrusts some more, moaning before finding the crook of my shoulder with his mouth and collapsing onto me with a cry that has me orgasming as his finger presses onto my clit a final time. With a final sharp spear, he pumps his fluid into me as if wanting to get it as deep inside me as possible. I close my eyes and let the tsunami of nirvana wash over me and flood my cells with light and strength, awakening the nerve endings that have been dormant since August.

The weight of him is heavy upon me as his tongue licks the crook of my neck to increase the pleasure of his orgasm. Nirvana pulses through my body for a long minute as his heaving breaths begin to steady.

"I'm sorry, angel," he finally breathes, lifting his head to meet my eyes. "I usually prefer to have much more sophisticated sex than that. It's just... been so long without you. I couldn't control the beast." His unwavering eyes stun me. "You unravel me, Jessynia. I'm not fully in control of myself around you."

I smile at him warmly. "Hey, I'm not complaining..."

"Next time, I will be more in control of your pleasure."

"Cam, it's like torture not seeing your face as you come," I finally whisper into the seam of his lips. "I dream of it every day."

"When I'm satisfied that you belong to me and to no other, you will watch me come every day of your life, angel. As I will you."

He smooths strands of hair off my face as he pulls out of me, keeping his body on top of mine as we melt into one.

Ten minutes later, we lie facing each other, unspeaking, our eyes roaming over each other as I smile at him adoringly.

"I want you to be with me, Jess. Nothing less than you being Mrs. O'Neill is acceptable to me." I soak him in as he continues to speak. "I've been with other women. Many of them."

I sigh out in exasperation. "Jesus, Cam, didn't you learn anything from the Tammy incident?" The thought of him with other women still sparks murderous thoughts in me.

"You're going to hear this, Jessynia. I've been with many women. That's how I know that you have to be mine. Because nothing I've experienced with anyone else comes close to the feeling that being with you gives me. Everything else has felt hollow and wrong. Fake. Empty. I've never been able to emotionally connect to a woman before you. I didn't even think I was capable of it." I gulp down the emotion I feel as he speaks. "I've waited for you for a long time," he continues. "I could get into a relationship with some woman if I wanted to, distract myself. It wouldn't be hard, but I've done that before. It's become intolerable to me. I don't want to resort to distractions anymore. Do you understand that? No one but *you* is bearable to me at this point."

"Cam, stop. I can't hear anymore."

He brings his lips to mine gently, the tenderness stunning me to my core. Breaking away from the electric kiss, he breathes, "Does this feel wrong to you?"

"No," I answer in earnest.

In fact, nothing feels more right.

And yet I know he can't claim me as his own... not while Jack, a man as dangerous as he is disturbed, is still hiding in the shadows, waiting to pounce.

But despite knowing the risk, I just don't know how to control my constant craving for Cameron.

"I can keep waiting if I have to," he says. "I can spend another ten years of life waiting. Do you want me to do that?"

"Of course I don't."

"Then I'm asking you to let me love you the way I need to. Not hiding away, not moments stolen in secret. I want to love you openly. I want to be with you in public. I want you to have my name. I want the city to know that you belong to *me*." I look down and he jolts my face up. "I'm not afraid of that man. I'm afraid of getting to the end of my life without ever having been with you. I'm afraid of marrying some woman I don't love because you won't have me. I'm afraid of having a child that isn't half of you. Those things are more terrifying to me than anything that he could do to me." My eyes mist at his words. "We're not waiting anymore, Jess. You belong to me now, and nothing will get in the way of us anymore."

I want to believe you, Cameron...

20

I LET OUT A BREATHY MOAN the following morning as lavender-scented suds slide down my body while I relish the warm water in the en-suite bathroom of my guestroom. The rainfall showerhead, which has clearly been designed by a team of experts in procuring pleasure, is currently turning my shower into some kind of tropical waterfall-type experience and I take extra long washing myself in the knowledge that I will miss this luxurious shower when I head to my parents' much more modest house for Christmas Eve tomorrow.

As I let the water rinse off the refreshing soap, my mind can't help but wander back to sliding up and down Cameron's cock last night as his eyes bore into me. Jesus Christ, it was one of the most erotic experiences I've ever had. The yearning in his face, the sinful lust in his eyes, the way he lost control and gave into the beast inside him... It's just beyond what I know how to resist. It's not lost on me that the fact that our sex is so forbidden is what also makes the pull of him so overpowering...

I shake my head to dislodge the thought, the delicious water soothing my body which feels like it's tingling all over. Accepting that all good showers must come to an end, I finally build up the courage to leave the delectable warmth and head out, swiftly grabbing a plush white bathrobe hanging on the back of the door as I do.

Tying the belt around my waist, I brush my teeth and run my wide-toothed comb through my hair before heading out to the bedroom to the sound of a knock on the door.

"Hello?" I sing.

"It's me," replies Cameron from the other side.

"Me who?" I reply playfully.

"The man who spent last night ravaging you."

I rush to the door and fling it open. "Shhh!" I admonish ignoring his mirth. I glance in the direction of the stairway. "Charles could be listening!" I whisper feigning outrage.

"He's out."

"Well, there's something to be said for old-fashioned discretion, sir!"

My gentle chiding dissolves as I notice he's freshly showered and wearing a polo shirt and dark-blue jeans that accent his dense frame in a way that is just ridiculously sexy. Not only does his damp brown hair caress his forehead in a manner that should quite frankly not be allowed, he smells indecent—notes of musk, wood and citrus float over my senses, making my mouth water. I smile at his outfit—he almost looks like a mere mortal and not the demi-god, the suit-wearing billionaire scion revered by men and women all over Manhattan.

He eyes me slowly from top to bottom. "Nice shower?"

"Amazing," I respond with a sheepish grin, feeling a little embarrassed after our intense sexual encounter last night.

"I would have liked to have joined you," he says, that rich voice of his rolling through me.

"Oh, I bet. I know what you get like in the shower."

"Indeed," he responds coolly, eyes narrowing as a fiendish smile escapes him. "My mother will be over in a few minutes."

"Okay."

"In the meantime..." He steps inside, turning to close and lock the door behind him.

"What are you—"

"Just something I didn't get a chance to do last night, beautiful..."

And with that I'm thrown onto the bed, the sides of my robe are parted and his head is suddenly between my legs, his talented tongue quickly finding the silky plane of my inner sex before spearing into me in a gesture that has my back arching and a hand grabbing his generous chocolatey locks.

"Cam," I squeal as his tongue finds my clit which he licks and sucks over and over, the strong, velvety muscle ramming rhythmically into the tight bud, leaving it throbbing, my hands grasping hold of the sheets. A high-pitched breath escapes me at the sensation of his strong jaw between my legs.

"Cameron," I moan softly which he seems to translate to mean *harder, faster, rougher*, his tongue ravaging my silken flesh as though it's some feast he can't get enough of.

He lifts his chin slightly, groaning, "I've been hard all morning thinking about your tight, pink—"

Suddenly, from what sounds like the bottom of the stairs, there is a cry. "Cameron? Jessie?"

I prop myself up. "Your mom!" I whisper as he continues his meticulous work without flinching, licking the clear gloss at the smooth entrance to my sex.

There are swift steps on the stairs and a hearty knock at my door.

"Cam!" I mouth, clutching his shoulder.

"Jessie, darling?"

"I... I... Val, I've just... got out the shower. I'll be... out in... a few minutes." I would roll my eyes at my stammering but it's a miracle I got those two sentences out at all without squealing.

"Well, come down as soon as you can. I want you to see someone."

Cameron's determined tongue spears into me, fucking my pussy which pulsates at the sensation of euphoria. I clasp a hand over my mouth as his thumb toys with my sensitive clit, building up an orgasm that I sense is seconds away.

"Okay, will do," I manage, breathlessly, writhing in an attempt to hold off the climax.

Another knock, more muffled this time.

"Cameron!" Valentina shouts.

Cameron responds to his mother's call by placing the very tip of his tongue on the tight knot of sensitive nerves and flicking up and down with devastating precision as pleasure mounts to fever pitch. The sensation of this strong, beautiful man's face so close to the slick entryway to my body is beyond what words are capable of.

"I... think he's... in the shower, Val," I stutter back.

"Okay, well, tell him he's wanted downstairs."

"Will... do!" I manage. "I'll be down in five."

"Make it ten," Cam whispers, and a few seconds later, a final flick of my clit by his tongue has me clasping a hand over my mouth as body waves of one of the most intense climaxes I can recall feeling ripple through me like a series of earthquake aftershocks. He gets up onto his knees, planting his hands on either side of my shoulders as he looks down, watching me as I close my eyes tightly and breathe through the nirvana rushing through my conquered body which feels like it's floating to the ceiling.

My palm drops to my flushing chest as I feel him lie down next to me. After a minute of heavy breathing, my limbs finally descend back to Earth and I manage to open my eyes, slowly turning my head to look at the deity next to me, lying on his side, arm bent at the elbow, head leaning on his hand. His smile is one of male satisfaction at his prowess and at the sight of the jelly-like creature he turns me into, sex wet and open, just ready to be taken by him if he so desires.

"Did you enjoy that, angel?" he murmurs.

"Enjoy it?" I say as I try to muster up the wit to form coherent sentences again. "Um, Cameron, just out of curiosity... How does it feel to be a god?"

"You turn me into one, Avery. There's no one I've ever wanted to pleasure the way I do you. I lie awake at night concocting different ways I intend to make you tremble."

"Oh, well, I'm glad I'm not the only one," I say, referring to the multiple nights I've spent thinking about how to best perform fellatio on him.

"Not to mention that watching your pure, breathtaking face as you come makes me very, very hard."

He reaches for my hand and slides it down his body to reach the bulging erection under his dark jeans.

I moan at the sensation of the thick cock straining in his pants and prop myself up onto my elbows. "Mmm, Cam, how about I return the favor?"

"I'm not sure my mother will be willing to wait that long..."

I breathe out in frustration. "I've been wanting to taste you for months. It's like torture at this point. Just for a couple of minutes?" I coax, licking his neck, my bathrobe open from the neck down allowing my round breasts to fall out.

"Hmm," he exhales hoarsely at the sensation of my teasing tongue, his fingertips finding my nipple, tugging it taut. "Tempting, but I prefer you take your time for that."

I sigh out in resignation. "No fair, Mr. O'Neill. There are things you've gotten to do that I haven't."

"Well, unfortunately, I need more control in bed than you do," he says, caressing the teat.

"Control? Cam, I turn into a drooling invertebrate every time I'm near you. If there's one area where you have more control than me, this is it."

"Good. And the more drooling the better."

"How about tonight?" I suggest, biting my lip.

"We'll see whether you've been a good girl today first..."

"Well, you're going to have to handcuff me to stop me if things keep going like this."

"Hmm, that's certainly on the agenda," he replies, a devilish glint in his eyes.

I shake my head and sit up.

"Jessynia," he says, sitting up and taking his phone out of his back pocket. "The moment took me last night. I wanted to show you this first." He taps his phone a few times and hands it to me. I look down at his STD results dated one week ago. Completely clear. "I just wanted you to see that," he says.

"Cam, I trust you," I respond. "I don't have mine. But I was tested in August after we... you know, and I'm clean too. And I haven't been with..."

"Anyone since?"

I blush. "Yes."

"I'm glad to hear it," he responds, a ripple of what looks like relief rolling through him. "The thought of another man touching your body gives me homicidal thoughts. You don't want to know about me?"

"No," I reply, my skin flushing hot as jealous ire swirls in my belly. "I'm not a masochist. I don't want ever to know about the other women you've been with, Cameron."

"Good. I like how insanely jealous you get, Jessynia. I like the way you burn with energy. I'm glad I'm not the only one that wants to rip the faces off the people you've been with."

"Well, you're not."

"If it makes you feel better, there's not a sexual act I've had in the last five years that didn't involve me imagining your face. Any woman I've touched since meeting you has been a distraction. Nothing more."

The irrational outrage at the thought of the many conquests he's had over the years tempers a little and I slowly breathe in and out. "I can live with that," I manage. "Look, I have to get dressed before your mom comes up again."

He lies down flat on his back, propping his upper back up on a couple of cream pillows and placing his hands behind his head as he watches me. "Don't mind me."

I make it to the white dresser on the other side of the room, pulling the long black metal handle to open a drawer.

"Turn around and look at me," he says.

"Cam, your mom's waiting."

"Your job is to be a good little girl for me today... so that you get what you want tonight, remember?"

I pause for a second and then swivel towards him, my breasts half-peeking out from the center of the loose bathrobe and my pubis on display for him to enjoy. "Just a warning, I'm not sure I'm designed to be a good girl."

"Oh, I know that," he responds. "Open the robe."

The edge in his voice has me standing to attention and I blush a little and pull apart the sides of the robe so that my hefty breasts are now fully exposed.

He responds with a moan and very slowly starts to undo the buckle of his belt before opening it. "Lose the robe, Avery."

"You're such a bad man," I utter with a shake of the head.

"You have no idea..."

I blush again—apparently blushing is the new bane of my existence —as I peel the robe off my shoulders, throwing it onto a chair standing against the mint-green wall.

He hisses his approval of my naked form. "Jesus, your body should be illegal. Your tits are fucking insane. Touch them for me."

"Cam...," I mutter, nervous about the show that this indecently sexual man wants from me and worried about the time.

"Do it."

I lift my slim fingers to my breasts, caressing the soft skin, slippery from the sexual workout Cameron just gave me. I pull at my nipples as I watch his twinkling eyes, massaging my ample breasts, my moist lips parting as I observe his arousal.

"Spread your feet apart." Upon my compliance, he unzips the jeans covering his large bulge. "Touch yourself," he directs.

I hesitate for a moment before gliding a hand down my taut abdomen to reach the silken entrance to my body. I use my plentiful wetness to massage the tight bud of nerves, panting slightly as my fingers add to the arousal of the orgasm I've just had.

He gets up, the greed of desire brewing in his face as he strides over to me and hitches me up against the wall so that my ankles are wrapped around his tight glutes and the back of my bent knees are in the inner crooks of his strong arms. He reaches down and releases his cock, the swollen dome heavy against the opening to its target.

"You want?" he asks.

"Yes," I nod with a hospitable smile. "Please fuck me, sir."

"Happy to oblige, my lady."

I gasp as he lowers me down onto his hard column which penetrates me in one swift, merciless thrust, the head of his cock hitting my cervix within a second.

He holds me with ease, smiling as he watches the awe in my face as he begins to slowly and purposefully pulse inside my delicate body which is already utterly enslaved to the prowess of his remorseless potency, completely deferential to his will and desire.

"Your body may very well make me lose my mind," he pants softly against my lips as his strong arms lift and then lower my receptive body onto him again and again, the walls of my sex stimulating him to his satisfaction.

"I hope so," I reply, beaming as I grip the preposterously hard curves of his broad shoulders while he pounds my slippery sex for a long minute, taking care to use force just gentle enough that my back doesn't knock against the wall behind me too roughly. I couldn't move out of the position if I tried, nor do I want to. Having this man hold and use my body feels like a privilege I could never tire of.

He contracts his glutes to better enter my insides as he studies my adoring face. "You have the world's most fuckable face," he murmurs, his eyes gleaming at my good-natured accommodation of his uncivilized needs.

I respond, licking the luscious curve of his bottom lip with a warm smile. "Well, I hope you remember that tonight..."

"Children?!"

I open my mouth in horror at the sound of Valentina's soft voice straining in irritation from downstairs. My mortified expression makes Cam break into a grin, his forehead dropping down to rest onto mine.

He tilts his head in the direction of the door. "Down in a minute, mother!" the billionaire tycoon shouts, wry derision in his tone despite the swollen head of his cock now resting on my cervix in a pause from his thrusting.

"You've got two minutes, young man. Then we're coming up!"

"Cam, we have to stop," I giggle as quietly as I can muster. "If your mother finds out what we're doing—"

"She'll probably throw a party," he responds dryly which has me chortling again.

"You have to stop," I whisper, trying to stop myself from laughing.

With his firm shaft still very deep inside my body, he closes his eyes tightly as he prepares to withdraw, clearly trying to resist the urge to ejaculate. He doesn't move, his respiration labored, his face exhibiting a momentary grimace.

"Okay there?" I ask with a smile.

"The problem I'm having, Avery," he responds in a rough whisper, leaning his lips onto my ear, "is that millions of years of evolution are demanding that I fill the inside of your tight little cunt with my cum."

"Well, I am on birth control, so please be my guest, sir," I respond as he pulls back to look at me. I raise my eyebrows cheekily and lean forwards so that my breasts tickle his chest and I'm able to lick his lips in the hopes of finally getting to watch his face as he orgasms.

"I would prefer that you weren't on birth control," he responds, pulsing inside me. God, his throbbing cock is so hard and thick and long. It fills me up so perfectly. And unlike with Jack, it only hurts a little. "I've been dreaming of impregnating you for some time now," he whispers.

I shake my head. "You're such a bad man." Secretly, I'm so afraid of this building desire I have to be impregnated by him.

He smiles fiendishly. "Admit it. You like me bad, don't you?"

I nod. "Cam, I want to see you come so badly..."

He shakes his head at my provocation "I'm still not quite sure you get to see that yet," he finally says as he lets out a low rumble of that pleasurable type of pain and slowly withdraws from my insides, placing me back down on the floor as he exhales loudly for several seconds. "I never knew I possessed self-restraint like this."

"Yeah," I pant. "I really think they need to take you to a lab and study you." I smile as his engorged cock points up at my face, just waiting to be tended to again...

"I need to be able to control myself around you. This is good practice."

"Isn't it hard to stop just as you're about to come?"

"Extremely. It will make me irritable all day... which only means I will fuck you better tonight."

"Mmm... That sounds kind of scary..."

"It will be."

My cheeks flush hot. "Cam, all I want is to watch your face as you come."

"I told you what needs to happen before you get to see that."

"Well, how about I try to change your mind tonight?"

His eyes narrow. "Be my guest..."

A few minutes later I head downstairs with Cameron behind me, excited to see Val whom I hear talking to someone in the sitting room at the front of the house overlooking the driveway.

As we burst into the sunlit room, I stop dead in my tracks at the sight of a woman I haven't seen for over three years.

"Evie," I stammer at the sight of Cameron's older sister, a woman who was like a sister to me before I got together with Jack and she stopped all communication cold, refusing to answer my calls, texts or letters. She even had her doorman send me away when I turned up at her Sixth Avenue apartment.

She gets up from the green and white lattice-print loveseat she's sitting on next to her mom. "Hi, Jess." As she starts to walk towards me, I brace myself for impact... but her face is soft, crumpled almost, and as she makes it within three feet of me, she swallows hard. "I've missed you," she utters softly, throwing her arms around me as we envelop each other in a strong hug that has tears falling from both of us.

"I've missed you too, Evie. You can't imagine how much."

"I thought you were coming tomorrow, V," says Cameron as Evie and I finally pull apart.

He kisses her on the cheek before they hug warmly.

"Well, you know me. I like surprises."

"How about some tea?" Valentina asks, her smile bright as the sun.

Two hours later, I sit holding Evie's hand in the sitting room as she finishes telling me about her short-lived relationship with Jack through a never-ending waterfall of tears and copious tissues to mop them up. Val and Cameron left half an hour ago to go for a drive with Silas and Francis.

Evie's beautiful, ethereal face quivers as she recounts the way Jack seduced her on Alex Frost's command, pretended he loved her and then dumped her mercilessly a couple of months later.

"Did he ever... *force* you?" I ask gently as she recounts the cold horror of Jack's actions while he was secretly dating her before we met.

"No. Never. Sometimes I wish he had done. I know that sounds crazy, but then I could have just blamed it all on him and not felt all this guilt about being so fucking stupid."

"You weren't stupid, Evie. At all."

"He was just... very convincing. I was so in love with him. I'd never been in love like that before. I would have done anything to keep him happy. All those things I told him I was not comfortable with, bit by bit, he convinced me to let him do them."

"Evie, you don't have to talk about them if you don't want to..."

"Jess, doesn't it make you sick to hear it?"

"Yes. It does. Sick. Nauseous. Disgusted... But I feel like maybe you need to get this out. You've carried around all this fucking shame for something that wasn't even remotely your fault."

She nods, her gorgeous brown eyes peering into mine earnestly. "He told he wanted to... sodomize me." I feel the floor fall out from under me. "I told him I'd never done that before and wasn't really keen to," she continues, "but he just hinted at how much pleasure it would give him and... I gave in. He didn't even pressure me. He just told me he would like it. I would have done anything to keep him happy."

"God, Evie, I'm sorry."

"Has he ever done that with you?" she asks.

I shake my head and reply truthfully. "No."

"Over the three months, his requests became more and more... degrading. He would tie me up. Make me lick his feet. He made me greet him by getting on my knees without talking. He used gags, put a dog collar on me a few times. Made me call him *master*, all the while keeping us a secret and convincing me that my brother was just jealous and didn't respect me as my own person. Jack said we couldn't go public because of Cam. I started to really resent my own brother."

"Jesus, Evie. I'm so sorry." While I know there is nothing wrong with doing any of these things when you are in a consensual relationship, in Jack's case, he knew that he would be dumping Evie after he'd humiliated her, which makes those acts unconscionable.

"Did he do things like that with you?" she asks.

"He was... dominant," I answer in earnest. "But not like that."

Truth be told, I can't even connect this cold-blooded reptile of a human with the loving, protective and passionate man I know him to be.

"He even told me that he loved me," she continues. "Then one day, he suddenly vanished out of the blue. I tried calling him for days. Nothing. I finally waited outside his apartment for hours and he... came out with... a woman. When I approached them and said I needed to talk to him, she started laughing. When I confronted him, he smiled and told me he was done with me and... to say hello to my brother from Alex."

"Oh my God," I utter, clasping my clammy palms to my face.

"I never told Cam that part, nor anyone else. I don't think I slept more than two hours a night for the next three months." As another tear falls from her vibrant eyes, I wipe it away with a tissue and tuck a strand of her wavy brown bob behind her ear to stop it getting wet. "A year or so later—he was with you by then—he came to apologize. He seemed really upset. He was crying, kept saying sorry. Said he didn't want to do it. Said he was ashamed, wracked with guilt. Him apologizing finally gave me peace, helped me to move on. I just wish he had been able to do it before meeting you. That whole year before he met you, I was basically a ghost. I was dead inside."

I drop my eyes as I try to temper my breathing.

"It *was* Alexandra Frost that put him up to it," she says through a clenched jaw, her voice suddenly hard. "I know that for a fact."

"I know," I respond, squeezing her hand. "She truly is some kind of soul-sucking succubus that has crawled out of the underworld."

"I'm not saying what he did is okay. It's not. Not even close. But it wouldn't have happened if not for her."

I nod.

"I think he really does love you," she says. "That's why he came to apologize to me. To atone, get a fresh start. I believe he meant to cut her out of his life for good. I think he did try. I guess he wasn't as strong as he thought..."

"Evie," I say with a soft sigh. "I wish you had told me all this before. It was awful when you cut contact with me like that. I was tortured over it."

"I was ashamed, Jess. Being used and dumped like that. It was the most humiliating experience of my life. I couldn't even face talking about it, even after he'd said sorry. Then hearing that you were with him... and hearing about how in love he was with you... It was really hard."

I nod and touch her arm. "I get it."

"It's so good to see you, Jessie. I've missed you so much. You can't imagine..."

"I've missed you too, Evie. I miss you all the time."

"You and Cam look good together. Real good."

"We're not... we're not together," I sigh. "I mean, not *really*."

"He's always loved you, you know? Do you love him?"

"I'm really trying my best not to."

"Afraid of Jack's reaction?"

I nod.

"If Jack can hold onto his humanity, then he won't hurt Cam," she says. "I'm sure of that. But if he gets sucked in by those people and loses himself like he did when he did that to me, he is capable of *anything*."

"What would you think if Cam and I started dating officially? Wouldn't you be afraid of Jack hurting him? I don't get how you and your mom can even want that."

"We want that because we remember what he was like before he met you. It was really, really scary, Jess. It was like a light had gone out of him, and it lasted for years. You brought the light back. You are his reason for existing. I don't think there's anything he could do about that even if he tried. And that kind of love is worth the risk."

This time it's Evie who squeezes my arm as I lose myself in the soft beauty of her earnest gaze.

21

"DO I REALLY NEED TO BE ESCORTED if I'm just going for a walk?" I lament to Aaron who is studying me from the kitchen as I put my boots and coat on in the mudroom.

Ten or so minutes ago, I watched Christian accompany Evie back to Val's house after she got a crying-induced headache and decided she needed a nap.

He lets out a sigh. "You'll stay inside the grounds?" he asks.

"Of course."

"How long will you be gone?"

"Just half an hour, forty-five minutes, tops. I really need some fresh air."

"Fine. But I want you to take my number. If you're gone longer than that, then text me and let me know or we'll be coming to find you."

"Sure." I sigh in resignation at the presidential-level of security. "What's your number?"

He picks up his phone and presses a button as mine starts to ring. "You've got it now," he says, hanging up.

"Oh, yeah, I forgot you had mine, stalker," I respond.

He smiles. "Watch your footing on that snow. There are patches of ice in places. Cameron will have my innards ripped out if you break a leg out there."

"Well, I will do my best to make sure you aren't disemboweled," I chuckle to his appreciation. "See you later," I say as I head outside and close the kitchen door behind me, my boots crunching into the fresh new snow.

I take a left at the end of the driveway and head up the copiously salted lane. Tall trees look over humungous futuristic houses dwelling behind bushes, hedges and evergreens on both sides. Black posts bearing cameras stand every fifty feet. A gray squirrel darts out across the lane and I watch it as it navigates the snow before scampering up the sinewy ochre bark of a glorious red cedar standing like a sentry over the house next door.

The air is crisp and the pine trees fragrant, cleansing the murky energy clinging to me from my two hours alone with Evie and her detailed recounting of her experiences with Jack. Even though I knew what he had done, hearing it from her, so raw, so dense in pain and humiliation, has left me gutted.

I trudge up the gentle slope, past an imposing wood and glass house to the right lurking behind a gate overlooked by another spectacular sky-scraping evergreen. As I glance at another cedar, I stop dead in my tracks, a misty gasp escaping me, chills zinging down my spine. I take a breath and slowly turn my head to see the man lurking behind a tree—Christian, I think.

But as my eyes pan back to meet the thick trunk, I see no one.

I glance all around, my mouth suddenly dry.

I'm sure I saw him...

As I stare at the colossal tree, wondering whether its trunk is wide enough to conceal a grown man behind it, I hear the chomp of tires coming up behind me and glance back to see Beth driving a black SUV. She stops beside me, her window rolling down. The lady looks just as glamorous as last night.

"Hello, Jess. Lovely day for a walk, huh?" she says in that confident, husky voice of hers.

"Yeah," I manage, shaking off the unsettling moment of dread I just had. "It's gorgeous. These trees are a dream."

"What are you up to now?" she asks.

"Oh, nothing much. Just thought I'd walk around a bit. Cam and Val will be back in an hour, I believe."

"Fancy coming in for a cup of tea?"

"Oh, I'd love to Beth, but I really need some fresh air. I've been cooped up all morning."

"Mind if I join you, then? There are some gorgeous paths through the forest behind the house I'm staying in. I'd love to show you..."

"No, of course not. That would be wonderful."

Ten minutes later, after Beth has parked and carried some stuff she bought inside her house, we head off into the forest at the back of her residence after I glance around furtively a final time, still feeling like I'm being stalked...

"This must be a little overwhelming for you, no?" she asks as we head up a narrow path winding up a tree-covered hill. "All these people, these security guards, the gates..."

"Yeah, it is a little *intense*. I consider myself to be a raging free spirit. My mom says I could dance before I could walk. I don't really like feeling..."

"Caged in?"

"Yeah."

"Oh, I get you," she responds. "It took me a while to get used to it too."

"I mean, I'm grateful to have this protection. I just wish I didn't need it. I have no idea how I got here, to be honest."

"You fell in love. It overwhelms all logic, all reason. Leads us down paths we could not have foreseen."

You can say that again.

We clamber up a small hill, over roots, stones and snow, trying not to slip on the occasional patch of ice. The tree canopies overhead have stopped most of the snow from reaching the ground, but there are spots where it has made it through and the sun's inability to reach those areas through the leaves and branches above has left the ground so bitingly cold that deceptively solid disks of ice have formed in parts.

"Whoops!" I exclaim as I slip, with Beth catching me in an instant, her arm gripping me firmly.

"You need boots like mine," she says, lifting her sole, a maze of black. I lift mine and see the grooves are much shallower. "Yeah, proper snowshoes will be going on my wishlist when I get back to the house." As we continue to trudge uphill, I ask, "Have you known Cameron long?"

"About five years," Beth replies.

"Really? I didn't know it was that long. He's so secretive about the other people in his life."

"I don't think he wanted you mixed up in this crazy world, Jess."

"Yeah, I guess that plan has gone awry."

She smiles. "I knew Jack too... before he was with you."

I stop in my tracks and search her eyes, anxiety seeping into my cells at the thought that she is one of the women he slept with at Q.N. "You did?"

"Yes. He's, um, quite the specimen."

My heart sinks at the compliment. "I suppose that's one way of looking at him. When did you meet him?"

"About six years ago. You hadn't met him yet, I believe."

"That's right. Was he... *nice*?" I ask.

"*Nice*?" she chuckles. "He was possibly the most charming man I've ever met."

"Yeah, that sounds like Jack," I mutter, wondering whether she's trying to provoke me.

"And, um, quite the physique, from what I remember."

I frown, stopping in my tracks again. She turns to face me, scanning my eyes keenly.

"Beth, you... you didn't meet him at... that place did you?"

"Yes, I did."

"And you slept with him?"

"Oh, no, no, no. Jack and I never had any sexual contact at all.

Never, Jessynia. I want you to know that." I shudder out relief from my body. "That would hurt you, wouldn't it?" she asks.

I pause for a moment, realizing how much the thought of Jack with another woman still affects me. "I guess I'm not fully healed from my marriage to the point that I no longer care."

"Well, I hope you do heal. Soon."

Breathing out a long sigh of relief, I start to head up again. "Have you been back there recently?" I ask.

"Good God, no. I haven't been back to that place for almost four years, ever since the creature from the underworld sprayed his foul scent all over it."

"Sebastian Gravier?"

"The very same."

I smile at her no-bullshit description, relieving some of the tension forming in my belly, though I can't help but notice the grimace of pain on her immaculately made-up face. It's amazing how women can know each other for such short periods of time before delving into the most intimate of conversations.

"I heard he's a sadist," I say.

"Yes. For him, sexual pleasure is greatest when he can cause pain to the person he's on top of. And the worst thing about it is that women line up for it. And go back for more."

"Yeah, it's a mystery, that one..."

"Indeed."

"Did you have a bad experience with Jack?" I finally ask as we continue our climb.

"No, not at all. He seemed to me to be one of the more decent people who frequented that demonic mob. Although I've since learned that he was blackmailing Cameron's father at the time..."

My stomach drops. "Beth, I'm sorry," I manage breathlessly as we reach the top of the hill overlooking a forested valley below. "It's my fault for asking. I'm just not sure how much more I can take hearing about Jack. I've spent the morning listening to what he did to Evie."

"That's okay," she responds graciously, her voice deep and composed, her accent exquisite.

"It's not you. It's just been... a lot." For a moment, I look down at the valley below me wondering how I ended up mixed up in the world of such people.

"Jessynia, I brought up Jack's physique because I wanted to see how you would react. I was concerned about the depth of your feelings for him after I saw how you were defending him last night."

"Oh." I let a tense breath out.

"You still love him, don't you?"

I glance down to avoid the look of concerned pity in her eyes. "I'm not delusional about Jack. Nor do I want to be with him. I just feel like I can't stand by and watch him just be lost to them forever."

"Jack is very, very seductive. You have to be very careful."

She pulls her scarf out from around her neck and lays it on top of a bench inside a small wooden shelter at the top of the hill with a perfect view over the snowy caps of the tree giants below us that lead down to a frozen stream in the distance behind which lies a misty sheet of white woods. She takes a seat on the bench and I sit down next to her.

"Well, I will not go back to him. Ever," I say as resolutely as I can muster.

"Stranger things have happened," she continues, eyeing me sharply. "I've seen smart, strong, principled women who have gone into *darkness* for men like him. Women no one would *ever* have imagined doing that."

"Well, I like the light. I'm not one of those women."

"I hope not. Not just for Cameron's sake, but for yours. That world is ultra-seductive. I should know. I was once engaged to Vallen Markov."

I pivot to face her, mouth agape, in shock that a woman who seems so shrewd and put-together could fall for a man whose picture they publish under the term *Psychopath* in the dictionary.

"Engaged... to Vallen?"

"Yes," she responds, her forceful gaze weakening.

"When?" I ask gently, "if you don't mind the question..."

"We split up four years ago. Were together for two."

"Two years? I'm amazed that cretin could hold onto a woman for more than two minutes." I shake my head at my clumsy faux-pas. "Sorry, I didn't mean to be rude. I just... can't stand that man."

"Oh, I feel the same, honey, believe me."

"You loved him?"

"Yes. I loved him, even when he cheated on me repeatedly. Even when he manipulated me, emptied one of my bank accounts, isolated me from my family and friends. Even when he abused me, not physically, but sometimes the wounds of emotional and verbal abuse leave deeper scars. I still loved him... or I thought I did. I thought that's what love was."

"God, Beth, I'm so sorry. That man is such a piece of human detritus."

"I was twenty-five when I entered their world. I was smart, well-educated, from a successful family. I should have known better. But that world is *very* seductive. I was insane with jealousy the first time he told me about the Society. I mean, smash-the-apartment-up insane. But he worked on me bit by bit until it suddenly didn't seem so strange anymore. Little by little, I was seduced by the thrill, the secrecy, hanging out with the richest, most powerful people in New York, observing their desire for me. We were one of the big *power couples* there a few years ago. Along with Steven Frost and his demonic wife, and Sebastian Gravier and his ex-wife, and a few others."

"Ex-wife? I didn't know Gravier was married..."

Her gloved hand brushes back a loose strand of her thick blond hair. "Yes, he's been *very* adept at erasing her existence from the history books. Rosie was sweet, gentle, totally besotted by him. *At first.* The daughter of billionaires. I'm sure that was her major appeal to Gravier... other than her innocence and purity. That's something he delights in taking from people. Sucks it straight out of them. It feeds that black hole he has in the place of a soul."

Beth takes out her phone, removes a purple glove and scrolls through some pictures, holding up a photo of an angelic-looking young woman smiling into the camera. She has brown hair that stops a couple inches past the shoulders accentuating delicate bone structure and luminous sky-blue eyes that are almost too large for her face. There's a button of a nose and the cutest of round cheeks. She's stunning.

"Why— I mean, what would a woman like that see in that maniac?"

"Men like that can be... very charming and very convincing when they see something they want. Gravier's father was an oil magnate from the Ukraine. He inherited his father's estate when he turned twenty-one, but marrying Rosie took his level of wealth and power into the stratosphere. She had inherited her own fortune when her grandparents died."

"And he got half when they divorced?"

She pauses for a few moments. "He got it *all* when she *died*."

My stomach falls out from under me. "How?" I ask, my voice collapsing under the weight of her words.

"Drowned... under the influence... a couple of weeks before she was going to file for divorce. She was secretly making plans to leave. I guess he must have found out. It was ruled a suicide."

"You don't think she really killed herself, do you?" I ask slowly.

"Well, they found fifty milligrams of diazepam in her system, enough to knock her out, disarm her at the *very* least. And Gravier was the last person who saw her. Says she was alive and kicking when he left for the night. Ultimately, they classified it as suicide based on the quantity of drugs in her system after he provided a list of *friends* who testified that she had been depressed and threatening suicide. It was all lies. She wasn't depressed. She just wanted out. She'd finally come to terms with what he was. He already had contacts in the police department by then."

"He killed her..."

"We don't know for sure, but let's just say that I don't think he was best pleased about the divorce in light of their air-tight prenup that would have left him almost nothing of her fortune. And sociopaths don't take rejection well. Causes severe narcissistic injury to them, from what Gabriel tells me. In the new will that suddenly appeared that we're supposed to believe she signed two weeks before her death, and that nobody knew about but him, and that had been witnessed by two of his friends and his lawyer, Vallen, she left her entire estate to him."

"God almighty," I manage, feeling blood drain from my face.

"That woman was some kind of angel. Not made for this world. She had tried to change him. To heal him. She believed he was redeemable. She saw the broken, abused little boy he was, saw the devastation his psycho mother had caused him. She believed him to be a good man inside. He just needed saving..."

I dip my head low as a single unexpected tear trickles over my waterline and onto my lip which I lick, the salty liquid entering my mouth.

"Turns out it was her that needed saving—from him," she utters solemnly. "They even found his semen inside her."

"You don't think..."

"That he fucked her when she was dying? That would certainly be his style. Or maybe while she was dead. I'm not sure what could give a monster like him more pleasure."

"God, that poor woman."

"Her parents never really recovered from it. Her dad had a stroke not long afterwards. Her mother was diagnosed with cancer a few months after that. She was their only child. Twenty-four years old. Same age as you, no?"

I nod.

"He didn't kill just one person that night," she continues. "He took out the whole family. I bet he loved that." She loops a strand of my wavy hair behind my ear as I feel my limbs wilt at the thought of Rose's demise. "I don't want to hurt you by telling you this story, Jess. I just feel that Cameron's desire to protect you has led to him hiding too much about these people."

I nod. "I think maybe we're past that point now."

"We are."

"Beth?"

"Yes?"

"Could you send me the picture of Rose?"

She frowns. "Of course I can. Put your number into my phone."

I do so and hand it back to her, feeling like I could drown in the deep emerald wells of her eyes.

“How did things end with Vallen?” I ask. “If you don’t mind my asking…”

“No, I don’t mind. You should know.” She takes the deepest of breaths before resuming slowly, her strong voice suddenly less vital. “Vallen had been eroding all my boundaries for months and months, convincing me of our special unique love, convincing me that the Society was good for us, that it would make us both powerful. He kept me in this pattern of withholding and punishment where he would withdraw his affections, constantly making me feel like I’d done something wrong, like I had to win back his approval.” She says it briskly, matter-of-factly, as if detached… or trying to be. “I ended up being demeaned and corrupted further and further until one day I found myself at the Society, maskless, being… fucked… by three men… at the same time while Vallen, Sebastian and nine other rich and powerful men sat around us in a circle, watching me as they drank cocktails and snorted coke off trays.”

I tremble, mute.

“I was the only woman in that room for three hours. It was one of those special *non-consensual* rooms where they go over what may happen to you and then make you sign that you consent to it before entering. You can use the safe word, but if you do so, you are permanently expulsed from the Society, which to most people has become their entire life by that point.

“I’d never been in one of those rooms before. They give you an end time but anything that you have signed to is fair game until that time comes. They explained what was involved and a lawyer even asked for my consent before we went in, believe it or not, with a written list of all the things that could happen to me in there and a list of all the men who could use my body. We decided on the time limit together. Three hours. And I signed!” She shakes her head, her body shuddering as if enraged by her own decision. “Signed my body over to them willingly, knowing what was going to happen, knowing they were all going to use me for their pleasure.

“All of those men fucked me that night, all of them except Vallen who just enjoyed the spectacle, instructing them on what to do to me.

"Gravier—whom I had grown to despise by that point, and he knew it despite my efforts to hide it—climbed on top of me as I was being fucked, and tied my hands behind my back so that I was even more powerless.

"One guy, who I'd never even seen before, was underneath me, fucking me like a fucking jackhammer while sucking on my breasts. I can still hear his moans. Still hear him calling me a whore. Another was... *occupied* with my mouth. And then as a final insult, once he'd tied my hands together so tightly that it felt like he'd cut off the circulation to my hands, Gravier starting sodomizing me with Vallen laughing *maniacally* as he watched him put his hands around my throat and start to squeeze, stopping every twenty seconds to let me get in a gulp of air before starting again. He leaned over and bit into the back of my shoulder. It felt like he was trying to get blood out of me. I had signed that I could be bitten as long as blood wasn't drawn. That's how enslaved I was by these people. The men were calling me *the whore, the worthless piece of...*" Her voice trails off and she takes a few moments to compose herself. "Their arms were so strong."

"Did you ask them to stop?"

"No. Not once. I would never have dared disgrace Vallen by saying no to any of them or showing the slightest resistance." Her voice shows signs of cracking and I restrain myself from putting a gloved hand on her arm, not knowing if she would want that. "Vallen had sold it like it was going to be the most erotic night of my life to have all these hot, powerful men desire me so much. Like it was something that would prove my love for him forever, that would turn me into a legend at that place. A goddess. But they treated me like an *animal,*" she exclaims roughly, a bitter bite in her husky voice. "Less than. A piece of meat. I had seen group sex at that place dozens of times but it was nothing like what happened that night.

"Once they had finished, they threw me in the back of one of their cars alone and dumped me at the apartment we were renting. I was so sore I couldn't walk properly. My wrists still ached from the zip tie. After half an hour in the shower, trying to scrub the feel of them off me, I looked in the mirror and didn't recognize myself. I dissociated. It was like my soul had left my body. At twenty-seven years old." She finally breaks down a little as she speaks and I put my hand on her arm. "I lay on the floor of that bathroom for hours, waiting for Vallen to come home," she whimpers, the sounds coming from her quiet and high-pitched. "I must have tried to call him fifty times. When I finally looked in the closet, all his clothes were gone. I went over to the office and saw it'd been emptied. Computers, documents, pictures, everything. He had got someone to empty it while I was being *used*. Then I saw the note. In the living room. On the table. I opened it." Her words come out staccato-like, as if she can barely face saying them. "And it said... in his handwriting...

"Dearest Beth. How does it feel to be damaged goods? One of Manhattan's most infamous whores? Unfortunately, I don't like filthy, used whores. And I certainly couldn't bring myself to marry one. You are henceforth permanently banned from the Society. We hope the memories of tonight will provide you with some comfort over the years to come. We'll be watching your every move. Speak about us to anyone and people will be visiting that cunt mother of yours in the night. It's been fun. V."

Every cell in my body feels like to weep for her, but I want to make sure it is a safe space for her to get this emotion out, so I gulp down the desire.

"I remember every single word of that note," she finally says, her voice little more than a whimper. "I read it a hundred times over the first month. That was his goodbye to me. It took me two years of trauma therapy to regain *some* pieces of my fractured soul."

My eyes roam over this intense woman's soulful oval face, at the short blond hair which she tucks behind her eyes with quivering fingers, at the torment in her watery eyes, mossy-green in this light, emitting earnest tears which drop onto her elegant ruby-red winter coat.

"Beth, I'm so sorry you had to experience those people. It was not your fault. At all. They are..."

"Monsters," she says, peering into me. "Vampires. I know that now. After a year and a half of feeling such intense shame that I used to cover up the mirrors in my apartment because I couldn't bear to look at myself, I finally started making a breakthrough and finding the compassion for myself that I had tried to show that *thing* I was engaged to. Cameron helped me a lot."

"He did?"

"Yes. He was going through his own trauma, but he was always there for me when I needed him. As a friend. We've never been anything other than platonic friends. I want you to know that."

I nod through another internal ripple of relief.

"That's why I feel the need to protect you, Jessynia. Because I know what they do to women in there if they sense those women are questioning their loyalty to Gravier. And because Cameron helped me to heal. And you helped Cameron to heal. Now I want to be part of the people that help you heal."

"You feel healed now?"

"I have my good and bad days. The support of this group has been... immeasurable. They've helped me so much. Francis and Remi. Gabriel. He and I have become very close."

"He's, um, quite the man," I say with a soft smile.

"Yeah, he sure is."

"Beth, do you mind if I ask you a question about Jack? I mean, Jack in that place..."

"No, of course I don't mind."

"Jack wasn't in the room when you..."

"No. In fact, other than Alexandra Frost who got to him when he was basically not fully formed—with the encouragement of Steven who has his own fetish for *innocence*, shall we say—Jack categorically refused to sleep with the wives or girlfriends of any other prominent members, including me."

"Did he do some of the extreme things that they get up to in there?"

"Not really," she responds, almost in surprise at the realization. "In fact, he was known for refusing to entertain the non-consensual areas, despite being... *requested* to, shall we say, by many of the female patrons."

The thought makes me sick to my stomach.

"I never heard of him doing things to degrade women excessively in some of those more hardcore rooms. He was also vocal about making the place less... *dangerous*. That's why he and Sebastian have always had such a fraught relationship. Jack's vision of a place that is a safe place for libertines and libertarians does not align with Gravier's need for control and his penchant for cruelty. Luckily for Jack, I believe Gravier is absolutely enthralled by him, just fascinated. In love, maybe..."

"Are you serious? You think he's gay?"

"Oh, no, no. He is most definitely not gay. The Society is extremely open-minded when it comes to sexual orientation. Anything goes in some of those rooms. Other than the fact that I've seen his, um, fervent lust for women in that place dozens of times, if he were gay, he would be able to express it openly. But there is something about Jack that he is just mesmerized by. I don't think it's a sexual thing. I think that Jack soothes something in him. I think he also knows that Jack could be a hugely powerful asset for that place, not to mention a huge draw... Maybe the biggest male draw that place has got." She studies my forlorn face. "I'm sorry to say these things to you, Jessynia. But you want to know the truth, right?"

"I don't want to. I have to."

She places her hand onto my padded black coat. "Gravier wants Jack by his side, and to accomplish that, he wants him completely broken, corrupted. Away from you. Gabriel thinks Jack is irredeemable, that he's just a young Vallen who will need a few years to turn deadly. I don't agree. His behavior was never as disturbing as the scum that have run that place in the last few years."

"That's why I have such a hard time just discarding him as a lost cause," I say, a sudden breeze frosting the air. "I know he's a decent person deep down when he doesn't have these people in his head."

"Yes. He is. But that doesn't mean he will *behave* decently. It doesn't mean he will ever get free of these people. They have contaminated his blood, and getting out can be... tricky. Even if he is more redeemable than the others, that doesn't mean he is safe to be around, at all. It doesn't mean he won't hurt you, or cheat on you, or lie to you, or put you in danger. You know that?"

"Yes. I know. I do *not* want to be with him. I guess I just don't understand why I still love him... and can't stop myself wanting to save him."

"It's because you are drawn to damaged and dangerous men like Jack."

"And Cameron?" I suggest.

"Yes, him too. The difference being that Cameron has spent the last four years trying to free himself from these people. Jack had a chance to break free when you started dating. He cut off contact. And he *chose* to go back. And this year, he has been... active there again, up to very recently. And that kind of magnetic pull they have over him is not something that even you, the woman he loves more than anything, can stop."

We sit in silence for what seems like an age, our eyes flitting between each other and the trees cascading down the hillside below us. A hawk flies low in the valley, the only sign of life in this most stunning of winter paintings.

"What about Cameron?" I ask.

"What do you mean?"

"Did he engage in some of the more extreme things at that place?"

She looks down. "Cameron is not the same man now as he was then. He was thoroughly *infected* by that woman."

I frown, waiting for further explanation.

Beth sighs. "I can't tell you intimate things about his former life, Jess. That would be crossing a line. You have to ask him about his time there yourself."

"Okay." After a few moments, I find her eyes again. "Beth, I'm so sorry that you had to experience those things."

"Well, I am doing much better now... *most* days. And I've become strong enough to know one thing with utmost certainty."

"What is that?"

"That they have to go down. And I'm willing to put my life on the line to make it happen."

"Yes," I say, sitting up straighter, my voice suddenly stronger, more resolute. "And I'll help in whatever way I can."

"We need Cameron to come forward, make a complaint about Alex.

If we can get Jack, even better. Those two are the big power players here. If one or both of them come forward, the other young men will too. And the women. Nathan's brother works for the district attorney's office. He can use his influence to push for prosecution."

"I'll speak to Cam about it after Christmas, and find a way to bring up the subject with Jack. We have to make this happen."

"Good." She smiles. "Cam was right."

"About what?"

"You're one hell of a woman."

"Well, I think the same is true of you," I say, losing myself in her earnest regard.

The shrill ring of my phone has me jumping.

Cameron.

"Where are you, beautiful?" he asks urgently. "They said you'd gone for a walk."

"I'm with Beth. We're... at, um, the top of a forest." Despite the gloom of the last few hours, I manage a small smile and an internal eye-roll at my ineptitude at describing our location.

"May I?" asks Beth.

"Good idea," I reply, handing her the phone.

"We're at Prospect Point, Cameron. We'll be coming down now." She hangs up after a few moments. "He'll meet us at the bottom."

We get up and begin to carefully maneuver down ice, roots and frozen earth in silence, trudging down for a few minutes until we hear crackles and thuds coming up the hill towards us. My heart almost jumps out of my chest at the sight of Cameron's stunning, competent frame walking towards us, like light flooding into the room after a blackout.

"Hello, ladies," he sings genially.

I feel like to throw my arms around him in sheer relief to see him after the heaviness of the last few hours with Evie and Beth.

"Hello, Mr. O'Neill," sings Beth playfully. "I love this girl."

"Most people do," responds Cam.

My voice is somewhat choked by the emotion of the day and I find myself unable to make light conversation like I usually can.

"Did you have a nice drive?" Beth asks Cam as he scrutinizes my face. If I know him, he can tell that I'm feeling a little sensitive just by the look in my eyes. He always could read me like an open book.

"It was great," he responds, not shifting his gaze from my face. "Let me help you down," he says to me, and without asking, loops his arm behind my back. There's something about his strong grip that always makes the world feel safer.

And there's a part of me that's aware how dangerous that is... and how similar it is to the dynamic I was in with Jack.

As we reach the bottom of the hill, Cameron turns to Beth. "Mom's making tomato soup and grilled *cashew*"—he glances at me—"cheese sandwiches for lunch, Beth. Fancy coming over?"

"I'd love to, Cam, but I've invited Gabriel over," she says with an almost imperceptible wink, which Cameron responds to with the subtlest of smiles. "But he wants to invite you two over for dinner at his place tonight. It'd be just the four of us. He knows you're leaving tomorrow, Jess. He would really love to spend some more time with you."

Cam looks at me. "Is that okay?" he asks.

"That sounds lovely, Beth. Thank you." In reality, after the day I've had, I would secretly love to just get in bed and spend a few hours alone to process everything I've heard.

"Great. Is 7 p.m. okay?"

"Perfect," responds Cameron.

"Should we bring anything?" I ask. "Dessert or anything?"

"No, just your gorgeous selves... and Cameron, if you want to bring one of your ridiculously divine bottles of red wine, I'm sure Gabriel won't complain."

"Will do."

"It was great to chat to you, Jess."

"You too, Beth," I respond as we hug each other goodbye.

As she heads down her driveway, Cam turns to look at me, raising my chin with cold fingers. "What's wrong?" he asks, his eyes shrewd. "I don't like that look in your eyes."

"Nothing. Just... lots of things came up today." I kick myself as I feel my eyes misting over.

"What things?"

"Evie and Jack. And then just now Beth told me about Rose. And about what Vallen did to her. Sometimes I feel like it's more than my soul knows how to cope with..."

"Jesus, I didn't know she would tell you all that."

"Well, I guess she wants me to know so I can better protect myself."

"*I'm* here to protect you now. You don't have to be afraid."

"Yeah, well, I really don't want to be one of those annoying women who rely on men to save her sorry ass." He breathes out heavily in frustration. "I want to know what I'm dealing with," I add as if to hold off the coming reproach.

"Even if it leaves you upset like this?"

"Yes."

We stand in silence, the winter air nipping at our cheeks as he watches me, towering above my five feet six inches, his eyes panning over my face, his respiration heavy.

Suddenly, in a move beyond thought and reason, I reach up to him, locking my fingers behind his neck and pulling him into me so that I can plant a strong kiss onto his full, pink lips. He reciprocates immediately, his tongue finding the seam of my mouth, delving inside a little, then a little more, until he is exploring my mouth, our tongues writhing against each other as his hands pull me into him.

A minute passes and we pull away breathlessly. "Cameron," I breathe, brushing my fingers down the side of his sensational face.

I suddenly want to tell him that I love him.

The words are desperate to come out. *I love you. I love you so much. I want to be with you. Forever.*

But I can't say them. Not until I sort things out with Jack. Instead, I kiss him again slowly—first his perfect neck several times and then his wicked mouth, hoping that he feels it in the desperate way my lips press against his and in the manner I look into him as we pull apart.

"Yes, Jessynia?" he says as I pull away, every fleck of color in his eyes incandescent in the wintry sun.

"Um, about that grilled cheese sandwich you mentioned..."

His smile burns into me. "Let's go, Avery."

22

LATER THAT EVENING I SIT ON CAMERON'S BED, watching him as he slowly draws the white cotton of his shirt over the chiseled ridges and valleys of his torso in preparation for the dinner that Gabriel and Beth have invited us to. As the thick ivory settles on his deep honey frame, his eyes lock with mine as he buttons it up from the top down, tucking the shirt into his slate dress pants. After days of seeing him in casual attire, the sight of him transports me to a vision of the scion from one of Manhattan's wealthiest dynasties standing atop the O'Neill tower in the Financial District—their flagship building, the only one named after the family.

From the bed, he picks up a muted blue tie with silver thread running through it, snakes it around his collar, his eyes evaluating me as his talented fingers loop the end into the loose knot he has formed.

I smile. "Do you really have to wear a tie?"

"Gabriel does not appreciate people coming to dinner dressed casually. He and Beth like to play dress-up for their dinner parties."

"Hey, I'm not complaining," I respond to the delectable sight of this mass of muscle dressed in his sexy suit.

"Good. Now you, my lady."

"I told you I don't have anything fancy to wear seeing as a *certain someone* did my packing for me and immediately forced me out of my own apartment." Every time I can make this man smile, it feels like my insides are jumping for joy. "How about I just wear this,"—I look down at my navy-blue bodysuit and black pants—"and add some jewelry and some lipstick?"

"Won't do, I'm afraid."

"Well, I'm sure they'll forgive me given the—"

"My mom has lent you a dress."

"What?!"

He goes over to the closet and carries out a black hanger from which dangles a long-sleeved burgundy velvet dress, tapered at the waist, with a slim ankle-length skirt and a sharp V-cut to the neck that seems to go down to where my cleavage would be.

"Mom says it should fit perfectly. You're the same size, I believe."

"Um, yeah, but not in the chest department. Your mom has cute little *bee stings* up top—*her* words. I don't think her clothes are appropriate for my body shape."

"Only one way to find out." He walks over to the bed and lays the dress onto the gray duvet cover.

"Get up," he says.

I don't comply, but shoot him a piquant look at the ludicrous amounts of alpha in his delivery. "Um, would it be possible to keep the use of imperatives to a minimum, sir?" The sides of his eyes crinkle in mirth as his gaze wanders to my lips. "They bring out a very non-compliant side in me."

"We can do this the hard way, Miss Avery, if you like?"

"And what is that?" I bite my lip.

Without a word, his strong hands pull me to stand up, tugging my pants down and off my feet and yanking my bodysuit up over my head.

"Um, excuse me, Mr. Caveman, I appreciate your enthusiasm and all, but—"

He silences me swiftly, his hand forming a merciless seal over my mouth as his body pivots behind me. Pressing his muscular pecs into my back, he clasps his other arm around my chest, his lips at my ear, his rock-hard erection pressing into my butt. "I've spent every day of the last four years dreaming about ripping your clothes off, Jessynia." The bite in his voice is dangerous. "Now that I finally have the right to, it's going to be happening a lot."

My core clenches in arousal, begging for his deviant invasion. I can't help how my body reacts to being dominated by his power, his ferocious male lust. I feel small in his dense muscles. Safe. Right. His right hand peels open the left cup of my black bra, his fingers caressing my round breasts, pulling on the nipple until it forms a hard point. He pulls his elbow back and tends to the other breast, uncovering it and working the teat until it is erect. He lowers his head, tilting me so that his tongue can find the nipple which he sucks on, pulling with his mouth, flicking before delivering a gentle nip with his teeth.

Still covering my mouth, he glides his free hand down my slim abdomen and into the black lace of my panties, over the hairless pubis and into the soft, silky folds, a deep guttural thunder escaping him as his fingers delve into the glossy juice designed to ease the entry of his throbbing erection into my tight body.

He slides his finger up and down the slick velvet guarding my sex, finding the tight nub of nerves and pressing firmly, then gently, sliding up then down, releasing his hand from my mouth just in time for a high-pitched whimper of reverence and submission to escape me. As he stands straight up, I see my chest flushing, my whimpers intensifying as he licks the side of my neck slowly with his strong tongue. It's all I can do to stop myself bending over the bed and begging him to fuck me.

His lips graze my ear, his fresh breath tickling my skin. "I believe you were complaining about my use of imperatives, my lady?"

"I was?"

"Yes, you were."

"Well, we're slightly in altitude. Maybe the lack of oxygen was affecting my brain."

I feel his cheek widen into a smile against my face as his fingers circle my clit. "Any complaints now?" he asks, his rich timbre seeping into me, changing the frequency of my cells.

I shake my head, tiny noises escaping me. "No... No more complaints, sir."

"If I'm not mistaken, you want me to fuck you?"

"Yes... if it's not too much trouble..."

"Mmm, I don't like to rush," he says. "They're expecting us in fifteen minutes."

"Cam, I really won't judge you if you want to fuck me quickly... and preferably very *hard*."

His teeth find my neck which he nips ever so slightly before he murmurs, "I like the idea of you being wet and ready all night, beautiful. I've been hard since this morning. I have a lot of pent-up energy. I'm going to conserve it until later when I can fuck you the way you deserve." He pulls his hand out of my panties.

"Um, Mr. O'Neill, I think leaving me in this state may be cruel and unusual punishment indeed."

"Good. I like the idea of you being in heat all night."

"Okay, well, don't complain if I get crabby over dinner," I whine playfully.

"Well, I went through something similar this morning, remember?" I think back to him fucking me against the wall and then withdrawing upon the arrival of his mother.

"Yes, but that was *your* choice. I'm respectfully disagreeing with the current course of action."

He leans his lips into my ear, one hand wrapping around my throat, and in the lowest of growls says, "I'll be more than making up for it tonight."

My sex clenches at his vow and the deep thunder in his perverse male voice. "Okay, sir," I smile. "So, about this dress..."

A few minutes later, he eyes me sternly, running his thumbs over the rich claret velvet of the dress cloaking my round breasts, sliding them from side to side until the nipples underneath rise to a point.

"You're right," he says roughly. "The dress looks indecent on you."

"I told you."

"I don't like the idea of that animal Gabriel seeing so much of you, but... in the circumstances, I will have to live with it. You'll have to let your hair down. When it comes to you, it seems I have a jealous streak that is highly uncivilized. I'd rather not end up assaulting one of my closest friends... which is what will be happening if I see him looking at your tits."

I break into a smile. "Well, he seems like a pretty sophisticated fellow, not the *rack-ogling* type," I jest.

"I know how that fucker's mind works when it comes to women."

"Well, maybe you underestimate him."

Cameron shakes his head at me slowly, deadpanning, "I'll allow my friend two glances. After that, he'll need medical attention."

"Okay, Mr. Caveman." I pull the hairband out of my hair and pull it so that it falls loose around my front. "Better?"

"More bearable," he responds.

I smile. "Okay. Let's go."

He follows me into my room and watches as I put on some long, thick over-the-knee black socks and apply some glossy nude lipstick, a dash of mascara, the tiniest brush of light-brown pigment on my eyelids and a bohemian-style pair of silver earrings with a line of semi-precious stones cascading from a small silver hoop.

"Fancy enough?" I ask.

"Your beauty is insane," he replies.

"I'll take that as a yes."

As we go to leave the room, he stops me in the doorway, bending down to lift the hem of my dress up, sliding his hand up my thigh and pulling my black panties down my legs, lifting my feet so he can pull them off.

"Hey!" I chastise as he throws them onto my bed, pulls me out into the hallway and uses my key to lock the door behind me. "Excuse me, sir..."

"I want your sex naked and accessible tonight."

"Cam, this is your mom's dress and you've left me kind of... you know."

"The dress is yours now, Jessynia. My mother wants you to have it."

"What? No! I can't do that."

"She hasn't worn it in five years. It brings back painful memories of my father. She says you having it would make her extremely happy."

"Oh, God, Cam..."

"Do you want to disappoint my mother?"

"No, of course not... but may I add that it's minus three degrees outside. It may be a bit nippy down there." I'm suddenly grateful that this dress is as long as it is.

He smiles. "Don't worry, Avery. I'll be thoroughly warming you up when we get back."

Before I can protest further, he drags me downstairs into the kitchen where he grabs a bottle of Bordeaux from the fridge. We put on hats and boots and head out. I'm grateful for the sting of cold air as we step outside, hoping it will cool my humming cells and the burning between my legs.

As we walk down the drive and take a left up the hill, I spot Christian, all in black, hovering around the front of Val's driveway, watching us in silence, his breath misting the air.

"Evening, Christian."

"Evening Mr. O'Neill, Jessynia. Need any help?"

"No, we're going over to Gabriel's. We'll be back in a couple of hours."

"Watch those steps, huh?"

"Will do," replies Cameron.

"Enjoy your night."

"You too, Christian."

"Bye," I say as Christian eyes me like I once saw a polar bear do a cameraman on the Discovery Channel.

Once we've cleared the driveway, Cameron turns to look at me.

"What?" I ask.

"Not fond of him, huh?"

"I... I really don't know the guy."

"But he makes you uncomfortable."

"I'm sorry. I don't know what it is."

"Aaron has been trying to get me to fire him for a while now too."

"Why?"

"He doesn't have any specific reason. Just weird vibes."

"You don't want to?"

"Apart from the awkwardness, he's been a great guard. Loyal, reliable."

"Yeah, I get it. I mean, I can be awkward as all hell in public too."

"Oh, I'll second that."

I give him a nudge with my elbow as we trudge further on up the hill, Cameron slowing down to accommodate my tortoise-in-a-wind-storm-like speed ascending the snow-covered hill. At times, he wraps an arm behind my back to help me go up faster. At others, he grabs my hand if it looks like I may slip. He is always watching, analyzing, ensuring my protection. It reminds me of the way Jack used to be. It soothes the deepest of needs in me—the need to feel safe, to be protected. I used to offer those things to myself.

I wonder when I stopped doing that...

"Are they a couple?" I ask as sparse flecks of pristine white, illuminated by the street lamps around us, dance in the air, performing the most epic of night ballets.

"Beth and Gabriel?" He pauses for a moment. "I'm not sure if either of them are really into doing the *couple* thing anymore, but they are very close."

"Why don't they want that?"

"There's a lot trauma there, on both sides. Plus, Gabriel has always been a bit... Let's just say I'm not sure if being with just one woman is really something he's capable of. Or at least, I've never seen him manage it before."

"Oh..." My stomach sinks for some reason.

I turn to look up at Cam to find the glimmer of a smile on his gorgeous face, lit up by just the haunting, ethereal light from the lanterns dotted around the complex. "Just so you know, Jessynia, I'm *nothing* like Gabriel."

I'm not sure why it unexpectedly unsettles me that Gabriel is not the monogamous type. I guess deep down part of me wonders whether being with a man like Cameron who has had so many sexual experiences and who has so many libertines as friends is just asking for trouble... in more ways than one.

"It's this one," he says, his gloved fingers clasping mine, leading me onto a driveway to the left near the very top of the hill. As he performs this typical boyfriend-type gesture, I could almost convince myself that we are just a normal couple going for dinner with friends and that the ghost of Jack isn't crouching in the dark shadows of the trees around us.

We head up the driveway past a black four-by-four covered in a thick layer of snow. Aaron pops out from a guest house just behind the car, sliding on a black coat, his hands locking with Cameron's in greeting.

He bows his head to me. "Jess."

"Hey, Aaron," I respond with a smile.

"I believe Gabriel asked if you wanted to join us," says Cameron. "You sure you don't? We'd love to have you, my friend."

"Oh, no, no. I'll leave you couples to it. I've salted the steps, but let me know if you need help getting up."

"Will do," Cam responds.

"I'll be keeping an eye out."

"Thanks, Aaron. Goodnight."

He bows his head to us and disappears back inside as we make our way to the end of the driveway and up the stairs to the right.

As we head up, the front door opens and Gabriel steps out. "Evening, children," he says.

"Evening, old man," replies Cameron.

"Sorry, we're late, Gabriel," I say with Cameron behind me. "I have a walking speed on par with a newborn sloth around here."

"Yeah, the snow really piles up in these hills," he replies. "And you're right on time, my friends."

As my boot hits the next step, I feel it slip and I stumble forwards, my hands hitting a step above, breaking my fall. I look down at the steps, thick with ice, not looking salted at all.

"Are you okay?" asks Cameron, leaning over me.

"Yeah, I'm fine. Sorry, born clumsy... and with an inability to pick out effective snowshoes."

"I'm having some decent ones delivered to your parents' house tomorrow," says Cameron. "I couldn't get them delivered here in time."

Before I have time to thank him, Gabriel walks down a few steps and reaches out his hand. I lift my gloved hand to meet his and he grasps it, squeezing it tightly as he and Cameron help me to my feet. "Okay there?"

"Yep. Thanks."

"Aaron!" Gabriel calls out. I turn to see Aaron emerge from the guest house. "When you have a minute, do you mind salting the steps again?"

"Sure, I'm on it."

On the deck, Cam and I shake off the dusting of snow on our outer clothes and head inside. Gabriel hangs up our coats and gives us house shoes to wear which Cameron exchanges for his bottle of wine.

As I inspect my wrist, which aches a little from the knock it just took, Cameron takes it in his hands, turning it to look at both sides. "Does it hurt?" he asks, skimming his finger over my soft skin which fizzes at his touch.

"It's fine," I smile, pulling away.

The living room is huge and open, coated in burgundy wallpaper with slivers of gold thread running throughout. There is a cream sectional surrounding a large coffee table with a thick slab of wood atop it.

On the walls are a handful of large oil paintings—one of a river running through a forest on a gloomy day. To the right is a sunset over the horizon, shiny waves fizzing onto a beach in the foreground.

And then I stop in my tracks as I spot the painting to the left on the main wall, at least twelve feet high by fifteen feet wide. It is the sinewy umber trunk of an oak tree, twisting out into a dozen or so main branches which each spawn their own smaller ones bearing leaves in hues of teal, sage and olive green. Behind the oak is a field and further beyond, tufts of grass leading to a sea of boisterous waves. If I didn't know better, I would say it was a view from behind the oak tree that Cameron took me to on Long Island.

"Jess?"

My mouth goes dry as I take in the painting.

"Jessie?"

Gabriel's voice.

I turn to him and see his eyes shift from me to the painting then back to me. "This way."

"Okay," I say.

Is Gabriel taking his power back from those people by displaying such a painting or is he haunted to the degree that he can't extricate himself from this imagery?

Maybe he just likes the painting, Jess...

Shaking off the ghosts of Q.N. which continue to stalk me, I follow the men into the dark, opulent dining room where we sit at a thick table whose top is a mixture of tigerwood and a clear, hard glossy substance encapsulating the wood divinely. Gabriel signals for Cameron to sit at the head of the table.

"I'll be with you in a minute, guys!" shouts Beth to the sound of clangs coming from the kitchen.

"Do you need any help, Beth?" I ask.

"No, thanks. I'm good."

"Wow, this table is beautiful, Gabriel," I say as he heads to a small bar nearby. "What is this clear material?"

"Epoxy resin."

"It's stunning."

"Apéritif?" asks Gabriel.

"Um, no. I get ridiculous if I mix drinks. I'll just stick to wine tonight."

He withdraws a bottle of red wine from his cabinet. "Cameron tells me you only drink sweet, sparkling white wine."

I grin and shake my head at Cameron. "Yeah, I am guilty of that one."

"Well, I have a red wine here that I'd like you to try," says Gabriel. "It's older and drier than what you usually like, but I'd like you to try something out of your comfort zone."

Cameron breathes out in irritation. "Gabriel," he groans slowly. "I'd appreciate it if you didn't take it upon yourself to educate this girl. I like to take care of the educating myself."

I roll my eyes playfully at his alpha-dom reaction to another man exerting his influence over the woman he's with.

"Just this once, my friend," Gabriel responds, pouring me a glass of dark blood-red liquid into a tall, round wine glass. He hands it to me, placing the bottle onto the table.

I take a sip. "Wow, this stuff is dangerous."

"You like?" Gabriel asks, glancing at Cameron with a provocative grin of amusement on his lips.

"It's amazing."

"Good."

He fills two cut crystal tumblers with malt whiskey over ice, handing one to Cameron sitting to my left and placing one to my right at the other end of the table. I can't help but notice his exquisite dress shirt—cornflower blue with tawny stripes of different thicknesses running from top to bottom above brown dress pants. His thick brown hair is neatly combed and his face freshly shaven. The muscles of his strong frame are obvious even under his shirt which is rolled up to reveal dense forearms.

He takes a seat opposite Cameron, finding his eyes just as Beth bursts into the room. "Sorry," she says as Cam and I get up.

"Don't apologize," Cameron replies kissing her on the cheek.

She turns to me and embraces me, looking me up and down. "Wow, you look *stunning*, Jess."

"Gift from Val," I say.

"You look like an angel."

"So do you, Beth!" I'm not kidding. She's wearing a skin-tight dark-blue robe with a plunging neckline which hugs her slim frame like a second skin. Her hair is tied into a tight knot at the back of her head and she's wearing a heavy smokey eye and crimson lipstick which has me wondering whether my lip gloss and mascara combo is a bit on the underdone side. "You look gorgeous."

. . .

Twenty minutes later I find myself laughing as Gabriel and Cameron spar verbally, busting each other's balls with stories of some of their questionable teenage antics as we tuck into dinner—gratin potatoes and vegetables accompanied by wild poached salmon for me and steak for the others, with Gabriel and Cameron tearing into crimson steaks so rare that they are almost blue.

"Yeah, you were *quite* the little shit back then, Gabriel," deadpans Cameron.

"Nothing much has changed, huh?" replies Gabriel in jest.

"No. If anything, things have taken a turn for the worse," says Cameron dryly to Gabriel's throaty laughter.

"How about you, Jess?" Gabriel asks as I swallow down a mouthful of lemony asparagus. "Did you get into much mischief as a child?"

"Well, um, I have heard from reliable sources that I could be a bit of a handful when I was in the mood."

"I can believe that," replies Cameron with a smile.

"I'm told I had a lot of opinions. I'm still waiting for the evidence on that one..." Beth chuckles and Gabriel breaks into a grin. "But to be honest, my parents were such incorrigible rebels that my brother and I often felt like *we* were babysitting *them*."

"Have they mellowed with age?" Gabriel asks, his teeth sinking into a thick chunk of bloody meat.

"I'm not sure how much mellowing I've observed of late if I'm being honest. They moved to Connecticut a while back and my mother now amuses herself by causing havoc around Westport." Beth chuckles. "She's decided that their recycling system is just wholly inadequate even though some say it's one of the best in the state, and boy, are they hearing about it..."

"Reminds me of someone I know," says Cameron with the slightest of winks that makes my insides shiver.

"Oh God, don't get me started on Tammy." I grin in pride at the sound of his hearty laughter. "So far, my mother has contacted the environmental protection department, the mayor's office, and about five local newspapers. The woman is like a freaking dog with a bone when she's got her panties in a twist."

I feel relief to hear all three of my dinner mates chuckle at my inebriated silliness.

"Good for her," replies Gabriel.

"Yeah, she's pretty cool," I reply finishing off my second glass of wine. As I place the empty glass down on the table, I feel the room spinning for a split-second which has me deciding not to touch the third glass that Gabriel is pouring me. "Though, um, don't tell her I said that. I actually feel like I'm channeling her some days which is just frankly... disturbing."

"She must be happy about your blog, no?" asks Gabriel. "How many visitors does it get a day now, ten thousand?"

"It got up to eleven thousand today. Any article I can't sell or don't want to sell, I stick it on there. I've actually had some online magazines contact me after reading stuff on the blog. I have no idea how so many people are even finding me. I just spend a few dollars a day on ads and then bug some journalist friends of mine and other bloggers to repost it on their feeds."

"Well, clearly people are resonating with your way of seeing the world," Gabriel says, a mischievous flame dancing in his eyes. "That could come in handy one day..."

"That's enough, Gabriel," chides Cameron.

I don't think Cameron knows how tempted I constantly feel to post an exposé of the calculated seduction of teenagers going on in Manhattan's high society.

"But she's proud of you?" Beth asks. "Your mom, I mean."

"Well, my dad's definitely more demonstrative about that kind of thing, but she hasn't disapproved yet, which in mom's language, means she's just brimming with pride on the inside."

"Well, that's something," she replies, getting to her feet. "I'm going to get dessert."

"Let me help," I say getting up to collect plates. "The food was amazing, Beth."

"Thank you, darling."

"I need a smoke," says Gabriel.

"I'll join you," replies Cameron.

I frown at him as I pick up his plate.

"Still just one a month," he counters to my silent reproach.

The men get up and head to the balcony just off the dining room to the right as I follow Beth to the kitchen and put our plates in the sink.

"Do you want me to stick these in the dishwasher?" I ask.

"No. I'll get to it later."

She pops a divine-looking open-faced pear tart in the oven and puts two glasses of water on the kitchen table which she sits down at. "Come join me, Jess. Let's leave the boys to it for a few minutes while this heats up."

I sit down opposite her, feeling much more unsteady on my feet than I usually do after just two glasses of wine. I watch as she reaches for a black cigarette case lying on the table, gracefully flipping it open and withdrawing a slim white cigarette from it which she lights with a golden flip-top lighter which makes her glossy scarlet nails flicker like hellfire. With the flash of the flame, I feel myself transported back to watching Alexandra Frost do the same at the bar in Richard's Hamptons mansion in August. As Beth pulls the white cylinder to her blood-red lips and inhales the pale smoke deep into the recesses of her lungs, a frigid chill rolls through the air like a bank of early-morning winter fog as I suddenly see Alexandra sitting before me, her glacial smoke-hued eyes narrowing in delight, her harsh features darkening as she peers into me, the tiniest of smiles registering on her thin lips. The racing of my heart is only matched by the sudden frenzy of my breathing as she eyes me keenly while taking another long drag, exhaling the ashy mist.

"Hello, Jessynia," she purrs, her beady eyes unblinking as she soaks me in, the tentacles of her malignant energy reaching towards me as they prepare to enter their prey. As her mouth opens, I see stains of crimson inside, remnants of a feast of blood which clash wildly with the ghostly pale curls of her white-blond hair.

I stare, paralyzed but for the internal tremor shaking my body, as the scene around me blackens and twisted trees invade the room, their branches and roots climbing up the walls like spider legs, infesting cabinets, snaking up chairs, sneaking up our table, roots encapsulating the wooden tabletop as she sits, peering inside me, unmoving, her unabashed darkness on full display.

"Jessynia?"

I feel a stab of pain in my neck as Alex's smile grows wider, more sinister, her narrow-set eyes gleaming as all blood drains from me.

"Jessie?" The voice is more urgent now.

And then there's a firm hand on mine, squeezing tightly, jarring me back through the looking glass and into Gabriel's kitchen. Beth's face zooms into focus as she eyes me with a mixture of concern and curiosity. "You with us, miss?"

"Yeah... sorry, Beth. I just... zoned out for a minute."

"You were totally gone there!"

"I'm sorry... I... I think this wine has gotten to me." I know it's impossible, but if I didn't know better, I would say I had been drugged.

She studies me for a moment as if bewildered, then says, "I was saying that I won't offer you a cigarette as I know you don't smoke."

"Well, I try my best not to. Don't always succeed."

"That's a gorgeous necklace you have there," she says, taking another puff. My fingers instinctively find the gold chain that Jack bought me. As much as I often forget I have it on, equally, I can't seem to take it off. Somehow it still feels like armor to me, protection from the world. "Present from Cameron?"

"Um, no. Just from another friend."

"You two look good together, you and Cam. He's different when you're around."

"Oh, how so?"

"He just seems... lighter. Like a weight has been lifted off him. Plus, he looks at you constantly. It's like he can't take his eyes off you. I've never seen him like that before. If you don't mind my saying so, it's hot as hell." She toys with her words deliciously.

I take in a big lungful of air and look down, slowly sighing it out.

"Worried about Jack?" she asks.

I nod.

"He's not the one you should be worried about." Her face is suddenly harsh, callous. I don't answer, feeling unnerved at the way her tone and demeanor can shift so abruptly. "The Society are the ones you need to be afraid of. Jack could maybe lose control and do something stupid, but when the Society wants to dish out pain, it is calculated to the minutest detail."

I take a sip of water. "Aren't *you* scared of them, Beth? Of aligning yourself with the resistance like this? Do you think they know?"

"They may know we spend time together, but they won't know how determined we are to take them down. We've taken a lot of measures to protect ourselves. Charles and Aaron have helped us set up systems to protect our phones, devices, homes. Aaron has tested them all. Once we can get those men and women to go the D.A. and get some journalists to cover the story, they won't dare do anything."

"But it was personal with you and... Vallen," I say. "Sorry, I don't like to say that thing's name, but you said he warned you never to speak out in that note. Aren't you afraid that they may take revenge on you if they find out how involved you are?"

She shakes her head. "You know a funny thing happens when you go through trauma. Sometimes the experiences you've had are so huge, so life-changing, so deep in their darkness, that as you start to heal, you kind of feel like you've experienced as much as life has to offer... and deep down you feel ready to let go." She looks down onto the table below her for a moment. "If I'm being perfectly honest, I've felt ready to let go of this life for quite some time..."

I shudder as she looks back up at me, her eyes suddenly hollow behind her immaculate makeup. "Beth, that would be giving them what they want."

"Well, if I lose my life speaking out about these people," she says, "then so be it. I have written my story up and have it with several lawyers. I hope some brave person would help me to get it out." She darts me a pointed look.

"Beth, you can't think that way. It's like you're resigning yourself to something happening..."

"I don't think it will," she responds. "Gravier thinks he has undying loyalty from his inner circle, but a lot of the people around him are not with him because they believe in him or even believe in the Society anymore. They are with him out of total abject fear of the consequences of defying him. Even a lot of those at the very top of that satanic place, the ones that perform the most heinous of acts for that man, they do it to survive."

"Do you think he knows that?"

"I think so, deep down. That's why he's getting messy, punishing more and more people, tightening the reigns. But if he keeps going like this, he's going to slip up and I just hope I'm around long enough to see the day when he's being led away in handcuffs."

"You will be."

She glances down at her flawlessly manicured hands. "If I can be around long enough for you and Cameron to be completely free of them, I can die a happy woman."

"I'm sure Gabriel would be extremely upset if anything were to happen to you," I say.

She looks back up, her dazzling jade-green eyes peering into me. "Gabriel and I have gotten very close over the last year." She takes a sip of water. "But he doesn't love me the way that Cameron loves you. I see it in his eyes."

"Maybe he just *can't* love that way, no matter who he's with?"

"Maybe..."

"You love him?" I ask.

She pauses and I observe a gulp in her throat. "I've decided not to give my heart fully to a man again."

I don't respond, aware of the depths of trauma she must have experienced to close herself off like this.

"Gabriel mentioned his father Luca the other night," I say. "His death. Can you tell me what happened?"

She takes in a final drag of her cigarette before slowly and methodically putting it out in a silver ashtray. "It's not the most pleasant of stories," she finally says. "How about we save it for another time?"

"Sure."

I'm suddenly startled to hear raised voices coming from the balcony and turn to face Beth, mouth agape.

She smiles at my reaction. "Don't worry about those two. They have always had that kind of relationship. I get worried if they get to the end of the night *without* having a huge bust-up."

I jump again at the sound of Gabriel bellowing and Cameron barking something back. "Good grief! Should we stop them?"

"No, let them get it out of their system. It's that Latin temperament, you know. Cameron half-Spanish, half-Irish. Gabriel half-Spanish, half-Italian. Fireworks are to be expected. This is their equivalent of a civilized chat."

"Oh, Lord..."

This time even Beth jumps at the sound of another yell from the balcony.

"Oh God, they're not going to start beating each other up, are they?!" I ask.

"You never know," she sings. "I've seen some ripped shirts in my time."

"Are you serious?!"

"I believe it's what happens when two dominant alphas attempt to reach a consensus."

"Oh God," I groan.

"I need to go to the washroom," she says. "How about you go and see if you can calm them down a bit?"

"Great..."

I get up and head to the balcony, sliding the glass door open. The men are sitting on opposite ends from each other, a small table keeping them separated, their faces mauve, their demeanor disheveled. They look up at me, their chests heaving in labored respiration.

Looks like I got here a minute before the shirt-ripping began...

"Um, I hate to be one of those annoying women who stop the men having their fun, but, um, the women feel that the night will be more successful if we don't have to get the first-aid kit out at some point."

I see Gabriel smile as he turns to look at Cameron who continues to glare at him for a few seconds until he shakes his head. "You know, Gabriel, I sometimes wonder how I ended up having a best friend who is such a total prick."

Gabriel grins, tipping his head. "Funny, I was just thinking the same thing."

"Um, I really don't want to cramp anyone's style," I say, "but I think what we need here is a bit of *yin* energy." I glance at Cameron who manages a smile at the end of a deep breath.

"Come join us, Jess," says Gabriel as Cameron makes room for me on the bench next to him beside one of two balcony heaters warming the air deliciously.

"I really don't mean to emasculate anyone," I say. "It's just that over the last hundred thousand years, women have developed an ingrained urge to stop the men around them from getting their heads caved in."

Amusement brightens Gabriel's eyes. "Well, we're not at the head-caved-in phase yet."

"*Yet* being the optimal word," retorts Cameron.

As Gabriel finishes off his wine, placing the empty glass down on the bamboo table between us, Beth appears, sliding open the balcony door.

"Um, I need help flambéing some sauce without setting myself on fire. Anyone care to lend a hand?" Her unflinching eyes settle on Cameron.

"Sure," he responds after a moment, getting to his feet, his hand clenching my shoulder as he steps around me. As he heads back inside, he turns around. "Be gentle with this girl while I'm gone, Gabriel. Otherwise, one of us will end up flying off this balcony. My money's on you."

Gabriel bows his head. "You have my word."

Cameron's gaze finds me as he slides the door closed behind him.

"You two have quite a *fiery* relationship," I say, the scene before me spinning once again. I take a sip of water from Cameron's glass on the table in the hopes of diluting the effects of the strong wine.

Gabriel smiles. "You mustn't mind us getting in each other's faces from time to time," he continues. "I only fight this hard with people I love..."

"Oh, the opposite of my mother, then."

"It sounds like it," he replies genially. "You've had a tough year, Jessynia."

Oh God...

"Is this the part where I get psychoanalyzed?" I ask gruffly.

His ensuing laugh is bold and fearless. This is a man that doesn't mind taking up space. "I guess it is. Though I'll try not to be a *prick* about it."

"Good!" I grin.

"Cameron's different around you," he says. "I see a light around him." I swallow hard as the handsome Gabriel peers into me, thick brown waves framing his piercing eyes and tanned face. "I imagine that must feel like a lot of responsibility on such young shoulders."

"Well, we're just taking it slow."

"Why slow?"

"Well, it just so happens that this man I love is also a sworn enemy of the man I'm still married to."

"Whom you still also love..."

I sigh. "It's just a fabulous spot to be in."

"These are two very powerful men, Jess. Strong, breathtaking, damaged men. They have energy that could light up Times Square. Being drawn to them is *normal*. It's nothing to be ashamed of."

"I'm just so afraid of Jack's reaction. And of hurting him."

He arches a brow. "He didn't seem to care that much about how much he hurt you."

"I know."

"That's not all you're afraid of, is it?"

He's right. In a place I don't often want to admit to, part of me is terrified of getting even more mixed up with the Society than I already am. I also realize that deep down, there is something in me that is afraid of Cameron. Not the Cameron I know now... but the one lurking in the shadows, the one that would emerge if he is overcome by memories and torment and demons.

The one who is *still* drawn to them.

My silence doesn't conceal the answer which must be etched on my face... and you don't have to be a renowned psychoanalyst to see it.

"You're tempted to walk away from them all, aren't you?" Gabriel asks.

"Yes. Sometimes."

"It would be the smart thing to do. But as I know well, when it comes to love, *very* few of us are smart."

"I've never really known fear before... or at least not since I was a teenager." He frowns but I press on. "It's oppressive, makes you want to run away."

"That's why we need to take these people down... so that no one else has to live like this."

"What do the Society think of Cameron?"

Gabriel runs a strong hand over the black tufts of hair on his strong chin, studying my face softly. "Well, Alexandra didn't take kindly to Cameron rejecting her and leaving. She's a typical empathy-challenged narcissist... in the clinical sense of the world. Rejection brings out the inner monster. And she felt something for him that she rarely feels for men anymore. I do believe she was... utterly besotted by him."

"I'm amazed a woman that cold can feel anything close to love."

"Yes, she is quite a case study. Unfortunately, Jack and Cameron seem to be the men she has felt the most for in her life. Other than Sebastian Gravier, that is. She certainly does seem to worship the ground he walks on..."

"What about the others? Do they dislike him too?" I ask.

"The big problem is Gravier."

"Why?"

"Because he abhors Cameron with a passion that never abates."

I gasp audibly as Gabriel says it.

"You didn't know?" he asks.

"No."

"I'm not sure that even Cameron knows the *full* extent of Gravier's *animus*. His hatred. We've tried to shield him from that knowledge as much as we can. I'm not sure we've succeeded."

"Why does he hate him?" I ask.

"Partly because Cameron walked away. But mainly because... Cameron has always been loved. He grew up surrounded by it. Not only was he loved, but he was respected, and given a safe space to be himself, to grow into his own person. His mother worshipped the ground he walked on. His father adored him. Same goes for his sisters, Lottie, Charles, my father, his entire extended family.

"Gravier never experienced anything like that. His mother abused him relentlessly, tried to mold him into something acceptable to her twisted standards, and before his death, his father just stood back and let her. When a child is abused by a parent, they don't stop loving the parent. They stop loving themselves. And if that goes on for too long, the psyche, the soul, they fracture. In his case, his soul is gone completely and the only solace that can relieve that void is feasting on the joy and life force of others." There's a silence between us as Gabriel studies my face before speaking again. "There's an old proverb... The child who is not embraced by the village..."

"Will burn it down to feel its warmth," I finish.

He smiles, watching me for a few silent moments. "That is how Sebastian engages with this world that has been so unfair to him. Causing misery and terror is medicine to him. Justice. It soothes him. And he is willing to burn down the entire world to get that drug, even if it means burning himself alive in the process.

"The trauma of being abused by a parent, an abuse that is utterly invalidated in our society, leaves you feeling lonely and cold in and of itself, and as you get older, you start to resent those that are loved so unconditionally like Cameron is.

"I think that's one of the reasons that Gravier has always been so enthralled by Jack. Jack grew up in a poor family, a criminal family, not a family where affection was shown the way it was in Cameron's. Then Jack lost his mother, his biggest source of unconditional love, when he was a young kid and his father's not one for showing affection, to put it mildly. Gravier feels a kinship to Jack because of it..."

"Would Gravier ever try to hurt Cameron?"

"Yes. Or the people he loves... which is why this year, we finally have to hit back."

I nod.

As this stunning man peers into my solemn face as if studying every square inch of me, I decide to ask Gabriel whether he left the note under my door. As I build up the courage to, I glance towards the little lodge below, thirty feet away, and inhale sharply as I see a man's face, his head and naked torso visible between the two curtains behind the small window facing the house. Aaron, I assume. As Gabriel turns to look in that direction, I see the man retreat and the curtains draw together, blocking him out.

Or did I imagine the whole thing?

This strong wine seems to be playing havoc with my sense of reality...

I glance at Gabriel who eyes me curiously. "You're jumpy, Jess."

"Yeah. Apparently." Though I don't remember being jumpy like this before June of last year.

As I look down and prepare to ask Gabriel about the note, there is a light thud of steps and the glass door slides open.

"Dessert's on the table, you two," sings Beth.

Gabriel and I watch each other for a suspended moment before I stand up, feeling him right behind me, his breath misting heavily on my neck as I step inside.

23

AN HOUR OR SO LATER, Cam and I stomp our boots on the mat outside Blackwood's side door before taking them off and hanging our coats up.

"Fancy an herbal tea?" I ask.

"Sure," Cameron replies.

I put the kettle on and place two white mugs on the glossy soapstone countertop, running my fingers over one of the frail white veins running through the thick onyx stone. I reach up and grab the wooden tea chest only to feel Cameron's dense frame envelop my back, his lips at my nape, a hand snaking around my side and over the blood-red velvet hugging my belly. He strokes my glossy hair to the side and begins to tenderly kiss the side of my neck, the heat of his lips warming my skin, spreading into the soft valley below.

"Did you enjoy dinner?" he whispers.

I nod, words eluding me as I feel his thick erection press into me as his other hand makes its way around my throat, holding it softly. In truth, between my vision of Alex Frost, Beth's comments about being ready to leave this world and Gabriel's insights into what Gravier thinks of Cameron, the moxie I've been trying get back these last few days is escaping me and I'm feeling paper-thin this evening.

This feeling of fragility is new to me—an unwanted, unexpected intrusion into my previously fearless life. Before finding out about Jack's affairs in June, I just don't remember experiencing this feeling. Even after my skiing accident when my body was falling to pieces, I always knew who I was, could always stand up for myself. I never had moments when I felt like I could crumble into the earth.

This is the last year I ever want to feel like this. My New Year's resolution is to claw back every ounce of the strength I've lost... and then some.

"I'm especially happy that Beth and I didn't have to take anyone to the emergency room," I say, dropping a sachet of spearmint tea into each cup.

I feel his soft breath of amusement on the side of my cheek. "I'm sorry about that."

"What were you arguing about?"

He exhales slowly, his teeth finding the shell of my ear. "I won't bore you with the details. Gabriel and I have always had a pretty... intense relationship."

"Yeah, *intense* is definitely one word you could use."

"I think the thought of your naked pussy waiting for me was putting me more on edge than usual." He reaches a hand down to my crotch, pressing the velvet over the sensitive knot of nerves as an avalanche of fire descends on me to the shrill whistle of the kettle. His teeth tug gently at my neck. I feel like he wants to bite. I can sense it in the forced restraint of his straining jaw muscles.

"Well, you've only got yourself to blame for that, sir," I counter, pouring hot water into each cup as my skin tightens at the low, unspoken threat in his words.

"You're right, my lady. The two-hour-long erection doesn't help a man keep his cool."

I swivel round to face him. "Two hours?!" He smiles as I hand him his tea, watching me from behind the cup as we take a sip of the fragrant infusion. "And how about now?" I ask.

He looks down at his watch. "I guess that makes it two and a half hours."

"Is that normal or are you a biological anomaly, Mr. O'Neill?"

"It's normal considering the state you left me in this morning..."

"I see. Sounds like it's been a *frustrating* day."

There's a smile in his sharp eyes. "Very."

A few minutes later, I turn to wash my cup in the sink to find his hand on top of mine, turning off the faucet. "Leave it," he says, lifting me up into his arms without asking and carrying me up one and then another flight of stairs as easily as if he were carrying a bag of groceries.

As we reach the landing separating our bedrooms, he sets me down, takes his key out of his pocket and opens the black door a few feet down at the very end of the hallway, his fingers interlacing mine tightly as he pulls me through, turning on a light and locking the door behind us. I'm amazed to see a narrow flight of stairs. I had thought we were at the top of this tall house.

He leads me up and opens a door to the left, pulling me through to a sight that has breath rushing from me. It is a loft, the same size as Cameron's bedroom, looking out onto the back of the house, but its slanted roof is made entirely of glass, as is the entire thick, solid wall, with just an iron girder forming the seam between it and the glass roof. In the corner stands a telescope pointing up at the inky sky, dotted with the incandescent light of trillions of stars.

As he leads me in, I look up in awe at them, more than I ever remember seeing in a night sky, with no city lights competing for their attention. "Oh my God," I say, stunned by the most awesome of the universe's light displays which go in and out of focus due to the potent wine Gabriel gave me.

I feel his gaze on my face. "You like it, angel?"

"I've never seen a room like it."

"Good."

I look up at the glass above us. "Where's the snow?"

"It's heated glass," he says. "Like you get in cars."

He pulls me towards the floor-to-ceiling window, to the right of which is a reinforced glass door with an iron frame that leads onto a wooden balcony enclosed by glass panels. The thick floor-to-ceiling glass wall stands a few feet behind the main wall of the house which is why—in addition to the forest beyond which stops you from being able to stand back far enough—you can't see this glass room from the back of the house.

I touch the window tentatively with my fingertip, checking if it is hot. It's cold.

Cameron smiles and moves behind me, his hand sliding over my belly. "It's only heated to two degrees," he says into my ear, pressing his left palm on top of mine so that it pushes against the glass. "You can see the little wires if you look closely."

"Oh yeah," I say as I spot the tiniest of horizontal threads running throughout. Leaning up against the window, I look out over the tops of what look like endless fir trees, their dark-green peaks swaying gently against the mesmerizing indigo of the night sky, illuminated by the moon—full, heavy, low in the sky. A blue moon.

"Oh my God, Cameron. It's so beautiful."

He finds my neck with his lips again, heating the air around us with his lust. "I like watching you discover things for the first time. Watching your face as you see sights like this is one of the most beautiful things I've ever seen. I want to always be there to watch you discover new things." His tongue leaves his mouth and licks my neck firmly as his hand delves into the top of my tight velvet dress, over my soft breast where he finds the nipple with a groan and pulls it to attention.

"Cameron," I moan as his fingers set my insides aflame.

He lifts my chin with his hand, his right finger pointing to the brightest spark in the sky. "Venus," he says.

"Are you sure?!"

"Certain. Would you like to see?"

"Are you serious?! Of course I would."

He releases his hold on me and walks me to the telescope in the corner. A minute or so of adjusting the lens and position passes and he finally guides me behind it. "Look," he says and I peer through the scope.

"It looks like a crescent," I gasp, observing a half-moon shape with a hazy glow around it.

"Yes. Through the scope you can see it wax and wane. Some days it's fuller than others, like the moon."

"I've never seen it close up like that."

"Breathtaking, isn't it?"

I nod, captivated by this mysterious planet as he pulls the top of my dress down past my shoulder, his lips finding the soft dip, nuzzling into the smooth light honey of my hot skin, stunning me with the reverence of his caress as my skin tingles in expectation of the stark expression of his uncivilized virility.

He releases me as I turn around. "This room is incredible, Cameron."

The plushest of muted purple rugs dominates the floor. There is a side table between two armchairs and a black ottoman against the long accent wall of dark green. A huge mirror hangs from it, six feet by six at least. There is a small room next to the door which may be a bathroom and a large black armoire next to that.

"I had this room made for you," he says, stalking me as I amble around.

"What?!" I swivel to face him.

He smiles at another of my ever-expressive reactions. "I made the architect convert half the loft space into this room after we bought the house because I know you like looking at the stars, and I knew one day I would bring you here to see it. No other woman has ever been here... other than my mother," he smiles.

"Cam, I feel like I could pass out at some of the things you say to me."

"That's the idea..."

He stands opposite me, quietly drinking me in. Cameron is one of those rare people I've met who, though kind and compassionate, can watch another person intently without flinching or having to look away and I feel my cheeks flushing at the sight of his glare.

"I like it when you blush," he murmurs, our eyes dueling... and him clearly winning.

"I think you'll find the tea steamed me up, sir."

"Hmm, I'm not so sure. I suspect you're going to be blushing a lot tonight, without the tea. And by the way, I like it when you call me *sir*."

He takes a step forward and grabs hold of my dress, pulling it up over my head without speaking and throwing it onto a chair against the wall. He moves behind me, unclasping my bra which he discards before continuing his walk, his fingertips skimming the skin on my waist, my back, my shoulder before finally he is in front of me, watching my face, his gaze unflinching.

There is the tiniest of groans as his eyes track the curves of my entirely naked body. I swallow hard as he runs his thumbs over my round breasts, gently stroking my nipples which harden into points for him. He studies my eyes silently as he plays with the soft teats, caressing, stroking, teasing and then tugging at both nipples.

"Those tits should be illegal," he says as a flush of pink blooms across my chest at the sensation of being totally nude and exposed in front of such a dominant man in his designer suit.

He walks around me again, slowly, deliberately, touching the pert cheeks of my derrière as he does.

"Those tits," he murmurs as he evaluates the body that he intends to use tonight. "That tiny waist. Those hips. That freshly shaven pussy. You have the single *most* fuckable body I've ever seen."

I shift a little as he comes to stand before me, contemplating me from two feet away as his hands form fists on either side of his lean frame.

Lifting one hand to my jaw, he uses his thumb to pry open my mouth, pushing it inside the pink opening. My lips tighten around it instinctively, trained by the months of fantasizing about performing fellatio on him.

"Not to mention those plump pink lips that were designed for grabbing onto my cock," he says. "And those big, innocent eyes that plead with me while I fuck you. You don't have any idea what you do to me..." He withdraws his thumb.

"I think I have a clue," I respond, biting my lip.

"Good. You were put on this Earth to be fucked by me, Jessynia. That is your purpose."

"I do have a brain, you know, O'Neill," I chide roughly.

"Well, you won't be needing that for the next short while."

"You know, you can be such an arrogant prick at times," I shoot back as he takes another step towards me, narrowing his twinkling eyes at me, his lips curving wryly.

"I suspect you enjoy my *arrogant prick* side, don't you?"

"Well, let's just say that with some of the *skills* you have, I can just about overlook it."

He glances down at my naked body before finding my eyes again, his voice low, his breathing quickening. "I like your defiance, Jessynia. I like your insolence. They make me very hard. I'm going to have a lot of fun trying to tame you to my satisfaction."

"I'm really not sure I like the idea of being *tamed*," I tease as he takes one more step towards me so that my erect nipples are now brushing against the cotton enveloping his hard chest.

"Good. The more you resist my need for control, the better." He runs his hand up my waist, finding the side of my breast. "You do know you are going to be my property very soon, Miss Avery."

"I didn't realize we were still in the eighteenth century, Mr. O'Neill," I respond, drowning in his blazing eyes.

"Well, if it makes you feel any better,"—he eases strands of my long brown hair behind my shoulders—"I was put on this Earth for similar reasons. To fuck you very, very hard. To watch your face as you come. To teach you what pleasure is. To impregnate you. Your pleasure, your happiness and your protection are my only purpose."

"Hmm, well, I guess we're even then..."

"I think so..."

And with that, we both edge forward and he takes my mouth for his own, charging his tongue inside. I don't even attempt resistance. I don't know if this is right or wrong. There is nothing I can do to resist this man now. My limbs weaken as his tongue ventures inside me, licking, sucking, writhing against mine as our hands venture into each other's hair, my fingers entangled in his dense locks as his tug at my long waves, perfecting the possession of my mouth to his satisfaction as he holds my head at the angle he desires.

I throw my head back as he whispers my name, kissing my neck softly, slowly tasting my jawline with his tongue, holding me possessively against his clothed rock-hard body. Our tongues find each other again, his the more dominant, fucking my mouth with ease.

As he pulls away, my teeth catch his gloriously carved bottom lip, biting the dark-pink flesh delicately until I feel it give a little. I pull away with a breathy moan, my eyes zooming in on the audacious indentations left by my teeth in his divine flesh. I've never felt an urge to taste someone the way I do him. Licking and sucking are just not enough when it comes to this man...

"Hmm... you like to bite too, huh?" he hisses, his eyes widening as he takes a step back, grabbing the knot of his tie and pulling the length out before sliding it off his collar. "Turn around," he commands.

I waver for a second before complying and feel him tug both my hands behind my back and start to tie them together.

I instinctively resist for a moment. "Cam, I—" My eyes find his as I pivot slightly, trying to pull one hand away from his grasp.

His eyelids drop as he scrutinizes my face, his arousal at the sight of my reticence apparent. "You told me you want to watch my face as I come," he says. "Your submission is the best way to accomplish that."

I don't answer but look at him nervously.

"Do you need a safe word, beautiful?" he asks.

I nod.

"How about... *Blackwood*?"

"Okay."

"Good. Say that word and I stop without question. Clear?"

"Yes."

"Now turn around." His stern command has goosebumps zapping up my arms.

I watch the dark embers in his eyes for a few seconds before turning so that he can finish tying my hands together. As he silently completes the task, I test the knot by pulling one arm up, but it's been expertly tied and my hands are immovable.

I swivel round to face him.

"Mmm." The deep thunder emanating from his indecent mouth

leaves my sex tingling despite the fear I feel at having my hands restrained by him for the first time. "I feel like I've been waiting to see you like this my entire life," he murmurs.

He takes a step back and reaches for the top button of his shirt which he undoes while watching me in all his moody dominance, then onto the next and the next, until he unpeels the thick cotton from his torso, leaving my lips parting at the sight of the immense mass of his huge shoulders, lean arms, his smooth, hairless pecs, and the deep grooves of his abdominal muscles. Reaching lower, he undoes the silver buckle of his black belt and pulls it off, throwing it to the floor before unzipping his pants and shedding the rest of his clothes. The sight of his thick length pointing upwards steals my breath.

I tremble internally at his naked form, elegantly masculine but for the primal deviance of his erect cock, the engorged dome of his head and the sack which hangs large and heavy above legs thick like tree trunks. His hands fist at his sides as he watches me take in the slabs of taut muscle gleaming in the crepuscular rays and shadows of the moon. There's no doubt about it: Cameron O'Neill has been put on this Earth to ruthlessly fuck women until he steals their sanity.

As my body succumbs to the sight of this most exquisite work of male art, he pushes his thumb into the wet mauve of my mouth. "I've thought about it very carefully, Miss Avery, and I've decided that you have been a good girl today." He withdraws his thumb.

"I have? Are you sure? I don't often hear that," I tease to a glimmer of wry appreciation from him.

"Well, there have been a few moments of insolence," he responds, eyes burning in dark amusement, "but overall, I can overlook it this time."

"That's a dangerous lesson to teach me..."

"I've decided to be lenient with you for the time being."

"Well, I'll have to show my appreciation for your generosity." I smile up at him, a smile he reciprocates in the way his almond-shaped eyes lift at the corners.

"Indeed." He pushes his thumb into the slippery heat of my mouth. "You know what I want from you, Jessynia."

As he withdraws his thumb, I swallow hard, trying not to fall under the weight of his desire. Without speaking a word, I drop to my knees onto the plush lilac-gray rug beneath us, looking up at him in anticipation, desperately hoping I can do the job justice and give this demi-god the pleasure he so deserves after dreaming of this moment for so long.

My lips part a tad as his eyes bear down on me, my deep, slow breathing forcing my chest out even further as I observe the thick erection pointing up at me, completely hard, engorged with blood, throbbing, huge, cut. Perfect. My mouth waters and I lick my lips instinctively.

He curls his fingers around his dense shaft. “Do you like seeing me hard?”

“Yes.”

“Yes, what?”

“Yes, I do,” I respond cheekily, knowing full well that he wants a *Yes, sir* out of me.

“I was expecting a *Yes, sir* or a *Yes, my lord*, Miss Avery.”

“I’m not sure you’ve done enough to deserve that yet.”

“Well, I intend to remedy that.”

“Good."

“Lick your lips,” he says.

I press them together, using the saliva between the seam to lubricate them.

“Open your mouth.” I acquiesce as he takes a step forward until the head of his cock is hovering an inch from my mouth.

“Look at me,” he murmurs. “Don’t take your eyes off mine. Understood?”

His words bring the ghost of Jack into the room... for just a moment until I shake him away.

With eyes locked into Cameron’s, I gently ease my lips over the smooth, firm head, using my copious saliva to slowly glide backwards and forwards over the sensitive dome as my tongue begins to caress his tip, my lips tightening their hold. He breathes deeply as I slide my lips further down his throbbing shaft, my wet tongue slipping, stroking, doing its best to stimulate this warrior-like man who is so worthy of the release he wants.

"Slowly," he says.

I comply and tenderly slide up and down, thankful for the thigh muscles I have from years of yoga practice which allow me to hold myself upright without my hands to help me balance.

I gently ease my lips off the column and take long, slow licks up and down his engorged shaft, on the underside and the sides, trying to keep as much of my tongue in contact with his sex as possible. He closes his eyes for a second, letting out a hiss of restrained pleasure as I tend to him with the utmost care and respect, my tongue communicating how I feel about his primal virility. The collision of his eyes with mine has thick glossy wetness pooling at the soft entrance to my sex.

"Jessynia..." he moans as I clamp my lips over his hefty length again and suck more fervently, saliva lubricating the fucking of my mouth. The fingers of his hand sink into my hair, slowly curving into a fist which he employs to pull me into him so that I take the full length all the way to the root. I try my best not to gag as the eager head of his cock hits the back of my throat over and over, filling it utterly.

To his sinful groan and a tightening grip on my hair, I begin to increase the rhythm, my head bobbing backwards and forwards over his dense cock as saliva drips onto my breasts. I whimper at the forceful thrust of his greedy lust as he fucks my mouth again... and again... again.

"Fuck, angel," he exclaims as I pull out and suck just on the tip, my juicy mouth wetting it with a glossy coat as my tongue darts out to lash him with licks of reverence and awe at his insane masculine beauty. "Mmm, the beast inside me wants to make you my slave," he utters as the underside of his cock slides backwards and forwards over my servile tongue. "I have to do my best to control him."

I shake my head just a tad and shoot him a look of mock-disapproval as I tend to just the tip with my tongue and lips, sucking, licking, desperate to receive a shot of his cum as a reward for my hard work. He watches me, his breaths cavernous, his glare indecent, as I gently draw in the smooth round head for long minutes, eager to do whatever it takes to make this glorious man tremble with deserved pleasure.

He finally pulls his thighs back a little, freeing my mouth so that the engorged tip is resting on the outside of my dewy, saliva-covered bottom lip.

"You're a goddess, angel."

I beam at the compliment, my tongue touching the tip as I finally taste a tiny amount of his pre-cum which has me moaning gently.

"Would you like me to fuck you?" he asks.

"Yes," I respond.

"Yes, what?"

"Yes, I would," I smile, provoking him playfully.

His lips curve as he shakes his head ever so slightly. "I will enjoy trying to get submission out of you, Miss Avery."

"I look forward to it."

Leaning over, he pulls me to my feet without a word before leading me towards the glass wall overlooking the forest, positioning himself behind me.

"Cam, are you sure no one could see us here?"

"Certain. It's impossible." He slides his hand over my taut abdomen before reaching down to my sex to check that I'm sufficiently wet to accommodate him. There is the tiniest of guttural moans as he feels the copious amount of gloss before wrapping his arm around my neck so that my throat is in its bent inside-crook, his outer arm taking the rigid press of the glass before us. He eases my upper body forward so that the points of my nipples stroke the glass as the sculpted cuts of his abdominals press into my bound hands.

He spreads my feet apart and, unspeaking, finds the wet entryway to my body with his cock which he slides up and down the slick velvet, teasing me cruelly.

"Ask me to fuck you," he orders.

"Please fuck me."

"Please fuck me, *sir*," he coaxes, cranky as all hell. Jesus, he's hot when he's irritable.

I don't respond.

"Say it, angel. I need it from you. I need that word." His breath is heavy on my cheek, his lips near my ear.

I stay mute again. Cameron's need for dominance isn't in question anymore, but that doesn't mean that I'm ready to accommodate it. As turned on as I am, I'm not going to be calling him *sir* in bed any time soon... even if part of me wants to. In truth, I fear that that word would not be enough, fear where he would need to go next... After the challenging and tormenting sex I had with Jack in the last few months of our relationship, I want to keep my power this time, even if deep down part of me wants nothing more than to submit to his sublime dominance.

"I'm very sorry, Mr. O'Neill. I'll need to see more from you before I start calling you that."

Show me what you're made of, Cam...

I feel him smile against my cheek. "Very well, my lady. Happy to oblige." His other arm wraps around my chest possessively as his large tip lies heavy against the soft pink of my pussy, threatening its invasion at the entrance to the tight hole he intends to take as his own when he so chooses. "I've never experienced resistance before," he whispers hoarsely into my ear, his rich voice a rumble through my flesh. "You have no idea what it does to me. Every cell in my body yearns for you, day and night." The grip of his arm around my neck tightens ever so slightly, pushing Jack's chain into my skin. "Imagining owning your soft little body is the only thing that has kept me going since August. Imagining your face. Your lips. Your eyes. Your pretty little cunt." I whimper as he squeezes again. "I like the way you look up at me. I like the purity in your face. The innocence. You make me feel like a man. You make me want to protect you. To take care of you so that you never have to work again if you don't want to. I fantasize about the day you are finally my wife and about the night I get to fuck you in that white dress when you are legally my property. I dream about the day I impregnate you and about what it will be like to fuck you as your perfect soft body begins to swell. Do you want that?"

I do, Cameron.

Every cell in my body wants to be possessed by him... but I can't make that promise yet.

"Hmm. How about you try to convince me of the virtues of being your property?" I suggest.

He breaks into the gentlest of breathy laughter. "Are you sure, Miss Avery? There are things I want to do to you that are not civilized at all."

"Good," I respond, my craving for him so acute that I need to know the darkness of his diabolical desires.

With a bestial groan, he enters me, forcing a high-pitched exhalation to rush from my throat as I dissolve into his penetration. He holds me tightly as he begins to drill my wet pussy, the thrust of his thighs and the might of his arms almost hitching me off the floor at times.

I whimper as his finger finds my clit, sliding and pressing firmly over and over with the utmost precision and competence, the rhythm matching that of his thrusts inside my accommodating body. My head tilts back to touch his shoulder. "Mmm.... It's so good, Cam. Don't stop."

"You like that, huh, baby?" he asks into my ear as he very slowly slides his thick length into me, then out, over and over, setting my insides alight with static and flame. I feel my body wilt under his possession as I listen to the slip of him entering my sacred flesh. "I like how much fight you have in you, Jessynia," he breathes into me. "It's one of the reasons I'm so *insanely* in love with you."

With his dick still deep inside me, I feel him undo the tie binding my hands before throwing it to the ground. I whimper as he pulls and twists my right arm behind my back, easing me forward so that my breasts are pressed against the glass wall and my face has to turn to the right, the side of my cheek flush with the cold glass as my left hand braces against it.

A sound, some mix of a gasp and a whine, flees the recesses of my body and I close my eyes as he pounds my sex, his growls becoming rougher as he restrains my arm with one hand while gliding his other up my chest and onto my neck where he begins to squeeze my throat.

The exposed side of my cheek receives the hot lash of his tongue as he fucks me, his lips finally locating the shell of my ear, nipping it slightly, his exquisite breath heavy on my face. "I'm going to take things very slowly so that I don't scare you, beautiful, but I intend to teach you the joys of submitting to me."

"Cameron," I gasp as he squeezes my neck a little tighter, causing his cock to swell further as he takes my soft wetness for his pleasure. There is a split-second of panic as I feel my throat constrict. I tell myself I will say the word *Blackwood* if he squeezes any tighter than this.

Come to think of it, that word is very close to home...

"Yes, angel?" he groans, a voiced exhalation of his unabashed arousal. The air is thick with it, the room and the moon witness to his devious way of fucking.

"My arm hurts."

"It's *supposed* to hurt, beautiful. Just a little," he reassures darkly, nipping the side of my neck with the alabaster bite of his teeth. The ramming against my cervix slows slightly. "Pain is a necessary part of submission."

I pull against his hand to release my arm but the vice of his grip is immovable as he continues to fuck me. I can picture the stark striations of his thick, lean arms as they contract, gripping me like a possession he won't let go of until he's ready.

"I'm not totally sure I'm the submissive type," I respond.

"No. You're not... yet. First I will have to teach you how to at least be somewhat cooperative." His hoarse moans intensify as he pulls out to the tip then enters in one swift stroke that has me wincing from the pain of the stretch as his body threatens to release his seed onto my cervix. "It's about balance, angel," he whispers gruffly into my ear. "I'm a *slave* to you outside the bedroom. My heart, my soul, my life, they belong to you. I have no power there. *You own me*. But I have to dominate you in bed, otherwise we will be out of balance. Do you understand that?" He tightens the grip around my throat further as his swollen shaft confirms his ownership of my body. "I don't need it every time. Just from time to time."

"I'm not sure I'll ever be the submissive type," I respond as my chest squishes against the cool glass.

"I know that, Jessynia. Luckily, I am as turned on by your resistance as by your submission. I look forward to you resisting me for as long as you can."

I whimper, shaking at the vice-like grip he uses to position me the way he wants me, my pussy open and available for him to enter at his leisure. His groans are rough but the way he uses his hands, even when he squeezes my neck, feels tender somehow, his fingers never using enough pressure to bruise me. There is a softness to the way he handles my body, as if handling some delicate flower that could disintegrate under his touch.

To the sound of another whimper of resistance, he says, "You know the safe word, angel. You can use it whenever you want."

"I want to give you pleasure," I say as his lips stroke the side of my cheek.

"I know that."

"But my arm. It hurts, Cam."

He releases it instantly, allowing me to brace myself against the glass with both hands so that my head no longer has to turn.

My eyes pan up to look at the pregnant moon in the inky star-dotted sky, enthralled by its sheer size, at the shadowy craters which I've never seen so clearly, a sight made all the more awesome because of the possessive way that the deity behind me is invading my body. There's a deep, long grunt into my ear as I look up at the stars which fall in and out of focus due to the intoxication of wine and desire.

I gasp loudly at the sudden flash of light zooming across the sky—a shooting star, the tail of a meteor, a comet burning up as it enters the atmosphere. Cameron's fingers curl around my throat and his mouth finds my temple as he looks down at the side of my face.

"It's beautiful, huh?" he whispers, his left hand cloaking the top of mine as my palm lies flush against the thick pane to brace myself against the impact of his drives into me.

"Incredible," I reply, in awe at the sight in front of me.

"I like fucking you while you're mesmerized like this... There's nothing more sublime." He slides his mouth down my neck and clamps his lips onto the bare skin in the curve of my shoulder, the shimmery blanket of stars and the moon above the only witnesses to our forbidden lust. I exclaim as I feel his teeth emerge from under his lips and begin to tug at my flesh, pressing harder and harder until he starts to bite, not enough to break skin, but enough for the pressure to hurt.

"You're such a bad man, Cameron," I whimper as his thrusting grows more urgent, his groaning intensifying as my flesh strains under his teeth.

I want to bite you, angel. I want to taste your blood.

In the heady throes of lasciviousness, I can't tell if he said that aloud or if Gabriel's wine has me hearing things.

"Just breathe into it," he murmurs as his teeth clamp down on my flesh again, hard and strong and merciless, the bite hungry, needy, deviant.

"Cam," I exclaim, pulling against him as the pinch stabs me.

He removes his teeth, his cock still sliding into and out of me. "I'm sorry, angel. My self-control hangs by a thread when I'm around you."

I know the feeling...

His hand wraps around my mouth, gagging me as his lips locate my neck again, this time clamping down as he starts to suck on that soft space in the curve between my shoulder and neck. He sucks harder and harder, pulling the muscle under my skin, the force of it pinching my collarbone, drawing at my warm flesh. I know the feeling well. Jack liked to do it, but with Cameron, it feels more forceful, more urgent.

It hurts.

At the sharp draw of my flesh and a pinch that sears me, I pull on his hand, freeing my mouth.

"Blackwood."

He stops instantly, slowing his thrusting as he does so, his mouth sliding up to my cheek. "I'm sorry," he pants. "I'm struggling to remain civilized around you."

"It's okay."

"How about we take things more slowly..."

I nod and he pulls out of me, carrying me over to the sturdy wooden table next to the wall, pressing my torso upon it. Lifting my leg up so that it bends at the knee, my inner thigh resting on the wooden surface, he climbs on top of me and penetrates me, his dense body immovable as he blankets my back completely, silent as he fucks my tight insides, the stretch so good as he slides into and out of me.

"Cam, the weight of you on top of me feels so good."

His lips slide against my temple. "Jessynia." He says my name with such yearning that I feel a tear well up in my eye from the force of it. "I can't live without you. You have no idea how much I need you," he breathes into me, his fingers threading into my hair as he holds my body in place for his pleasure. "My need never ends. It follows me day and night..."

"I need you too," I breathe, looking down at the curving veins in the oak tabletop beneath me.

"You do?" he asks.

"Yes."

"Good." He pushes my fingers flat onto the table, his hand heavy on mine, pressing my palm into the dark, glossy wood. "I will be erasing the touch of any other man from *every inch* of your perfect body. Is that clear?"

I nod as he fucks me slowly, first in silence before growling perverse threats and carnal promises into my ear. His hand glides between my torso and the table, locating my clit which he tends to as he slows his thrusting to a gentle slide, the only sounds exchanged between us being exhaled breaths and the slip of his sex entering and exiting mine.

He uses my wetness to trace circles, to slide in all directions, to pinch, to tease, to caress, until I feel my body begin to undulate.

"Don't stop," I moan.

"I need you to come, angel." He keeps going, building pleasure, leaving my breathing fast as he slams into me while edging me closer to nirvana.

"I want to hear you moan, Cameron. It will make me come."

"Say please."

"Please."

He presses again, this time growling into my ear ferociously as he does so, the full expression of his fiendish virility taking me over the edge as ripples, then waves, then the unleashed tsunami of ecstasy blasts through my cells and I exhale the surge of hot, electric pleasure that courses through me, leaving me high and light, my limbs feeble as I dissolve into the wooden table, barely conscious as he uses my ravaged body to pleasure himself with, pounding rhythmically for a long minute before finally releasing a guttural cry and collapsing onto my back, his slippery chest slick with perspiration, enveloping me completely as he heaves out his release.

A minute later, while still recovering from the full display of his prowess, I am lifted into his arms and onto the soft rug. A moment later, I hear the door of the armoire creak open. Swiftly, a quilt is upon me and his hot body lies down next to mine, his lips nuzzling into my neck.

As our panting subsides, we dissolve into each other, skin slipping, limbs intertwining, eyes opening for short moments, our gazes soft, focused.

A while later, we watch the glistening of infinite stars above as we lie entangled in each other on the thick rug of this warm room, illuminated by the haunting gray of moonlight.

Our eyes meet for a moment and I break into a gentle smile at the indecent way he is still looking at me. "What?" I ask.

"I've spent four years dreaming of you naked on your knees with your hands tied behind your back."

"And, um, was it what you imagined?"

"Better."

His finger gently traces the crook of my shoulder where he was sucking earlier. I can't see it but I'm sure it will leave a huge welt.

I shoot him a look of chastisement. "I would like to point out that I am going to have to wear high-neck sweaters for the entire time I'm at my parents' place, sir."

"I do sincerely apologize for my lack of self-control, my lady. I couldn't resist the urge to mark you."

"Mark me? I'm not a prize Jersey cow, Mr. O'Neill. I hope you're not fantasizing about branding irons."

He pauses for a moment. "I don't think you want to know."

I shake my head into his smile as he shifts his leg over mine so that his cock lies heavy on my thigh, erect a mere twenty minutes after releasing his seed inside me. The hefty column rests against my skin.

"Jesus, Cam, I don't think my body can take much more tonight," I say as I feel the weight of his greedy erection. "I suspect I'll have to be treated for internal injuries if we go again."

He smiles, wiping a strand of sticky hair off my face, his fingers brushing my forehead. "I'll show you mercy until tomorrow, Avery."

I beam in response to his promises of pleasure tomorrow—the last time we will see each other until... God knows when.

"Do you have to leave tomorrow?" he asks. "Can you not tell your parents you're spending Christmas with my family?"

"You ask this despite having met my mother?"

His smile only lasts a moment before his expression darkens. "Every time you leave me, I deal with the fear that I won't get you back."

I watch him earnestly, unsure what to say. "You'll always get me back, Cam."

"You know what I mean, Jessynia. I'm not talking about having you in my life as a friend. That would not be acceptable to me. I want you to belong to me. My body aches every minute that I'm away from you. It's inside my cells. I get through it by focusing on the day you finally become my wife. If I don't marry you, my entire life will have been in vain."

"Cam, stop..."

He tightens his grip on the side of my face. "I love you, angel. I'll wait... as long as it takes, but after you file for divorce in March, you won't owe him anything ever again... and as I told you before, at that point I intend to make you *beg* to be my wife."

A heady brew of anxiety and anticipation rumbles through me as I stare into vivid eyes that burn almost burgundy in the low light. "You're so good... for such a very bad man, Mr. O'Neill."

"I'm glad you think so."

As he holds my face, I close my eyes, my body exhausted, desperate for sleep as I fade into the protective warmth of this sensational man.

"Cameron!"

"No!" he shouts, grimacing as if in pain, his stiff, muscular frame writhing and shaking in the dark next to me.

Jesus...

"Cam, wake up!"

A rough, rabid groan escapes him as he twitches as if in agony. "Stop!" he shouts. "No!"

"Cameron! Wake up!"

Grasping his tense shoulder with my hands, I shake his body to wake him, but within an instant, before I can even react, I'm thrust onto my back. Winded, I reach my hands up as his thighs straddle my legs and his hands wind around my throat.

Fuck...

"Cam! Stop!" I manage over strangled breaths as he tightens his grip, leaning his torso towards me. In the moonlight, I see his eyes just about open but know he isn't there.

I strike his chest. He doesn't flinch.

Please, Cam...

As the pressure of his burning hands constricts my neck, breath leaves me and I start to panic. I grasp his hands to pull them off, but they are immoveable, as if made of stone.

Find the pressure points...

As he leans his head into my neck and a glint of light illuminates the tips of exposed teeth, a split-second flash from my numerous self-defense classes has my hand forming a first which careens under his bent outer arm and into the side of his throat at full force. His grip eases a tad, allowing me to punch his throat again. As his hands release my neck, I bite down hard onto the fleshy part between his thumb and index finger which has him stopping his assault, the sudden cessation allowing me to grab his hands and push them away from me.

The agony in his twisted features subsides, leaving a furrow in its place as he zooms in on my face, finally registering where he is as he wakens from bleak darkness buried within deep recesses of his being. "J... Jessynia..."

I push his chest with all my might and he climbs off my body, watching me, eyes wide, face grimacing, as if in a pit of confusion as I get up and shuffle back to the glass window, clutching my throat.

"What ha— I thought you were—" he starts, getting to his knees.

"Stay back!" I shout.

As he studies the hand around my neck and begins to register what just happened, his head drops, his forehead finding his hands. "Jesus, no," he whimpers, his voice a low, empty cry of despair, his body heaving for a dozen fraught seconds before his misty eyes finally meet mine. "Oh God... Did I hurt you?"

I don't answer, but hold my neck as I watch over this damaged man's descent into devastation, slowly realizing that the wounds of his trauma are much closer to the surface than I had thought.

"I'm sorry. I'm so sorry. Jessynia. I would never do anything to—" Silent tears tumble onto his face as he buries his head in his hands again, his body tight, tense, bound by the ties of torment. It's a sight I could not have imagined—this man, this scion, one of the gods of Manhattan, worshipped and revered everywhere he goes... broken.

"It's okay," I finally say, coming to realize that there are forces at play here that he isn't even close to being free of.

"Your neck... Does it hurt?" he asks, as if struggling to meet my eyes. I've never quite seen this depth of hollow pain in his face.

"It's okay," I answer, still clutching my neck to soothe the imprints his crushing pressure left behind. "You just really scared me. I thought you were going to—"

He hangs his head low, sinking trembling fingers into his thick, wavy chestnut locks. As a stream of silent tears flows down his face and onto the sculpted grooves of his body, I get up. I take a few tentative steps towards the rug he's sitting on and sit down at the side of it.

Through tear-strewn eyes, he finds my face, searching it, a look of shame in his eyes that I haven't seen for so long. He slides his hand over and puts it onto mine, squeezing it firmly. I let him. "I'm so sorry."

"I know, Cam."

"I'm going to get help," he says with sudden resolve that breaks through the torment. "I will fix this. I promise you. Please don't give up on me."

A tear falls from my eyes as I begin to speak, rubbing my neck as if to reassure myself that this will all be okay. "Has this happened before?"

He pauses before speaking. "Twice. With Olivia. That's one of the reasons I didn't let her sleep in bed with me for the last year we were together. I've never let another woman sleep in my bed since... other than you. I thought this thing was over."

"You still have nightmares, don't you?" I ask softly. "A lot of them..."

He shudders out a heavy breath. "Yes. But... I never thought I would do that to you... The thought of hurting you is just... I'm so sorry. I'm broken."

I edge closer to him. "No, Cam. You're not broken. You just... have trauma trapped in your cells. We all do. We need to get it out. There are therapists that can help—trauma therapists, somatic therapists. They can help both of us."

The lonely desolation in his striking eyes stuns me. "I'm a ghost without you, Jess. I can't see the light. I will fix this, I promise you. Please don't give up on me."

The shadow of Jack leaves the haunting chill of goosebumps prickling my skin. I've heard him say those words.

"I won't give up on you, Cam, but... you don't need me, not really." I can't be the only reason another man doesn't descend into darkness.

"I'm going to heal," he says. "I'll do whatever it takes, even if that means going to the police and exorcising this thing inside me..."

I put my hand on his. "It's your decision. But I'll be there with you, no matter what."

24

EARLY THE NEXT MORNING, we sit in his car parked a few houses down from my parent's Connecticut home in the suburb of Westport. The heavy snowfall that has blanketed the windscreen in the ten minutes since Cam and I arrived has left us in a private enclosure where the outside world has faded to white, barely seeming to exist. Cameron and I never usually have trouble finding things to say to one another, but he was quiet on the drive over here, grave, as if pulled into fear.

"You can come in, Cam... if you want," I suggest.

His usual strong, vibrant face looks almost pallid today, like a ghost or some unearthly creature. "No. I can't see them today." The bleak candor of his delivery rips me to shreds, causing a pit to form in my stomach.

"My parents love you, Cam. Like the rest of the world, they're giddy every time they come near you."

"I love your parents, Jess... but I can't face them after last night."

"Look, stop. We're dealing with *trauma*, here. *All* of us. We don't need to add shame to the mix. I can't handle you feeling like some monster. What happened... wasn't within your control."

"I'm going to get help," he says adamantly. "For the nightmares. I've made an appointment to see a doctor. I will fix this fucking thing once and for all."

"I know that. We both need to heal... as do all the people who have dealt with that group. We'll take some time to get better, to get treatment and then everything will be alright. I promise. Do you believe me?"

He pauses for a moment, the grim shadows in his face stunning my senses. "It will? I'm afraid that maybe you think I'm too fucked up."

"I don't think that," I answer earnestly. "I'm dealing with trauma too. I know what it's like... I know *I* can heal. I know *you* can too."

"Beth has put me in contact with someone who helped her too. I'll see him next week."

I nod as he searches my eyes, his anguish twisting my insides. "I want to be with you, Jessynia... once I'm healed," he says. "Do you still want that?"

I put my hand on his arm. "Yes. I want that." He breathes out audibly and his body unstiffens. "But, Cam, I don't want you kept in limbo while I sort things out with Jack. I'm still too afraid of what he'll do. That means we are not together now. I need a couple more months to handle him and prepare for the divorce. He said he will grant it if I wait till March. That will give us some time to get some help too. We owe ourselves that, so that we can be healthy together."

He nods. "If you talk to that man, it has to be by phone, and I want to know about it days beforehand. I want to be there to help you. I want security on standby."

"Okay."

"I'm only calling my team off while you're here because your father agreed to hold you to the conditions—no walks outside alone, no going out at night, no driving alone. And if you leave the house even just to go into the driveway, your parents have to watch you. Do you still agree to that?"

"Yes. I promise."

"Your brother definitely won't be coming?"

"No, he's with his girlfriend's family in SoCal. But my godmother

Barbara is here. And she can kick any man's ass into the next century. You've never met her, right?"

"I've heard about her."

"Well, she's a force to be reckoned with."

"Once you go back to Manhattan, you will have a guard watching you to make sure Jack hasn't picked anything up about where you've been the last few days. Okay?"

"Yes."

After two pings on my phone in quick succession, I reach into my purse to pull it out and see a message from my mother:

Are you nearly home?

I answer:

About ten minutes away.

"Cam, I have to go."

His grave regard has my heart stalling.

"Please don't take any calls or texts while driving," I say. "You need all your wits about you in these conditions. And text me when you get back. I'll be worried until I hear from you."

He smiles, a sudden shimmer of silvery light peeking through dreary clouds. "Do you remember at college when you used to force me to text you when I was just going two hundred feet across campus back to my room?" he asks.

"Yes."

"And remember you turning up at my room at 1 a.m. shouting at me the one time I forgot and switched my phone off."

I smile. "Boy, I was an opinionated little loudmouth back then."

"Back then?" He arches a brow. The levity of the gesture has me feeling I will get him back.

I grin. "Promise me?"

He nods.

A minute goes by in the silent white cocoon of the snow-wrapped car.

"Cam, I have to go."

He turns on the engine and pulls out, driving me to the front of the house. After getting out and getting my things out of the trunk, Cam and I trudge over the powdery snow to the driveway of my parents' house.

"You sure you don't want to come in?"

"I can't," he replies, his breath misting the air, causing an ethereal cloud to frame his insanely beautiful face. "Jessynia..."

"Yes."

"If by some miracle that man ever gets near you and asks you if you and I have slept together, you tell him no, okay? You deny it. I don't give a fuck about his feelings or my safety, but in the event something goes wrong and I'm not, or my men are not, with you to protect you, you lie. That man is much more dangerous than you realize."

I nod, trying to soak in every inch of his face, terrified that for some reason I may not see him again.

"Goodbye, Jessynia."

"Bye, Cam."

He lingers for a moment before turning and trudging back to the car, getting in as I make my way up the driveway to my parents' berry-red front door, adorned with a festive wreath beside a sign hanging from the brick wall next to it saying *Beware: Cranky lady with a very short fuse inside. Knock at your own peril.*

After ringing the bell, I look at Cameron in his black SUV. He watches me until the door of my parents' house opens, at which point, he drives away.

His departure leaves trepidation rattling through my belly.

"Where's Cameron?" asks my mom, her irritated tone in sync with the very apt welcome sign.

"Hello to you too, mother."

"Did you invite the poor man in?"

"Of course I did. Good grief, mother, what are you wearing?" Her bright fuchsia kaftan with its huge bell sleeves and clashing lime-green embroidery around the neckline plucks me out of my melancholy, making me smile from ear to ear as I envelop her in a hug. "I bet they can see you from space!" In truth, I love that my mom has the guts to wear whatever the hell she wants. Her unusual outfits with their shocks of clashing colors used to be a source of endless embarrassment when my brother and I were kids, but now I see the power of unabashedly owning and expressing your individuality.

"And he didn't want to come in?" she presses as we pull apart, ignoring my question with her usual dog-with-a-bone obstinacy.

"His mom is expecting him back for lunch. Lottie is arriving today. He couldn't stay."

"Oh… pity," she moans glancing down the street as if hoping he will be back.

"Um, well, *I'm* here, mother."

"Well, come in, darling."

I allow myself an internal eye-roll at my mother's maternally-challenged attempts at being unconditionally welcoming as I put my bag in the living room and follow her into the kitchen where my dad jumps up and envelops me in a bear hug.

After being grilled by my mom about Cameron and insisting we are just friends, all the while receiving moral support from my father in the form of muttered comments and copious eye rolls, I hear my gorgeous godmother Barbara's resonant voice booming downstairs.

"Where's my girl?" she sings.

I get up as she enters the kitchen, crushing me in a hug. Her husband Frank appears behind her, kissing me on the cheek and ruffling my hair with his hard-working fingers.

"Men, huh?" he scoffs as I pour them both a cup of tea while they take a seat at the kitchen table. "Don't they just *suck*?"

"Frank!" jabs Barbara.

"Well, it's the gorilla in the room, dear. Never ignore the gorilla. It only gets bigger and nastier."

"It's okay, Babs," I smile.

"I couldn't believe it when your mom told me," continues Babs. "I had to have a stiff drink after that one."

"Make that two of us," adds Frank.

"Four," responds my dad.

"When you and Jack came to the restaurant you seemed so…" Barbara stops mid-sentence as I lower my eyes. "Oh honey, I'm sorry."

"That's okay," I reply, forcing a smile.

"How have you been?" she asks.

"Well, it's been... hard. Like all separations, I guess."

"Has he been in touch?"

"A few times. In writing mainly. I've asked him not to call."

"Well, I have a few choice words I'll write to the little shit," replies Barbara.

"And I can muster up a few as well," adds Frank. "First word *Piss*. Second word *Off*. Third word *Ass*—"

A disapproving jab to the arm from Babs at his drôle attempts to cut the tension has him stopping and sitting up straight in mock-compliance. "Oops, I've set off the beast," Frank jests.

I giggle at my gorgeous, zany godparents whose warmth and zest take the edge off sitting at the kitchen table that Jack set next to me at this time last year for Christmas which we spent drinking questionable coconut-milk eggnog and grazing on copious amounts of nuts as Jack humored my family by watching the ubiquitous Christmas movies and partaking in some of the silliest games known to man.

Not to mention ravaging me mercilessly in every corner of my bedroom, the proximity to my parents and the risk of being caught seeming to turn him into an animal as he fucked me silently against the wall, hands restrained behind my back over my desk, against the window, in my little closet, and in bed when my legs couldn't stand anymore.

As I'm hit with the memory of him fucking me quietly from behind against the door of my bedroom as my parents walked up and down the stairs just on the other side, that deep, weary sense of despair overwhelms me as I realize that he was sleeping with both Alexandra Frost and Lydia Bulgova at that point. And God knows who else at that place...

"Sweetie?" My godmother's voice finally registers.

"Sorry, I was just..."

"The guy is a fucking idiot," says Frank. "And he'll realize that soon enough. Like most idiots do. And you can then tell him, *Sorry, I don't date morons*."

I smile at Frank and squeeze his hand. "Enough about me. How are you guys?"

The next few days pass in a haze of champagne, spicy teas that no one would ever touch outside the holiday period, dried fruit, silly hats, and the ubiquitous Christmas movies, games and songs. Christmas dinner was a fest of insanely delicious Seitan turkey which Barbara made from scratch accompanied by mushroom and red-wine gravy, green beans with almonds, roast potatoes and a sweet potato and marshmallow casserole that Frank insisted on because it reminds him of his mom's cooking, and which my father didn't hesitate to playfully express his utter contempt for.

There has been a fair amount of nipping, mainly between the couples but also directed at whomever is in earshot, with my über-liberal parents getting under the skin of the more conservative Frank and vice versa. Babs and I made sure to give people a verbal whipping on the numerous times one of the three decided to inject some off-limits political digs into our politics-free holiday week and I haven't hesitated to stick up for Frank whenever my parents gang up on the poor guy. Two against one is never a fair fight.

I've spent a few hours on the phone to my friends. Kevin has been regaling me with knuckle-biting tales of his straight-laced family who are lovely but don't seem to fully get the ostentatious personality of their boy Kevin. Stella has spent the week engaging in hate-sex with an asshole lawyer from a competing firm. Maddie has been flitting between her dad and her mom who is still bitter about her dad's choice of a woman a mere five years older than Maddie.

I haven't had the guts to tell my friends about the nights I spent at Blackwood with Cameron. They think I've been with my parents this whole time. I'll tell them when I see them on New Year's Eve... or maybe a few days later once we're all sober. I've never kept anything from them before. It feels so lonely to do so.

I've done my best to throw myself into writing as well as finishing the novel I started in Blackwood which Cameron insisted I take with me, in part to distract myself from text messages from both Cameron and Jack that leave me feeling jittery.

At just after witching hour on December 30th, a day before I am due to return to Manhattan, I find myself wide awake, unable to sleep after unsuccessfully trying to shake off the nightmare I had this night involving a rabid, bloodthirsty Sebastian Gravier, a leather strap and some other *toys* I won't mention in a room at Q.N., Manhattan. I peer outside at the layer of snow blanketing my parents' privet-hedge-enclosed back garden as I switch my phone on, sighing in relief that there isn't another message from Jack.

I have tried just not responding to him at all, but every time I do, he tells me he's losing control, and I panic and respond as briefly as I can. I can't shake off the fear that if I cut him off for good, he will become like one of them—like Vallen or Steven, or worse, like Sebastian, whose pain led him to switch off his humanity entirely to the point that he now has to take people's souls to sustain himself, one of the living dead. Maybe other people would just sit back and watch it happen, but I can't. It would break me into pieces...

Abandoning the report I'm reading about the alleged effects of EMF radiation on health, I instead spend half an hour studying the effects of trauma on the mind and body, as well as dominance as a trauma response, trauma and nightmares, and then various forms of therapy, alternative and otherwise. After saving some links, I look up some local self-defense classes for women, finally settling on an eight-week Saturday morning course starting next week in SoHo near Kevin's apartment which will give me an excuse to go see him more often than I have of late.

As I switch off my laptop and decide to give sleep another try and shake off this unbidden sense of trepidation I'm suddenly feeling about going back to Manhattan, there is a vibration from my phone. I take a breath, assuming it's another message from Jack only to see Cameron's name.

Jessynia. I'm tormented by what happened. The thought of hurting you kills me. I would never do anything to deliberately cause you pain. I want you to know I'm sorry to the depths of my being. I'm getting help. I'm going to fix this problem once and for all. Yours, Cameron.

I hate that he's awake so late, and that he sees himself as some problem case. That will not help him. Without thinking further, I press the call button, my heart leaping as I hear his voice.

"Jess," he breathes, as if in relief.

"Cameron," I whisper. "I can't talk loud. Parents are asleep next door... and my mom is on her crabby pills again."

"Why are you up so late?" he asks, his voice, weary, showing signs of that weight and exhaustion I heard when I first knew him at Brown.

"I couldn't sleep. What about you?"

He doesn't answer.

"You had another nightmare, didn't you?" I ask.

He remains quiet.

"Cam?"

I hang my head, my heart aching at the thought. Nightmares like the ones I have had this year are new to me too. I had bad dreams before finding out about Jack's affairs and the Society, but never were they this vivid, nor did they leave me sitting upright clutching my chest, sure that someone was in the room watching me...

"I've been studying trauma," I say softly, not wanting to push him away by making him sound like something that needs fixing. "There are so many resources and experts out there that can help... We're going to heal all this. I promise."

"Jessynia, I need you to know how sorry I am about—"

"Look, stop. I know it already. Don't say it anymore. Okay?"

"You forgive me?"

"It wasn't you, Cam. It was pain trapped inside. There's nothing to forgive."

He breaths out heavily. "I miss you. My body wants you with me." The deep richness of his voice never fails to affect me. "I can't relax without you. I feel like I'm constantly trying to find this thing that's disappeared. It's torment being away from you at this point."

"You have to give me a couple more months. We can use that time to try to heal so that we are in better shape to..."

Shit!

I swivel round to the sound of a faint but clearly irritation-fueled knock on the door, turning to see my mother standing in the doorway in her thick nightdress, squinting into the light of my room, hair wild like overgrown heather on a heath.

"Shit. I've woken the beast," I whisper into the phone, deliberately loud enough for her to hear.

There's a gentle snicker from Mr. O'Neill.

"Young lady." Somehow my mother manages to whisper and shout at the same time. "Is four o'clock in the morning *really* an appropriate time to be making phone calls?"

I hear Cameron chuckle at her irate tone which, thanks to my mom's badass personality, can't help but sound amusing.

"I'm very sorry, mother. I thought I was being quiet."

"Well, you weren't!"

"Did I wake you?"

"No," she groans reluctantly. "I was already awake. But if you keep this up, you'll wake up your father and then I'll have to watch him yawn all day. That'll annoy me no end."

"Heaven forbid!"

She stands in the doorway, waiting for signs of my capitulation.

"Give me one minute," I whisper. "I need to say goodbye."

"I'll give you three, then I'm coming back in."

"Thank you, Mom."

As she pulls the door closed, she stops. "Oh, and, um, say hello to Cameron for me," she says, a knowing smile brightening her eyes.

"How did you—?" She grins at me impishly. I guess my mother knows me better than I give her credit for. "Goodnight, Mom."

"Goodnight, daughter."

On the soft click of the door closing, I whisper, "My mom says—"

"I heard." His energy is suddenly lighter which floods me with relief.

"I have to go otherwise the mom from the black lagoon will be back."

"Can I speak to you tomorrow?" he asks gently.

"I'll call you once my godparents have left. I have to go. You need to try to sleep."

"You too, Avery. I want you in bed." There's a dangerous bite to the way he says it.

"Okay, goodnight."

"No. I want you in bed *now*."

"Cam, I have to—"

"Get in bed," he orders.

I capitulate, pulling my covers over me. "I'm in bed."

"Good. Now you are going to do exactly as I say."

"Cam, I can't. My mom will kill me if she hears me."

"You don't need to talk," he responds. "Just listen and follow my instructions."

I feel my skin go clammy and my sex begin to tingle at the indecent assertiveness in his voice.

"What are you wearing?" he asks.

"Pajamas," I whisper.

"Take them off."

Without thinking, I obey his command, my sex starting to pulsate at the arresting force of his tone.

"Done?" he asks after a moment

"Yes. You?"

"I'm naked," he replies. "Lying on my bed."

I swallow hard at the vision of his formidable silhouette glistening in the moonlight, shimmery lilac rays bouncing off the pronounced ridges and valleys of his hard body.

"Are you lying on your back?" he asks.

"Yes."

"Good. Tease your nipples," he directs, "until they're hard."

My hand reaches down to my breasts which I caress gently with my fingertips before finding the teats and toying with them.

"Pull on them."

I acquiesce to his demand, pulling both so that they stand to attention. The dominant, moody tone of his so sinfully sexy that I lose all rational thought when I hear the whispers of the brooding beast that he's constantly trying to control.

"Are they hard?" he asks.

"Very."

"Now lick your fingers," he says, his breathing heavier.

"What?" I'm really not good at phone sex. I always feel more nervous than sex-goddess-esque when I'm on the phone.

"I won't repeat myself," he replies sternly.

I blush, despite no one being able to see me, as I put my middle and index finger into my mouth.

"I want to hear you sucking them."

I lick my fingers with a whimper, hoping he can hear.

"Louder," he instructs.

I comply to the sound of a hoarse groan from Cameron. "Good. Now slide your fingers down to your pussy."

"Okay," I reply quietly as my fingers delve into the pool of thick, clear syrup around my soft sex.

"Are you wet?"

"Yes."

"How wet?"

"Very."

"Wet enough for me to slide straight through your tight little slit?"

"Yes."

"Good," he moans, exhaling loudly. "Bend your knees and part your legs, wide."

"Okay."

"Now I want your fingers inside you."

I hesitate for a moment, not used to doing this of late.

"Do it," he instructs upon my silence.

I accede to his desire, inserting one and then a second finger an inch into me, unable to stop myself from throwing my head back and exhaling audibly at the sensation. If I close my eyes, I can almost feel the head of his cock entering me.

"Slide in and out."

The tiniest of breathy moans escapes me as I pull my fingers back and then insert them again, just an inch, but enough to imagine this glorious man inside.

"I like hearing your pleasure," he responds. "Let me hear it."

I pant into the phone, loud enough for him to hear but not loud enough that my mother could hear from the next room.

"Do you like that?" he asks, his breathing heavy.

"Yes," I reply, succumbing to pleasure that I have not been able to give myself for so long. Since splitting up with Jack and saying goodbye to Cameron in August, I have not really been able to touch myself or bring myself to orgasm like I used to do so easily. Stella even bought me a special new talk-of-the-town vibrator to help solve the problem, and while it did, it still felt like my libido had been castrated compared to the heady years of daily sexual exploration with Jack. Finding pleasure again with Cameron has felt like watching a dry riverbed fill with water, the tepid liquid lapping at its sides, burrowing into arid earth, splashing, whirling, bringing plants to life around it, giving replenishment to wildlife nearby. It has felt like coming back to life.

"Are you hard?" I whisper.

"Very. My hand is around my cock. The head is pointing towards me."

"Mmm," I breathe.

"I'm gripping my shaft tightly, sliding my hand up and down, imagining your warm wet cunt sliding down onto it," he groans. "Would you like that?"

"Yes," I breathe. "So much."

"Mmm. The thought of your wet juice sliding down my cock makes me very hard."

I whimper, wishing he were on top of me.

"Touch your clit."

I slide my fingers over the wet velvet and up to my clit as his low moans intensify, the cadence quickening.

"The next time I fuck you," he pants, "you will be handcuffed and blindfolded..." I shudder with a mixture of fear and arousal. "Unable to see as I impale your soft body. Do you want me to fuck you?"

"Yes."

"Say it. Say *Please fuck me, my lord.*"

"Please fuck me..."

"My lord."

Silence.

"My lord," he repeats.

I defy his command again. I hate to ruin the moment by not acquiescing but deep in my bones, I fear that his need for total dominance comes from his trauma and I can't engage in it until I am sure. Plus, the fact that I will not lose my power like I did with Jack ever again.

"You're still defying me, huh?"

I don't answer.

"I like your defiance, baby. I like the challenge. It drives me insane. But there will come a point, once I have made you my wife, when you will be my slave... just as *I* am *yours*."

I'm too aroused to engage my brain enough to form the words needed to tell him off. Instead, we stop talking, listening to each other pant and groan, him loudly, me very quietly, the pace accelerating as our pleasure syncs and I arch my back to the thought of his arousal.

As pleasure mounts to fever pitch, I whisper, "I'm going to come. Can you come too?"

"If you were with me, I would come down your throat. Would you allow that?"

"Yes."

"And you would swallow every drop."

"Yes. Come for me, Cameron," I whisper. "As loud as you can. I want to hear."

He respects my wishes, grunting and grumbling to the sound of his hand working his cock until he finally releases a guttural cry that allows my body to release the tension I have been building up, a tiny high-pitched exhalation exiting my throat as the warm, bubbling buzz of bliss floods my cells, trickling into the furthest extremities of my body, lighting them up as his thunder of pleasure softens, turning into a pant and then a breath and then a sigh of desperately needed release… for both of us.

My legs quiver as they fall flat onto the bed and I open my eyes, half-expecting him to be on top of me.

Our panting softens until he murmurs, "If being apart from you involves nights like this, I can live with it."

"Cam," I say softly, breathlessly. "You made me come so hard."

"You have no idea the depths of pleasure you're going to experience, beautiful. I intend to open up a new universe inside you."

"Cam, I have to go," I whisper. "My mom has the ears of Border Collie."

He pauses. "Goodnight, Jessynia."

"Goodnight."

I pull the covers tightly around me as I close my eyes, dissolving into the warm glow of his powerful aura, sleep consuming me in an instant.

25

THE NEXT MORNING, I SIT CROSS-LEGGED ON THE BED in the guest room that Babs and Frank have been staying in, watching her pack as Frank hands her items of clothing which Babs has now banned him from attempting to fold. They are shortly returning to the gorgeous riverfront restaurant on Long Island that Jack and I went to just four or so months ago.

"You sure you don't want to spend New Year's Eve with us, sweetheart?" asks Barbara.

"Cut it out, Barb," retorts Frank gruffly. "She's a young woman. She shouldn't be spending it with two batty old crones like us."

"Speak for yourself, old man!" she shoots back, leaving me in fits of giggles. "I still know how to have a good time."

"Oh sure. You, some Prosecco and The Bee Gees on a loop. Party of the century."

With that, Frank dodges a tube of toothpaste that goes flying across the room courtesy of my godmother.

"Ooh, she's still feisty this one," laughs Frank, tossing it back into the suitcase on the floor.

"Next time I won't miss!" barks Babs.

"How about I leave you two young ladies to it?" asks Frank.

"I think that's best, Frank," I laugh.

"Philip asked if I could help him shovel some snow off the sidewalk. Do I have time?"

"You do," replies Babs, shooting the poor guy an unimpressed look. "I'm going to speak to my girl for a while."

"Okey-dokey."

He shoots me a sneaky grin as he leaves the room, shutting the door behind us. Barbara groans as she gets up off the floor and comes to sit next to me on the floral blanket.

She strokes a lock of my loose hair and loops it behind my ear, touching the two silver hoops in my lobe as she withdraws her hand to place it on my baggy boyfriend jeans. "You get more beautiful by the day, baby," she says, studying my face. "Boy, those eyes never get old."

"So do you, Babs."

"Pfff," she says with a dismissive smile. "I'm starting to feel old. Sometimes I don't recognize the chubby old broad staring at me in the mirror."

"Hey, don't say that. Society has taught us that women over a certain age have no more value. It's *total bullshit*!"

"Yeah. They really have it in for us wise old gals."

"And you're not feeding into that horseshit!"

She smiles. "I'll try not to, my sweet."

"And anyway, your tongue *definitely* hasn't aged..."

"That's true," she laughs.

"That's what matters!"

Then her expression suddenly becomes more serious. "How are you coping really, darling? You seem a little quieter than last year."

"Oh, I'm okay," I say after a pause. "The last few months have been... tough at times. Seeing Cameron again has felt like a burst of light."

"I can't wait to meet this young man."

I smile. "You'd like him. He's, um, quite the man, to put it mildly."

"What do you think is holding you back from being with him? Is it just Jack?"

"Jack hates him with a passion"

"So? He can't exactly kill him. I know it's Manhattan, but it's not the Wild West either."

"I don't think he would kill him. But maybe he could hurt him. Injure him in some way. Plant something. Damage his reputation. Get him arrested. God knows..."

"And maybe your imagination is running away with you?"

"Yeah. I've just seen a lot of... strange things this year. I don't feel as safe or as fearless as I use to feel."

"That's *totally* normal after divorce, honey. I've seen many friends of mine go through that period of self-doubt afterwards. Don't you worry. You'll get that girl back. That feisty little thing who used to shout at people when they yanked their dog's leads too roughly and poured a bucket of rainwater over that bully's head in the yard..."

"God, I'd forgotten about that," I chuckle. "Mark O'Brian. What a little *shit* he was. He's in prison now, apparently."

"And I bet you he never forgot that little ten-year-old girl who dumped that bucket of freezing-cold water on his head."

I smile.

"That little force of nature is still in there," she continues. "As you heal, you will reconnect to her, darling. And she will come back to you. I promise."

I squeeze her strong, hard-working hand. "It's not just that. I'm afraid that if I get together with Cameron, it will push Jack over the edge and he will end up in the clutches of some... conscious-less people and... criminals. Permanently. He always tells me that I'm the only one that stops him from losing his humanity."

"Boy, that is one hell of a responsibility to plunk on someone else's shoulders. He shouldn't be doing that."

"I know. But I feel like he has no one else to stop it." I breathe out in exasperation, feeling overwhelmed by my unrelenting need to protect him. "Babs, why do I care so fucking much? Why do I feel like I have to constantly sow this safety net under him?"

"Because that's who you are, sweetheart. You are a beautiful soul, an old soul. Caring, compassionate. When you love, it's with your *whole* heart. And you want to save the people that you care for. But when you get to be my age, you understand that you can't. Only *they* can save themselves... if they want to. And not all people *really* want to be saved."

"I know," I utter in resignation.

"And do you know what happens to the woman who stands under the man while trying to sow a net underneath him? He sometimes falls slap bang on top of her. And she ends up crippled while he gets up and walks away. You understand?"

I nod. "I know all this, Babs. My brain is telling me to let go. But this is the same man who nursed me back to health for months and months. And I just feel like I'm watching him dancing on the edge of this cliff and he just keeps getting closer and closer to the edge, and I'm the only one who can see it and it's my job to stop him because if I don't, he will... *fall*."

"Sweetie, Jackson has made you think you are his only lifeline. It's a manipulation tactic. He cannot put his fate on your shoulders. That's too much weight to bear."

"I know. You're right." I don't dare tell her that sometimes I feel that Cameron is also on the edge of that cliff...

"I love you, my sweet," she says in that gorgeous sonic boom of a voice of hers. "But that chapter of your life is over. And you can't start a new one until you've fully let go."

I nod.

"How are you getting back, darling?" she asks. "Frank said he doesn't mind driving you."

"Cam is forcing me to go with his security guy, Aaron. He won't take me all the way back, just to the Upper East Side. I'll get a cab from there. They want to scope the place out, make sure Jack doesn't have anyone outside the building."

"Isn't Cameron going back to Manhattan?"

"Yeah, but in a few days' time."

She studies me, cupping my face as I feel the tiniest tremor of uneasy angst undulate through my body. "What is it, darling?" she asks.

I smile at her. This gorgeous woman knows me too well. "I just have anxiety about going back to Manhattan."

"Why?"

"I don't know. I just have this feeling of trepidation, like... something is going to go down when I get back."

"Nothing is going to go down, and if it does, me and Frank will be over there in a shot, guns blazing, to sort things out. They'll need a SWAT team to stop us." I giggle and squeeze her hand. "I'll miss you, my darling," she says. "We all love you, even that Rottweiler of a mother of yours."

I grin. "I know. I love you too."

"And you, my girl, don't need anyone else's light to feel whole. You never have. Just you mind that."

I throw my arms around her, losing my face in her thick, wiry hair, rich in the aroma of coffee and vanilla. Right now, I feel like I wouldn't mind if I never let go.

After seeing my godparents off, I sit watching TV with my dad in the living room while my mother potters around in the kitchen making deliberately loud clanging noises to express her disapproval of the movie dad and I chose after we outvoted madam two to one.

We watch an animated snowman flying through the air, a scene from a movie from the eighties that reminds my dad of his childhood. I must have watched it every Christmas since my birth. I'm pretty sure he plunked me in front of it when I was still in diapers. I could certainly do with a year off, but I know how much dad likes watching it with his kids, so I'm happy to sit next to him with my cup of tea, my eyes flitting between the screen and his soft, handsome face.

As I take a sip, out of the corner of my eye I see a vehicle pull up in front of the house and a man get out. It's a mail delivery truck. I get to my feet as he makes his way down our freshly cleared driveway.

"You've got mail," I sing as my father presses pause. "I'll get it." I open the door and greet the gentleman merrily. "Morning!"

The man glances down at the thick envelope in his hand. "Jessynia Wilder?"

Taken aback for a moment, I pause before saying, "Yeah, that's me."

"Sign here please, miss." I do as instructed. "Have a nice day," he says, handing me the envelope.

"Same to you. Happy New Year."

I close the door and lock it as my ever-nosey mother appears next to me. "Is that for me?" she asks, eyeing the envelope.

"Um, no, it's for me." I don't recognize the sender's name nor address in Manhattan.

I rip open the hard outer envelope to an internal shiver as I pull out the smaller envelope inside with one name written on it—Jessynia, written in distinct writing. Jack's writing.

I take a breath to steady myself as the ponderous weight of his energy hits me through this piece of paper I've been delivered.

"Well?" The boldness of my mother's raspy voice is unsettling at times.

"Oh, it's... it's Stella," I lie. "She said she'd send me a letter about her holiday escapades."

"I'm trying to watch a movie here, ladies," chides my father.

"Sorry." I place the letter behind the outer envelope so that my name is hidden from view. Heading towards the sofa, I say, "I'm going to read this in my room, Dad. I'll be down in ten, okay?"

"No worries, sweetie."

I kiss him on the cheek and ignore my mother's never-ending curiosity as I head upstairs into my room where I close the door behind me and sit on the patchwork quilt over my bed.

I slowly tear open the letter, terrified that it may be Jack confronting me because he knows about my stay at Blackwood... but based on past behavior and Jack's sledgehammer way of expressing himself, I am sure I would have received a barrage of calls and visits if that had been the case. If he knew, the entire street would know about it at this point. Hell, the entire city of Westport, most likely.

My heart twists in my chest as I pull out two thick sheets of white paper, his scrawl a brilliant expression of elegant madness.

I draw in a breath as I start to read.

. . .

Jessynia.

I hope this letter gets past your parents. I know what they must think of me.

This holiday has been the darkest of my life. Even the Christmas after my mom's death felt less hollow than this one.

I have ached for you every minute. I have looked for you in rooms, praying you would walk through the door.

I have missed sharing looks with you, missed caressing your hand under tables, missed watching your breathtaking face as you open gifts with that boundless enthusiasm of yours.

I've missed carrying you through snow, pouring you glasses of wine and watching terrible movies with you lying in my arms. I miss watching you laugh until your sides ache. I miss pinning you against the wall as you accommodate my never-ending hunger for your body.

This emptiness I feel is something I thought I had lost when I found you. I don't know how to handle it some days, other than to fall into darkness completely so that I don't have to feel anything.

I sense that's where I'm headed without you. There's a pull there that I don't know how to resist anymore.

No, Jack.

Please try.

My eyes mist over as I continue to read.

I remember the first time I saw you. It was on campus. You don't know this but I spent weeks watching you before I finally plucked up the courage to talk to you. I've never felt so terrified to talk to anyone as I was you.

The first time I saw you, you were studying a bulletin board. Your turquoise scarf was wrapped around your neck. Your hair was hanging over your denim jacket. You were wearing black leggings and Doc Martens.

I can't explain what it was, but you stopped me mid-stride from a hundred paces. I was mesmerized by you. Your light. Your presence.

Then you turned around and I saw your face. It was the single most beautiful thing I'd ever seen. And those eyes. They were huge. Lumi-

nous. Glistening. The color of your scarf. Then you saw a friend and smiled and wrapped her in a hug.

I knew I loved you that second, before I'd even spoken to you. I knew I had to be with you. I felt like I knew you. I felt like you would understand me. You would see me in a way others couldn't. I wanted to protect you from the very start. Wanted to keep you safe.

My asshole friends would make fun of my attempts to talk to you. I tried about a dozen times before I finally managed to. I know I probably seemed like a cocky prick to you, but I was trembling inside. I still do when I'm near you.

Finding out that your physical beauty is nothing compared to how beautiful you are as a person changed something inside me. It altered my DNA, turned a light on in what had felt like a decade of darkness.

A lump forms in my throat.

Going to London wasn't something I needed to do. I could have done everything from Manhattan. I did it because I knew you would be spending the summer there, and I hoped that I would finally convince you that I was worthy of being with you.

The first time we made love, I knew I could never be without you again. I felt something I had never felt. I finally understood what the term even meant. Watching your pure, innocent face as I entered you was something that still haunts me. I'd never felt this desperation to ensure another person's pleasure. I'd never felt this constant craving to be inside someone. Every time we made love, it soothed me. It felt like returning back to something I had thought I had lost.

I know maybe I've given up the right to say such things after what I've done. I can't fully explain my need to self-destruct. I wish I could control that side of me. The side that has ripped away something that I never thought a piece of shit like me would ever experience.

But I love you, Jessynia. When you are sick, silly or disheveled, I love you the same. Even when I haven't understood you, I've loved every part of you since the day we met.

There is no moment of respite for me from the pain of being without you. No distraction I've tried takes the edge off the beauty of sharing my life with you.

I know you don't trust me anymore. I don't blame you. I no longer trust myself.

But I feel shifts, angel.

I see through people that once controlled me.

I want to get out.

I need to know you are there, that you can see me.

If I know you are there, I can make it.

Please don't abandon me for good. I will be lost.

A ghost.

Please tell me you're there, baby.

I love you.

Yours, Jack.

I break down in silent sobs as I finish reading, tears spilling onto the page, mixing with the black ink which fuzzes on the paper.

Jack, why?

How do I do this?

I crawl into bed, the sheets and pillow now a tissue for my tears, and let the gnawing ache wash through me, crying quietly for arduous minutes that leave me hollowed out, until I finally stop and stare silently out of the window at the dismal cloak of gray outside.

As the deep discomfort begins to subside, I contemplate the world that both Jack and Cameron were drawn into at such a young age. Yes, they are grown men now and responsible for what they do, but it's not so easy when someone gets their claws into you when you're young and undeveloped, not yet fully formed as a person. Those types of experiences change something inside you.

As my pain turns to disbelief and then to irritation and then to rage, I think of Alexandra Frost and that place, those people who think nothing of toying with people's lives for the sheer sadistic thrill of it.

A whirling maelstrom of outrage and fury pulls me in, rabid ire pumping through my veins, making me want to claw the hellfire from my body at the thought of these corrupt people.

I burst to my feet in a shudder of wrath, my skin hot as I open my laptop and begin to type an email to my lawyer, my fingers tapping the keys frenetically:

Hi Donald,

Happy New Year to you. I hope you have had a lovely, relaxing holiday time with the family.

Hopefully, you won't get this till you come back to work, but I want to update my divorce petition to include the name of one of the women Jack had an affair with. Could you change the name of AAA to Alexandra Frost?

No rush at all. Next week is fine.

Thank you very much.

Happy New Year.

Jessynia Avery-Wilder

26

"TEN, NINE, EIGHT, SEVEN, SIX, FIVE, FOUR, THREE, TWO, ONE... Happy New Year!!!"

The cramped bar-restaurant in the heart of Hell's Kitchen, Manhattan, explodes as the clock strikes midnight. Kevin, Maddie, Stella and a few other friends of ours envelop each other in sloppy hugs before embracing random revelers at adjacent tables. We all lift a glass of bubbly as Kevin's friend Larry toasts to health and happiness to the sound of a pop of streamers going off behind him and the obligatory *Auld Lang Syne* drifting across the room.

"To good friends... and fresh starts," adds a giddy Stella in a stunning berry dress, darting a pointed look at me as she says it.

"To fresh starts!" our entire table shouts in agreement.

After another half-hour of drunken merriment, some of our friends decide to call it a night, leaving Maddie, Kev, Stella and I to finally catch up on our holiday adventures.

"Honestly, anyone who tells me that hate-fucking isn't the best fucking there is has no fucking clue," slurs an inebriated Stella to the hysterical chuckles of the rest of us. At this point in the night, we're all so hammered that the vaguest trace of wryness in any sentence can set us off.

I grab the glass of champagne from her and replace it with a glass of water with a few sorry remnants of ice cubes bobbing on the top. "Drink, madam," I say.

"Though the bastard's now ghosting me," she adds, which has Kevin sputtering his expensive booze down his unshaven face.

"Good!" shouts Maddie over the rousing eighties' pop music that this little establishment is famous for playing. "You said he was an insufferable prick, anyway."

"Oh, yes, he is quite the prick," responds Stella smoothly to my and Kevin's laughter of derision. "A very *talented* prick."

"Um, didn't the *very talented prick* try to blackmail you over some mess-up you'd made?" I ask.

"Yes, he did. How do you think I ended up sleeping with him?"

"What?!" yells Maddie. "He blackmailed you into sleeping with him?"

"Oh, no, of course not," responds Stella. "That was just my counter offer. What he really wanted was for me to talk my client into settling for less than she was worth."

"And did you?"

"Most certainly not. He accepted the sex in exchange for no longer blackmailing me and talked his client into giving my client what she wanted."

"Well, at least someone got something out of it."

"Oh, yes," she purrs.

"God, why is sex with people we hate so good?" asks Kevin. "I slept with my asshole of an ex—who I hate even more now, by the way—just before Christmas and it was *the* hottest sex we have *ever* had."

"Oh, why did you sleep with that fucker?!" I chide. "You said you were never speaking to him again after the shit he's pulled this year."

"Yeah, I know. I was about to spend the week with my family. I'd put on five pounds. I was weak. What can I say?"

Stella and I look at each other with knowing smiles. I'm feeling so grateful for my worldly, non-judgmental friends. Besides, I'm hardly one to give advice on how to move on from an ex.

"Oh, I get it," adds Stella. "It's all that hellish rage just bursting to come out. I slept with Ian once after he cheated on me..."

"What?!" shout Maddie and I in unison at her revelation of sleeping with the man she once called the love of her life, the man who finally knocked down those walls she had kept up for so many years, who taught her to trust again after her challenging childhood with that revolving door of stepfathers—the man who she caught sleeping with a mutual friend of hers, breaking her heart, stopping her from being able to form deep emotional bonds to heterosexual men, for now, in any case. I am hoping that will change with time.

"Why didn't you tell us?!" moans Maddie.

"Why do you think, sweetie? I was ashamed as hell of letting anyone know."

"We're hardly ones to judge," says Kevin. "I mean all three of us could write a book about how not to hold onto your dignity in a relationship."

"Hey, speak for yourself!" I throw back at him as Maddie throws a crumpled-up piece of napkin at him. I follow suit, leaving a laughing Kevin holding his hands up in surrender.

"So how was it?" I ask Stella. "With Ian..."

"It was so good I almost felt bad about dumping his wallet and house keys down the toilet before leaving."

Her deadpan admission has us in fits of hysterics again, no doubt aided by the Veuve Clicquot we've been sipping all night.

"You did not!" I sputter.

"Oh, I sure did, baby. He's lucky I restrained myself from chucking his phone down there as well. I just wish I could have seen his face when he found them."

"Did he say anything to you?" I ask.

She clears her throat as if about to give an important speech. "He texted *Well done. Very mature. So now we're even.*"

"Are you serious?" exclaims an outraged Maddie.

"Yep. And I responded *No, baby. We're not even. Not even close.*"

"Good!" we all shout.

"Never heard from the fucker again. Let me tell you, that one act was better than the six months of therapy I'd had before. I highly recommend it."

"God, you guys are making me feel better about still brooding over Jack."

"Hey, breakups are a mess, sweetie," responds Stella. "We get it. It's not all black and white like it is in movies. It's a big steaming pile of spaghetti and we're all just trying our best to wade through it."

"Yeah. You know, I did something dumb this week," I say.

"Ooh, do tell," replies Kevin.

I hunch down a little and peek around the room to check that no one is eavesdropping, lowering my voice to library-level volume. "I sent an email to my lawyer asking him to add Alex Frost's name to the divorce petition."

"Oh, God, Jess, are you sure that's a good idea?" asks Maddie.

"No. It's not," I reply. "I just get so fucking sick of that woman getting away with the stuff she does. I feel like someone has to take a stand against her and her monstrous ways at some point."

"I thought you were going to wait till March to file," says Stella.

"I am. And I'm not going to keep any of the cheating stuff in the petition. We have a prenup so it makes no difference at all anyway. The lawyer told me it's good therapy to get it out."

"You don't want to mess with that Frost bitch," says Stella.

"I know. I was just really upset one night and... that happened. I'm going to email the lawyer tomorrow to tell him to ignore my last email and pretend he's never heard of Alexandra Frost."

"Yeah, well the Frost bitch deserves to be publicly outed," says Kevin, "but you don't want her or that paranoid psycho husband of hers on your ass."

If only Kevin knew about my unforgettable art gallery meeting with Steven Frost...

"Do you trust this lawyer?" asks Stella.

"Yeah. My parents have used him for thirty years."

"Well, I'm guessing he's used to late-night emails from irate soon-to-be divorcées," responds Stella. "Just make sure you send that email retracting the name tomorrow."

"I will."

"Ladies, I think I'm gonna have to call it a night," says Kevin, stifling a yawn. "I have to get back to SoHo somehow."

"Me too," says Maddie.

"Make that three," I add. "Do you want to spend the night at mine, Kev?" I suggest. "I could make my famous banana and walnut pancakes in the morning..."

"I'd love to, sweetie, but I have to get some stuff done tomorrow."

After saying our goodbyes, Stella and Maddie head uptown in a cab they've miraculously managed to flag down as Kev and I set off arm in arm down Ninth Avenue in the direction of our apartments a few kilometers away. Hoping to be as lucky as our friends and nab a cab, both of us flail our arms wildly at cab drivers who ignore us in glorious nonchalance.

"Turn your light on, then!" shouts Kev, as another cab without its *occupied* lights on rolls past us to the beeps of urgent car horns, the fast tread of tires and the guffaws of drunken revelers walking by.

"They can't hear you, lovely," I laugh.

"Oh, they can *feel* the energy," he retorts.

A couple of blocks down, as we reach West 30th and head into Chelsea, a black SUV pulls up beside us and a window rolls down. "Need a ride?"

"Aaron! You said you would take the night off!"

"Orders of Mr. O'Neill."

"Oh my God!" I exclaim. "Please tell me you did not spend New Year's Eve outside waiting for us to finish drinking!"

"Part of the job," he responds with a warm smile.

"That's terrible. Oh, God, I feel so bad!"

"I hate New Year's Eve with a passion, Jessynia. This was way more enjoyable to me than all the usual schtick I have to sit through."

"Christ, are you sure?"

"Always," he responds.

"Okay, well, this is my friend, Kevin."

"I know that," he responds. "I suspect you two need a ride..."

Kevin and I glance at each other, unable to believe our luck. "We'd love one, Aaron. Thanks so much."

"Get in."

We get into the large vehicle and buckle in while I introduce the men to each other more formally.

"Did you two have a nice evening?" Aaron asks.

"Amazing," responds a slurring Kev. "I haven't laughed this hard since I found out my ex had developed a one-inch bald patch."

The bald Aaron chuckles. "Maybe he'll end up like me..."

"Oh, no. Your baldness is *hot*."

"God, Kev," I groan, bumping him with my elbow.

"I mean you look like The Rock."

"The Rock?" Aaron repeats dryly, eyes crinkling in amusement.

"That's a compliment, *believe* me." Aaron chuckles. "I mean, most men look hot with a shaved head," slurs my drunken friend. "Not Gary though. He's handsome from the front but from the side, he has a head shaped like a grape that's been stepped on."

I can't stop myself from laughing, watched in the rear-view mirror by Aaron whose eyes twinkle as I chuckle uncontrollably.

"No, seriously," continues Kevin, deadpan. "He's not one of those hot, sexy bald guys like Vin Diesel or something. When he loses all his hair, he's gonna look like a kumquat on a stick."

After another fifteen minutes driving at a snail's pace in the ridiculous Manhattan traffic, I try to catch my breath as we pull up at the end of my block. Aaron turns around to look at me, grinning as I attempt to pull myself together. He and Kevin have made me laugh the entire way back to my place. "You okay there, miss?" he asks.

"Yeah, sorry, too much champagne," I explain, finally composing myself.

"I checked the block out a couple of hours ago," Aaron says. "It's all clear. I'd still rather not pull up right in front of the building. We'll watch as you go in. And you text me once you get inside and lock the door, otherwise I'll be calling you. Okay?"

"Yes, sir. And you don't mind dropping Kevin off?" I ask.

"Of course not."

"Unless, Kev, are you sure you don't want to spend the night at my place?" I ask.

"I'd love to, Jess, but—" he lowers his voice to an almost-whisper —"I actually have a *friend* coming over in half an hour."

"God, I should have known!"

"Well, what can I say? I'm a popular guy."

"Oh, well, you enjoy. And Aaron, please go home after dropping Kev off. I won't be able to sleep if I know you're spending the night out here."

"You won't be going out again tonight?"

"Definitely not. Nor tomorrow. I've decided to spend the day sleeping and catching up on emails and bracing myself for the year. I bought all my groceries for the week this morning."

"Okay. I'll give you a day off tomorrow as long as if you do decide to go out, you give me a call. Agreed?"

"Agreed."

"I'll let Mr. O'Neill know you've arrived home."

"Oh, dear," I groan.

"He insists on knowing your every move."

"Mmm, that is *so* freaking hot," responds Kevin, positively swooning. "I wouldn't mind being possessively stalked by the world's hottest billionaire."

"Okay, that's it," I laugh, kissing Kevin on the cheek before leaving the car. "Goodnight."

"Goodnight," they say in unison as I close the door behind me and head a block down to the entrance of my building.

I turn to see them drive off and head inside, past tonight's concierge-less front desk and up the stairs. As I reach my apartment, I wrangle my keys out of my purse, turn the key in the lock and go in, grappling for the light switch and turning it on before locking the door behind me.

Pulling out my phone I text Aaron:

Arrived safely Mr. Rock. Going to bed. Happy New Year.

On pressing send, I take a deep breath and look at the dozen or so messages I've got tonight wishing me a Happy New Year—my family, Babs, a few yoga, college and journalist buddies, Maddie's mom, Cam's family, my musician friend River and even my friend Sean, the Brooklyn plumber who still texts me every month or so to ask how I am. After sending each one of them a brief message back in my drunken state, I build up the courage to look at the messages I've studiously been trying to ignore—from Jack and Cameron.

Both messages say more or less the same thing: in a nutshell, I belong to them and this new year will prove that. I don't answer Jack's message, but send Cameron a reply—nothing too strong, but wishing him a Happy New Year with a few silly emojis that hopefully remind him of some of our offbeat in-jokes. I hate sending superficial messages like that to Cam. I have so much I want to say him, to both of them, but I'll have to tackle that job tomorrow when I'm sober and coherent.

Putting my phone on the kitchen counter, I head to the bedroom and strip off my clothes, chucking them into the laundry basket and glancing at my shoulder in the small mirror on the wall next to the door. Cameron's *branding* has finally gone but for the tiniest remnants of purple and orange that you could only make out if you really looked for it. Even though the deep violet welt has gone, for the most part, I still feel the tension on my skin as Cameron pulled with his mouth as if wanting to taste blood.

I shake off the thought and pull on a clean ankle-length cotton nightdress over my naked body and some matching fluffy teal socks to protect from the cold winter bite permeating the apartment building.

I head over to the phone on hearing it beep.

Kevin:

This Aaron guy is hot. Definitely straight sadly.

I respond:

I hope you didn't harass the poor man!

Kevin:

He seemed more amused than harassed. Besides he could crush my neck with one squeeze of his hand.

Me:

Good! Leave the poor man alone!

Kev:

He's just dropped me off.

Me:

Ok. Going to bed. Enjoy your night.

Kev:

Will try. So drunk. Hope I can perform. He's drunk too apparently so hopefully, he won't judge.

I send him a laughing emoji back followed by a *Be Carefree* and put my phone on silent before plugging it into the charger on my desk.

Hearing a light tapping coming from the unlit living room, I glance over to see if I maybe left the window ajar before going out.

It looks closed.

Best to check.

I hum as I walk through the long, dark room to make sure that the window is indeed closed.

But as I get to it, my hairs stand on end and an icy bolt of panic thunders through me as I spot a dark form behind a shelf to my right and a black silhouette in the reflection of the window in front of me.

I pivot in a flash.

No.

The gasp escapes my throat before I even register what's happening.

Cold terror crushes my chest, primal fear invading every one of my cells as the masked figure standing against the wall of the L-shaped living room takes a step towards me.

From behind a hand comes over my mouth.

"Don't you *dare* fight," the voice snarls into my ear as the second man in front of me steps forward.

The scream doesn't have time to come out...

27

I FELT IT BEFORE I SAW IT.

The needle.

Going into my arm.

Terror masked the spike of pain.

My legs kicked as he held me.

My eyes widened as the other man approached.

On the edge of consciousness, I recall little things now.

The stranger's breath on my ear.

His powerful hand over my mouth.

A scream muffled.

Limbs limp at first.

Then like jelly.

Then no strength at all.

Slumping to the floor.

Whimpers escaping me.

Pulse hammering.

Breathing quickening.

The man stopped me from falling hard, easing my fall onto the floor.

The side of my face hit the varnished oak.

I wanted to fight, but I couldn't move.

I tried not to drift out of consciousness.

My mouth was so dry.

Eyelids were heavy, half-open at best.

Then a large set of black shoes in front of me.

"She's out," said the voice behind me, no panic therein. "That was easy."

The feet in front of me splayed out, knees bent.

A man crouched down.

All in black.

Even the gloves.

I couldn't see his face.

I closed my eyes so he couldn't see them opening.

He lifted my arm and pulled me, laying me face up onto the unforgiving wood.

Then a monitor around my arm, another on my fingertip.

Sharp beeps.

There was a male voice.

A timbre deep like the rumble of a truck through my torso.

"Tachycardia, to be expected. BP within range. O2 sats normal."

Did I know that voice?

I smelt the vague hints of his cologne. The scent seemed familiar to me.

"We'll check her again in the car."

Then a strong hand on my face, smoothing hair out of it, squeezing my cheeks together to the sound of clicks coming closer.

Then the stamp of a metal heel.

"Hands off, Isaiah. You know the orders."

A rush of relief to hear a woman's voice.

"Just making sure she can breathe, Grace. No harm in that."

"Get her in the case." Anger roughened the woman's elegant voice.

The case?

Relief vanished but I was too inert to gasp.

I recall pieces of time coming in and out of focus.

The constriction of claustrophobia.

The desolation of darkness.

The helplessness of being carried.

An object.

A thing moved about.

Barely human.

Then a hint of cold air.

Voices, hushed.

A car door slamming shut.

Muffled sounds, clicks and thumps.

A case unzipping.

Then I was lifted.

The relief of artificial light.

They lay me flat, my head melting into something soft.

Hands were upon me.

A monitor on my arm.

I couldn't open my eyes.

Sentences floated about here and there.

Or did I dream them?

"BP normal. Tachychardia's resolved. Slight O2 drop. Within range."

"Glenn will check her over when we arrive." Calm order in the woman's voice. "Make sure she's in the recovery position."

Then we were driving.

My body swayed with bumps and turns as the miles accrued.

Roads lit up, then dark.

So dark.

I couldn't measure time.

Minutes, perhaps.

Maybe hours.

And then the crunch of gravel.

A man carried me in his arms.

A building.

Quiet corridors.

Doors opening.

A bed.

Melting into the mattress.

Falling endlessly.

People entered the room.

I couldn't see them.

Couldn't open my eyes.

Hands were upon my arm.

Fingertips on my wrist.

I felt the brush of cotton as the top of my nightdress was pulled down an inch.

Then the cold shock of a metal disk on my chest.

A woman's voice, unknown to me. "Heart rate a little fast. Nothing to be alarmed about."

"When will she wake up?" A man.

A voice I know.

I couldn't match it to the face.

"It'll be a few hours."

"She'll have to be monitored. If something happens to her, it will start a war."

"I'll stay with her." The woman's voice from the apartment.

Thank God, the woman's voice.

More words, now forgotten as if never uttered, and then the tread of footsteps leaving the room.

The click of a door closing.

I sensed the woman crouch down next to me.

Smelt her poisonous perfume.

It invaded me.

The hard tips of her fingers moved hair from my face.

Stroked it.

"Jessynia," she said, an ache in her voice. "I'm here."

And now... a bed.

A room unknown to me.

Heavy.

Can't stay awake.

Falling...

28

THE SOFT WARMTH OF THE BED IS THE FIRST THING I BECOME AWARE OF.

My eyes open, widening, blinking as the taupe wall comes into focus.

To its left, a window covered in a burgundy drape.

Birdsong beyond.

My stomach twists and breathing frenzies as I realize it was not a dream.

Insidious fingers of cold horror wrap around me, crushing me as I realize I have lost time.

I move my fingers, contracting them into a fist before releasing them, then wiggling my toes.

"Good morning, Jessynia." The woman's voice, the same that rang out in my apartment, shatters the silence, leaving me trying to sit upright, my weight born by one hand against the mattress, the other clasped to my beating heart for comfort, my respiration brisk and audible.

She gets to her feet from the leather armchair opposite my bed. Her hair is auburn, just a tad lighter than the curtains. Her eyes are a swirl of green and umber like shimmering discs of browning moss in the forest. She is in her mid-thirties by the looks of it, with maroon stiletto nails and wearing black pants and a long black shirt, rolled up to the elbows.

I pan down to her shoes—black leather with silver caps on the toe and short matching spikes sticking out of the slim heel at the back.

"You were in my apartment." A tremor shakes my voice.

"Yes. We thought it best I be there."

"*We*? Who is *we*? Where am I?"

"There are people who wish to speak to you, Jessynia."

"What people?"

"You'll see soon enough." The harsh bite in her voice frosts the air.

"And so, what, this is their solution?!" I want to shout but my lungs are tight. "These people can't just pick up the phone?"

"No," she replies stiffly. "We are beyond that point."

I pull the covers off me with quivering hands, rage rushing into me like water filling a dam as I get out of bed. As my feet hit the floor, I stumble forwards, my palms breaking my fall as it transpires that my legs have the strength of a newborn foal's. Sharp pain stabs at my weak ankle as I get to my feet.

"The effects of the sedative will have fully worn off within a few hours," the woman utters coldly. "In the meantime, I suggest you get back into bed."

"Back? Are you insane?!" I manage, picking myself up off the floor and leaning against the wall. "What am I doing here?!"

I grab hold of the curtain and pull it open to see a huge patch of gravel and woods beyond. The sun has risen high in the sky. It must be at least 11 a.m. if not much later.

"What is this place? Where the hell have you brought me?! Do you realize this is kidnapping?! Do you people have no limits?"

"I'm not the one you should be shouting at, Jessynia," she snarls. "If you were smart, you would speak to me with a *bit more respect*. I am one of the people ensuring your protection."

"My protection? From whom?"

"You seem to have antagonized some very powerful patrons."

"*Patrons*? So I suppose this house belongs to the Society? Is this one of your *entertainment* buildings?" I would air quote the word, but I can barely feel my hands.

"Yes, it is. And there are razor-wire fences twelve feet high all around the property with guards on every gate, so if you want to make it out of here in one piece, I suggest you cooperate."

"What happened to me?" I ask, my feet almost numb.

"You were given a sedative and brought here. No one touched you, Jessynia," she says, her glare earnest and severe. "Nor will they at *any* point while you are here. Non-consensual sexual acts are *strictly* banned by the Society."

"Well, I don't consent to being here either!"

"It doesn't matter whether you consent to that or not. The only power you have here is being Jackson Wilder's wife. That is what is keeping you safe. Beyond the aforementioned tenet, your wishes and boundaries are irrelevant."

I glance up at the seams where the walls meet the ceilings for signs of cameras. "Are they listening to us? Watching us?"

"No," she replies stiffly. "There are no listening devices in our rooms with the exception of the parking area, the corridors and the front entryway. Our patrons don't come here to be spied on."

"No, just kidnapped, threatened and stalked if they step out of line."

"There is a price to pay for what we can offer, and our rules have become stricter in recent times. It is for the protection of our patrons."

"Protection?" I scoff. "I think you mean *control*."

A stark double-knock at the door sends my stomach flying into my chest.

"Come in," says the woman.

As if in slow motion, the door swings open and a tall, stocky man enters carrying a small wicker bowl and a plastic bottle of water which he places on the table next to the wall to my left.

He pivots to face me, his gaze cunning, assessing my fear, my intimidation at his presence. I inch back on the bed as his lips twist into a sinister smile.

"She slept through the night?" he asks, presumably addressing the woman while keeping his shark-like stare trailed on me for every syllable.

I know that voice.

"Yes," replies the woman.

The man looks to be in his early thirties—huge and well-built with buzzed brown hair, light cocoa skin and the deepest of large brown eyes which appraise me mercilessly. He glances down at the nipples that I know are poking through the cotton of my nightdress, a consequence of not having a bra on which makes the fabric constantly brush against them, turning them into hard points. He exhibits no signs of shame at the brazen way he is appraising my body.

"Mmm." *Did he really just groan in arousal?* "She needs to eat. She'll be having a long day."

"How about you address me directly?" I challenge, feigning bravado as he can no doubt detect from the wavering in the pitch of my voice. "And tell me what I'm doing here."

The neanderthal smiles, taking a step towards me, his eyes wandering over my face, a hand scratching the thick neck peeking out of his white collar. "You are going to eat now because we need you functional for the rest of the day. Is that *direct* enough?"

"No. It's not. What do you mean by the *rest of the day*? I want to go home."

"What you want is irrelevant. The sooner you understand that, the better." He picks up the bowl and the bottle of water, taking steps towards the bed as I inch back on it. He places them on the duvet cover next to me. "Now eat."

"No," I return resolutely, indignation brimming within me.

His smile is callous, not reaching his eyes. "I'd heard you had quite the character. There's nothing I enjoy more than getting submission out of some naïve little girl like you who actually thinks she has some power."

I don't answer, my eyes boring into him, wishing this were a fair fight and I could unleash my fury on his sorry ass.

"Now eat!" he growls, his raw resonance making my body vibrate, unleashing a few seconds of that primal fear I felt back at the apartment.

I glance at his large black shoes. “You were in my apartment,” I say as it hits me that his was the voice of the man who touched my face.

He smiles. “I must say I did enjoy seeing the fear in your face when you first saw me. It was quite... *superb*. I shall remember it.”

“Your name is Isaiah,” I say.

“Clever girl. I like it when people come in here thinking they can use their brains to manipulate themselves out of here. When they think they can outwit us or that they have some power. It just makes the shock and horror they feel when they realize they don’t *even more enjoyable*.”

“I’m not trying to outwit anyone,” I retort.

“Oh, please do,” he responds. “It will make your *willing* submission all the more victorious. Now eat!” I peer down at the bowl to see it filled with pieces of fruit. “Or do I have to hold you down and force-feed you?” he continues. “I’m certainly game if you are, though I can’t ensure things wouldn’t get a little *messy* in the process.”

“I don’t feel well,” I say, realizing the extent of my nausea from the previous night’s alcohol as well as whatever they used to drug me. “I shouldn’t eat at all.”

“You can throw up later if you need to,” responds the man, taking a step towards me. “But first, you *will* eat.”

I glance at the woman who tips her head in the direction of the bowl of fruit, her allure as severe as an arctic winter.

They watch me as I take hold of the bottle, unscrew it and take a sip, ensuring that the water stays down, drinking until half the bottle is gone. I reach my hand into the bowl and pull out a slice of apple which I bring to my lips before biting down, the crunch breaking the silence. Then some grapes as nausea hits me again.

“I can’t eat any more. I’ll be sick.”

He eyes me fiercely, his chiseled features hard as nails. “They’ll be by at noon,” the man says, presumably addressing the woman but locking his glare on me. “Give her some time to get ready.”

“Get ready for what?” I ask.

"You'll see," he responds.

"You know there are people in my life who will be contacting me today," I say, trying to shout but failing under the menace of his presence. "You realize they'll get suspicious if I don't answer."

"But you *are* answering, Jessynia," he responds with the most duplicitous of smiles. "You have been answering *all* morning. We have your phone and are making sure no one suspects you are not at home. That includes your family, friends and *other people* who have a keen interest in you."

I take a sharp breath in.

Oh God, has Cameron texted me today?

Did they see it?

"Well, you don't have the right to do that!"

"Unfortunately, you signed away your rights when Cameron O'Neill brought you to Quercus Velutina. That was not a smart move in hindsight."

"Well, I've never told anyone about this place. No one! Isn't that what you people wanted?!"

"We are taking that into consideration."

"This kind of thing you're doing is just making everything more dangerous for everyone, including yourselves."

"No, Jessynia," he replies, shaking his head slowly, his cavernous voice leaving me feeling like I'm falling through air. "Not for us. No one can challenge our power anymore. And it increases by the day." He glances down at my body. "You have an hour to wash, if you wish to, and get dressed. Your clothes are on the table." He tips his head towards the table to my left opposite the window. "There's a washroom behind that door." I glance at the door to the left of the table. "We'll be back in an hour. Make sure you are ready. Tardiness is *not* acceptable here."

"Ready for what?" I ask as he leaves the room. "Ready for what?!"

"Just do it, Jessynia," snaps the woman as she reaches the door, her tone some discordant mix of a command and a plea. "It will happen, whether you consent or not. I highly advise you not to force me to dress you. You will *not* like that." She steps into the doorway, turning to look at me a final time. "We will be back in an hour. I suggest you lie down once you are ready. Rest a little."

"Is your name Grace?" I ask, remembering the name uttered in my apartment.

She pauses for a long moment, grim shade lurking in the sharp angles of her face. "Yes," she replies, closing the door behind her, the click of the lock turning in my stomach.

29

THE FEAR OF MY BREATHING BECOMING TOO SHALLOW hovers just above me as panic begins to seep into me like heavy rainwater into soft earth. Tentatively getting to my feet, I head to the window to see a spattering of expensive cars parked on the gravel around the place. Beyond it is a thick patch of long grass, and further still, a wood of deep green and dark shadow that encircles the outside of the house.

Inspecting the windows, I see that metal lattice is sandwiched between the two panes of thick glass. Only one window can be opened, its frame sturdy and new, bearing two handles, each fastened by a robust-looking black lock. I pull at the handles, yanking and tugging, releasing my frustration only to find that they move a quarter-inch and no more no matter how much energy I exert.

"Fuck," I mutter, turning around to scan the room, checking the walls, the ceiling, looking for signs of the tiniest of hidden cameras. The room is almost bare—no pictures, no mirrors, no ornaments, no plants, no devices, no cupboards, no boxes.

I lift the edge of the mattress to see that the bedframe is comprised of a solid block of wood. The headboard is a thick cross-section of a mammoth tree. I pan round to the two hefty black armchairs in the corner to the right of the door, then to the table with the bowl and clothes on it opposite the window and... that's basically it. Precious little to hide a camera in.

I head over to the table which looks like something you would see in a modern art museum. It is a solid block of clear epoxy resin—something I know only thanks to Gabriel—housing thick pieces of what looks like olive wood based on the warm caramel color and the distinctive umber swirls within. My fingers skim the top of it as I observe the wood entrapped within, a sight I last saw on the compound.

On top of the table lies a pile of black garments. I lift one up expecting a top and sweatpants or something of the sort, but instead unpeel a long black ballgown, sleeveless, tapered at the waist with a straight skirt. The thin shoulder straps plunge down to meet at the lower back, which would leave my back from the bottom of my ribs up completely exposed. While the round neckline is high and would cover my cleavage, with its thin satiny material, it would still be frankly indecent on someone with my naturally ample breasts with nipples that so easily harden into points.

"I'm not wearing that," I whisper, the room the only witness to my distress.

I glare down at the table, expecting to see a bra and panties, but there is only one garment left—a pair of black lace panties with the tag still on, presumably to show they are new.

How considerate of them.

I shake the dress to see if a bra is hidden inside. Nothing. My breathing starts to shallow once more at the thought of facing Isaiah wearing a dress like that which will reveal my back and whose thin material will show off the shape of my breasts underneath so immodestly.

Throwing it down onto the table, I thrust open the door to the washroom and find it almost bare but for a showerhead attached to the ceiling above an ivory bathtub in the corner. To the right stands a sink below a brass-framed mirror next to a towel rack bearing three plush burgundy towels.

Opposite the sink is a toilet and hanging from a hook of twisted brass on the inside door is a burgundy bathrobe, tag on and tied at the waist. The walls are a collage of squares of various shades of gray, taupe and beige, and the floor is a mosaic of earthy hexagonal tiles.

To the left of the washbasin sits a ceramic ledge built into the wall holding two small wicker baskets—one filled with toiletries, another with makeup, all small and in packaging suggesting they are new.

I glance all around, searching for signs of a camera. Nothing. I pull the mirror away from the wall, checking behind it. I check the shower-head, toilet. Nothing.

Maybe she was telling the truth...

After taking a short body shower, I wrap myself in the bathrobe and head back into the bedroom. Wondering if Grace is out there so I can voice my concerns about the dress I'm supposed to wear, I try the bedroom door handle only to find it locked as I'd expected.

I tap against it a few times. "Grace? Are you there?" I ask, trepidation making my voice quiet.

No answer.

I grab the panties from the table and pull at the tab swiftly so that the plastic strip breaks. I go to pull them on, but stop myself.

"This is insane," I blurt out, wanting to cry, but refusing to let myself for fear I won't be able to stop. I need all my wits about me if I'm going to make it out of here intact.

As loath as I am to wear the panties they've picked out for me, the alternative—wearing nothing—is even worse. I pull them on under my bathrobe before picking up the dress and letting it hang in front of me.

I don't want to wear this fucking thing...

With the alternative—wearing a bathrobe that can be pulled apart at the front with one tug—being unthinkable, I look around a final time for cameras, see none, and throw the bathrobe onto the bed, quickly shoving the dress over my head, feeding my hands into the loops so that the soft black straps settle onto my shoulders and the shimmery ebony fabric of the dress falls onto my body. It fits me like a glove. It could not have hugged the contours of my form any better than if it had been made by a team of couturiers. I glance down and see my breasts weighing heavy underneath the silken fabric, little bumps in the satin revealing the taut nipples beneath. It looks indecent.

Heading to the washroom, I brush my teeth and run a comb through my hair so that I can pull it forwards to cover my chest. I glance at the makeup they have so kindly left for me to put on.

No way in hell am I wearing that.

As I head back to the bedroom, flashes of frenzy arrow through me as I try to take slow breaths and tell myself everything will be okay.

To no avail.

In an instant of insanity, I find myself with my ear pressed to the bedroom door as I listen for noises on the other side. There are occasional thumps and bangs and at times bars of soft music drifting through the air, though in my uncoordinated state, I can't tell if my brain is conjuring up the sound to soothe me. Same goes for that vague hint of musky incense in the air which I can't figure out if I'm imagining.

I head to the window, pulling on the handles again which still don't budge. Not sure what I was expecting. I could try breaking the window but it has a panel of metal lattice sandwiched between the panes and it wouldn't be a quick maneuver. It would take minutes of smashing and pulling to get out, enough time for someone to hear the commotion and come through the door.

I look around the room anyway to see if there is some heavy object I could use to break the glass. The table is a solid block of resin and wood. I could barely shift it, never mind lift it. Same goes for the leather armchairs with their thick wooden legs. The wicker baskets won't do it, nor will the plastic bottle. The toiletries are all travel-sized.

It's as though everything placed in this room was designed to stop you from being able to find a way out. I fight the insidious intrusion of icy fear as I wonder if others have been kept here against their will.

Looking for signs of life outside, I see only the occasional bird fly overhead, unknowing witness to a dwelling concealing dark secrets that the elite of New York don't want revealed.

I pick up the bottle from the bed and drink before forcing myself to finish the bowl of fruit so that I at least have a little energy in case I need it. My head falls onto the dark-purple pillow as I hold another around me for comfort. Although there is snow on the ground outside, inside the room is warm, heated by a short strip of radiator along the bottom.

In a lonely moment of fear, I bat away tears as I think of Cameron... and then Jack. Do they even know I'm here? Is Jack part of this whole thing? Does he know about me and Cameron? Or is this Gravier's way of declaring war on him?

The thought of Cameron's father pops into my mind.

These monsters kill people...

A tear falls from me despite myself and I bat it away in an instant, closing my eyes as I try to just breathe in the hopes that whatever happens next will lead to me getting out of here.

As I grip the pillow tightly, I close my eyes and imagine lying in Cameron's strong arms so that I don't succumb to the panic hovering over me, spying on me, just waiting for an in so that it can invade my insides and steal my sanity...

30

FIFTEEN OR SO MINUTES LATER, just as my heart is starting to beat more evenly, there are sounds—the metallic clicks of lone footsteps getting closer. The dull rattle of the lock has me clutching my chest and sitting up to attention as Grace enters the room carrying a pair of black shoes which she places next to the door.

Relief undulates through my flesh at the sight of her, though I don't know why.

She glares down at me, assessing me gravely. "You finished the food," she says, glancing at the bowl.

"Grace, what am I doing here? I'm scared. Do you understand that?"

"You're not wearing the makeup."

"No. There's no way I'm wearing that!"

"Yes you are."

"No! I want to go home."

"That is not an option. The faster you comply, the easier things will go for you, Jessynia."

"I'm not dressing myself up like some... goddamn Christmas present for these people. I'm not consenting to any of this!"

Her tall, sturdy frame edges towards me. "Consent is an irrelevant abstract in your current situation," she barks. "You either comply or you will be made to comply and you will *not* like it. Now get up!"

"Can you at least tell me what's happening here?"

"You will know soon enough." She heads to the bathroom, returning with the small basket of makeup. "*Up*!" Her voice is suddenly harsh, hateful even, leaving me feeling hollow and cold.

I get to my feet, my barely-there feet.

"Come here," she orders. After a moment's hesitation, I acquiesce, following her to the resin table on which she places the basket, her hand movements as graceful as those of a ballerina in a grand pas. "Come closer," she says.

"I don't want to."

"You comply or they will make you. How easy your experience is here is in your hands."

"Who are *they*?"

"You will find out soon. And they will not be pleased to see you unprepared."

Bitter fear mists my skin. "Unprepared for what?!"

"It is your choice." Her tone is brutal, but her eyes suppliant almost, as if at odds with the words she is speaking.

I can't read this woman. Is she five personalities in one?

Afraid of igniting the ire of my captors, I take a final step towards her, barefoot and feeling tiny in my almost five feet six inches opposite this towering woman who in her pointed black heels must stand at least seven inches taller than me.

She tilts her head from side to side, studying my jawline, before lifting a stilettoed fingertip and running it down the curve of my cheekbone, the tip of her nail dragging on my soft skin, sending a ghostly chill into me. "You have the most exquisite face I have ever seen, Jessynia. And I have seen a lot of beautiful people in my time."

I balk at the compliment and the unauthorized intrusion into the boundary of my flesh. "Yeah, well, being good-looking, as *you* say I am, is not much of an achievement. But then I don't suppose that one's character and values are virtues in a place like this."

"No, they are *not*." She narrows heavily made-up hazel eyes at me.

"In fact, the virtuous ones do not seem to do well here. Purity is something that is coveted at first and then corrupted with vigor... until it is extinguished like a flame."

She lifts a hand, stroking my long hair behind my ears on either side before glancing at my necklace, sliding her hand down to lift and inspect the gold chain—Jack's chain. "Stunning," she breathes. "You may leave that on."

Turning to the basket, she pulls out a tube of mascara from a small, black cardboard box. There is a muted pop as she withdraws the black wand from its slim metallic casing. She opens up a small mirror and holds it in front of me, handing me the wand. "Put it on."

I take the wand from her with fingers that feel as though they are not my own and apply the black bristles to my long brown lashes, watching them as they transform from natural to something I would wear at a dinner party.

I hand her back the wand. "Are we done?"

Silent, she takes a small black palette from the basket, removing a plastic hygiene film from it before taking a brush and swirling it in a powdery russet disk. "Hmm, they even purchased the cruelty-free stuff, just for you."

"How considerate of them," I respond stiffly. "I'm so happy they are aware of my purchasing habits."

Remind me to thank them later.

"Close your eyes," she orders, placing the palette on the table.

I glare for a moment, frowning in incredulity before closing them to feel the whisper-soft swirling of delicate bristles on my eyelids, one then the other. After what feels like an age, she stops and I open my eyes.

She studies her work, the tiniest quiver of satisfaction seeming to register in the face of this undecipherable woman as her gaze meanders to my cheeks and the sides of my face.

"Your skin is flawless," she says, turning to the basket and pushing a tube of foundation aside. "It doesn't need help." She does the same to a compact of blush. "You blush very easily. We won't be needing this."

Instead, she pulls out a tube of lipstick from a carton, sliding off the golden lid and swiveling the base to reveal a gleaming crimson cylinder with a diagonal tip. The thing is the color of blood.

"I'm not wearing that," I say as I spy the deep glossy scarlet they want applied to my lips. "I never wear colors like that!"

"And why not?"

"Because they look indecent on lips like mine!"

She tilts her head again, contemplating my lips as she licks hers, her eyelids heavy. "Yes, you do have a very plump, pink mouth." She looks down at me in cold relish as my brows furrow at her inappropriate tone. "I imagine Mr. Wilder and Mr. O'Neill must have enjoyed it *greatly*."

Winded, I take a step back, arms wrapping around my waist as she confirms what I had feared—they know about me and Cameron.

"I... I... don't see what Cameron has to do with this," I lie, trying to find out if her assumption is just a theory or if her words are founded in certitude.

She shakes her head slowly, her aura suddenly sinister. "We know, Jessynia." My stomach lurches. "Denial would be a *weak* tactic that would lose you all respect. I highly recommend you employ something else when they come. Now *open your mouth*."

The words take me back to the dozens of times Jack has said that to me when I have been on my knees in front of him, fixing me with that same assertive glare. I comply instantly as if through years of ceaseless conditioning and detect the tiniest glimmer of a groan as she lifts the glossy crimson cylinder to my lips.

"Wider," she directs, transporting me back to Jack's commands as he looks down at me, his hard cock preparing to enter the wet warmth of my small mouth which readies itself to suck until he decides it's time to stop so that he can fuck me until satiated.

I part my lips further and she leans her head in towards me as she starts to stroke the slick blood-red pigment onto my lower lip, her eyes focused in what looks like... arousal.

Jesus. Is everyone permanently in heat around here?

She takes care to follow the contours of my lips, angling the tip to cloak the corners of my mouth, her face now close, obtrusive spicy perfume radiating off her.

"Press your lips together," she says as she pulls away. "Hmm," she murmurs as I comply, taking in my face. "Breathtaking. They will be most pleased."

"Who will? Who's coming here?"

"You will see."

"I don't want to see. I'm scared. I want to go home."

If I didn't know better, I would say a momentary flicker of pain had warped her face. "That option is not on the table now."

"Will I go home later?"

"That decision is not in my hands… but no physical harm will come to you while you are here." She looks down at her watch before marching to the door where she picks up the shoes she placed down earlier.

"What time is it?" I ask.

"Almost noon. We've had special shoes made for you. Low and steady to accommodate your ankle."

"My ankle? How do you know about these things?! What, do you have a file on me or something?"

"Several."

"Well, I'm flattered, but I'm really not that interesting!"

"I beg to differ. So do many members of the Council. They find you captivating in the extreme."

She hands them to me—ebony open-toe leather slingbacks with some kind of gemstone detailing around the buckle. The soles are soft with just the tiniest lift at the back, an inch at the very most.

"Put them on."

I bend down and slide my feet into them, the opening at the tips allowing my glossy peach nails to pop out. She eyes them with a nod of apparent approval, her gaze trailing down and then back up the dress which clings to my slender legs, coats my thighs like a second skin, hugs my slim waist and provides little modesty for my breasts.

"I need a bra," I say, looking down at the teats she is eyeing so indiscreetly.

"The decision to omit the bra is final."

"Decision? What, did you have a meeting about it?"

"Our president gave me a list of his preferences for your attire."

"President?" I shudder at the thought of him. "You mean Sebastian Gravier?" She doesn't respond, glaring at me defiantly. "Do you hear how *insane* that sounds?!" I shout. "He has no business deciding what I wear! Have you people lost all sense of reality?!"

"Your dress is backless, Jessynia. A bra would ruin the effect. Plus, we do not allow them at Q.N. The building is thoroughly heated. You will not be cold. Most people find they get too hot in here."

Suddenly a sound. My eyes dart to the door. I hear footfall, distant at first, then louder, closer. Multiple people. Wisps of words drift through the air. Voices deep.

"I'm scared," I whisper to Grace, hoping she has some humanity left and can somehow protect me.

She glances back at the door swiftly before turning to look at me, narrowing her eyes, and in the lowest of voices, whispers, "They feed off fear. Don't show it. It is like a drug to them. It will whip them into a frenzy. Hide it as best you can."

I frown at her, unable to understand whose side she is on, or whether she even knows it herself... Is it like Silas and Beth said? Is her allegiance to them a question of her very survival?

The shuffles grow louder until they stop and I watch in slow motion as the handle to this room—a black sphere with vines carved into the metal—turns, causing my heart to race violently as is if my body were one throbbing pulse.

An abrupt blast of air is sucked into the deepest recesses of my chest as figures file in one by one in silence, taking up position opposite me, eight feet from my bed. I can't conceal my distress as I scan the eyes of people all known to me and more terrible than I would have ever wanted to see again.

Grace takes up position to the left of the group. Next to her stands Vallen Markov, then Steven Frost and to the right of him, his wife, Alexandra Frost, her angular face harsh, her eyes blazing, a firestorm of enmity, as though having to restrain herself from attacking me. If looks could bite, my neck would be pouring blood.

They pin me with their glares to the harrowing soundtrack of more footsteps approaching. Another man enters the room, a man whom I have never seen before—mid-forties, tall, eyes that look almost black, a short beard, dark-brown hair that reaches his shoulders, and dressed in the type of ornate tunic that Silas had been wearing back at the compound. His eyes widen as he looks at me, as if pleased with what he sees... or maybe just pleased with the distress I can't seem to conceal.

I'm doing my best to ignore the sinister creature taking up position in the center and instead track Isaiah, the neanderthal from before. He enters last and closes the door behind him, walks behind the figures and places an emerald half-bottle of wine on the window ledge before taking up position to the far right next to the bearded man.

Unease invades me at the sight of another stranger—tall, very short ashy-brown hair wearing a dress shirt, open at the front, and dress pants.

Though this man is entirely different from the others.

He is wearing a full-face mask.

It is molded leather, matte and obsidian. The features are strong, unsettling, the brows furrowed, the mouth an eerie slit. His muscles are obvious beneath his shirt and his chest rises and falls visibly as he stands, feet slightly apart. For a split-second, I think it could be Jack. It isn't. He's too short, around six foot one from the looks of him, his hair a little too dark, and he doesn't possess a physique that is as densely muscular. I try to see his eyes through the slits in the mask but can't make them out.

In any case, I am wholly distracted by the sight of the final man who comes to stand in the center of the line—a man who has filled my nightmares of late.

A man I had hoped to never see again.

Sebastian Gravier.

The sight of this legendary Manhattan monster so close has the room spinning for a moment.

Freshly shaven, his long pale-blond hair tied into a tight bun at the back of his head, he is wearing black dress pants and a loose white shirt, open at the top, the sleeves rolled up to reveal densely muscular forearms and a thick black band on his left ring finger. His shoulders are broad, strong. I had forgotten how tall he was, easily as tall as Cameron and Jack.

His eyes are a kaleidoscope of grays laced with hints of the palest ice-blue, discs of lucent smoke which gleam as he watches me shift back on the bed, watches me try to stop my chest expanding in fear and to keep my composure, concealing the terror I feel. The corners of his mouth lift the slightest amount as he takes in the intimidation that I am clueless as to how to obscure.

To my endless chagrin, I've never been good at the *sang froid* thing. Jack once told me that the fact that my face shows all of my emotions in glaring detail would get me into trouble. He tried to teach me his implacable stare, how to keep your jaw muscles from tensing and your eyes from widening, but even in front of him, I was more likely to burst into nervous laughter when I tried practicing it than to keep a straight face. Except now, I don't feel like laughing...

"Hello, Jessynia," says Gravier, his voice rich, deep with a hint of gravel at the end of words. The accent is expensive, the sort you would expect to be bred on the Upper East Side and not in a young offender's institute in Illinois. When he speaks, his eyelids drop just a tad as though he's savoring each word, or more so savoring the effects of his words on his interlocutor, his target, his prey. "Did you sleep well?" His tone is of cold curiosity.

I shake my head, trying to find my voice which I know will emerge small and high-pitched, my diaphragm weak, stopping me from claiming my usually rich timbre. Swallowing down my nerves, I utter, more softly than I want to, "Sleep well? Your people drugged me! I didn't sleep. I was knocked out!"

I glance to the left to spy Vallen's toothy grin before locking eyes with Sebastian, his smile more subtle as he cocks his head slightly to the side like I'm sure I've seen a vampire do in a horror movie right before ripping out the throat of the human in front of him.

"The inconvenience is regrettable," Gravier responds, his voice so measured it could almost put you into a trance. "Unfortunately, we had little choice seeing as you would not have cooperated willingly. Nothing was done to you while you were asleep," he says coldly. "Nor will it be without your written consent while you are here. Such a thing would have the gravest of consequences at our Society."

"Oh, yeah, you're such an *honorable* group of people. I'm not consenting to being here!"

"Recent events have made it unavoidable that we talk to you directly."

"And so this is your solution?" I manage, trying to pretend that my mouth isn't as dry as dust, that my insides aren't now quivering and that I don't feel like to burst into tears at the sheer visceral overwhelm I feel. "What do you people want from me? I didn't tell anyone about the Society. No one! Isn't that what I was supposed to do?"

A shake of the head by Alexandra Frost has me glancing in her direction. Her breathing is heavy, her glare bestial, a lion stalking prey, ready to feast.

"We appreciate that, but it seems you have been less than discreet about a matter that you were warned *very clearly* about." Gravier speaks slowly, deliberately, no ums and ahs, no filler words, fidgeting or signs of self-consciousness. His imprint on the world is outward only.

"Yes, I had believed that we had come to a clear understanding about the consequences of mentioning my *wife* to other people when we had our chat at your friend's little art exhibition," spits out Steven Frost.

I swallow hard. "Well... my friends and family have known for months, before our little *chat,* and they promised me at the time not to repeat the fact that your wife spent months screwing my husband"—I pause for a moment, waiting to see if he reacts which he doesn't—"and they have all kept their promise."

"We're not talking about your *friends,*" Steven growls, his features blackening, leaving cold despair seeping into my skin.

As I scan my brain, my mouth goes dry and raging butterflies, rabid flecks of black, flutter in my stomach as I wonder who he means. Cameron's friends at the compound? Do they know about them? Oh

God, does he mean the lawyer I emailed? They can't know about that, can they?

Fuck...

"You have been *very* indiscreet *indeed*," Steven hisses.

I gulp hard, my voice choked again as I try to cloak my terror in a fragile veil of affected self-assuredness and pasted-on righteous indignation. "Look, I've dealt with enough verbal pretzels in the last few hours to last me a lifetime. Can you please speak plainly and tell me who you are referring to?"

"We're talking about that cunt lawyer you emailed," Steven snarls as Alexandra glowers at me, taking a small step towards me, a movement that has Vallen Markov grinning, his dusty-brown eyes lifeless, as frigid as sea air in the depths of winter.

"How do you know about that?!" I search his eyes, indignant at the affront that comes from feeling violated. "Did you hack my emails?"

"Unfortunately, no," replies Sebastian. "Mr. O'Neill has done a good job making sure that your email and phone are impenetrable—well, until now that is..." My heart stalls at the thought that they have my phone. "Your lawyer has not been as careful with *his* security systems."

I try to breathe as I find Steven Frost's savage glare again. "I... I was... upset that day," I stammer, praying I don't succumb to one of those panic attacks that plagued me in my late teens. "I let my emotions get the better of me. I was going to email him to retract my statement *this morning,* if you had given me the chance..."

"And we're supposed to believe that?" barks the ever-elegant Alexandra in a tight, long indigo ballgown that puts her lean frame on stunning display. A very rare glimmer of indignation registers on her usually inscrutable face, cracking the glacial façade that she has worked so hard to erect around her.

"It's the truth," I respond.

"I. Don't. Believe. You." Her words emerge haltingly, like the first wax melting under the wick.

"Of course you don't," I say with gusto that is almost entirely fabricated. "You don't have honor or morals, nor do you know what it feels like to trust anybody. I'm telling the truth. I can email him now if you like."

"That's already taken care of," responds the bearded man with the long brown hair, his stare lascivious and indecent. "I suggest you don't undo our correction."

"What do you mean *taken care of*?" I ask.

"We mean that you emailed him this morning to retract your defamatory accusations," he responds nonchalantly.

"You said you didn't have access to my emails..."

"That was before last night," he replies. "Before we gained possession of your phone."

As panic permeates me as they confirm that they have my phone, I start to scan my mind furiously to recall the contents of it. I deleted Cameron's messages and the handful of pictures he has sent me since August the day after he dropped me off at my parent's house, but haven't deleted the messages he's left since, nor the photo he sent me yesterday—his lean, sculpted body under a white sheet that shows off every dense bulge from his torso down.

Not to mention that I now have Beth's number in my phone. And Gabriel's. And Silas's. Not under their real names, but still...

A sudden thought causes my breathing to shallow.

The picture of Rose.

Oh God, did I delete it from my phone? *Jesus, I can't remember.*

"Yes, we've had quite an enjoyable morning indeed contacting your friends and family," says Vallen Markov, imparting his trademark dead-eyed smirk. "Mr. O'Neill has been quite vocal about his affections for you this morning and his plans for you this year. We have had a great deal of fun conversing with our old friend. It has brought back some quite potent memories of his... singular tastes."

I inhale swiftly, this time not managing to keep it under my breath. "You have no right to do that!"

"Right? Your husband has rights too, Jessynia," Vallen replies, his eyes wandering greedily down to my chest before feasting on the distress in my face. "You are still his property by law, and despite our best efforts, he is still utterly contaminated by his affections for you.

Though that may change when he is informed about the extent of your betrayal with a man who was once a *brother* to him." He grins darkly as he finishes the sentence.

"They are not *brothers*," I counter in indignation. "That ended when *she*"—I gesture towards Alex—"got him to seduce and dump Cameron's sister as part of some sociopathic game of chess. And as for betrayal, I don't think I need to tell you about the *dozens* of times my husband cheated on me during our marriage. I don't think he has much moral high ground to stand on there."

"Hmm," Vallen smirks. "You can certainly share your rationalizations with him. See how he handles them..."

"So, is that what all this is about?!" I yell, or try to, my throat still tight. "Me emailing my lawyer? Lawyers are bound by attorney-client privilege. He couldn't tell anyone if he wanted to!"

"You were told to keep my *fucking* name to yourself!" Alexandra snarls, her composure cracking like a pane of glass in a tornado. I've never seen this side to her. The narcissistic injury. The ego monster unleashed. It's chilling to behold her type gripped by narcissistic rage so closely.

"Are you serious?" I reply. "You spent *months* fucking my husband, even after I told you that it ripped my insides out and *you're* upset? How do you think I feel? Plus, you know, I don't want to burst your little bubble, but it's not exactly like you've been discreet with your amorous *adventures,* Alex. Even if I went around telling people, it's not like that would be ground-breaking news around Manhattan."

"You smug little bitch!" she hisses, her angular face hard as nails.

"I mean it's not like I also told him that you're some sort of... soul-sucking ephebophile with a penchant for undera—"

Quick as a snap, I'm forced to brace myself, lifting my hands up and recoiling as she takes a breakneck step forward, raising a sharp hand to strike me.

She is stopped mid-air by Sebastian to the right of her, the vice of his strong fingers snaking around her forearm roughly, stopping the descent.

She turns to face him, breathing heavily. "He won't like that," Sebastian growls with a slow shake of the head, his dense muscles gripping her mercilessly until she shows signs of simmering down. I look at Steven who doesn't even glance in her direction. If I didn't know better, I would say he couldn't care less about the force with which Sebastian is dominating his wife.

As her breaths become less ragged and the harshest edge of her rage begins to dissipate, at least on the surface, she takes a step back, regaining her position, her unblinking ash-hued eyes dueling with mine.

So clearly the woman has a spinning ball of fury inside her just below the surface of her sanguine shell. I mean, I guess I deserve some of her wrath, but I'm finding it difficult to feel compassion for someone who delighted in seducing my husband when he was in his mid-teens, and then again when we were living together as husband and wife. Not to mention the carnage she's left in marriages all over the city.

"Tsk, tsk. That was not very civilized, Jessynia," chides Gravier, the ghost of a black smile on his face. "I think you owe our honorable friend an apology."

I glance at the masked man who shifts his stance before turning to face Alex, my face contrite. "I sincerely apologize if my mention of your fetish for innocent teenage boys offended you, Alex."

Vallen snickers under his breath as Gravier narrows his eyes in amusement.

"Innocent?" she sneers, a flush of coral pink appearing on her flawless tanned skin as she rakes back a loose lock of her distinctive curly golden hair. "I've been a young teenage girl myself, Jessynia, and I know full well that there is nothing *innocent* about them." I shudder at the grimace of pain in her face as she spits the words out as though in contempt at the universe and all the wrongs it has inflicted on her. "I bear more scars from the days of my so-called *youth* than from anything that has happened to me as an adult."

"And so, what, instead of getting help for your trauma you decide to poison other young people, spread your pain to them?!"

"Well, it has worked for me so far."

"It's not a solution, Alex! You're just spreading pain around to others."

"Spare me the lecture, Jessynia. And spare me the spiel about the innocence of teenage boys. I would have thought you would have lost your illusions about them given your own experiences." Her eyes widen in delight as I flinch at her utterance.

"What do you mean?" My mouth is dry and I swallow down the lightheadedness I feel, placing both hands at my sides on the bed to steady myself.

"You know full well what I mean," she murmurs slowly, her thin nude lips pouring out murky smog that invades my lungs. Her countenance is suddenly lighter, a thing of dark glee. "Or have you forgotten your unfortunate incident in Albany?"

I don't move but for a tear that immediately spills onto my cheek and trickles down the milky skin where it hovers on the edge of my jaw before dropping onto my breast. Another appears in my other eye, teetering on my waterline as I remain locked into Alex, my bottom lip quivering for a second before I stop it by biting it gently.

How could they know about that?

As the woman who shared my husband with me feasts on my anguish, I think back to summer camp in an area of wilderness near Albany when I was a few weeks into seventeen. One of the camp leaders—an older boy of nineteen years, smart with neat hair combed to the side—had asked me to help him carry a bucket of potatoes to another area of the camp, leading me on a "shortcut" through a patch of forest on the outskirts of camp. At that age, two years feels like a decade. He felt like the adult who was taking care of us. I remember the innocence, the naivety, the stupidity of mindlessly following this boy who had been such a great leader all week, so polite, so attentive, so keen to help us out. I recall how he stopped, placing our buckets down on the forest floor, the confusion I felt as he brought a hand to my face and moved in to kiss me, the rage that erupted in him as I pushed it away and stepped back. Within an instant, he had grabbed me, turning me, pushing me against a tree, his chest against my back, grappling at my shorts, his hands near the button, tugging at it as I writhed and tried to scream through the hand over my mouth. I recall scratching deep into the flesh of his hand, him wincing just a moment, his other hand loosening a tad, allowing me to bite into his index finger. I remember the flesh giving way under my teeth, the faintest taste of blood in my mouth. Suddenly there were voices nearby, loud enough for him to let me go. I ran through the forest to the camp where I broke down and told one of the women running it what had happened.

Then whispered havoc as his parents were called, as were mine to take me home. There were discussions between adults and camp officials asking for my version of events, kindly at first and then with suspicion, with insinuation, with hostility as the story he span was made of entirely different yarn to mine. His family were rich and influential. They insinuated that I had slept with other boys there, had led him on. The rumors spread like wildfire in the sweltering depths of summer. I had not touched another boy at that camp nor done anything but kiss a boy up to that point. In fact, I was a virgin until the age of nineteen.

After much covert conversation, it was decided that the police would not be called but that he would be banned from the camp. I don't know who made the decision, but it was concluded that the fallout from me going to the police would be too great for me to bear. When I got back to school after summer, rumors had been spread about me. I don't know what caused me more trauma—his attempted assault, the sudden loss of innocence or the shame and recrimination I was made to feel afterwards. And to avoid the pain of it all, my parents stuffed it away and it was never spoken of again.

As I grew older and started college, I started self-defense classes and for three years arranged classes for other students on how to stay safe.

And then I fell in love... and those things stopped.

I know one of the reasons I fell so desperately in love with Jack was that he always made me feel so safe, so protected from the harsh shadows of the world, from the figures lurking in back alleys, from the dangers of other men. He would appear, his cruel glare hounding them into backing off if they stepped too close to me. He would arrange for cars to pick me up, would insist on paying for cabs when the subway would have done just fine, and would force me to do boxing and kick-boxing practice at least once a week. He forced me because I had stopped doing such things myself, so sure that he would always be there to defend me, keep me safe. Gradually as I spent more time in his strong, possessive arms, I let go of my fear of the world, of men. I melted into him, sheltering in his power without even knowing I was doing it. Losing myself in the impenetrable bubble of his visceral strength was effortless—so effortless that I didn't even realize that I was willingly handing over all my own power and self-reliance the entire time we were together.

NOW I WANT IT BACK.

"How do you know about that?" I ask, static from the unbidden memory leaving my senses screaming as I eye her and then Gravier who watches me as if in utter fascination. There was no police report filed and no one knows that story apart from Maddie, Stella and the people at the camp. I never told Cameron nor Jack, always afraid that Jack would perhaps seek revenge on the person who had tried to take part of my soul from me.

"We know a lot about you, Jessynia," responds the bearded man gruffly. "And we also know about some of the disturbing plans that our *enemies* are conjuring up behind the scenes. I think you know what I mean. They seemed to have dragged you into something that you have no idea the perils of."

"Indeed," adds Gravier, his glare brutal. "For all of his raging desire to protect you, Mr. O'Neill seems to have brought you closer to danger."

"Closer? I was already in danger! It wasn't two weeks ago that *he* set his psychopathic nephew on me!" I shout, signaling towards Vallen with a tip of my head. "What had I done wrong *then*? I had done *nothing* wrong and you still targeted me."

"Yes, that was most enjoyable," says the voice behind the black mask.

I shift back on the bed, clutching my neck as the man slowly bends his head towards the floor and pulls his mask off as if in slow motion, lifting his eyes to lock with mine, a corrupt, perfidious smile twisting his pale face. Ilya. I pant overtly at the sight of the man who almost seduced me in a depraved plot to forever contaminate my peace of mind and turn me into a pawn in some wretched, ungodly war. His ashy-brown hair which once hung below his ears has been cut extremely short and brushed to the side like an angelic little schoolboy. The juxtaposition between his respectable outward appearance and his inner malevolence could not be more unsettling.

"It was very enjoyable indeed," he repeats, his smile now a grin, matched only by his uncle Vallen's. "Pity it had to end when it did. Maybe I will have a chance to correct that at some point in the future..."

"What is he doing here?!" I shout at Sebastian, tears starting to roll down my face like droplets of rain down a window pane as that feeling of violation I felt at the apartment sends my cells into a frenzy. "Do you realize what he tried to do to me?! What had I done then?!"

Fat drops of salt water fall onto my chest as my eyes dart around the room, my distress now on dramatic display for all to see. I spot smiles of malicious delight on the faces of everyone other than Grace. Sebastian Gravier tilts his head, eyes wide with relish, studying the human emotions that some of these specimens of the living dead can only mimic in an attempt to fit in with society. Vallen starts to snigger as I somberly look down at the black satin under my hands.

I am startled by a groan from the bearded man with the long hair and glance up to find him breathing deeply, scrutinizing my face with glee, making no attempt to hide his arousal at my pain. "She is exquisite," he growls. "We have to have her. She has to submit."

I grimace at his words and wipe away tears with shaky fingers.

"Hmm... your presence seems to be quite distressing, Ilya," says Sebastian, voice low, his eyes trailed on mine for every syllable. "I suggest you make your way to the Oak Room. We shall be starting soon anyway."

Ilya bows his head at the order before making his way out of the room.

As I sniffle away tears, Grace appears before me with a tissue, crouching down to dab my face to correct any fallout that could besmirch the impeccable makeup she applied earlier. "Stop it!" she commands within inches of me, though her eyes are soft, pleading almost, a sight those behind her can't tell.

"Leave it, Grace," murmurs the bearded man. "The tears are most sublime."

"Agree," says Steven Frost.

She stands up and moves back in line as Gravier speaks. "Are you ready, Jessynia?"

"Ready for what?" My voice is so damn soft...

"We have been working on your husband for a while now, trying to free his mind of the hold you have over him." There is a bitter bite to his voice. "Nothing seems to take the edge off it, sadly. We have made the decision to invite you to join us as a last resort, in order to avoid us having to declare you fair game."

"*Fair game*?" I say. "What does that mean?"

"It means you will be considered one of our enemies," replies Gravier coarsely. "And we will take appropriate measures to ensure our survival. You would *not* want that."

"Where exactly will I be going?"

"You will be witnessing one of the initiation ceremonies that our female members have the pleasure of experiencing before being let into our inner circle," replies the bearded man as I instantly think of that final night Beth spent in this place. "We believe that it is something that is quite *enticing* to most women."

"Well, I don't want to see it!"

Gravier eyes me sternly before looking over at Grace and then Isaiah. "She's tense. Give her something to loosen her up."

"What?! No!" I protest.

Before I have a chance to speak again, Grace is before me, grabbing my upper arm and yanking me to my feet, her strong fingers on my flesh making my skin crawl. Isaiah takes the glass bottle that he had put onto the window ledge and unscrews it, handing it to Grace before reaching into the inner pocket of his black jacket to take out a small silver box which he opens, removing from it a single sky-blue pill.

He moves to stand in front of me, glowering from his superior height, ten inches taller at least. "Take this," he instructs lifting the pill to my mouth and shoving the bottle into my hand.

"No! What is it? I'm not taking it."

"You either take it willingly," he responds acerbically, "or we will tie you to the chair and force you to swallow it. Nothing would give me more pleasure than to bind your hands to a chair and pry your mouth open."

"Please," I pant. "I don't want to."

Grace takes out a syringe from the upper pocket of her black shirt, removing the slim plastic cap and pushing slightly so that there is a squirt of liquid. "You take it, or we will use the same means as before and the effects will be more potent..."

"The pill won't make you pass out," says the bearded man. "It's just something to help you relax. Low dose. We have all taken them before. So have the two men in your life... dozens of times."

In that bitter, dead-end type of defeat, I take the pill from Isaiah's thick finger and put it into my mouth.

"Drink and swallow," he orders.

I bring the bottle to my lips. The wine enters my mouth and I hold it there for five long seconds. As I do so, I think of Rose and the pills her so-called husband gave her.

"We will be inspecting your mouth when you're done," Isaiah barks as Grace recaps the needle and returns it to her pocket. "Swallow!" I finally swallow the pill and remove the rim of the bottle from my lips, staring at him pleadingly, hoping I can ignite some remnant ember of humanity that he must have had at some point. "One more sip," he presses.

I bring the dark-green rim to my lips again and take another sip just as I start to feel my heart racing and a raging flood of euphoria filling my system.

"Open your mouth," he commands.

"I feel dizzy," I pant, not complying as I hand him back the bottle and sit back down on the bed, clutching my chest, my mouth parched, my skin clammy, covered by a dewy mist.

"She's swallowed it," replies Grace.

"What did you give me?!"

"Just something to relax you," replies Gravier, his keen eyes contemplating me callously. "Just let the feeling float over you."

The juxtaposition of the euphoria hitting my brain, like the most intense of orgasms, mixed with the terror of being out of control in front of these people has a tear trickling onto my cheek.

"I can't breathe," I whisper.

"You can breathe," responds Gravier. "Just relax and enjoy the feeling."

I pant, light-headed, steadying myself against the bed.

"I think she likes it!" cackles Vallen sinking his fingers into his hair which appears to come alive like a sack of slithering snakes.

"You gentlemen may depart," directs Gravier.

Upon his command, Vallen and Steven bow and leave the room, leaving behind Grace, Alexandra, Isaiah and Sebastian.

"Help her to her feet," Gravier says.

Grace pulls on my arm and yanks me up. The room spins for a moment before steadying as Sebastian turns to leave, followed by Alex. Grace snakes her arm behind my back and Isaiah grips my upper arm as they walk me to the door.

There is a corridor with walls lined with deep wood illuminated by soft spotlights above that flash in front of my eyes which can't seem to focus no matter what I do. The brisk pace of the others and my unsteady gait has me losing sight of them.

Isaiah relinquishes his hold on me, taking up position behind us as my shaky feet make it down another corridor where I begin to hear music, or to be more precise, chanting, in Latin maybe, melodious string instruments accompanying it. We pass doors of various deep colors with symbols carved into them, just like those at Q.N. in Tribeca.

They lead me in silence into a small room with cloaks and masks hanging from black hooks. Grace dons an indigo cloak, Isaiah a black one, before removing their shoes and reaching for masks on adjacent hooks. Grace puts on a plain half-mask that matches her cloak while Isaiah puts on a full black one like the one worn by Cameron in Tribeca, though somehow the features seem sterner and more sinister than the one I remember; I wonder for a moment if it really is or if my memory is playing tricks on me. I shudder at the well-rehearsed spectacle of them raising thick hoods over their heads, the shifts of color in the velvet leaving their cloaks pulsing and alive.

As they stand in front of me, unspeaking, I try to calm my breathing and not lose my wits completely. My body feels warm, fuzzy, euphoric almost, with a high buzzing through my brain like the most delicious of wines. If it wasn't for the fear I feel, I would enjoy it but the combination of this and being out of control has alarm bells ringing throughout my cells.

Grace heads to a cupboard fixed to the wall on the left and pulls out a half-mask, distinct from the others, for this one is not made of leather, but of a shimmery silver fabric with crystals of some sort adorning the outside curves. I'm too disorientated to offer resistance as she places it onto my face and pulls the chord behind me to the sound of footsteps entering the room.

I turn to see a man wearing a black half-mask and black cloak with the hood down, a thick strip of gold embroidery in the shape of vines running down the center of it. I know from his sheer bulk, the ashy-blond hair and the strong jaw that it is Sebastian who is turning to face me.

I can't see his eyes but feel his glare stroll over my face, onto my exposed lips, down my neck, over my breasts, waist and legs before shifting up.

"Acceptable?" asks Grace.

"Very," he replies. "She'll need a cloak. Her body is highly distinctive. It would not be wise for all members to recognize her."

Grace pulls a burgundy cloak off a sinewy black hook and stands before me. "Lift your arms," she barks, setting the firework from hell off in my brain. I comply and feel the thick velvet nestle onto my warm skin. She pulls the hood up over my head.

Isaiah doesn't attempt to hide his groan at the sight, leaning into me to take me in. I can't tell where he's looking through his thick mask but I suspect it's my lips, the only part of me now on display.

"Good?" asks Grace.

"Perfect," replies Sebastian.

31

GRACE GRIPS MY UPPER ARM FIRMLY as we leave the room and head further down the corridor. At the end, a black door is half open and a glow burns from inside to the sound of languid chanting accompanied by some deep string instrument.

We pass two security guards and enter a large, dimly lit room in the center of which lies a black ottoman with some cushions on it, as long and wide as a king-sized bed. A woman stands before it, cloaked in ivory velvet with a matching half-mask on her face. Two feet away stands a dark table with a silver tray on it adorned with various objects that I can't fully make out in the gloom of the room. Next to the table stands an armchair of black leather.

For a second, I think I'm imagining things as I see the twenty-five or so people standing in a semi-circle to the right, all cloaked with masks on, silently facing the lone woman whom I fear will be on the menu tonight. There are armchairs and loveseats scattered around a few feet behind the patrons next to side tables adorned with drinks and snacks and other things my blurry eyes can't make out.

Upon entering, I am pulled to the left by Grace and come to stand between her on my right and another woman three feet to my left who watches me from behind her burgundy mask. I'm just praying it isn't Alexandra Frost. On second thoughts, the woman is standing next to three cloaked men. Their cloaks are obscuring the bottom half of their faces, but from their build, it looks like they may be her husband, Vallen and Ilya.

My dry throat constricts at the thought.

To the right of Grace stands Sebastian Gravier and to his right, his lackey Isaiah. On either side of the door we came through stand two more masked security guards wearing black suits over what must be steroid-induced bulk.

I glance at the main wall to the left bearing an ornate wooden engraving of a mammoth oak tree. The tree itself is stained almost black, just like the one at Q.N. in Tribeca, though this time it is at least twice the size, a silent witness surveying the sordid revelers below like some kind of revered deity.

The room is lit up by imitation oil lamps attached to each wall which cast unsettling shadows all around. The walls are connected by a rich hardwood and sheathed in opulent wallpaper with a backdrop the color of merlot and sumptuous vines of silver and gold thread weaved throughout.

On the wall to my right behind the patrons, the lamps above allow me to make out hooks from which hang various items you would expect from this place, but which stun nonetheless due to the casual way they are displayed. There are ropes, ties and handcuffs of various sorts as well as what look like shackles, whips and ball gags. The sight of them has my limbs wilting.

There is a slight waft of incense in the air, nothing too heavy, but it still adds to the nausea I feel from the drug they forced into me. I turn to Grace. "I don't feel good."

She glances behind her and takes a glass of water from a table against the wall. "Drink this."

I take it from her and gulp down the icy water, trying to quench my raging thirst.

"Better?" she asks.

I shake my head. "I don't want to watch this."

She leans her head in towards me, and in a whisper that only I could hear over the chanting utters, "Just breathe, Jessynia."

I frown behind my mask and watch as her inscrutable leather façade turns towards the center of the room.

We play our roles as unspeaking witnesses for long moments until the chanting finally subsides and out of the corner of my eye, I observe Sebastian Gravier stride towards the center of the room, the thud of his bare feet echoing around this now-silent hall. The strip of gold vines running down the center of the cloak and along the hem glistens in the moody light.

He stops a few feet away from the woman, watching her for a few moments behind his mask before turning around to face the semi-circle of people behind him, filling the room utterly with his potent energy.

"Hello, my friends." His voice is so deep, so self-assured that it seizes every ounce of your attention whether you want it to or not. "It has been an honor to spend the year with you and we are privileged to have you here on this first day of what will be an eventful new year for Quercus Velutina."

Raucous applause rings out around the room.

"I would like to thank you for wearing your masks for the first stages of today's celebrations to accommodate our guest who will be present for a short while." Masks turn toward me and I inhale sharply at the sight, wondering if they know who I am. "We are hopeful that sometime in this new year, she will be able to experience her own initiation into our family."

The energy of the fervid applause causes my skin to flush hot.

Like hell, Gravier.

"This year will be a year of growth for our beloved Society, of strengthening our bonds, of ensuring the survival of freedom." He speaks slowly, measuredly, as if chairing some business meeting. "Freedom to be ourselves. Freedom over our bodies. Freedom to experience the offerings of life as we want to, just as our forefathers declared when they created this unique Society of free-thinkers."

Yeah, Rose has tasted your idea of freedom.

"We have never been more united, nor more certain of where we need to go. Part of this year of growth is initiating new members into our inner circle. Members who have shown themselves to be loyal to us, who have proven their fealty and honored their vows of discretion and fidelity.

"Our honorable friend here"—he takes a step towards the unmoving woman and pats her on her cloaked shoulder"—has been requesting the opportunity to be initiated into our inner circle for quite some time, as you know. After a *unanimous* vote, she finally has the chance today. Do we support her in her desire?"

"Yes!" The deep, multi-tonal cry of many voices ricochets around the room.

"You know what will happen today, my friend?" Sebastian asks, turning to face the woman, feet slightly apart and hands locking behind his back. The scene shakes before my eyes and I blink a few times to refocus, my flesh warm from the drug despite the grotesque scene playing out in front of me.

"Yes." Her voice is faint.

"Louder, please."

"Yes!"

"It has been explained clearly to you?"

"Perfectly."

"And you are consenting to today's entertainment of your own free will?"

"I am."

"And you wish to finally be part of our family?"

"I do." Jesus, she sounds like an automaton, desperate for approval from its human master.

"How much?"

"More than *anything*."

"This is *not* a non-consensual room and you may stop at any time you want. The safe word is *White Oak*. Is that clear?"

"Yes."

"Yes, what?" His tall form stiffens under his black cloak.

"Yes, my lord." She bows her head to him.

A shiver slides through me. I had this same exchange with Cameron not long ago. Did he ask for my reverence spontaneously or is it part of his programming after witnessing *entertainment* like this? Jesus, was he channeling Sebastian Gravier when he requested those words?

"But if you stop before the final bell," Gravier continues, "then you will forfeit your opportunity to become part of our inner sanctum. And you will revert to being an ordinary member of the lowest order until you have once again proven yourself to be worthy of more. Is that understood?"

"That won't happen."

"You are sure of that?"

"Yes, my lord."

He takes a step toward her, pulling down her white hood to reveal loose strawberry-blond hair that shimmers like strands of rose gold. He pulls the seam at the center of her pale cloak, slowly and carefully opening it up, revealing her ample breasts, her sand-hued skin. He pulls further to reveal her neatly trimmed pubis before finally walking behind her and withdrawing her cloak from her tall frame completely in a gesture that has me clasping my quivering hand over my mouth at the sight of him exposing her in front of the entire room.

"You have worked hard I see," says Gravier who, from the angles of his mask, is sliding his gaze slowly down and then back up as he appraises her lean, strong body.

"Yes, my lord. I wanted to make sure you were pleased with what you saw."

"Hmm, we shall see... We have faith you will perform to our satisfaction. Don't we?" he shouts turning to the spectators.

"Yes!" The boom of voices enters me roughly.

"Turn around. Don't be shy. The others deserve to see the results of your hard work."

She slowly turns counter-clockwise to the sound of groans and claps of approval from the men and the women. From a distance, she looks like Cameron's ex-girlfriend, Olivia. I'm sure it isn't, but my eyes can't quite focus and the duplicitous drug is playing treacherous tricks on me.

As she pivots back around to face Gravier, he asks, "Are you ready, my friend?"

She nods.

"I need verbal consent," he retorts.

"Yes. I'm ready." Her mouth moves under her silver half-mask. There is not a sliver of hesitation in her voice.

"You are certain?"

"One hundred percent."

"Very well. All gentlemen here have been tested and cleared by our doctors in the last five days. Those that haven't been tested shall use sheaths. Clear?"

"Clear!" The voices of men ring out like the most chilling of choruses, though this time the sound is deeper, rougher, more urgent. I see some men shift slightly, their body language desperate, yearning as they emit bestial groans, craving the release this woman is offering.

The sound of music begins—light chanting accompanied by medieval-sounding string instruments, faster in pace this time, emitted by speakers hidden in the shadows near the ceiling of this dimly lit room.

"Libertas est potestas," Gravier bellows, turning to face the crowd, his powerful voice resolute, earnest.

"Libertas est potestas!" the room shouts, and as the sharp voice of the woman to my left floats over to me, I realize with a shiver that it is indeed Alexandra Frost.

"To Quercus Velutina!" shouts one man.

"To Quercus Velutina!!"

And upon the cry, the scene before me begins to shake as Gravier turns to face the woman and removes his ebony cloak, throwing it onto the armchair nearby to stand completely naked before her. He pulls the band out of his hair, letting it fall loose around his shoulders, the thick golden strands luminous in the gloom of this somber room. His skin is pallid and although I can only see the back and side of him, his body looks as muscular as any I have ever seen in person. Every groove, every ridge, every trough is clearly defined. There is no sag, no unintended hollow, no weakness. Not even Jack, a mass of defined muscle, can surpass the sheer bulk of his muscles.

Without a word from him, the woman drops to her knees and looks up at him, opening her mouth as Gravier glares at her from behind the darkness of his unnerving mask. As he pivots slightly, I see that he is fully erect and... very big. She proceeds to edge her plump lips over the engorged head of his cock, sucking on only the tip for a long minute before taking him deeper into her mouth. Other than his solid erection, he seems to exhibit no sign of pleasure at all as she gets to work, sucking and licking with a zeal and enthusiasm I didn't think existed outside the handful of porn movies I've watched in my life. He is unmoved, watching her as if analyzing her work rather than taking pleasure in what she is doing to his body.

She licks and sucks, not taking her eyes off him, as groans and exclamations from the men and women resound around the room. I see a man step forward, barely able to restrain himself, caressing the bulge under his thick cloak.

Cruel chills creep up my back, a spider advancing, as Gravier pulls out of her, holding her chin. "Get up, my friend."

She obeys.

"Bend over. Face the door. Face down."

She submits again and climbs into the ottoman, facing in our direction before bending over so that the side of her face is pressed against the leather. As Gravier moves onto the ottoman behind her, I see his full form in the dim light.

He is huge. Long. Thick. Erect.

Both Jack and Cameron are far bigger than average, so big that I have struggled to accommodate them at times, but even they can't surpass this man for size.

He climbs on top of her, pressing her head down firmly with his strong hand as he licks the golden skin over her spine from top to bottom, just as Jack did to me in that Hamptons house, before grabbing hold of his dense erection and entering her slim body to her squeal, leaning over her back, hemming her in as he lifts his head and begins to look in my direction, the thrusts of his muscular body hammering into me as he does.

For a second, I think he needs something from Isaiah or Grace, but he keeps looking, the twisted masculine features of his unnerving mask bearing down on me as his hair falls around his face, his look all the more savage for it. In my intoxicated fervor, it feels like his mask is coming towards me, like it is moving, the malevolent features twisting, talking to me...

I feel a glimmer of that claustrophobia I felt the last time I was at Q.N. with Cameron and take a step backwards. I sense Grace turn to look at me for a moment as I try to breathe while the ground bounces and the room begins to spin.

"He's staring at me," I mutter, realizing I said it aloud.

I know I can't tell because of his mask, but I know by the exact angle of his head that he is looking at me. Not Grace, not Alex—the angle would be slightly off. He is fucking this woman while watching me.

I feel my skin flush hot, claustrophobia constricting my chest as I take another step back. This time, Grace turns to grab my right arm as the elegant Alexandra Frost darts behind me, grabbing my left arm and forcing it into an armlock as her right arm contracts around my upper chest, her hand finding my mouth, clamping down on it roughly, muffling my shout as I wriggle to free myself. In response, she pulls my arm up higher behind my back until it pinches, the ligaments straining. I stop at the threat of pain.

I once learned how to get out of armlocks in self-defense classes but it's been so long and I'm so uncoordinated that I can't remember. Between Grace's hold on my arm and Alex's ire which seems to be giving her the strength of ten men, I am stuck, caged in as Sebastian fucks this woman while watching me as Alex's unmasked mouth closes in on the side of my face.

"Don't you dare move," she hisses into me, a serpent zeroing in on its prey. "You're going to watch this."

I spot masks turn in my direction and perverse laughter straying from them as Gravier rubs his hands up and down the woman's back as he studies me while fucking her docile body.

He tips his head in the direction of someone to my left and nods. The man removes his cloak and hangs it on the hook behind him, leaving his dense body uncovered. Despite the mask, I see from the light-brown hair that it is Vallen who strides up to the pair, and takes up position before the woman who lifts her head promptly on his arrival, opens her mouth wide and lets him penetrate it as she begins to perform fellatio on him to the sound of applause around the room.

I guess I missed the part where there is some kind of accomplishment going on here.

She sucks avidly, with Vallen lifting his head back in pleasure, showing the emotion that Gravier seems incapable of.

"Are you enjoying this, Jessynia?" Alex asks, her grip over my mouth loosening as she finds my throat.

I pull against her only to have her and Grace grip me more tightly. "No. Let me go, Alex!"

"You will be watching, Jessynia. This will be you one day."

I struggle again but she yanks my arm up and I exclaim at the harsh pinch, stopping the fight. "I will *never* consent to this."

"Hmm. That's what all of the women who come here say... until they watch it a few times and realize that there is no greater honor than being the vehicle of pleasure for men like these."

"*Honor?* You people are insane."

In the drug-induced stupor I'm in, the sight of Vallen and Gravier both penetrating this woman is some grotesque monster of restless flesh. Vallen turns his head in my direction, a grin twisting under his half-mask as the floor falls out from under me.

Alex's growl into my ear is a devious chant. "It is no secret that Sebastian considers you his most coveted prize. He desires you greatly, you know. Do you have *any* idea what a privilege it is to have a god like him wish to make educating you his own personal project?"

"Privilege?" I scoff, the glow of a thousand candles lighting my loaded cells up from the inside. "I guess I missed the *privilege* part, what with all the drugging and the kidnapping and forcible confinement." I realize I slurred the last few words and that the sight of Vallen's back in front of me seems to be transforming into that of some perverse form of the underworld.

"Not to mention Vallen," she continues in that elegant accent she has worked so hard on cultivating, "who would kill at this point to be able to defile you."

"Oh, lucky me. Every psychopath in New York wants me..."

I feel her lower cheek widen against mine as if she is smiling. "You know, watching them fuck you at the same time, little girl, will be one of the greatest thrills of my life. And if your husband and your lover could join in as well, well, that would be quite sublime."

I whimper and try to pull away again, only to have her tighten her grasp on me.

"Need help restraining her?" an impatient Isaiah asks from behind.

"No, I've got this," Alex responds. "She has no strength left."

No strength? I'll show you strength, you bitch.

Gravier turns his head again and nods towards the man to Alex's left. The man removes his cloak, confirming that it is indeed Steven Frost, her very own husband. I shift my gaze, wishing I could see Alex's face as she watches Sebastian and Vallen withdraw from the woman and her husband climb onto his back and position himself underneath her on the ebony ottoman, impaling her without a moment's hesitation as he kisses and licks her neck while Gravier climbs back on top and begins, I assume, to sodomize her. And then Vallen, positioned in front of her mouth, makes three...

Sordid applause rings out around the room as I watch the eerie "entertainment". This incarnation seems gentle, respectful almost—no grabbing of hair, no insults. Their hands are gentle, tender almost, with what seems to be a calculated avoidance of the whips, gags, shackles and handcuffs of various types hanging from the wall like some taunting menace.

But what these people aren't aware of is that I know what happens when they are done with someone. I know how they treated Beth. I feel the ghost of her in the room and the imprints of her final night at Quercus Velutina as I watch this shiny infomercial designed to make you feel as though you too will be safe with them... when the truth is anything but.

As Steven Frost grunts loudly in pleasure and begins to suck the woman's pale brown nipples as he fucks her to the sound of her delight, I sense Alex's grip on my neck tighten.

"Are you enjoying this, Alex? Is it nice seeing your own husband fuck another woman?"

"I've accepted this part of his life." Her fingers wind around my neck, the sounds coming from her the low thunder of wrath.

"Yeah, you sound *fine* with it, Alex."

She pauses for a moment as if to get a hold of herself. "Well, in return, I take my own pleasure wherever I want... and with *whomever* I want." A sear of torment chars me at the thought of her and Jack. "And as you know," she continues, "I have no shortage of supremely talented men lining up to take away my pain."

"Well..." I pause to find my voice. "Judging by the bitterness in your voice, you don't sound like you're enjoying the sight, no matter what bullshit rationalizations you are feeding yourself."

Her pungent perfume permeates my body as her devious mouth presses against my skin. "He's not the only man around here whose pleasure at the hands of another woman I have endured. Watching your husband fuck women here is one of my greatest thrills and also one of my deepest sources of pain."

"*Your* sources of pain? Are you serious?"

The tempo of the chanting increases.

"Yes. As women, it is our burden to endure pain."

"Maybe you're just hanging around with the wrong men, Alex."

"Hmm. Have you ever experienced two men at once, Jessynia?" she asks, her thin, pale lips locating the entrance to my ear as if wanting to pour her poison into me. To my silence, she responds, "I didn't think so. You must have thought about it though, no? Thought of solving your little dilemma by asking your husband and your lover to share?" She tightens her grip on me as I attempt to squirm free. "It seems like the most obvious solution to me. Being ravaged by those two men at the same time is something most women would *kill* for. In fact, I frequently suggested it to both of them, a very long time ago. Your husband was game." A note of amusement ambles from her lips. "Your *lover* rejected me, however. Wouldn't give me the full expression of what I wanted. You know, I've never really forgiven him for depriving me of that particular experience. I only hope that I get to watch him and Jack pleasure you at the same time one day. That would certainly make up for the insult, especially if Sebastian were permitted to join in..."

"Well, it's important to have dreams, Alex," I sneer.

On the utterance of her name, the sudden strike of a gong rings out around the room, and upon its muted clang, the other patrons begin to remove their cloaks as a heaving mass of bodies begin their distorted dance.

Women around the room drop to their knees while others offer their bodies up to the men around them, bending over, lying on rugs, lifting legs against the wall. A few men approach the blond woman in the center of the room and begin to stroke her as Gravier thrusts harder and harder, the dense striations of his pale muscles heaving bestially before he finally pulls out of her and ejaculates onto her back, his mask turned in the direction of Alex and I as he completes the domination of his test subject.

"Mmm," Alex groans. "He's something else, isn't he? I've been with many men, Jessynia, and I can confidently say that no pleasure I've ever experienced with *any* man surpasses that I have felt when being the vehicle for our president's needs. And that *includes* your husband. The day I watch Sebastian begin to teach you the dark pleasures he knows will be one of the greatest days of my life."

A naked woman, all soft olive curves and easy grace, saunters up to Gravier and hands him a black robe which he puts on while another wipes down the woman's back as I spy a man taking up Gravier's position behind her.

Sebastian ties the rope around his robe as he slowly strides towards us, stopping a foot in front of me, eyeing me from behind the menacing obsidian façade, a devious smile on display under his half-mask. In my drug-addled state, between Alex's grip, the venomous invasion of her words and the pseudo-human face in front of me, I feel unsteady, like

I'm falling through space into some black hole. The Society's leader doesn't speak for the longest time, his mask eating into me, its features contorting under the potion I've consumed.

"Did you enjoy that, Jessynia?" he asks.

"No, I did not." My voice quivers again. "I want to go home."

He doesn't move as my gaze finds the dark slits in his mask as I try to block out the moans and writhing in the sordid shadows around me.

"Take her back to the room," he finally says, departing as Alex releases her grip on me and Grace pulls my arm, walking me out and back down the corridor as Gravier enters a room to the right and shuts the black door behind him.

As we make it back to that same room I was in before, Grace rips the seam of my crimson cloak open and pulls it off me, leaving me in my supportless black dress. I glance around and see several new bottles of water on the table, one of which she grabs and gives to me. I drink half of it down.

"Eat," she orders, gesturing to a bowl that is restocked with fruit and nuts. "Someone will be in to see you soon."

"Who?"

She doesn't answer.

"Who?" I repeat.

"He just wants to talk," she whispers. "Don't let him inside your head."

32

AFTER DRINKING SOME MORE WATER and eating some fruit, I lie down on the bed, hoping the heady euphoria and nausea from the drug will begin to subside and things before me will start to become unblurred. I lift my fingers to my neck, feeling the pulse slightly steadier than before.

I close my eyes for what was supposed to be a moment, but as I open them, I realize from the depths of my stupor that I must have lost time as I awaken to weighty footsteps getting louder and louder until the clack of the lock spikes through the room and the door gently eases open. I have no idea if I closed my eyes for seconds, minutes or hours.

I sit up and get to my shaky feet at the sight of Sebastian Gravier entering the bedroom, freshly showered, his long, damp hair falling down his muscular neck, stopping just below the tops of his shoulders. He is dressed in black pants, black shoes and a black shirt which hangs loosely over his broad shoulders, the top few buttons undone to reveal slabs of pale muscle below.

He closes the door behind him as I edge to the window. "What do you want?" I ask.

"Hello, Jessynia."

"When am I going home?"

"We haven't had an opportunity to have an honest chat with each other in private. We will need to do that first." He takes a slow pace towards me. In fact, everything that this man does seems to be by design, as if in total control at all times.

"What about?"

"Sit," he says, gesturing towards the two armchairs in the corner of the room to the right of the door.

"No."

He smiles coldly and takes three more steps towards me, edging to within a few feet of me, hands linked behind his back as I step backwards until the window ledge prods my back.

"Perhaps you would prefer I stand right over you as we talk? I can certainly do that if you so desire..."

The very thought of it has insidious tentacles reaching into me, moving my body towards the black armchair in the corner where I sit down, watched all the while by him.

I stiffen as the reputed sadist pulls the second one around so that he's sitting opposite me, three feet away, leaning back into it, one leg crossed over the other as he observes me in eerily composed stillness for what must be a minute before finally beginning to speak as I frown into him. "Did you enjoy the entertainment?"

"No. I did not."

"Hmm. I wonder if you would have the guts to admit it to me if you did..."

I shake my head as I take in his singular face, the blur from earlier dissipating, finally leaving my vision somewhat clear. With him sitting so close, the full realization of his outer beauty takes me aback. He has a rugged oval-shaped face, carved in lean angles, a high forehead, a strong jaw and blade-like cheekbones that curve upwards to meet the seam of his upper ear.

His eyes are large and the most singular gray color—not the dull, smokey ash of Alexandra's eyes, but eyes of the most luminous icy gray, the color of a glacier in the light of sunrise. There is something otherworldly about the light behind them—specks of pale lucent blue dancing in a smokey crystal sphere with what look like flakes of gold around his pupil. Other than the slight shadowy hollow around them and the hint of mauve under his waterline, they look like they could belong to some otherworldly creature with starlight for eyes. His lashes are long, his nose straight, perfect. His cheekbones angle down to meet full lips above a strong dimpled chin.

Gravier is in his mid-thirties at least, with a face as rugged and masculine as his bulky body, in mesmerizing contrast to the ethereal shape and color of his eyes. To me, it feels like what it would be to peer into the eyes of Lucifer, morning star, the fallen archangel, the rebel, supposedly the most beautiful of all angels, the pinnacle of physical perfection, able to tempt the hardiest of souls from their paths. He is a study in contrasts—his beauty an insidious cloak obscuring the depraved beast within.

His muscles are thick and defined, filled with knowledge and the experience that a man in his mid-to-late thirties has acquired—an experience and competence evidenced by the sheer force of his glare and his obvious awareness of his rare beauty, strength and power.

He has a way of watching me that is unfamiliar to me. I've been contemplated by dominant, lustful men before—Jack and Cameron being just two of them. I'm used to feeling the weight of gazes of yearning and arousal, of glares of possessiveness, of stares of protectiveness, but Sebastian's gaze is different. It is of cold yet deep curiosity, reptilian almost, as if studying some species that is not his own.

When he looks at you, you feel him on you, the weight of his deviant thoughts imprinting on your flesh. His gaze is of scrutiny and fascination, and entirely absent of any semblance of self-consciousness. He thinks nothing of tilting his head forwards or to the side to evaluate different parts of your face and neck, his expression impassive despite the most focused of eyes. Not to mention that he shows *no* sign of any embarrassment at having bared his body to me not long ago, been seen fucking that woman no less. In fact, it is me who fidgets and blushes under the weight of his unquestionable energetic dominance over me.

I watch as his gaze prowls over the curves of my cheeks onto my lips and then down my neck. Unlike Isaiah, he at least has the decency not to stare at my breasts under my silken black dress, but then again, he doesn't have to. The supreme masculine aura is so affecting that I feel its weight on my delicate female body even as he observes his distance. His unrelenting stare, one that would be so inappropriate in everyday society, penetrates me in a way that has me feeling like he's inside me.

"What do you want?" I ask, trying to sound tough in the face of his implacable composure.

"You sound nervous," he responds, eyes narrowing. His voice is so deep and resonant, as if having served him for centuries. "Not only that, you look frightened, no matter how hard you try to conceal it. I know the look very, very well. I can spot it from across a room. You can't hide your emotions from me, Jessynia. I see into you, much further than most people, whether you can accept that reality or not."

"Well, I'm not here of my own free will, Sebastian." I swallow hard, unconsciously inching into the black leather against my back. "Forgive me if I'm a little ruffled at being, you know, kidnapped and held against my will. I suppose I should be taking this all in my stride? I guess I don't possess your sang froid. Sorry to disappoint."

The icy diamonds in his irises glisten at my attempt to put on attitude despite my inner unrest. "You don't have to be afraid," he says coldly. "I think we've made it clear to you that you will not come to any physical harm at our Society today."

Today?

"When am I getting out of here?"

"Sometime later."

"Well, you realize I could report you for kidnapping?"

He smiles. "Yes, you could. I suppose whether you do so or not all depends on how attached you are to your loved ones. Your actions once you leave this place will be a true test of your affection for them." He places both feet flat on the floor and leans into me as I breathe in sharply. "Your Godmother Barbara made it back home safely, I'm glad to hear," he says, the softness in his voice so discordant with the menace in his eyes. "Though the stupid woman does still insist on sweeping the leaves off that deck overlooking the river. Tsk, tsk. Not very smart at this time of year. It's so easy to take a spill in that icy water.

As for your brother, he does enjoy his late-night walks near the ocean. That ocean water can be *so* unpredictable..."

I bring my hand to my thundering chest, unable to stop myself shaking. "If you go anywhere near my family, I'll—"

"You'll *what*, Jessynia?" The room falls into cold shadow. "Please amuse me with your hollow threats." His cadence is slow and melodic, as though talking about the lightest of subject matters, so at odds with the darkness of his words.

I swallow down the rage building up inside me. "Please tell me what you want," I repeat, feeling my face flushing, a sight which has his lips twisting ever so slightly at the corners.

His silvery eyes lock with mine. "We have worked with Jack to bring him fully into our fold where he belongs. He *should* be one of our greatest assets. But no matter what we have tried, his loyalty is to *you*, not us. That brings his position here into question. Not only that, but he seems to be contaminated by your love of... *principle*." He spits out the word with contempt as if it makes him sick. "He doesn't share our vision for the future of our Society."

"You mean, he doesn't agree with your scorched Earth tactics? Well, maybe he has a point... Maybe these tactics you employ are just making things more dangerous for everyone."

"Thank you for your in-depth analysis, Mrs. Wilder, but the loyalty of our members must be to our Society above all else. *You* are what is stopping Jack from embracing us fully. *You* are the block and that barrier needs to come *down*. The easiest and safest way to accomplish that for yourself and all the people you care about is you joining us."

"And what if I don't want to?"

"We believe you will... You just need a little time to get used to the idea," he suggests, his gravel-tinged voice as deep as the ocean.

"Jack and I are getting divorced, Sebastian. I'm not going back to him, especially not when he is still wrapped up in this demonic cult."

He almost laughs. "Demonic cult." He smirks, repeating the words slowly as if gleefully toying with each one, contemplating all the elements that make up their meaning. "You're a very brave woman.

Most people would not dare to disgrace the place I have worked so hard to build up with such a label."

"Well, you don't seem like the type that needs to be pandered to." A sudden wave of nausea hits me and I rest my arms on the firm sides of the chair, needing their support as strength ebbs from my limbs. "At least you know how I feel about it, if you didn't already."

"We are already aware that you are not seduced by power. Your purity is captivating and as it turns out, is also what is so problematic here. It seems to be what is stopping you from joining us like every other good wife does..."

"Well, I'm sorry to disappoint. I must be a very bad wife."

His smile is a dark threat. "Luckily for us, we know what your greatest value in life is."

"Oh? And what's that?"

"Safety." My chest tightens at the low, frigid way he says the word, as if icy air were being exhaled from his lungs.

I swallow down the threat I'm anticipating.

"And there will come a point," he continues, his features suddenly harsher, his brow creasing as his words come out rough and impatient, "when you understand that the *only* way for you and your loved ones to be safe is if you devote yourself to your husband... and to *us*. The others that you have recently been foolish enough to frequent would happily lead you down a very dangerous path. You have *no idea* how dangerous. Out of respect for Jack, we are choosing not to declare you an enemy, but if you continue to align yourself with forces that would seek to hurt us, then even Jack won't be able to stop you from being declared fair game. You, your friends, your family."

"Leave my family out of this! And my friends! They have nothing to do with this!"

His thick muscles flex as he props his bent arms onto his muscular thighs, invading the neutral space between us. "It is *your* choice what happens, Jessynia. You are at a fork between two paths. It would be wise to choose your next step carefully and not follow *fools* who have no idea of the dangers that lie ahead. I have faith that you are smart enough to make the right decision."

I can't stop my face from falling as I wonder how much he knows. Did they have me followed to the compound? Does he know about the resistance? Or is he just bluffing?

"What people are you referring to exactly?" I ask in a weak, transparent effort to find out exactly what he knows.

"I'm referring to your lover and his friends." I swallow hard, frowning as I lose myself in the sinister shadows of his face. "No need to feel embarrassed, Jessynia," he smiles. "You're in pain. Mr. O'Neill can help with that pain. I understand completely. In fact, I have watched in delight as it has played out. Personally, I think that Jackson deserves a little dose of karma for his *many, many* indiscretions. Maybe he will better understand the sanctity of marriage once he understands the pain of betrayal."

"The *sanctity* of marriage?" I scoff. "How many married couples were in that room watching each other screw other people? Maybe you need to have someone explain your *sanctity of marriage* theory to Alexandra Frost the next time she's watching Steven fuck some other woman?"

He narrows his hollow eyes at me. "The vast majority of couples have the wit to comprehend that allowing their partners to explore pleasure with others within the structure that we offer is highly preferable to them doing it behind each other's backs in the outside world... as *all* couples do... or *want* to do. We believe that you and Jack can find that balance here as well."

"Really? And what is in it for me exactly? You clearly don't know me very well if you think I could ever enjoy watching my husband touch another woman. The thought of him sleeping with Alex left me *tormented* for months. I was out of my mind with rage and jealousy. I could barely eat or sleep. Can you understand that? I will never be one of those women that can get on board with something like that."

"That's because you believe it's all about his pleasure. It isn't. Today was about our men initiating a young woman into our inner circle, but our Society is for the pleasure of *both* men and women." He rubs a strong finger against his dark-pink bottom lip. "We know that you like sex, Jessynia. No woman who marries a demanding man like Jackson

Wilder or takes a lover like Cameron O'Neill doesn't. But we don't believe you have fully understood the depths of pleasure that your human body can attain. And you would have access to that pleasure here, access to experiences most people could not even dream of."

"You don't think that I've experienced pretty much everything with Jack, already?"

"No, I do *not*," he snaps. "Jack is in love with you. It's a grave mistake that many make in life. And it means he will never allow himself to do the things he really desires to do to you because he is afraid of hurting you, or scaring you, or having you think ill of him. And as a result, he is not allowing you to experience pleasure the way you should be... nor is he allowing himself to feel the pleasure he wants when with you... Hence why he needs us."

"Well, I... I don't remember having any complaints with him."

"No, but you haven't realized one tenth of your sexual power, Jessynia. You don't even seem to fully realize what you were designed for, put on this Earth for. There's an innocence to the way you look at people that is in abject contradiction to the depraved depths of your sexuality. To your face. To your body. You may be the most sublimely sexual creature I've ever seen, and I have seen a *lot* of people."

I recoil in my chair, wrapping my arms around my waist, my gaze sliding between his rugged face and the white-gold tips of his blond hair that caress his shoulders as he leans into me. "You don't have the right to talk to me like this," I manage weakly.

"You function in this world using your brain, using your principles, your compassion, when in reality your sole purpose is to be fucked constantly. And fucked by the most competent men this world has to offer.

"You seem to be in *total* denial about your outrageous beauty and the power you have over men, a power you have not even begun to take advantage of. Two of the most powerful, most breathtaking, most sought-after of men in Manhattan are in love with you. Men worshipped all over the city. In the case of Mr. O'Neill, he is the scion of one of the wealthiest dynasties in the country. A billionaire god on this Earth. Every woman wants him, and this man wants you and *only* you will do. We know with certainty at this point that he feels nothing for the other women he distracts himself with. That is power that you *do not fully appreciate*."

I gulp down my intimidation as I feel the bulky mass of his torso edging closer to mine, inch by inch.

"I also desire you *greatly*, Jessynia," he murmurs, leaving the air dense with his devious desire. "In fact, there is no one on this Earth whom I desire with more fervor." I feel my throat tighten as his hypnotic gaze pins me to the firm leather behind me. "I have spent many a night contemplating your pleasure, your submission. Contemplating tying a leather strap around your wrists, contemplating what it must be like to have you look into my eyes as I enter you. Or watch your face as you allow yourself to come while a depraved man like me is inside you. I want to peel you apart, Jessynia, layer by layer. I want to penetrate you. I want to fill your soft, fertile body."

"And I suppose Jack would just stand by and watch this happen?" I stammer, energy trickling from me.

"Well, he certainly wouldn't be the first man I've convinced of the virtues of allowing another man to fuck his wife. Very few men agree to it at first—men are a greedy, selfish lot, you see—but once they see the potential, then giving up their wives and watching another man enjoy and educate them becomes one of their greatest sources of pleasure. It may even be the opportunity for Jack to do something that he has never done with you."

"And what is that?"

"Sodomize you." He says the word softly, tenderly almost, in grotesque discordance with the violence of the word.

I start to breathe faster, my cheeks flushing as he tilts his head to the side, his lips curving upwards in pleasure at my reaction. I try to swallow down the shock I feel at his boundary-less way of conversing.

"That is how Jack usually verifies total submission from the women he has," he continues. "He uses it with *everyone*... except you. You can tell a lot about a man's feelings for a woman from the things he does or does not do to her in bed. And in this case, I know everything there is to know about the depth of his love for you. I would bet that he's never even tried, has he?"

I stare at him, unable to stop the shock of violation manifesting on my face. "Well, it's lovely of Jack to have filled you in on the intimate parts of our relationship. That's another thing I'll have to thank him for."

"Jack never told me that. It was just something I had suspected. Thank you for confirming my suspicion."

"*What* do you want?"

"I want your submission. I want your loyalty. I want your sex." His gleaming eyes widen in fascination at the tiny gasp I emit. I notice his thick tongue licking the seam of his lips. I wonder if he even knows he's doing it. "We don't force people here," he murmurs slowly. "I want you to submit to me. I know that beyond your learned outer expression of outrage and revulsion, that deep down, in a place that you can't face admitting to yourself just yet, that you want to know what it feels like to have the tongues of multiple men on your body at the same time, to have a group of men hold you down, enter you, driven insane by their desire for you.

"I know that you want to know what it would be like to slide your soft body onto mine as you stare into my eyes. To be pleasured by the experience of my tongue. To experience sex with an older man, a man who knows what he's doing in a way even Jack doesn't. A man who can educate you in the darkest of pleasures, pleasures which will blast your world right open. I know I've come to you in your dreams, Jessynia. I know you want to know what it feels like to have my body climb on top of you, pin you down, tie your hands to posts so that you are at my mercy. I know you want to feel me slide into and out of you... over and over again. I know you want me to teach you levels of submission that will bring you ecstasy like you could never imagine." His eyes burn into me like hot embers on my flesh. "I believe you also want to experience the joy of submitting to the pain I like to inflict, to wince under the bite of my teeth into your soft flesh. I know a small part of you wants to climb onto my hard cock right now, to feel the ecstasy of being dominated by a *monster* like me."

I shake my head at him despite euphoria still warming my insides from his drug, leaving my body tingling at his words, my sex clenching. I feel my nipples contracting into hard points from the contact with the satin of the black dress. He glances down at them and smiles.

"I know what I do to you, Jessynia. You can't hide from me." I swallow hard. "Our first time would not be in a public forum as you saw today. It takes at least a year for most people to build up to that point. It would be in private, in my bed, your eyes looking into mine as I help you to admit the truth about your need for dominance and depravity. And then at some point, Jack could certainly be invited to join. I believe I could probably also overlook my revulsion for Mr. O'Neill in this instance. It may in fact be the only way to soothe my enmity for the man. To keep him out of danger. Wouldn't you like to know what it feels like to be pleasured by all three of us at once?"

"You can dream all you want, Sebastian."

"You are a *submissive*, Jessynia."

"No. I am not."

"Yes, you are. Not in life, but in sex. You're just too proud to admit it to yourself. Your ego won't allow it. But you would not be with men like Jackson Wilder or... Cameron O'Neill"—his eyes are cold as he exhales Cameron's name—"if you were not. You know deep down what it means to be the property of men like that. You know that they require submission. It is non-negotiable. Dominance is the currency they use with women. You haven't picked just one man like that. You have picked two, back to back. And you feel more for these two men than for any others you have ever experienced despite their ruthless dominance. Despite how disturbed and dangerous *both* of them are.

"In our Society, you would be worshipped. I am not the only man—or woman for that matter—who considers you their ultimate prize. You and Jack would be powerful beyond your imagination. And that power could be extended out to other things that you hold dear... other causes. We have members in powerful positions all over New York and our power grows by the day. Join us, Jessynia, and I will personally make it my job to educate you, to help you feel pleasure you could not even conceive of."

"Sure," I respond, "until one day when I step out of line or speak up or question something and get thrown out like a piece of trash."

A malicious smirk sneaks onto his lips and he holds it for what feels like an eternity. Spikes of static zigzag over the bare skin on my arms as I peer into him, frowning, breath bated as I wait for him to speak.

He finally does, unblinking, reaching into me with his words as he leans back in his chair. "I see that you have been talking to Beth Vass."

"I... I..." I want to feign ignorance but am afraid of him catching me in a lie.

"We are aware of how indiscreet and... *problematic Ms.* Vass has become of late," he sneers. "We intend to remedy that in due course." He allows the silence between us to lengthen and I buckle under his glare.

"Well, I don't know who you're talking about."

"Tsk, tsk, tsk." He shakes his head. "We know a lot more than you think, Jessynia. Your desire to protect her is admirable, but we will get on a lot better if you don't insult my fucking intelligence!" He snarls the last words, his eyes blackening as he does so, the energy of his broad body shifting as if bringing in a cloak of fog with it.

How does he know? Did they spy on who was entering and leaving the compound?

I squeeze one of my hands for comfort as the tiniest glimpse of the black evil that lingers inside that breathtaking outer shell of his comes to the surface like crude oil releasing from a crack at the bottom of a lake.

There you are, Gravier.

I see you.

He takes a breath, his face morphing again, the murk dissipating from the room. Over the course of the next silent minute, his eyes eat into mine, swirls of lucent ice dancing around a sphere of onyx that contracts and expands despite the light remaining constant. I square my shoulders in defiance, maintaining eye contact, albeit blinking about five times to every one of his.

As he seems to realize that he can't stare me down, he begins to smile. "I admire your spirit, Jessynia. Your guts. I *rarely* feel fascination towards humans anymore. I lost my illusions about the filth that is humanity before I had hit puberty. But you're different. I like the naïve way you still believe in people despite being smart enough to know better. I like your strength. I like your defiance. They will make your submission even sweeter."

I shake my head at him slowly.

"As for Ms. Vass, no doubt her version of events is tainted by the disgrace of her expulsion."

"Well, you like to paint this place as some den of pleasure that you walk away from scot-free. But there are people who have been through trauma as a result of things that go on here. Many people. Do you care about them?"

"That woman was disloyal to me after we welcomed her into our family. She chose her fate. She is responsible for her situation. It's called *consequences*. It's a word that worthless cunt will *soon* understand the *meaning* of."

I shudder at the thought of Beth being in his crosshairs. "Is there ever a point when enough pain has been inflicted?" I ask. "How much more do certain people have to go through?"

He leans into me, knees bent, the underside of his forearms coming to rest on his thighs as he rubs the knuckles of one hand with the fingers of the other. "I used to show mercy to people who hurt me. It was not a good idea in hindsight. She was warned of the consequences of speaking out. She will pay for her decisions. Of that I can personally assure you."

"Hasn't she paid enough?"

"Oh, no. Not *nearly* enough."

"And what about Cameron?" I ask.

"What about Cameron?" he replies, his eyes black frost.

"Has he suffered enough for your liking?"

"Suffered? That man was born into this world with every possible privilege that a human being could possess. Not to mention that he has been worshipped like a god since the day he was born. Surely a little suffering is divine justice."

"And so, what, you want revenge for him having what you should have had? It isn't his fault that his mother loved him, Sebastian."

He smiles. "Hmm. It sounds like you must have been talking to Gabriel. He does so enjoy sharing private stories from my childhood. He has quite a colorful one of his own, but I don't suppose he's shared his dark past with you, has he? Much easier to focus on me, I assume, and ignore his own perverted sins." The smooth words pour out slowly like thick black tar. "How is he doing? My old friend... I know it's been hard for him since his father's death. I'm amazed he has the fortitude to discuss my life after that."

I swallow hard, trying to unravel what he's insinuating. I can't play dumb about having met Gabriel. I just about got away with it last time.

"There are ways to heal, Sebastian." I scour his eyes, trying to detect if there is any shred of humanity left in him that could hear the message. "Ways that are effective without transferring your pain onto others."

"Are there? I'm not so sure, Jesssynia. You know pain, I have no doubt about that. But you don't know *hell*, and until you've burnt in its fires with no way out, your advice is hollow. As it is, I've found that transferring my pain onto others is the *only* thing that soothes the restless rage just a little. Nothing else comes close."

"Even if that involves taking out someone's father? Did killing Joseph not satisfy your desire to hurt Cameron?"

He narrows his eyes at me. "His death was ruled an *accident*, Jessynia."

"An accident?" I frown.

"Yes. An accident. May I ask who it is that I have to thank for this *vile* accusation? Silas? Francis? Gabriel?"

As he names the people who I spent those few days with at the compound, my stomach sinks to the floor in wretched dread as something comes into such clear focus that I know it to be a certainty. "You have someone on the inside, don't you?" I ask.

His lips slowly widen into a chilling grin as he rubs a hand across his strong jaw. "You're a very clever girl, but I'm afraid that would be telling. We can't have that."

"Who is it?" I ask to a beam in his eyes. "Christian?"

It has to be Christian. There's just something so off about him.

He breathes out audibly, feigning pity. "It could be, Jessynia. Although the ones we usually suspect the least are the ones who are closest to us. Those make the best informants by far, I've discovered."

I feel my body weaken as I run through the list of people who were there those days, all the people dearest to Cameron:

Christian, Silas, Francis, Beth, Remi, Charles...

Evie...

Aaron...

Gabriel...

Could it be one of them?

Oh my God...

"Who is it, Sebastian?"

"I'm afraid the only way for Mr. O'Neill to protect himself is to cut every single person that is left in his life *out*."

"Who is it?" I press.

"You never know... Perhaps Mr. O'Neill is not the only person around here who has a dear loved one willing to betray them in exchange for some pieces of silver..."

Kevin...

Maddie...

Stella...

"You lie!" I feel the unexpected trickle of a tear on my cheek. "No one in my life would *ever* do that."

"I'm glad you're so sure, Jessynia. It must be nice to have such strong bonds with your friends."

"Who is it?"

"I admire your persistence, but I'm afraid it would be most ungrateful of me to reward loyalty with *betrayal*," he snarls.

"Loyalty?" I scoff as the thought of Rose blasts into my mind. "I know what your version of loyalty is—"

Stop, Jessynia.

I manage to refrain myself before I say something to waken the beast again.

Or maybe it is too late... He eyes me curiously, the underside of his arms resting on his thighs as he rubs one hand with the other, his fingertips finding the thick black ring on his left hand, his ring finger. His muscles are so dense under his loose shirt, his shoulders so broad, caressed by tips of pale-blond hair, his dark roots framing a breathtaking, rugged face.

His bulky frame leans into me further as I feel myself recoil into the chair. "Hmm. I saw something somewhat... *disturbing* on your phone this morning," he says, his deep voice suddenly soft, entirely incongruous with the unspoken threat therein. "I feel like I can read your mind, Jessynia. Can you read mine? What am I thinking of?"

I know instantly that he's thinking of the picture of Rose that Beth sent me. Before I wasn't sure if I had deleted it. Now I know I didn't. It wasn't in my camera folder, but in one with media received. And I didn't think to check there... or rather I just thought I would have more time before I had to take care of it.

"What am I thinking of?" He lowers his chin a tad, his warrior-like chest and shoulders rising and falling as he takes deep, silent breaths, his eyes dueling with mine as I try not to crack and break down under the sheer pressure of his hawkish glare, his presence, his power.

"You're thinking about a picture," I respond.

"Good. Of whom?"

"Of your dead wife."

Your murdered wife, Gravier.

His displeasure seems to quieten like the air after a rain shower. "I'm glad to see you have the guts to face saying that to me," he responds. "I thought I had lost my ability to be surprised, but I must admit I was taken aback when I saw my poor ex-wife's picture on your phone. Courtesy of Beth, no doubt?"

My voice escapes me.

"Why do you have it?" he asks.

The silence between us lengthens.

"Why?!" he barks, fire rising in his chest, turning the room as black as soot.

"I wanted that picture because... she reminds me of me... and because she's been erased. After her death, you erased her from existence, and if one person at least sees her picture, then she's not forgotten. Not erased."

"And what exactly makes you think she deserves to be remembered?"

"Don't we all? Or did she commit some cardinal sin too?"

"Yes, she did."

"And what was it?"

"*Betrayal.*" His voice is a thunderous growl betraying an avalanche of bitterness.

"Wanting to leave you is *betrayal*?"

"Yes, it is."

"No, it isn't. It's part of relationships. Most break down at some point, and we have to let that person go."

He shakes his head slowly. "I don't usually accept life lessons from women a decade younger than me, Jessynia. You are testing my patience."

I shift in my chair, my skin suddenly clammy. This is about the time I should be shutting up but I want to know more about Rose. "Did you love her?" I ask.

He pauses, smiling at my persistence. "Love her? I once loved someone. Long ago. Loved them desperately. Worshipped them. Wanted their approval with every fiber of my being. I never got it. No matter what I did. And then in the split-second it took for my love to finally turn to hate, I seem to have lost the ability to love. I understand the concept. I see the fools around me feel it, but... I don't. So, to answer your question—no, I did not love her. But I respected her purity very much... until she chose to betray me, that is."

"And you feel no remorse?"

"Remorse? The police did a thorough investigation and it was determined that the poor thing committed suicide."

"And is that what happened?"

He narrows his eyes at me. "Have you ever watched someone die, Jessynia?"

"No, I can't say that I've had that pleasure."

"Well, I have, unfortunately. And let me confirm that there *is* no greater pleasure. There is a primal fear that is just exquisite. There is that moment when the poor subject realizes they've been drugged. Their eyes widen and they start to stare at you in shock. It's just perfection. Art. Then by the time they realize what's happening, their limbs no longer work like before. They try to get to a phone, but they can't. They try to turn over, but nothing seems to work. Adrenaline allows them to open their eyes just a little. The terror in their face is like nothing else." He groans as if in pleasure.

"When people think you don't know what they are up to, they are willing to do anything to keep up appearances until they have a chance to get out... Dinner, wine, music and dancing, even. I find that a rich, sweet sauce with elements of crunch and a little bitterness, along with a glass of expensive, full-bodied red wine can mask the flavor of even the most potent of pills. These days they make powerful pills so small..."

I feel my eyes start to water as I picture Rose's face as she realized she was going to die by his hand.

"Removing the clothes of someone who can't cooperate can be problematic. A very sharp knife is most useful if you're getting impatient. Lifting a woman into a bathtub has never been a challenge for me. You know, when a person has been drugged and can only drool a little, they still try to fight. They can't move like we can but they twitch and grimace and groan trying to stop the inevitable. It is just sublime. And that plea in their eyes... sensational.

"I suppose that I should really have restrained myself from saying goodbye like a husband should say goodbye to his wife, but that expression of pure horror... It was just so mouth-watering. Then the eyes widening as you climb on top of dead limbs... Then watch them choke under water... not too much. It's very important to take one's time, enjoy the process. But experiencing someone as they are suffocating and then being brought up for air over and over... I fear that I may not ever be able to reach such heights of pleasure.

"And then the final moment... The shock and horror on their face as you reach ecstasy while they realize their light is being extinguished forever, eyes wide under the water, their last breath witnessed by their own personal demon. I do fear I have developed quite a taste for it. It is just transcendent, divine, a thing of God himself. I look forward to repeating the experience."

Rose's face in that bathtub suddenly appears before my eyes as clearly as if she were sitting in the room. I see her beautiful face under the water, brown hair floating, blue eyes open, with Sebastian being the last thing she saw of this world...

"Oh, but not with you, Jessynia," he says coldly. "Don't fear. I have other plans for you. You are a much more vibrant and fascinating creature than my poor late wife. It turns out that purity without an edge becomes *extremely tedious* over time. I much enjoy watching you navigate this world. I enjoy watching you broken and trying to put the pieces back together. That is not something I believe I will ever tire of."

I can't stop a tear from spilling onto my cheek at the thought of Rose trying to break free. She was so close. She just didn't realize until too late that beneath his exquisite façade, there is some kind of monster lurking inside.

As the tear makes its solitary path over the curve of my cheek, onto my jaw where I feel it linger, teetering like a glistening dewdrop clinging to the tip of a leaf, Sebastian's eyes lock with mine as he extends his hand forward and brushes his thumb against my jaw to wipe it away. Numb from the pain and overload of hearing about Rose, I don't move, letting his hand linger on my face for a moment, wiping my jaw before bringing his thumb into his mouth and licking my tear from it.

He closes his eyes tightly, tipping his head back, breathing out the deepest of groans, as if the taste is bringing him to ecstasy. He finally opens his eyes, panting slightly as if in post-coital bliss as another tear trickles down my cheek to the sound of a single pair of heavy footsteps heading towards the room.

An abrupt knock on the door shatters the grotesque intimacy.

"Come in," Sebastian says, not hiding the rapacious yearning in his eyes.

Isaiah enters, speaking curtly. "He's here. He's been informed of recent events."

"Good," replies Gravier. "Bring him in."

33

"WHO'S COMING?" I ask, anxiety rushing through me like a raging torrent.

Gravier smiles in response. I feel the weight of his gaze on my face as I look up at the door to the sound of swift, heavy footsteps approaching. The thuds stop for a moment, causing my breath to hitch as Gravier gets to his feet, standing to the side so that I have a clear view of the man entering the room.

On a sharp inhale, I see the man's tall, dense form enter the room, his stormy energy filling it entirely.

He glances at Sebastian for a second before turning to me, his face all shadow, engulfed by the all-consuming bitter poison of wrath.

My shaky gaze flits to the light gold of his skin, to the sandy hair with its pale tips, to the broad forehead and razor-sharp cheekbones and those blue eyes, incandescent in the afternoon light streaming through the window.

The rage stiffly contained in his intimidating physique dizzies me.

Jack.

I pan down the arm of his brown leather jacket to his left hand. He's still wearing his wedding ring, the gold pressing against the phone he has gripped in his hand.

My phone.

Jesus...

He knows about Cameron.

"She wasn't harmed in any way," says Sebastian to Jack who doesn't unlock his glare from mine, his chest rising and falling fast.

"Yeah," I respond, trying to once again channel my inner badass to deflect from the trepidation I feel at Jack's unrelenting ire. "No harm, apart from, you know, the kidnapping and the illegal confinement and then the unwanted sex show, no harm at all."

Sebastian's icy eyes betray a split-second glint of malicious amusement. Jack's hard face, on the other hand, shows nothing but cold, bitter fury.

"We'll leave you two to... have a chat," says Sebastian to Jack. "You have a lot to talk about." He turns to Isaiah. "Tie her hands behind her back. Maybe she will learn to respect her husband a little more like that."

"What?!" I shout, getting to my feet as Isaiah descends upon me. "No!"

I put my hands out to stop him, but he grabs one arm easily, using it to spin me around and pin me to the wall. I squirm and fight, but his grasp is immovable.

"Let go of me!" I shout as his knee and elbow pin me to the wall.

He ignores my plea, instead retrieving some kind of tie from his pocket which he uses to bind my hands deftly as if having done so a thousand times before.

He finally releases me and I swing around to face the men. "No harm, hey, Sebastian?" I shout, my eyes flitting between him and Jack whose rage doesn't seem to have tempered in the slightest. For a split-second, my intoxication has me seeing masks on both of them. I'm clearly nowhere near as sober as I had thought.

"We want you with us, Jack," Sebastian says firmly, putting his hand on the pronounced curve of Jack's shoulder. "*Both* of you. Your wife seems to have forgotten who she's married to. I would suggest that it may be time to remind her."

"Agreed," Jack replies cruelly, enmity infesting the word.

Sebastian glances at me a final time, his usually impenetrable face not concealing his malevolent satisfaction as he leaves the room after Isaiah, closing the door softly.

As their footsteps grow dull, my husband, a man I haven't seen for four months, takes slow, silent steps towards me, his face a thunderous grimace of recrimination as he slides my phone into the back pocket of his black pants.

I retreat a step until my tethered wrists are pressed against the taupe wallpaper enveloping the walls of this old building that has seen way too much. As he makes it within two feet of me, my outrage at the handcuffing turns to fear at seeing the malice in his eyes and I whimper in distress. "Jack, stop. Please..."

The plea comes out meekly, a high-pitched cry that he ignores as he thrusts his body onto mine, one hand slamming into the wall next to my head as the fingers of his other hand wind themselves around the front of my throat. He presses his dense torso into me, the sheer weight of it compressing my chest, taking my breath away.

"Stop!" I cry as his legs part mine. Abject fear makes my eyes widen, lifting, locking with his as I pant, my arms pinching from the pressure of his bulk pushing me into the wall. I had somehow forgotten the daunting power of his muscles, his thick, brawny shoulders, the defined ridges of his pecs under the dark-gray shirt peeking through the sides of his jacket.

His thumb grasps my jaw as his lips approach mine, his eyes a blaze of frantic azure flame. "I warned you in August that if you went *anywhere near* that fucking man, that there would be blood," he growls, his thick erection pushing into my crotch. "Do you remember that?!"

I cower, still dizzy on my feet, as he roars his rage into me leaving an avid beat of electric current pulsing through my cells, a grotesque consequence of the lingering euphoria I feel from the little blue pill.

"Jack, stop," I cry, an eruption of tears escaping me.

"Do you know what it did to me to read the messages that that man sent my *wife* this morning?!"

I don't answer, taciturnly imploring him to calm down behind tearful eyes.

"Do you?!" he roars.

"Jack, stop. Please."

He pounds the wall behind him again.

"Yes, I know what it did to you. I've been through it, Jack. Not with one woman, but many. Remember? Except we were still *together* at the time."

His breath is heavy on my face as he repositions his hand on the wall, strengthening the cage around me, the storm showing no sign of stilling.

"That is *not the same*!" he snarls into me.

"I'm sorry," I utter softly, trying to temper his fury.

"Sorry?" he sneers. "I warned you about the *consequences* of going near that man. Do you remember?"

"It wasn't planned," I shoot back through a seemingly interminable waterfall of tears which spill onto the thin black satin covering my breasts, causing my nipples to harden opposite his chest.

"It wasn't planned by *you*. Maybe it *was* planned by *him*." He lifts my chin roughly, his lips making their way to within an inch of mine.

"I was in pain, Jack. I didn't mean to see him again. I tried to stay away from him."

"Tried?"

"Yes."

"Well, trying isn't *good enough*!" he rages as I shrink down in front of the beast off its leash, nausea flooding me from the drugs they forced into me. "What did he do to you?" he asks bitterly.

I don't answer.

"What. Did. He. Do. To. You?!"

I cower as I look into the ravenous eyes towering over me. The intimidation is not just about his superior height and strength, but the overpowering Viking-like aura that clings to the man. I feel his thick muscles flex under the leather of his coat, see his chest expand until it feels five times the size of mine, see the striations of his forearm twist, aware he could snap my body into pieces with a flex of his wrist if he wanted to.

I peer into the raging tempest in his blue eyes above strong, wide, angular cheekbones framed by thick dark-blond hair, strands of which glisten like gold in the hazy sunlight beaming through the window.

With knees slightly bent, his dense erection presses into my clit, stimulating me constantly, arousing me against my will.

"Did he fuck you, Jessynia?" he asks coldly.

My voice is gone. I don't want to lie. I want to tell him the truth. I shouldn't have to hide it. But I'm terrified, especially being here in this house with my hands bound, unable to move, not knowing if I will get out.

I glance at the bed to my left as Cameron's words float before me. *Deny it.*

"We kissed," I respond to the sight of an eruption of hellfire in his wrathful eyes.

Well, I guess that part is true...

"You expect me to believe that's all?"

"You can believe what you want, Jack."

His grip around my neck tightens. "I'm going to ask you again... Did that man fuck you?"

"No," I whimper, the panic of his compression forcing the lie from me.

"Don't fucking lie to me!"

"I'm not."

"You expect me to believe you spent three days in the same house as that cunt and he didn't touch you?"

"Well, we weren't alone," I manage, my voice little more than a whisper.

"Hmm. Maybe it's better you not tell me. I have so much rage inside me... I'll end up doing something that can't be undone." A tremor of angst rumbles through the stiff mass of his body. "Do you know what it does to me to know you spent time with that man? To know that his lips touched yours?"

"Yes, Jack," I shudder, my drug-addled mind conjuring up a ghostly drip of blood running down his face. "I know that pain. What, do you think that you should be able to cheat on me for *months and months* and never experience anything like that yourself? Would that be fair to you?"

"I saw the messages that that cunt sent to you this morning. He's clearly in love with you... or wants you to think that for some reason. He seems to think he has a chance at being with you. That means you must have given him a reason to think that, despite what I warned you in August. Do you know what it did to me to read those messages? Do you?!" He bangs the wall hard.

"You're scaring me, Jack. Please stop."

"What do I do with this, Jessynia? With this rage? *You* tell me. How am I supposed to get rid of it? *How*?!"

A trickle of tears escapes me again as his vicious eyes bore into mine, his labored respiration showing no sign of abating, his face grimacing in turmoil as the grip on my neck tightens.

"He was trying to protect me..."

"Protect you?!" he snarls.

"Yes. These people were trying to intimidate me. He wanted to protect me and then—"

"It isn't *you* who needs protection anymore, Jessynia. It's *him*." He growls the word like a wounded animal. "He's going to *pay* for this," he snarls. "On my blood, I promise you that."

"No, Jack, please. He wasn't trying to hurt you."

"You're so *fucking* naïve, Jessynia," he spits out. "You don't get it. That man wants his revenge on me and he will happily use you to get it."

I shake my head. "That's not what he's doing here. He doesn't want to hurt either of us."

"No? Well, he's hurt me, so it looks like his little plan has worked so far, even if you are too fucking blind to see it."

"If he had just wanted to hurt you, he wouldn't have respected my request to stop contacting me for months!"

"What happened at that house of his, Jessynia?" he growls. "On Long Island. Did he touch you then?"

"No," I say, swallowing hard, too afraid to tell him the truth. I'm not a good liar. I feel my chest and face flushing hot as his face twists into a grimace, his suspicion flaring across his beautiful, harsh features.

"If I find out that he touched you—" Just as he looks on the verge of committing a crime, I see him glance down for a second, and then again, his brow creasing as he releases his hand from my throat, his eyes widening in confusion as he grabs hold of the delicate gold chain hanging around my neck—*his* gold chain, the one with our initials engraved into it.

He stands up straight and looks at it in bewilderment before grabbing it to inspect it closer, tugging it round roughly so that he can see the clasps, his panting loud as he zooms in, I assume, on the letters J-J that he had carved into the gold.

His demeanor shifts instantly, turning from the riot of rage to utter puzzlement as he peers into me in confusion. "Why do you have this? Why are you wearing this?"

I don't answer, my voice lost under the weight of his turbulence.

"Why?!" he asks roughly.

"I always wear it," I reply.

He shakes his head, scouring my eyes before reaching down into his back pocket from which he withdraws my phone, holding it low enough that I can see the screen below me as he swipes to unlock it before going into my gallery to look at my photographs.

Photos from last night appear on the screen—Stella and I embracing, Maddie kissing me on the cheek, our table cheering as we hold aloft glasses of wine. He zooms in on my neck in the picture and on the glistening gold chain around it.

He swipes further back—pictures of me, Babs and Frank in the kitchen at my parents' place, then me and my dad on the couch and does the same, focusing in on the little golden chain.

Further back still—me with a yoga buddy at her place, with a journalist buddy at a coffee shop, then a goofy selfie I sent to Kevin, all with the chain. He swipes further and further back looking at every picture with the necklace until he gets to the final two pictures in the folder—one of Jack and I on the beach in the Hamptons the morning before I found him being blown by Alexandra Frost, and then finally a picture I took of him in January this time last year that I haven't yet found the strength to delete from my phone. It was in Costa Rica, in our own private little bungalow. Jack was naked when I took it, but the picture is him, waist up, lying on a sun lounger, one arm bent behind his head, another resting on his sculpted chest. He is grinning broadly in the picture, tanned and gorgeous. I remember making him laugh when I took it.

He looks down for a moment and then back up at me as if hunting for something in my face. "Why do you wear this?" he asks, breathless.

I pause for a moment before speaking. "I've always worn it, Jack," I respond softly. "Ever since the day you gave it to me. I've never taken it off. Not once."

Fast tears tumble onto the wide planes of his devastating face as he watches my eyes, the storm subsiding, his aura softening, replaced by his distress at the sight of my tear-strewn face.

"Why?" he asks.

I swallow down the salty tears that trickle into my mouth. "Because I feel safer when I wear it. And because it helps me feel that you are with me. I still need to feel you near me, even if I can't say it to you anymore."

He lifts his hand to my face, cradling my jaw, rubbing tears from it with his thumb as he leans his face towards me so that our eyes are inches apart, swirls of light feeding off each other.

"Do you think I wanted this, Jack?" I cry through messy tears. "I didn't. All I ever wanted was you. I never wanted anything else."

I couldn't count the number of heartbeats that pulse in my chest as he watches over me, tears spilling relentlessly down his breathtaking face. I feel a hand slide up my arm, skimming my shoulder, then neck until it finds the back of my head as he leans his face into mine, gently finding my wet lips with his, offering a caress that sends a shockwave spearing through my inebriated system.

He presses his pink lips against mine, watching me as he does so. I don't flinch. Maybe it's the drugs making me hot and delirious, weakening my resolve; maybe it's the sheer relief of seeing his fury abate; maybe it's the dark need this man has always stirred in me; or maybe it's that unremitting yearning I feel to be back with the husband I adore and that I can't ever be with again...

Whatever the reason, I allow him to kiss me, allow his tongue to find the seam of my lips, to lick the length of them, to push inside me, to taste me, opening up my mouth as the strong muscle dances against mine, licking deep into my mouth, a groan escaping him as he fucks my mouth, his fingers delving further into my hair, pulling, angling my head the way he wants.

He pulls away from me as if analyzing me, scrutinizing every minute movement of my face, looking for signs of something—resistance maybe. In my desire to get away from here, I try not to convey it, and instead look up at him, eyes soft, despite feeling unsteady on my feet, the high of the drug-induced nirvana now turning into what I pray will turn into the more mellow buzz of intoxication.

"Open your mouth," he says, narrowing his eyes, scrutinizing every inch of my face.

I comply. I don't want to. Not like this. But I want to get out of here. And that won't happen for as long as the beast has control of him.

"Look at me," he says, his thumb sliding across the black satin over my nipple. "Keep your eyes open."

I obey his instruction and he slowly slides his tongue along the length of my lips, his eyes fixated on mine for every second of the kiss that tastes of the salt of my tears.

"Hmm," he responds, his arousal apparent.

He pulls away and pushes his thumb into my mouth. "Suck," he says.

I pause. I don't want to do this, but I have to get out of here, and submitting to him is the only way I know for sure to make that happen.

I clamp my lips around his thumb, sucking gently as he exhales in arousal. He presses his body into me, his hard erection prodding the tight knot of nerves between my legs.

He removes his thumb and slides it across my jaw, his other hand cupping my breast. He watches my eyes from an inch away before standing back up and spinning me around. I feel him undoing the knot binding my hands together. Upon freeing me, he crumples the tie up and shoves it in the pocket of his jacket.

"I'm getting you out of here," he says resolutely, intertwining his fingers with mine. "You let me do the talking. Is that clear?"

I nod and he leads me towards the door, opening it.

We step into the hallway...

34

JACK GRIPS MY HAND TIGHTLY as he leads me down the dark corridor.

As we reach an open space with several doors, my heart nearly jumps out of my chest as we are cut off by Isaiah who appears from one of them, quick as lightning.

He positions himself square in front of Jack, his burly frame arresting our advance. "Where are you going, Jack? Sebastian hasn't given the order to release her yet. He won't be happy."

"Good," Jack growls, his hand dominating mine as he pulls me, increasing the pace as he brushes past him.

"Jack!" Isaiah's booming voice calls behind us as we walk through a seemingly endless maze of corridors, each feeling darker than the next. As we head down another, I see bright light at the end of it and what would appear to be a foyer. There must be many windows leading into it, letting in natural light—a skylight perhaps, an exit, surely.

As we approach and I begin to feel the bright hope that comes with the anticipation of freedom, Jack and I stop dead in our tracks at the sight of the formidable silhouette of Sebastian Gravier appearing at the end of this tunnel, blocking it completely. I turn around, a gasp escaping me as I see Isaiah behind us, blocking the way back, pacing towards us steadily.

Jack pulls on my hand as we slowly walk towards Gravier, his thunderous features coming into view as we approach, made all the more sinister by the backlighting which leaves his face a contortion of harsh shadow.

"We haven't finished with her yet, Jack," growls Sebastian, his thick muscles tense under his black shirt.

"Get the fuck out of my way, Sebastian," counters Jack.

"Your loyalty is with us, Jack. Not with her nor anyone else."

"There is no one else that exists to me but her. Now get the *fuck* out of my way!"

I glance up at Jack's fiery profile, a whimper escaping me as we get within ten feet of Gravier and stop. I pull back on Jack's hand to stop the advance, but he seizes it more firmly. The men glower at each other, unspeaking, years of secrets, many dark and painful, exchanged in this silent death duel.

"I had planned to speak to her again," Sebastian finally says.

"This is *my* wife!" Jack roars. "*My* property. The rights of a husband over his wife overrule those of the Society. Those are *your* rules, Sebastian. Remember? *Yours*! You enshrined them in the regulations when questioned about your behavior towards your wife, or have you forgotten?"

Sebastian's eyes darken, his demeanor terrifyingly cold. "Don't bring up my wife *ever* again."

"Then leave me to handle *mine*. We're done here, Sebastian. This girl belongs to me. I'm taking her back. You go near her again, and it will start a war. Am I making myself clear?"

As Gravier's heinous glare flits between me and Jack, he slowly takes a few steps back, giving us enough room to leave this infernal tunnel and enter the bright white foyer. A large black front door stands to the right with two guards positioned in front of it. Not even Jack could make his way past men of their sheer size.

"We're leaving, Sebastian," Jack says firmly as I glance at the gravel parking lot through two small windows on either side of the door.

"There are consequences to every action, Jack," responds Sebastian stiffly.

"You're right, Sebastian. For *everyone*."

They war in silence some more before Gravier finally turns to face the guards, nodding at them slowly before chilling me with a glare that could freeze the air around us.

Jack pulls me towards the front door as the two guards step aside. Without a backwards glance, he opens the door and pulls me through and outside as a blast of frigid air rushes into me, stinging the skin of my bare arms, a welcome reprieve from the oppressive confines of that place. Taking off his thick jacket and putting it around my shoulders, he leads me across the gravel to his car which beeps as he presses the fob that he withdraws from his pocket.

"I have your keys," he says as he opens the passenger door. I get into the large black SUV before struggling to click my seatbelt into the buckle with my shaky hands. Jack gets in and helps me buckle it before driving down a lane through a dense patch of woods. At the end of it is a closed metal gate. A guard stands next to it and another in the doorway of a small lodge to the right of it.

Jack slows the car to a stop fifteen feet from the gate, waiting, watching silently for signs of movement. One guard is talking into a cellphone, peering at Jack as he does so. After ten seconds with no movement, Jack puts the car in reverse, rolling back twenty feet and stopping before revving the engine.

Fuck...

Just as it seems he's going to use his car as a missile, the guard in front presses a button and the gate slowly opens. He stands aside and Jack drives through swiftly, silent as he begins to navigate these quiet roads, clear of snow but for piles of slush lining the shoulders.

I notice him glance in his rear-view mirror repeatedly as we drive past thickets of snow-capped woods, past fields and meadows blanketed in a gleaming layer of white, all the while my nausea starting to build.

We make it onto a larger road, and I see signs for Newton, Andover and Lafayette. We must be near Stokes State Forest, a popular hiking spot in Sussex County, New Jersey, a rural area about fifty or so miles to the north west of Manhattan. I remember hiking around here a couple of times with my dad and brother when I was a young girl. I hadn't foreseen one day revisiting the area like this...

As Jack continues to drive with urgency past service stations, restaurants and a hotel, the loathsome spectre of nausea from Gravier's drug reignites and I realize I'm about to throw up. "Stop the car."

He glances at me. "What's wrong?"

"I'm gonna be sick."

He pulls over onto the shoulder and I get out, the black heels Grace gave me pressing into the slush on the side of the road. I barely notice or care, consumed as I am by the misery of nausea. I feel Jack's strong fingers pulling my hair back off my face as clear liquid fills my mouth and I lean over, waiting for my body to eject my stomach contents.

It doesn't happen.

Instead, I begin to shiver in the icy air as I stand back up. "I can't," I say.

"Are you ready to keep going?" he asks.

I nod and we return to the car and set off. Ten or so more minutes later, I beg Jack to stop again. This time he pulls over onto the side of the road, checks both sides are clear and does a swift U-turn in the opposite direction.

"Where are we going?" I ask meekly, hoping not to throw up all over myself.

He doesn't answer, speeding down the road for a minute before taking a left down a smaller road. We drive for ten or so minutes as nausea builds until we get to an even narrower road, finally turning right onto what is little more than a path through a forest.

Jack pulls out his own phone from his jacket pocket. "It's me," he says, his face grim. "I need the house to myself for a few hours. I'll be there in three minutes." He hangs up and puts the phone back in his pocket.

"Where are we going?" I ask.

He ignores my question. I should be demanding answers, but that's the thing about nausea. It's such a foul sensation that wraps its fingers around your body so tightly that you don't have the energy to care about anything but making it stop...

As we drive over bumps in the rough path, a black gate approaches, opening automatically as we reach it. "Where are we?" I ask, unease seeping into me.

He doesn't answer, continuing to drive until the road opens up and a large house looms before us. It's not large like the one I've just escaped from, but still must have three or four bedrooms and ample space for parking all around. It is a modest wooden and brick construction, two stories tall and totally enclosed by the dense forest around us. Two cars—one pickup truck and one SUV—are parked to the right of it on a patch of dirt.

As Jack pulls up in front of the house, two men exit the front door, each carrying a large box of something. They head towards the pickup truck and slide back the thick black cover on the back of it, placing the boxes on the bed of the truck before pulling the cover back over it.

"Stay here," Jack orders as he gets out and strides over to the men. On closer inspection, I realize that I recognize one them—one of the men following me in the subway that day in August. They glance over at me from time to time as Jack talks before finally getting into the truck as my husband makes his way back over to the car, the sight of him sending trepidation into me.

He opens my door, unbuckles my seatbelt and urges me out before looping a dense arm behind my back. He pulls me forward and I push against him to stop the advance. "What is this place?" I ask.

He eyes me sternly, ignoring the question as he picks me up and carries me in his arms to the front door, entering before kicking the door shut. I glance to my right and see a sparsely furnished living room full of boxes and a handful of small black bags laid out on a table. I'm able to look for just a second before Jack carries me swiftly up the wooden stairs opposite the front door.

We head to the left into a sparse bedroom—cream walls, a basic queen bed with a wooden frame to the left, some mismatched wooden tables and chairs to the right and a gray rug on the floor next to the bed.

The window has a thin sheet of lace over it between two thick brown curtains and overlooks the front of the house.

Jack carries me into the en-suite bathroom to the left of the door and places me down on a rug between the shower and the toilet. I slump down on the floor, the affliction of nausea annihilating my body, leaving me listless and desperate for relief yet unable to vomit. I don't even know if being sick will help me at this point. The pill they gave me will have dissolved by now. It's in my blood. God knows how long this is going to last...

Jack grabs a glass from the sink to my left and fills it with water. "Drink this. It will help you vomit," he says.

"I don't know if vomiting will help me. I think it's too late."

I peer up at him to see his face shift with the realization of what I'm saying. "They gave you something in there, didn't they?" he asks.

"Yes," I respond, watching his expression harden.

"When?" he asks grimly.

"About an hour ago, I think. I can't tell. How long will it last?"

He takes a breath as if to calm himself. "Another few hours."

"Oh, God. I feel like shit. Will vomiting help?"

"No."

"I want it to stop, Jack." My eyes meet his which soften.

"There's nothing you can do," he says, pain twisting his face. "You have to wait it out."

I turn to face the toilet bowl, waiting for a few minutes, hoping something will come out in the vague hopes of getting relief. It doesn't. "It's not working," I say. "I can't get back into that car. I feel too sick. It's horrible."

I try to get to my feet but am wobbly as I do so, barely able to feel my limbs. Without speaking, Jack lifts me into his arms and carries me out and into the bedroom, laying me down on the large bed dominating the room. He lifts the tan quilt cover and I slide underneath it and sink into the mattress, praying that this feeling goes away soon. Jack heads to the bathroom, brings back the glass of water and sits on the side of the bed, cupping the back of my head, lifting it a little. "Drink this."

I take a few sips only to feel sick, stopping with a shake of the head. "No more. I can't."

After a pause, he places the glass down on the pine nightstand, bare but for a small lamp, pulls his jacket off and throws it onto a table opposite the bed. He lies down next to me, getting in bed, his head hitting the pillow beside me, his somber eyes contemplating my face, a face ravaged by the drugs, sickness and torment of the last twelve or so hours of my life. His strong fingers tuck an unkempt lock of my hair behind my ear, his fingertips lingering as they do so. His wrath seems to have tempered compared to before but I catch his expression hardening at times, only to soften a moment later, the internal struggle registering in the angles of his face.

"Do you feel better?" he asks finally, looking at my parched lips.

I shake my head. "Do you know what they gave me?"

"What did it look like?"

"It was a tablet."

"What color?"

"Light blue."

"They gave you ecstasy."

I inhale sharply, although deep down I knew it already. Not that I had taken it before, but the euphoria, arousal, panic and disorientation go so far beyond the effects of the occasional joint I've smoked that I knew what it was before he said it.

"It's not the stuff you get on the streets," he continues. "They have access to pure MDMA. They cut it with speed themselves, have a guy who compresses different cocktails. Some of it's cut with cocaine, others with acid or ketamine. The blue one is pure but very low dose. It's the mildest of the lot that they make. Thank God they only gave you that. For all our sakes."

"Did you know they were going to do this?" I ask.

He pauses for a few moments before speaking, his face hard. "They had talked about it before. I told them *no*. I didn't know what they would do last night. I only found out today, just before finding out about you and... *him*. Do you know what it does to me to know you spent those days with him, Jessynia? Do you know that it rips out my insides?"

I look down before finding his eyes. "I wasn't trying to hurt you, Jack. He took me away because..." I stop as he shudders, a shadow darkening his treacherous features. I'm so scared of him and Sebastian going to war that I can't tell him about Cameron saving me from Ilya Markov. "I was in pain, Jack. So much pain. He helped me."

"Helped you? Is that supposed to be a joke?" The grit in his voice drives through my besieged body.

"Jack, do you realize how many times you cheated on me? Do you understand what that did to me? You ripped my fucking heart to pieces. You're not some innocent victim in all this!"

"That isn't the point, Jessynia."

"Maybe it is. Maybe when you do that to someone, you can't expect them to behave the way you want them to anymore. Maybe there are consequences to doing what you did..."

"I can't allow this," he utters through clenched teeth. "You know that about me. You know that when a man goes near you, I want to rip him to pieces. I want to take him out and his entire family. Is that what you want?"

"Well, Cameron and I aren't together," I reply, swallowing down fear.

"And you want to be?" he asks, narrowing his eyes at me.

"Well, being with my husband is not much of an option for me anymore. Unless I lobotomize myself so that I can cope with you sleeping with other women. Is that what you want for me? To turn into one of those Stepford Wives who pop pills to turn off their pain? To lose everything that is sacred to me about being in a relationship?"

"But not *him*, Jessynia. On a good day, I can just about cope with the idea of you being with another man, but not *him*."

"I knew him before you, you know? He was one of my best friends."

"That makes no fucking difference here," he replies, his eyes rough on my face.

"Did you know we were friends when you first approached me? Is that why you wanted to be with me? To hurt him?"

"No. I did not know that," he responds resolutely. "Do you think that I would marry you, spend years inseparable from you, as part of some ruse to hurt someone else? I told you in the letter how I first saw you. Did you read it?"

I nod.

"I was obsessed with you from the second I set eyes on you. I wrote the truth in that letter. As soon as I saw your face, I knew I had to have you. I had no idea you even knew him. When I found out you were friends, I thought about staying away, but we'd spoken by then, and I couldn't. You were like a drug to me, Jessynia. You still are. It had fuck all to do with him."

"Well, I have the right to have friendships, Jack. You don't get to dictate those things anymore."

He grimaces. "You being with him is *not* an option, Jessynia, nor will it ever be. I warned you in August not to go near him again, remember?"

"He was trying to help me. He knew that they were... He knew I was on their radar. He wanted to protect me. Can you understand that?"

"Protect you? Like *today*, you mean?"

"Well, he couldn't exactly have predicted something like this."

"Has it occurred to you that he is trying to *protect* you from the people that *he* introduced you to?" He takes a deep breath as if trying to calm the storm. "I was informed today that he took you to Tribeca in August," he says, his body tense as if trying to contain rage. "You *hid* that from me, Jessynia."

I swallow hard. "Well, I decided I had the right to know what my husband had been doing for the last six months of my marriage."

"And it was *him* that walked that you into that place," he sneers. "*He* is the one that has put you in danger."

"I had to beg him to take me."

"You begged him after he told you about it, didn't he? Didn't he?!" he shouts.

"Stop," I say, cowering, my body retreating into the illusionary shield of the quilt. I would get up and get out of there but I still feel so sick.

"He didn't *have* to tell you about that place. Especially if he was *so* concerned about your safety. He chose to. Do you see that?!" he bellows.

I whimper at the violence in his tone. "You're scaring me."

"*He* told you about that place. *He* put you on their radar. *He* is the one you need protection from. Have you ever considered that hurting you may be his way of getting revenge on me?"

"Revenge? You mean for what you did to his father and to Evie?" I ask in defiance.

He drops his gaze for a moment before finding mine. "I see your friend takes pleasure in exposing the most heinous of my acts, ones I've long repented for. I imagine he talks less of his own disturbing behavior. Of his own perversity." He leans into me, a storm brewing. "That man is *fucked up* beyond belief. I've spoken to his ex."

"Olivia?"

"Yes."

"When?!"

"Last July. I wanted to understand what I was dealing with when I found out you'd been speaking to him."

"What, and she just handed over all their intimate secrets?"

"She's not like you, Jessynia. She can be bought easily."

"Well, you had no right to do that!"

"*Right?*" he snarls. "I had *every* right to know about the man talking to my wife!" he barks. "Not that I didn't already know how disturbed he was."

"Did you sleep with her?" I ask, nausea making me shiver.

"No. I did not touch any woman from June when you first found out until... that night..."

"When I saw you fucking Alexandra Frost on the balcony. *That* night, you mean?" Dew mists my eyes at the thought.

"Yes. Until that night."

"Do you think that was easy for me?"

"No. I don't. The thought of what you had to see makes me sick to my stomach. But it doesn't change the fact that Cameron O'Neill is fucked up beyond belief. Violent nightmares, disappearing acts, trauma. Pathological dominance. He doesn't use dominance the way I do, Jessynia. He requires it. It's a need. It's part of his fucked-up psyche and I won't have you ripped to pieces by him."

I look down, trying to breathe through the sudden sensation of my throat constricting, an unbidden memory of Cameron straddling my body and crushing my neck in the dark.

"You've seen it, haven't you?" he says, his eyes wide, searching mine. "You've seen that he's sick in the head."

"No," I lie, a flush coming over my cheeks as I do so.

Jack's eyes narrow. "Did he hurt you?"

"No," I reply instantly, though as I say it, deep down in some place I don't want to look at, I realize it isn't true. "Anyway, if you talk to anyone's ex, they will have a whole bunch of shit to say about them."

"Not like this."

"He's suffering from trauma, Jack. As we all are."

"Whatever the reason," he snarls, "he will *never* go near you again. I am going to make sure of that myself."

"And what do you suggest instead? That you and I join Gravier and his demonic little cult? Become one of those couples in that place... Would that be better for my wellbeing?"

"I want to find a solution. I want to be your husband. I still wear my wedding ring. Every day. Whether there's another woman..." He stops speaking as he sees the flinch of pain on my face. "It still hurts you, doesn't it? The thought of me with other women..."

I don't answer, but the *yes* is written in the quiver of distress in my eyes.

"Good." He breathes out a sigh of what seems to be relief. "I can't stand the thought of you not caring anymore. It torments me. Jessynia, the connection I feel to you is like nothing I've ever felt to another human being..."

"Since Cameron?"

He frowns at me. "Yes. We had it once."

"And what happened?"

"I made a choice."

"And you still stand by that choice?"

"It's a choice there's little going back from."

"Maybe there is. He managed it. The only other option would be staying with you and accepting that you go to that place and that those people are part of our lives. Is that what you want for me?"

"Is it an option?"

"Well, let's see. Does it mean that I would be able to sleep with whoever I want there?" I ask. The very thought of it makes me sick, but I want to know how far Jack is willing to go to accommodate that place in his life.

"No, it does *not*!" he growls. "No man in that place will ever touch you."

"I didn't think so. But I'm supposed to go through the pain of seeing you do it..."

His glower softens on my face, his breathing tempering.

"I spoke to Beth over Christmas," I say softly. "Do you know what they did to her at the end?"

He looks down for a moment, letting out a long, silent breath as his gaze finds mine again. "Yes. I know what they did to her. I did not approve of that course of action and I was vocal about it. I still don't approve. I don't participate in those kinds of... acts. She didn't deserve what happened to her."

"How can you want to be around people that do things like that, Jack?" As I speak, I feel energy seeping from my limbs like sand from an hourglass. "Please make me understand this."

There is a long silence before he speaks. "I'm pulled back to them, Jessynia. I don't know why. It's stronger than me. I've tried to fight it... so many times."

"You'll never be able to stop it, will you?"

"I try. Every day."

"Well, like you say, Jack, *trying isn't good enough*."

"I want you, beautiful. I crave you every minute of every day. I crave your body. I crave the way I feel when I'm inside you, that way you look at me. There is no feeling that comes close to it." He lifts his hand to my face, stroking the flushed skin over my cheek.

"I can't, Jack."

"Because of him?"

"No. Not because of him. Because I can't go back into that cycle." A tear falls from me as I say it.

"I'm out of balance," he continues. "I feel rage inside me. It's stuck in my cells. I can cope with finding out that that man spent time with you only because I'm with you. Your presence soothes me, Jessynia. It always has. Your face. Your body. Your mind. Your beauty. The way you look at me. But I won't be able to handle the thought of him telling you he loves you when I'm no longer near you. I'm afraid of doing something we will all regret. I feel rage that needs to come out... Rage that is stronger than me."

"Well, I told you I'm not with him."

"Prove it to me." His eyes zoom in on my lips as he leans towards me.

"How?"

"You know how."

"No. I'm not proving anything to anyone."

"I need you to give yourself to me. It's the only way I can get back in balance."

"I don't *give myself* to people anymore, Jack. I did that for a long time, remember? I never said no to you before last June. Even when I was tired or sick or still sore from the time before. I thought that loving you and keeping you satisfied would be enough for you to stay faithful to me. It wasn't. I'm not doing it ever again."

"Fine. I want you to submit to the pleasure I want to give you."

I swallow hard as his thumb begins to caress my lip, setting off fireworks on my skin as my sex begins to contract gently. I know it's partly the drug but the barest touch of my skin by him leaves sparks dancing like solar flares.

"I know you want me, Jessynia. I know you're wet. I know you want me on top of you as I slide inside your body. I want you very badly."

"So?" I manage, my breathing becoming audible. "Maybe always getting what you want from women isn't the way it should be. Maybe resistance is healthy in your case."

Without speaking, he pulls the covers off me urgently, climbing on top of me, his lips finding my neck as his eager erection prods me from behind his pants. He kisses me gently, his lips the softest of caresses on my neck, his tongue emerging, licking the light honey of my skin as I lean my head back, every cell in my body alight, desperate for release.

"I can heal us, baby," he murmurs as he kisses me with a tenderness that I had forgotten he was capable of, the silk of his lips caressing my skin with reverence. "Please let me..."

I let out a moan of pleasure at the sensation of his hard form on top of me, at the thick erection pressing between my legs. His kisses are so soft, his touch one of awe, as if handling something so fragile that it could break into pieces.

Suddenly his lips find my mouth, pressing, pushing until his tongue emerges to lick the seam between my lips before delving inside. As his tongue dances against mine, I begin to feel claustrophobia at the dominance of his body despite my arousal.

Jessynia, wake up.

As Cameron's face flashes before me, I push on Jack's chest hard, forcing him out of my mouth, a gesture he responds to by pinning my hands to the bed, glaring down at me.

"No, Jack! You don't get to do this! You don't get to cheat on me for months and months and then have me submit to you like every other woman does. I'm not like every other woman. Those privileges expired when I caught you fucking Alexandra Frost."

"I need you, angel," he says, the heady lust in his voice passing from his body to mine. "I'll go insane if I don't have you."

"No. I'm still not fully sober. I can't think straight."

"I'm not in the habit of being turned down," he snarls.

"Well, maybe being turned down is good for you. Maybe never hearing the word *No* is part of the problem."

The grip on my wrists tightens.

"You told me you love me, Jack. Prove it to me. Stop."

His eyes burn into me as the heavy pulse of his erection rubs against my clit, arousing me despite myself. His breathing becomes deeper as he stares into me, mesmerizing me with the deep wells of glacial blue in his eyes as he rubs his body against mine, his mouth brushing my lips, his limbs dominating me entirely. With a final pulse against me, his body softens as if in release, collapsing onto me, his lips at the crook of my neck as he heaves, his body weighing a ton on my delicate frame. It is a weight so oppressive and yet so wanted. The feel of him is a drug I fight to resist every day.

Finally, his breathing steadying, he looks up at me before climbing off my body.

"Thank you," I respond, breathless at the sight of his arousal.

"You're the only woman on this Earth I would do that for. Mind you, you're the only woman who has ever said no to me, made me wait, put up a fight. That's part of the reason I'm so insanely in love with you, Jessynia. It's why without you my soul is lost. It's why I desire you to the point of insanity."

He grips my cheeks with one hand as my body begins to weaken. As the drugs are wearing off and the nausea subsiding a little, they are leaving behind insidious fatigue.

"I will free myself from these people, baby."

Wake up, Jess. "You said that last summer," I manage.

"I meant it *then*. I *still* mean it. I'm not free yet, but their power is waning. I will get free. I need you to believe me."

I feel my eyelids close as fatigue of the most unyielding kind invades my cells. "I have to sleep for a while."

He nods. "I'll stay with you."

I feel his breath on my cheek as his forehead dips to touch mine. His eyes are the last thing I see before the stupor of sleep and intoxication takes me.

35

"I HAVE TO HAVE YOU, JESSYNIA."

My eyes blink open to the sight of Jack's naked torso coming into focus as he climbs on top of me, his shirt discarded somewhere, the solid muscles of his shoulders and chest bearing down on my slim body. His hands delve into my loose black dress, peeling it open to uncover my breasts which he devours with his tongue, licking and sucking on my nipple like some animal desperate to discharge its energy.

No, Jack.

My lips don't move. My whole body is inert, my mouth dry as he hitches my dress up and pulls my panties down past my feet.

I try to move my hands but they are immobile, paralyzed. With the hem of my dress now around my waist, he climbs back onto me, lifting my knee. I gasp internally as I feel the tip of his rock-hard erection lying on my pubis.

"I need your body," he whispers roughly into my ear.

I try to shake my head, but my listless form doesn't cooperate. Using his legs to part mine further, his hand eases open the folds of my sex to a grumble of satisfaction at the copious juice he finds which he uses to circle my clit with.

"If you give yourself to me, I won't hurt him..."

Jack, we can't.

He bends both my knees with his hand, my feeble legs unable to move of their own accord as he positions his cock at the juicy entrance of my sex.

"Your body is mine, Jessynia. It always will be." His rough threat shakes me, but I can't move other than to open my eyes as he cages me in, his gaze peering into me as he slowly pushes his cock inside my body, watching me through the lens of his invasion, his dominance, his victory.

He elicits a whimper from me as his lips come to land on mine, his breath stroking my face as he rams himself inside my tight sex. "You are my wife, Jessynia. Your body is *my* property alone. You will understand that before the day is over."

I lie immobile, trying to move, or speak, or do something as he pleasures himself with the insides of my body, barbarous growls emerging from his throat as he hammers my cervix again and again and again. He licks into my mouth as he shifts the angle of his thrusts, his athletic form dominating me entirely.

"You like that, don't you?" he whispers, eyes gleaming in delight as he reclaims my body as his own. "You're dripping wet. You can't hide what I do to you."

Jack...

As he thrusts deeper, pinning my hands above my head, grunting as if about to come, the realization of what is happening slides into focus and Cameron's face appears before me.

No.

Within an instant, I find myself panting as I open my eyes, relief undulating through me as I see Jack, fully clothed, lying next to me on the bed, his eyes tender as he watches my face.

"Bad dream?" he asks, his brow creasing.

My breathing steadies as relief overtakes me. "How long have I been out?" I ask, sighing out, grateful that he respected my wishes.

"A couple of hours."

"Did you sleep?" I ask, realizing that the light from outside is much dimmer, the sun setting in what must be late afternoon.

"No. I took a shower and stayed with you." I glance at the damp tips of his thick blond hair that I used to delight in threading my fingers into when he would enter me.

I place my hand down on the pillow next to my head and his palm blankets the top of it, his fingers interlacing with mine so hard that it almost hurts.

"Do you feel better?" he asks.

"Yes," I reply, realizing that the fog of intoxication and nausea has subsided. "Much better. Jack, I want to go home."

He lets out a slow breath. "I will take you home, but you will not be seeing that man again. You'd better not test me on this one, Jessynia."

"I want you to stay away from him," I respond. "He wasn't trying to hurt you."

His face darkens.

"Jack?"

Silence.

"He still loves you, Jack."

"You don't say that, Jessynia!" he snarls, causing me to flinch.

"He does. I can't explain the different ways he tries to protect you. But he loves you."

"And I suppose he shows it by telling my *wife* that she will belong to him this year?"

"Maybe... Maybe he's trying to protect me for you... because you can't."

"How kind of him," he sneers. "Ripping my heart to pieces has been for my benefit, it seems..."

"I didn't say that. But anyway, if we were to get back together now, could you *promise* me you would *never* be unfaithful again?"

"When I married you, I vowed to be faithful. I meant it. I managed it for two years before they... If it weren't for... *them*, I would be. I'm sure of it."

"But you're not free of them, are you? So, you won't be..."

"I've tried, baby. I always try. That place is the only way I know how to cope."

"Well, maybe you need better coping strategies, Jack..."

He glares at me, unspeaking. "I can't have you go near him ever again. I already fear that once I'm away from you, my wrath will consume me..."

"I have the right to move on too, Jack. I mean, you're not gonna tell me that you haven't been sleeping your way through Manhattan since we separated..."

"But not *him*."

"Do you think it's fair that you get to cheat on me for months, ending our marriage and then dictate who I'm allowed to be close to after our marriage falls apart?"

"Yes, I do," he utters coldly. "You're my wife and I have every right to dictate that. And I slept with those women to cope. Nothing more. I didn't feel anything for any of them."

"Other than Alexandra Frost," I say, watching his eyes darken.

"Yes, other than her. Though her hold on me is not as strong as it once was."

"You're sure about that?"

He doesn't answer, his gaze meandering over every line of my face.

"Maybe there's another way," I finally say.

He frowns.

I shake as I muster up the courage to utter the words. "You and Cameron file a complaint against Alexandra Frost for statutory rape."

His eyes widen and he gets up in a shudder of incredulity, pacing the room before turning to face me, his massive bulk bristling. I sit up, still queasy but ready to make my case.

"I've already told you that you live in some fantasy land, Jessynia. You have no fucking clue how dangerous these people are. Not to mention that they have infiltrated the police. They have high-ranking officers as members. Are you aware of that little fact? And do you *seriously* think the D.A. would prosecute statutory rape against the wife of one of the most powerful men in Manhattan, with all the other shit going on in the city?"

"Maybe. If there were enough of you."

"Is this part of the *plan*? Cameron and his little gang... Is this their big trump card? Because let me tell you, it will *fail* and leave the people who make the complaint hung out to dry, fodder for whatever retribution Gravier decides to dish out at his leisure."

"It's not a plan. It's just an idea. *My* idea," I lie. I don't want Jack knowing about what the resistance are hoping they can pull off. I can't be certain that he won't repeat it. "What she did was wrong, Jack. You were fifteen. It was a serious crime."

"Well, I hate to burst your little bubble, Jessynia, but I wasn't exactly complaining."

"Maybe not then, but I don't think you fully realize the extent of the damage caused by her seducing you at that age. The power and influence she and those people have had over you has... shaped things. And they had no business doing that."

"Has it occurred to you, Jessynia, that if they wanted to punish me, the best way to do it would be to hurt the *only* woman I've ever loved? It is *not* an option. Not for me. Not for him. Unless he wants to see you dead, that is. Because that is what these people are capable of in their quest for revenge. Or is that part of his plan? Would your death be his way of getting his full revenge on me? You need to get this insanity out of your head. There is no justice with these people. That's not how the universe operates. Plus, they have a whole plan for what happens if someone denounces their operations. A way to wipe all record of themselves off the map with the press of a button. And they rehearse it constantly to make sure nothing will ever go wrong."

"And so why are you still wrapped up with these psychopaths? You have to make me understand this."

He leans his muscular body against the wall by the window, eyes dueling with mine. "I don't know. Maybe I'm more like them than I care to admit."

"No. You're nothing like them."

"Maybe I want to self-destruct," he shrugs. "Maybe they accept the side of me that I hide from the world. Make me feel like less of a freak."

"You're not a freak, Jack."

"You don't know how dark my thoughts go, Jessynia. How violent. How much rage I have to contain."

"We all have dark thoughts."

"Not like this."

"And what happens if Sebastian decides that you're no longer an asset to him. You realize he can turn on people overnight?"

"I don't know if I care that much anymore. I'm in pain. Every day. Every day I look around and wonder where you are. I feel like I'm floating, untethered. Like something is constantly missing. I don't know how to stomach this pain much longer. Maybe he's meant to put an end to me."

I feel my breathing shallow. "No, Jack. You know that would destroy me. You can have a life... without me. Without them."

"You're so sure about that..."

"Yes. I am. You need to get away from them. Once you're away, you will start seeing light again. I promise you. You won't need me to feel it."

He sits back down on the bed, finding the back of my head with his hands, pulling me towards him, his face dipping into mine. "I love you, Jessynia. Nothing about that has changed. I feel you with me every second of the day. I crave your presence constantly. It's beyond anything I can control. I want you to know the things about me that I've kept hidden. The thought of getting my marriage back is the only thing keeping me in check, keeping me from spiraling out of control. I know how badly I've messed this up. I know deep down I have penance to pay. I know I deserve what I'm getting. But I can fix this. Just give me more time."

I feel my eyes mist at the solemn plea in his savage glare. "More time won't change things, Jack. I can't put myself through this fear of you cheating anymore. I can't lose any more of my soul."

His fingers sink further into my hair as that wave of harsh energy that ebbs and flows with Jack returns. "You being with Cameron O'Neill is *not* an option." The bite in his low voice makes me quiver. "And if I ever find out he is near you again, I will tear each limb from his fucking body."

"Well, I... I won't go near him," I say, aware of the ache in my chest as the words come out. I don't know if I mean them, but I can't help but panic at the thought of Cameron getting hurt because of me.

"I'll be having a chat with your *friend* shortly."

"What?! No! I don't want you going near him."

His grip on my hair tightens, the tension pulling at my skin. I whimper, trying to pull his arm away with both hands, but it is immovable.

"That's no longer an option," Jack says coldly. "The severity of what happens to him will depend on you respecting my wishes. What happens to him is in your hands, Jessynia. I assume you don't want his *blood* on them."

I feel fast tears dripping onto my cheeks. "Just leave him alone... and I will too."

"I'm going to have men watching your place."

"What?! Jack, no. I don't want that!"

He squares his shoulders, bending a knee to sit straight in front of me as the fingertips of his other hand lift the two circles at the bottom of his golden chain. He freezes me with his glare. "I don't want you taking this off. You are *my* property, Jessynia. *Mine*. You always will be. No one will go near you again without my knowing it."

Without asking, he pulls my head towards him and kisses me hard on the lips, holding me firmly in place so that his tongue can penetrate my mouth with ease. I don't resist. I'm too afraid to resist. Afraid of not getting out of here, and mostly afraid that if I do, he will take his anger out on the one man I know I have to protect... no matter what heinous theories Jack has about his motives.

As his feast on my flesh grows more fervent, I pull away hard. "I need to go home," I urge as he pulls his tongue from my mouth, panting heavily. "I have to call my family today. They'll start getting suspicious if I don't call."

"You will be calling them, but you will not be calling *him*. Not today, nor ever again. You have made it very clear to him today that you will never see him again."

"What?" I respond faintly, feeling blood drain from me at the thought. "What did you say to him?"

"I will be having my own talk with your friend in the near future.

There are things I know about him that he will not want exposed to you. In the meantime, *you* have told him very clearly that you no longer trust him and to never come near you again. For his safety, he better not *ever* think those messages were not from you. And if you attempt to undo what I have done, then one day, he will be walking down a street and will not make it to the end of it. Whether he survives or not, his life will never be the same. I'm not fucking around here. If I find out that he has become close to you again, there will be blood spilt all over Manhattan." He pulls my face into him. "Is that clear?!" he snarls, his roar utterly wild.

I pull against his grip. "Once we're divorced, I have the right to see who I want, Jack."

He leans into me, the storm in his face raging. "See, that's where you're wrong. Divorce or not, you will always belong to me, and if that man goes near you, the price he pays will be *great*." I gulp down tears that trickle down my cheeks and into my mouth. "And I know one thing you would not survive is having a man's death on your conscience. His... or mine."

His eyes track the tears falling down my face and onto the black silk over my dress. I can't say anything else to antagonize him until I get out of here. All that matters is getting home.

"I want to go home, Jack."

He slowly loosens the grasp on my hair, the furor in his face dissolving slightly as he gets to his feet. "Stay here," he says after a moment. "I'll be back in a minute."

"You're taking me back?"

"Yes," he responds stiffly before leaving the room and closing the door behind him as I get to my feet, relieved to find them strong, the ground now firm beneath me. I walk over to the window and see Jack leave the house through the front door and approach a man in the driveway—one of the men from before. As they stand talking next to the pick-up truck, I realize that Jack is just wearing a T-shirt and sweater and I pivot in an instant to see if his jacket is still here.

At the sight of the thick brown leather draped over the table, I run over to it, checking his side pocket for my phone which I retrieve with shaky fingers, heading back over to the window so that I can keep an eye out for his return.

The phone shows just seven percent battery and as I swipe to turn it on, I see missed calls and messages from family and friends.

I scan them speedily:

No worries. Let's chat tomorrow.

Same to you gorgeous.

Have a great day.

Call me tonight darling.

I flick through the conversations, looking at the messages written in my name to the people dearest to me: explaining to my mom that I'm at lunch with Stella and can't talk; to Maddie, Stella and Kevin that I'm spending the day with my aunt and will call them tomorrow; wishing a Happy New Year to Babs and River and Sean and Mason and my yoga and journalist buddies, former boss, former professor and a dozen other innocent people who had no idea they were conversing with the inner sanctum of Quercus Velutina.

And then I turn to Cameron's message folder... to find it completely empty, every message erased. Not only that but his number is blocked. I unblock it without thinking. Maybe I shouldn't but Jack is wrong if he thinks he's going to decide who is and isn't permanently banned from my life.

Clicking on my scheduling app, I program a message for Stella that she will receive at 9 a.m. tomorrow morning, typing as if chased by ghouls.

Stella. If you're getting this message, please call me immediately. If you can't get through to me, I need you to know that I was taken, first by Sebastian Gravier's group, a society called Quercus Velutina, the Black Oak Society.

They took me to a house near Stokes State Forest on the morning of January 1st and held me there against my will.

Jack took me away from there that same afternoon to another house in the area. It's in the

forest. I don't know where. Some of his men are here.

He says he will take me home now. It's about 4pm on January 1st. If you get this message and you can't reach me, please call the police and the DA's office.

It has to be people you trust there. I love you. Jess.

I know maybe it's a lot, but it's just a safety net. Once I get home safely, I will delete the message so that she never gets it. I don't want my friend mixed up in this unless there's no other choice.

I glance outside to see the men still talking, but slowly moving towards the house.

Shit...

Just as I'm about to put the phone back in Jack's pocket, a message appears on the screen, causing my heart to stall.

JESSYNIA, PLEASE TALK TO ME.

Cameron...

I DON'T UNDERSTAND.

I'M DRIVING BACK TO MANHATTAN NOW.

I KNOW SOMETHING HAPPENED.

I NEED TO SEE YOU.

I shudder at his words, my vision blurring for a second.

I will never be able to tell Cameron what happened today.

I know it would start a war.

As I contemplate texting him back to tell him that I don't want to see him—the only option I have to keep him safe—I shiver in fear at the sight of Jack walking back inside the house.

To the heavy thud of footsteps on the stairs, my trembling fingers just about manage to delete Cameron's messages and block his number again as I get to Jack's jacket, sliding the phone back into his pocket.

I make it to the window just as he opens the bedroom door. He stands filling the doorway, watching me before glancing at his jacket and then back at me as my heart beats out of my chest. He takes a few steps forwards and slides it onto his tall frame, before walking over to me and pivoting me so that I'm standing opposite him.

"Look at me," he says.

I comply, trying not to tremble as I'm held hostage by the deep blue in his fierce eyes.

He glides a hand up the black silk of my dress, over my hip, up my waist, sliding over the side of my breast and up my neck where he cups my face, leaning into me. "You want to go home?" he asks.

"Yes."

"To our place?"

"No. To mine."

He shakes his head. "It's not safe there."

I nod. "I know. I'm going to ask Stella to help me find a secure service apartment straight away. She does it for her clients all the time."

"Why won't you come back with me, Jessynia? I can keep you safe. What's more, you being back with me will ensure that the people you *care* about are safe as well."

I swallow hard at the implied threat against Cameron. Part of me thinks I should go back with Jack. It would certainly solve some of my problems. And I have ached for his passion, power and protection so feverishly over the last few months. But going back would also turn me into a prisoner, someone staying with an unfaithful man out of fear for my life and for those of others. I can't go back to him like this...

"I can't Jack. I can't put myself through this anymore."

He breathes out slowly, his irritation apparent. "I'm stationing my men on you."

"Well, I don't want that!"

"I don't care whether you want it. It's happening. He will *never* get near you again. Is that understood?"

I glare at him, unspeaking as he lifts my chin up, his fingers sliding up my nape, curling into my hair. His lips, the only soft part of his body, find mine, sliding against them, kissing them, sending savage waves of electricity coursing through me despite myself. I don't want to kiss him, or at least not powerless like this, but I want to get out of here, and I want to quell his wrath over Cameron, and me rejecting him would do nothing but ignite it.

His tongue finds the seam between my lips, licking firmly, prying my mouth open as his thumb slides over the hard nipple under my black dress. He groans his appreciation of my submission, his tongue venturing deeper into me, his body pressing against mine. As I feel the hard press of him against my belly, I pull away, pushing against his chest.

"I want you to take me home, Jack."

He shakes his head slowly. "I'm not used to being left unsatisfied, Jessynia. You know that *very* well..."

"Well, I'm not consenting to any more than this, so you have no choice."

He watches me darkly for a few moments until I see the corners of his eyes lift, his demeanor softening. "I like that you say no to me, beautiful. No one else has ever done it. Your strength is a drug to me. It's one of the reasons I'm in love with you to the point of being ill." He breathes heavily, contemplating my lips as he holds me against him. "I'm getting you back, angel. You belong to me. I'm going to heal myself and free myself from these people. I intend to become the husband you deserve."

I don't answer, staring up silently at this most savage and competent of men. "Can you take me back home?"

He releases his frame from mine, rubbing his thumb over my swollen lip before pushing it inside my mouth, evaluating me as if for signs of resistance. Satisfied with my compliance, he withdraws his thumb, watching me in silence for what feels like a minute as his strong fingers caress my jaw and neck. "You need a sweater," he finally says. "Stay here. I'll get you one."

As he leaves the room, I turn to look out the window at the forest beyond, my eyes roaming over the snow-capped woods of deep green, shadow and secrets.

As I take in the majestic tree sentries all around, I feel tingling in my body, starting at my fingertips and slowly trickling through my cells, little by little, up my arms, across my shoulders, down my abdomen and into my toes. A fiery crackle of white-hot energy floods my brain as I curl my fingers into a ball and release them, feeling power seep back into me, my body alive with flame and light.

I feel strength return to me—the strength I lost back in June when I found out about his affairs, and the strength that has seeped from me ever since like blood dripping from an unhealed wound.

I see the fearless woman locked inside that room in the labyrinth, only this time I see the passageway clearly. The paths are lit up and I can see how to get to her. I have the key. And I am going to let her out.

To the sound of slow, heavy footsteps approaching the door, a fizz of electricity sparks through me like a live wire out of control as I finally feel that bold woman I had lost coming back to me, my resolve solid, my sense of self returning... and with it, there is only one thought:

They have to go down.

EPILOGUE

"Are you sure he doesn't suspect you?"

"Certain."

"Good. Let's keep it that way. We wouldn't want our precious informant to be uncovered before the plan is in motion."

"As long as I can be there to see his face when he finally finds out... I've been waiting to see the smile wiped off that smug face for a very long time."

"Indeed. The girl knows there's someone on the inside now."

"He'll never suspect me. I'm the last person he'd ever think it was. There are others he'll start to doubt first."

"Good. Perhaps you could even sow a few tiny seeds of doubt in his mind... I would very much enjoy watching him turn on the people who love him the most..."

"Well, I've certainly sown a couple over the years."

"Yes. Seeing him broken and alone would be quite sublime."

"I'm on it."

"But be careful. You are privy to information that only she knows at this point. We don't know how much she's going to tell him. You can only repeat what he tells you and no more. Don't mess up."

"Oh, I won't. I've been waiting to see him taken down for years. To pay for what happened. It's fueling my every move at this point."

"I can see you're as eager as I am to see justice served."

"Oh, yes. And when the time comes, I would very much like to be the first one to draw blood."

"Hmm... I think I'll have to take that pleasure for myself. As you know, my contempt for him and all the privileges life has granted him has become a tumor I need to excise. But once I've finished with him, you can have your fun. I want the end to be very long. Very drawn out."

"My knives are already sharp. Disfiguring that perfect fucking face of his will be one of the highlights of my life."

"Hmm. I will certainly have to watch that."

"What about the girl?"

"Well, I think it's only fair she watch over him as he takes his last breath. He does so rely on her for support. Don't you think?"

"And she'll be allowed to live? I'd certainly volunteer my services to eliminate her as a possible threat. As long as I'm given free access to her for an hour beforehand."

"Hmm. I understand the temptation, but I very much enjoy her alive."

"You're sure she won't go to the police?"

"Certain... once I've made it very clear that if she breathes one word, then the other man she loves will be next. And then her parents, then her brother, then her aunt, then her godmother, then her friends and then everyone in her life, until it is just her left in her own solitary cell in hell."

"She certainly seems to crave safety and protection above everything else."

"Yes. Those are her highest values. And once she understands that she and every person in her life will be safe once she finally joins us, you never know... We may finally be able to bring her into our family where she belongs."

"Now, wouldn't that be poetic justice?"

"Yes. Most poetic..."

ALSO BY MONIQUE EDENWOOD

Thank you so much for reading *Black Oak Burning*, the second novel in the Black Oak Series.

The third novel in the series is called *Black Oak Scorched* and will be released on April 30th 2021. It is now available for pre-order on Amazon.

Please see "Announcement about Book 3 in the Black Oak series" below for some more information.

About *Black Oak Scorched*

I did everything in my power to resist Cameron's ceaseless craving for my flesh. The depth of his desire and the fervor of his attacks on my will was merciless, wearing me down as I struggled under the weight of Jack's possessive need to reclaim me and his surveillance of my every move.

Not to mention Sebastian Gravier's increasing desperation to have me submit to him so that he could educate me in the dark pleasures of the Black Oak Society that have been so carefully crafted by his wicked deviance.

What the resistance didn't know is that as they were finalizing their plan to take down Quercus Velutina once and for all, the Society were mounting one of their own, with brutality and betrayal that no one could have ever imagined.

Despite the victory of his bloodshed, Sebastian's restless hunger for suffering and revenge never abated, and once Cameron made it clear to Jack that he intended to take me for his own, Gravier finally got what he had ached for—Jack declaring all-out war on Cameron, restless and ready to hand down his own special brand of justice.

He thinks he has won, but the war will not be over until Jessynia belongs to me and me alone. And my yearning for her and my need to possess her soul will never end....

Black Oak Scorched is the third novel in the Black Oak series and is the first book in the series featuring multiple narrative points of view.

For mature audiences.

WORD FROM THE AUTHOR

I would like to say a huge thank you to those who have joined the Black Oak Series and enjoyed these characters and stories. I couldn't even begin to express how thrilled and honored I am to have people read the books and resonate with them.

When writing book one, I really wanted to give a complex and multi-dimensional representation of infidelity that wasn't black and white and that didn't reduce complex and flawed humans to just being good and bad or weak and strong.

I have known many people in my life who have tried to forgive an unfaithful partner and I know it is one of toughest things we can do. I see people who do that as incredibly strong and really wanted to explore that dynamic with the book.

I wanted to continue this theme in book two because while I absolutely love reading books with super sassy, badass female leads and find it totally thrilling to channel their strength for a while, occasionally when I read those representations, I feel a tiny bit disconnected as myself and the many amazing women I have been lucky enough to know in my life are super strong and feisty at times, but also have moments when we are much more flawed and vulnerable.

We can sometimes get knocked off balance and feel torn and

struggle to find ourselves at times. At other times, we allow people to influence us and we find it difficult to trust our own judgment, so for me, it was very important to show that side of being human—the vulnerable side, the side that doesn't always know which way to turn, the side that questions their decisions and feels compassion for those that don't always deserve it.

I believe that sometimes we need time to regain our strength and I love exploring the darkness that all of us feel at times as well as our complex human weaknesses and I hope I did that with this book.

If you have liked the book and are ever inspired to leave a very quick rating or even a very short review, please feel very free to. It does help independent authors tremendously and I can't express how greatly appreciated it is and what a huge difference it makes.

Having said that, just having people read it means more to me than anything else.

Thank you once again for taking this journey with me and please feel free to reach out to me on Facebook if you have any questions!

Thank you again so much,

Monique

ANNOUNCEMENT ABOUT BOOK 3 IN THE BLACK OAK SERIES

When I first published book one, *Enter The Black Oak*, I believed that it would be a trilogy because I saw it as the story of just Jess, Jack and Cameron.

In writing the very long book two, the Black Oak universe became larger and more complex than I had initially planned, with the introduction of some new characters and storylines.

When I first started, I had a vision mapped out for book 3, but after working through it in my mind for many months, I have realized that it would be impossible to fit the remainder of the story into just one more book.

This series of books means so much to me and I really want to avoid cutting out important chunks of content and story in order to fit the confines of what I had originally planned.

I have also been asked by many readers over the last few months to provide some chapters from the narrative point of view of Jack or Cameron or both, and adding another book or two to the series would allow me to do that. I know that is something I would delight in writing (and reading!).

I have made the decision that the Black Oak series will be longer than a trilogy. I currently am not certain if that means four books or five books.

I did not make this decision lightly. I put my heart and soul into every line and I would not increase the length of the series for any other reason than because I feel in my writer's soul that I have to do that, and because I believe that the stories and characters deserve it and that it would serve the readers.

I am hoping that if you have read book two, you will be as curious about the new characters as I am and excited that they will be explored more!

If you have any questions, please feel free to contact me on Facebook or by going to my website Contact Us page.

Thank you,

Monique

ABOUT THE AUTHOR

Monique Edenwood is a British-Canadian author based in Vancouver, British Columbia.

Her love of the magical trees and forests that she grew up surrounded by helped to inspire her first novel, *Enter the Black Oak.*

When she isn't writing or reading, she loves hiking and cycling around beautiful Vancouver and is a lover of 80's music and epic fantasy.

She is passionate about helping people take a well-deserved break from their daily lives for a short while with the help of some very memorable fictional boyfriends and loves exploring the intimacies and complexities of relationships.

For more information or to contact the author, please contact her on Facebook (facebook.com/moniqueedenwood) where she is very active, or at www.MoniqueEdenwood.com.

For updates on the Black Oak Series, feel free to visit Facebook.-com/Entertheblackoak.

Monique absolutely loves hearing from readers of the Black Oak series and tries her very best to respond to every comment she gets.

Printed in Great Britain
by Amazon

57378112R00293